OPERATION: LOST PRINCESS

SUPER AGENT SERIES, BOOK 4

MISTY EVANS

Beach
Path
Publishing
LLC

Operation Lost Princess, Super Agent Series, Book 4

Copyright © 2020 Misty Evans

ISBN 978-1-948686-23-5

Print ISBN: 978-1-948686-99-0

Cover Art by Fanderclai Design

Formatting by Beach Path Publishing, LLC

Editing by Patricia Essex

Please Note

1

FORTY KILOMETERS OUTSIDE OF MOSCOW, Russia

ACE. KING. QUEEN. JACK. TEN.

Ryan Smith spread the cards in his hand just enough to see the five-card sequence was the same suit. Hearts.

In a rundown cabin in a desolate part of the former Soviet Union, maybe, just maybe, the rotten luck he'd had for the past week was about to change.

Stuck in this frozen wasteland, Ryan had cursed Conrad Flynn a hundred times in the past two days. This was Flynn's job, training a group of American spies in SERE—Survival, Evasion, Resistance and Escape—not his. Even the special ops team, there to teach the new recruits advanced survival techniques that could only be learned in the harshest surroundings, could have handled this op on their own.

Given the choice, Ryan would've rather faced a firing squad than train rookie spies. Too many years of fieldwork had made him hard, given him an edge, and matching nightmares to go with it. Even though he was in charge of the American spies

I

stationed throughout Europe, he didn't have patience for those who hadn't already earned their keep.

But Conrad was laid up at Georgetown University Hospital with food poisoning and had asked Ryan to stand in for him. Since Ryan was heading to the trilateral nuclear arms reduction summit in Moscow tomorrow, it only made sense for him to take Conrad's place. Point was moot. There was nothing Ryan wouldn't do for his best friend and CIA colleague.

Glancing across the cracked, green Formica table—standard equipment for a secret CIA outpost—Ryan's friend and UK SIS counterpart, Truman Gunn, wiggled the toothpick in the corner of his mouth. Barely a millimeter of movement, it was enough to tell the CIA's Director of European Operations what he wanted to know.

His luck was definitely improving.

If only luck were enough. Facts, details, careful analysis—those were Ryan's tools to obtain the complete story in any situation. After spending the past twenty-four hours watching Gunn train new recruits and play endless rounds of poker, Ryan had picked up on the British spy's unremarkable, but all-too-telling, tick.

Damn time something went right for me. Even if it's only a hand of poker.

Sliding his winning cards together, he laid them face down on the table while Gunn continued to stare at his. The other players consisted of Lawson Vaughn, leader of the special ops team Pegasus, and Conrad's latest recruit for his spy army, weapons expert, Josh Devons. The rest of the group had holed up in the bunker under Ryan's feet with Call of Duty and a bottle of cheap Russian vodka.

Both Lawson and Josh had folded and were studying Gunn. While Devons seemed content to play poker in the inhospitable surroundings, Lawson tapped the table with a restless thumb. His wife was in America, heavily pregnant with their first child and ignoring doctor's orders to take things easy. He wanted to call the op quits and head back to America. Ryan couldn't blame him.

Icy wind whistled through the windows, rattling the panes. Lawson's cell phone rang and he snatched it off his belt. Reception in this area outside Moscow was iffy at best and they used a SAT phone to talk to Langley or Vauxhall Cross if needed, but every once in a while, cell phones worked. When they did, all the men felt less isolated. Less like they were in the Arctic Twilight Zone.

Lawson rose from the table to seek out privacy, eyes lighting up as he saw the name on his caller ID. That meant only one thing: the person on the other end was Zara. Pegasus's commander left the room, and Ryan wondered what it would be like to have someone back home who loved him. Who waited for him. Who called to hear his voice, no matter the time or place.

Gunn wiggled his toothpick and Ryan held in an impatient sigh. The edge that kept him in the spy game wasn't conducive to relationships or training spies, but it did give him an advantage at cards. "Today, Gunn. Or Lawson will be having grandchildren before we finish this."

"Keep your underkecks on, mate." His eyes never left the cards in his hand.

Another minute passed before Lawson returned, looking morose, and going for the fridge.

Ryan caught his eye. "Zara okay? That baby giving her grief?"

Grabbing a sports drink, Lawson opened the top and flipped the cap into the sink full of dishes. "She's fine. Baby's fine. Z's pissed Flynn wouldn't let her come on this training op. Can you imagine a seven-months pregnant woman out here in Siberia?"

"Forty clicks from Moscow is not exactly Siberia, even

3

though it feels like it. And Zara is Flynn's top operative. She could give birth and take out a terrorist cell at the same time."

Lawson sighed in disgruntled agreement. "She kept going on about onion-topped castles and me finding some *krasavits* to replace her. Whatever a *krasavits* is."

"Pretty woman" Ryan translated.

Lawson rolled his eyes. "Zara won't admit it, but she worries about me, and right now, she's worried about the baby. Her stress level is in the stratosphere. When I get back, I'm putting in for vacation. I gotta do something to keep her calm or our baby will be here next week."

Sometimes Ryan wished someone—besides his mother—would worry about him. "I'll talk to her next time she calls, okay? Put her fears to rest."

"Um, Smitty?" a disembodied voice called from behind Ryan's chair, a definite strain in the three syllables.

Ryan glanced at the opening in the floor. The hatch led down to a surveillance room under the house. Del, the CIA's top-shelf computer tech, had made himself at home there with an impressive array of computers, printers, and assorted gadgets.

The cabin and bunker had been used as a KGB debriefing location during the Cold War by the Soviet Union. For years after, it sat empty in the inhospitable terrain and only recently had been "acquired" by the CIA as a secret outpost. A satellite dish on the roof fed information in and out of the bunker, but once the trap door was closed and a rug and crappy kitchen table placed over it, an unexpected guest or casual observer would never realize an entire communications hub was right below their feet.

"What is it, Del?"

The tapping of computer keys filtered up from the space. Del cleared his throat. "We've got company."

As if controlled by the same puppet master, Ryan, Truman,

and Lawson stood in unison. Josh stayed seated. In the back of his brain, Ryan made a note to talk to Conrad about Josh's lack of fight or flight instincts.

"Who is it?" Ryan demanded. No one should have known they were there except a select few big wigs at Vauxhall Cross and Langley, and the place was too isolated to attract attention from the main road.

Del's chair squeaked. "Not sure. Red Lada Riva, circa 1993 maybe? Turned off the main highway thirty seconds ago and is headed in this direction. Fast."

Ryan and Truman exchanged a look. Unexpected Russian visitors could be a problem. A big problem.

Josh scratched his buzzed head. "What the heck is a 'lot of Riva'?"

Apparently *weapons expert* didn't translate to *foreign car expert*. Ryan kept his exasperation in check and called up his composed director of operations persona. A mixture of body language and voice tone suggesting Ryan was omnipotent. "Not 'a lot of' Riva. Lada Riva. Russian auto. Didn't they teach you anything at the Farm?"

"Uh, Smitty?" Again Del's voice rapped against Ryan's nerves. "The Lada's being followed by another car, approximately one kilometer behind it."

Shit. So much for his luck changing. *Next time I see Conrad, I'm kicking him into China.*

Lawson drew his handgun from a shoulder holster while Ryan mentally checked off the number and types of weapons they had total. International incidents were to be avoided at all costs, but the men's security was his biggest concern.

"Give me more to go on, Del." He knew the answer to his next question before he asked it, but asked anyway. He hadn't made it to director without being one-hundred-and-ten-percent thorough with Every. Fucking. Thing. "Friend or foe?"

Not waiting for the answer, Lawson ran for the front room.

Truman motioned Josh to get into the bunker with Del. Josh ignored him, but he yelled at his teammates below and the Call of Duty noise ceased.

Del swore under his breath before he cleared his throat and called up to Ryan. "Cops."

Before he could respond, the distinct report of guns echoed over the whistling wind. While they sounded like insignificant fireworks in the distance, there was no ignoring the fact they were both significant and dangerous.

Double shit.

He considered and discarded the idea of all of them hiding. If the cops snooped around, they'd find the Range Rovers in the barn and know someone was there. They'd take the place apart and discover the hidden door and bunker. Explaining why a group of American and British spies were hiding in the abandoned, former Soviet bunker was harder than meeting the cops head-on and diverting suspicions with a fictional story.

Fluent in Russian and fictional stories, Ryan figured he could send the cops on their merry way in five minutes. Tops.

Over the next thirty seconds, he worked at securing the place. By the time he looked out the curtained window in the front living room, Lawson and Josh stood positioned in covert spots in the living and dining areas. Ryan's winning poker hand was still on the kitchen table, which now hid the trap door.

The Lada was coming in fast and hard down the long, narrow snow-filled lane. It fishtailed, kicking up ice and snow before stopping abruptly in front of the house. Sirens sounded in the distance. When the driver's door flew open, Ryan saw a brief flash of white blonde hair and panicked eyes before the female driver slipped and fell to the ground in a heap of red material.

His body moved before his brain kicked in. Grabbing the latch on the door, he threw it open in time to see the woman rising to her feet on four inch stilettos that matched her red dress.

Her very *short* red dress. Under which was the most incredible set of legs he'd ever seen.

Runway models would kill for those legs.

His brain skittered to a stop. *Black hole alert.*

Ryan shook his head. *Forget her legs, idiot.*

The woman staggered, reaching a hand toward him, eyes pleading for help, and once more his body moved of its own accord. He took two half-running strides to get to her, ignoring Lawson's yell of "what the hell are you doing?"

A strong wind buffeted Ryan's hair and clothes, and stung his eyes, as he grabbed her hand. It was small inside his larger one and cold as ice. Bringing her in close, he steadied her against his body, keeping her upright as her heels—who the hell wore stilettos in the Russian outback?—sunk into the snow.

She clung to him as he shuttled her into the safety of the house, the little voice in his head echoing Lawson's question and asking him if he'd lost his damn mind.

Without a word, Truman sprinted past and jumped into the car. The Lada disappeared into the dense woods on the east side of the house.

Good man.

Ryan shut the door and released the woman's hand reluctantly, telling himself his reluctance was only because he was afraid she'd fall.

The voice in his head laughed.

"Do you speak English?"

She nodded, but the action made her sway. Was she drunk? High?

He grabbed her forearm and she locked her knees and gave him another pleading look. "I need...help. Please."

Although strained, her voice was rich and strong. Her

Russian accent was light as a feather, almost nonexistent. In fact, she sounded more American than Russian. Nothing clouded her eyes. They were crystal clear and bright with adrenaline.

Not drunk or high.

Scared?

Didn't matter. What mattered was why she was running from the cops.

And if he was seriously going to go through with hiding her from them.

Cuz, shit, he could work a miracle every now and then, but this...

This was shaping up to need more than your everyday miracle.

Problem was, he didn't have time to play twenty questions and find out who she was and what was going on. A blue and white police car had just found the entrance to the driveway.

Sirens blaring, the VW Passat slowed, crawling over the snow encrusted, rutted terrain. The lights on the top flashed a red spotlight on everything they touched inside the cabin and out, a giant eyeball searching for its prey.

The woman saw the flashing red lights too. She stepped toward Ryan and away from the spotlight, swaying again in the heels as she murmured something under her breath. Her words were so soft, he couldn't make out what she said. Without warning, her eyelids drooped as if she were going to pass out.

He grabbed both of her shoulders, held her still. When she didn't look at him, he shook her a little. "Who are you?" He thought he was entitled to at least know that before he put his life on the line for her.

"I'm an American," she whispered. "I was told the CIA could help me. *You* would help me."

She knew he was CIA? What the hell?

Ryan dropped his hands, and before he could ask another question, she tipped, falling face forward. Right smack into him.

He caught her before her knees hit the floor, but she was dead weight. Getting both arms under her body, he lifted her like she was a bride. Her short fur coat—as useless as her dress and shoes in the current winter conditions—fell open, and the action fired up his already pounding pulse.

In the space of a heartbeat, the analytical compartment of his mind logged her flawless skin, slender neck, and luscious curves the coat had hidden. Breathtakingly beautiful.

And then his gaze froze and his brain stuttered.

The shit just kept coming.

Above her left hip, a red stain, darker than the red of the dress, was spreading under the silk.

Her body was not only dead weight, it was hot. Regardless of her cold hands, she was burning with fever. She'd been injured. Shot by the cops? Infection didn't set up that fast. The injury had to be older. Either way, she was losing blood and must have been running on pure adrenaline.

She blinked once, twice, trying to focus, and half-smiled up at him. Not saying a word, she slipped her slim fingers into the deep V-neck of her dress that showed off her cleavage to perfection.

Immediately, Josh stepped to Ryan's side, gun drawn, as if he expected her to pull a weapon.

What she slowly inched out of her bra was a weapon of sorts, but not one Ryan ever expected to see.

The shiny metal object swayed under his nose as she showed it to him. "Proof," she mumbled, pressing it to his chest.

Even through his heavy knit sweater, the touch of the thing made his skin crawl. He frowned down into her eyes, searching their now cloudy depths. "Where the hell did you get that?"

In answer, her eyes, so pale blue they were ice-like, fluttered closed once more, and her body went completely limp, the key sliding back into her palm.

His shit meter went sonic.

Josh stuttered, cleared his throat. "Jesus, is that what I think it is?"

Ryan nodded and took a deep breath, staring at the oversized key. It wasn't just any key.

In the slim hand of the beauty in his arms lay a titanium launch key to an Intercontinental Ballistic Missile. A weapon of mass destruction.

With no time to hide her in the bunker, his choices came down to two: risk an international incident over a woman he didn't know, or open the door and hand her over to the cops now exiting their vehicle with guns drawn. One cop crouched behind his car door, aiming a gun at the cabin, while the driver walked towards it.

Conrad, I am so going to kill you.

Ryan caught Josh's eye, nodded once, and headed for the back bedroom, Miss Legs secured tightly in his arms.

2

Anya Romanov Radzoya had been raised on Russian fairy tales. *Vasalisa the Beautiful* had been her grandmother's favorite story, but Anya preferred stories about her ancestors, real Russian princes and princesses. They didn't have happy endings, but the men and women in her family had lived fully and loved every minute of the drama, beauty, and strife.

When she woke, naked, in a strange bed with the handsome American spy sitting beside her, she dared believe she'd fallen into one of her family's tales of daring and intrigue. Staring at the man who watched her intently, a tingle of anticipation ran up her spine.

Had she done it?

Had she escaped Ivanov and found the man who would save her grandmother from certain death?

The key. Anya's anticipation turned to panic as her memory came flooding back. Her gaze searched the room. *Where is the key?*

She tried to prop herself up and felt a sharp burning in her side. The damn cut from Ivanov's antique dirk. The Golden

Weapon, he called it. The slice of the dirk, a warning. If she didn't do what he wanted, there would be consequences. Consequences to her *and* her grandmother.

Anya slipped back down into the sheets, a cold sweat breaking over her skin.

As if he guessed what she was looking for, the man leaned forward and opened his hand. Large and calloused in a few places, it was a strong hand, and if she remembered correctly, a warm hand.

Nestled inside that strong, warm hand was her prize. Her proof of President Ivanov's treachery, and the required show of faith to the CIA.

She reached out to take it, but the man pulled it away, balling his hand into a fist.

He scanned her face, assessing what he saw with guarded interest. "That cut is infected, and you lost a good amount of blood. That's why you passed out. I patched you up and smeared some antibiotic cream on it. Keep the wound dry and covered, and you should be fine in a couple of days." In the dimly lit room, his eyes were as dark as her favorite Baltika beer, and his voice just as smooth. "I can't wait to hear how you got that."

Under the cotton blanket, she ran a hand across a thick bandage on her left side. Outside of her grandmother, no one knew about her blood clotting disorder. In her haste to get to Moscow, she'd forgotten her blood reconstitution kit, and she'd chastised herself repeatedly since Ivanov wounded her.

Forget the wound. She was naked. Had the American spy taken off her dress to stitch her up?

Her cheeks heated. *Of course he did. He barreled out the door to save me, caught me when I fainted, and he's sitting by the bed, waiting for me to wake up.*

He's the man with my key.

Anya was passionate about a lot of things. Her work on the Human Genome Project, and her other genetic mapping projects at GenLife Laboratory in Arlington. Her grandmother —the last of Anya's family—and the secrets Grams had insisted the two of them keep. Hiding from the past, which had now caught up with her.

At twenty-six, though, those things—the very cornerstones of her life—had kept her from learning much about men. Their glances and open appraisals were a sign they found her attractive, but she'd worked diligently at her job, hung out with her grandmother, and worried about her secrets every time she received a hang-up call, or a strange vehicle followed her for more than a few blocks.

Besides the fact she was a mess of paranoia and lived with constant dread as her best friend, she didn't have time to play mating games. No friends. No boyfriends. It wasn't just her defective blood screwing up her life. Her family's dark past, with all its secrets, murders and betrayals, kept her from sharing even the basics about her life with anyone.

This American spy, however, seemed like a decent guy on the surface. He'd helped her so far, after all. He didn't trust her, that was obvious, but could she blame him? He was a spy and she was a stranger.

He wanted to know who she was, why she was here...he wanted to know her secrets. Past and present.

So not going there. Not yet.

Doveryai, no proveryai, Grams would caution. Trust, but verify. Except Grams, being the paranoid woman she was, always changed it to *don't trust until verified.* Subtle but important difference.

Anya's voice croaked when she opened her mouth to speak, her throat so dry, she could spit wool. Embarrassed, she licked her parched lips and swallowed.

The movement wasn't lost on him and his gaze dropped momentarily to her lips. Her cheeks heated more. Nerves, she told herself. It was only nerves.

How she got hurt—hell, why she was in Russia in the first place—was a complicated story and not one she intended to share with just anyone. Maybe someday, she'd tell it to her granddaughter as a fairy tale, but until then...

She shivered under the blanket. "The police, what happened to them? Why didn't they arrest me?"

The man studied her face for a moment as he chewed on the fact she hadn't answered his question. "I sent them after your car. They found it in the woods a kilometer from here and believe you walked off and left it to avoid capture. The sun has set and they couldn't find footprints even if they tried in that dark forest. Why were they chasing you?"

"I was speeding."

One of his brows rose. He didn't buy it, although it was a plausible answer. The damn police had nothing better to do on M9 than harass speeders. Luckily, they hadn't caught her and figured out who she was.

He jiggled the hand holding her key. "Where did you get this?"

Like her great-grandmother on the Radzoya side who'd survived Hitler's invasion of Leningrad during the Second World War, Anya prided herself on being careful and shrewd. The spy who'd promised his help would be the only man she would discuss any of this with. "Are you Solomon?"

Nothing changed in the man's face and yet she sensed him tensing. "Solomon who?"

Anya's stomach tightened. Her knee wanted to bob with a fresh rush of nerves. "You are CIA, right?"

He didn't answer, his face staying flat, neutral.

"You know. *Solomon*," she insisted, panic setting in. This guy wasn't her contact, so..."Your boss?"

At this, the right corner of his mouth quirked up ruefully, as if he were trying not to smile. "Solomon—" he said the name with a funny emphasis "—is not here. I'm filling in for him. You'll have to talk to me."

The panic hit full force. No Solomon? Now what? She chewed her bottom lip, praying for a lightning strike of inspiration.

The man leaned in, turned serious. "Where'd you get this key?"

The hint of his smile had made her want to see more, and his eyes...they nearly swallowed her in their brown depths. So different from the mad blue eyes of Ivanov. Even though he didn't trust her and didn't like her asking for Solomon, this man's eyes told her she was safe with him.

Anya drew in a deep, cleansing breath. *What would Grams do?*

As if her grandmother whispered in her ear, the answer came. *Make him see you as a person.* Not exactly a lightning strike, but she'd take what she could get.

Anya held out her hand, sincerely wishing for a do-over. "My name is Anya."

Her wish was granted. He gave her a strained smile, seeming slightly surprised, and shook her hand. "Ryan."

For a moment, he looked younger, less worried. She liked him better that way. Unfortunately, she couldn't divulge where she'd gotten the key to anyone but Solomon. He and the key were her fail safe. "Where's my dress, Ryan?"

He hesitated and glanced away. "You won't be wearing it out of here." His tone was soft, apologetic. "The side seam ripped when I was trying to examine your wound, um...discreetly."

Was he blushing? She rolled onto her side, gritting her teeth against the pain, and patted his knee to let him know it was okay. She wasn't mad about the dress—although she was blushing again, too, since he'd seen her naked—but she needed clothes. Time was running out. She had to tell Solomon about what she'd discovered and get back to Moscow before Ivanov realized she was missing. "Perhaps you have an extra sweater and pair of pants you'd loan me?"

His gaze landed first on her hand perched on his knee, then rose to her face. "Information, first. Clothes later. You need to take it easy on that wound for now."

Tough guy with a heart again. Drawing her hand back, she ignored her tight stomach and the recurring urge to bob her knee. She could be tough too. "Solomon first. Then information."

"Did Solomon send you to steal it, or did you do that on your own, Cowboy?"

Cowboy. Yes, that's what she was now. American men loved cowboys. Some of the women she worked with did too. Even her grandmother loved cowboys and watched old Clint East-wood movies. Ten-gallon hats, grand gestures, and vigilante justice. Although Anya preferred TV medical dramas and sitcoms – she'd learned most of her Americanisms from them – she'd be the best damn cowboy this side of the Atlantic if it meant saving Grams and bringing down Ivanov.

Sitting up carefully, she gestured at her bandaged wound, the blanket drooping low on her chest. "Thank you for doctoring me, Ryan. I owe you my life."

His focus dropped to her exposed skin, but only for a second. Then it was back to eye-to-eye contact, serious expression, tight frown. All business once more. "It wasn't life threatening, but you're welcome."

Little did he know.

She swung her legs out from under the blanket and over the edge of the bed, keeping vital parts covered. Even though it cost her some pain, the move claimed Ryan's full attention. She forced a bright tone into her voice while he stared at her legs unblinking. "Please, Ryan, I have to talk to Solomon. It's a matter of national security."

At that, his eyes went hard. He was tiring of the game, whether he liked her legs or not. "When and where exactly did you meet Solomon?"

"I've never met him, per se. I've only spoken to him once. Briefly."

"Who are you working for?"

"Sorry?"

His jaw tightened. "Why were the cops chasing you for speeding, and not for having this key?" Said key dangled from his hand. "I want answers."

Handsome, but bossy. "Why?"

"The safety of my men depends on it."

"I am not a threat to you or your men."

"You bring an ICBM launch key and a pair of Russian police to my door, and you don't think you're a threat?"

Okay, he had her there. "I'm sorry. I don't know how to do this spy thing. But I have to talk to Solomon. Now. My grandmother assured me he could help."

"Then you're up a shitcreek, sweetheart, because he's not available."

"Fine. Give me back the key." She stood on wobbly legs, determination locking her knees so she didn't fall. "I have to get back to Kremlin Palace before I'm missed."

"Kremlin Palace?" He eyed her with new curiosity. "You work there?"

A knock on the door startled them. The man she'd seen rush out to her car before she'd fainted walked in without waiting for an invitation. He wore the same expression as Ryan. Closed, flat, hard to read.

Ryan stood as if anxious for the piece of paper the man handed him. As Ryan read, the man approached Anya, held out her passport, and bowed ever so slightly. "Princess. A pleasure to meet you."

Oh, God. He knew? Her passport was under her American name, Anya Radcliff, and her American identity had been built by the best her grandmother's money could buy. How had they discovered her true name so easily?

They're spies, Anya. Duh.

Taking the passport, she refocused. The man's accent pegged him as British. That could work in her favor. The Brits respected bloodlines and royalty. Maybe he would take her to Solomon.

She returned his nod. "Please call me Anya. And you are?"

"Truman." He stepped back to stand at the door again. "At your service."

Ryan glanced up at her and back to the paper several times, as if trying to make the facts in black-and-white mesh with the woman. A little unnerved, Anya sat, covering her legs, and lifting the blanket higher around her breasts. What was on that paper other than useless facts? Her date of birth. Her bloodline. The death of her parents all those years ago. Her move to America with her grandmother…

Did it tell him red tulips were her favorite flower? That she could whistle the entire second movement of Tchaikovsky's Symphony No. 4, or that one whole drawer of her desk at work was filled with chocolate bars? That her life was all about helping people uncover the mystery of their gene pools?

Did it tell him President Ivanov had kidnapped her grandmother, and was blackmailing Anya to stay by his side and play the dutiful princess during the summit meeting?

Finished reading, Ryan returned to the chair and scooted it close to the bed. So close their knees touched. Another tingle of anticipation—or was it dread?— rolled down her spine as he drew out an oversized cell phone. "Well, Princess—" he used the same funny emphasis as he'd used before "—I think it's time we call Solomon and get this situation straightened out."

Finally, they were getting somewhere. Anya nearly laughed with relief, her stomach muscles unknotting. This was no fairy tale, but somehow, someway, she would rescue Grams and bring President Maxim Ivanov down.

3

As RYAN DIALED Conrad's number on his encrypted cell phone, he wondered what it was like not to be the responsible one. To be the one making the mess, instead of cleaning it up. He was tired of putting out fires. Tired of fixing what was broken. Tired of pretending it never bothered him.

He'd been cleaning up other people's messes since the age of eight. His father had left his mother with two kids, a fat mortgage, and an empty bank account, and Ryan, being the oldest, stepped up to do the duties his old man left behind.

In high school when his younger brother decided his absentee father and alcoholic mother were good reasons to start the chem lab on fire, Ryan went to the principal and school board and talked them out of pressing criminal charges. The unruffled but impassioned negotiator was born.

When his mother lost yet another job, Ryan enrolled her in A.A. and gave up basketball to get a second afterschool job. By college, he'd already earned a degree in Most Responsible with a double major in Peacekeeping and Troubleshooting.

Along with a foreign affairs and international law degree— all earned on scholarship—he'd attracted the attention of

Susan Richmond at the CIA. Off-the-record, he negotiated a verbal agreement with her to help him with a few family matters before accepting her recruitment offer. Her word had been gold back then, and his mother had found a government job while his brother got into MIT and graduated, thanks to a special mentor Susan arranged. She took Ryan through the CIA's training camp and put him on the fast track to management in the world of Central Intelligence.

It had been a hell of a ride on the spy train and, now, at thirty-three, the negotiator was burned out.

But when he glanced up and saw the Russian princess smiling at him with anticipation, he knew he'd meet the cops at the door, smooth talk them in his fluent Russian, and send them on their way all over again. In fact, if called for, he'd draw the gun from the small of his back and shoot to kill.

It's what he did. He rooted for the underdog, cheered for the renegade, helped the damsel in distress. Never mind that his logical mind told him she wasn't any of those. His gut said different.

Pushing the chair back, Ryan stood and walked away from those killer blue eyes and dazzling smile. The service was there, but even with his high-tech, encrypted phone, it took time to connect to the other end.

Conrad's wife, Julia, answered. As young spies in Susan Richmond's group, the three of them had been stationed together and spent many nights in different parts of the world listening to music, drinking wine, and coming up with new ways to recruit assets for the United States government. For codenames to use with the assets, Julia had immediately designated her and Conrad as the ill-fated Biblical couple, Solomon and Sheba. Ryan had steered away from damnation and went with his favorite rock guitarist instead.

"Sheba, this is Eddie." He made sure to emphasize the names, even though Julia was no longer a spy, but had defected to the FBI. While Ryan's secure phone wouldn't allow their conversation to be picked up by unwanted sources, he wouldn't jeopardize Julia or Conrad by using their real identities in front of Anya.

He didn't trust her and she already knew his first name— what the hell had he been thinking offering that up so easily? —as well as Truman's, *idiot*. "I need to talk to Solomon."

Julia hesitated, then said, "Solomon's not available. Is there something I can help you with?"

Conrad wasn't available? A seed of unease opened in Ryan's gut. Julia must have known Ryan was filling in for her husband, even if she didn't know details of the op. "Sorry, Sheba. I need to talk to Solomon. Immediately."

Julia lowered her voice to a whisper. "He's in the hospital and I can't talk right now. Neither can he."

The line went dead. Ryan held the phone away from his ear and stared at it. Had Julia just hung up on him?

She would never do that. She would never leave him hanging unless...

Unless something big was up with Conrad.

Was he *that* sick?

Shit, shit, and more shit.

Conrad wouldn't go to the doctor, much less enter the hospital, even if he was dying of bubonic plague. Like Ryan, he hated hospitals almost as much as he hated terrorists.

Ryan added a new worry to his ever-growing list.

"Is there a problem?" Anya asked.

"No," Ryan lied. "Solomon's going to call me—" The phone rang in his hands, caller ID labeling it 'unknown number'. Ryan knew who it was. "Back."

He punched the connect button. "Hey, man."

"What'cha got?" Conrad's voice wavered ever so slightly.

The unease in Ryan's gut expanded. For a second, he forgot about Anya, the cops who were probably still watching the place, and the ICBM launch key in his pocket. A dozen different questions and smart-ass comments ran through his head, all intended to get a rise out of Conrad so he'd know just how sick his friend was.

But the moment wasn't right for any kind of personal exchange. The facts, the full story, would have to wait. "An unexpected package arrived here today for you, *Solomon*, apparently with some information you requested?"

There was a slight pause. "Where did the package come from?"

"The Kremlin."

On the other end, Conrad did the math. "Attractive package? High end?"

Ryan stole a glance at Anya. In the bare room, she stood out like a neon sign. A beautiful, sexy-as-hell neon sign with legs that could...

Black hole alert. He cleared his throat and looked at the cracked and peeling paint on the far wall. His brain started working again. "Affirmative."

"Huh. Glad she found you. I meant to call you about this, but I got waylaid by this stupid food..." Conrad's voice wavered again, like he was straining against some ugly pain. He coughed. "Does the package have something of interest for us?"

That was an understatement of Russian-size proportion. "Package won't share with anyone but you."

"Ah." Ryan heard him shift in the bed. "You near the package?"

"Yeah." He hit the speakerphone button and held the phone between him and Anya.

Conrad cleared his throat. "This is Solomon. I can't help you right now, but my friend there can. Tell him what you know. Don't be afraid."

Anya bit her lower lip, eyes scanning Ryan's for duplicity. Her voice came out strong but strained, as if she were at war with herself and pissed as hell at Conrad, and trying not to show it. "What we talked about, it's bigger than I expected. Ivanov..." She stopped herself, drew a steadying breath. "I brought proof that I've been inside his quarters, but he has my grandmother. I tell the wrong person what I know, and she dies."

She started to say something else, but Ryan drew the phone away and held a finger to her lips to shush her.

Was that true?

Even though no one should have been listening to the conversation, he wasn't taking chances. Anya had stolen a Russian nuclear missile launch key, and assuming it was to a working ICBM, she was probably being hunted all over Russia at that point. Didn't matter that Russia had gone high-tech years ago, or that, like the U.S., they'd upgraded all their weapons to computerized systems. Or the fact, also like the U.S., they claimed to have reduced their stockpiles extensively and were not pursuing the new "bunker-busting nukes" as rumored by various sources.

Yeah, right.

The current president was over-the-top paranoid about security and boasted he owned the largest and most expensive weapon museum "arsenal" in the world. At this point, a speeding ticket was the least of Anya's worries.

Or his. "Solomon, do I have your permission to extract the information from the package?"

No hesitation on Conrad's end. They'd played this game many times before. "Absolutely. Whatever information the package contains should be given to you."

Ryan raised a brow to see if Anya understood. Her face was inscrutable, but her body language wasn't. Pissed was putting it mildly.

"I have information that can bring the down president." Her voice was loud. Too loud. A sheen of tears brightened her eyes and she took another fortifying breath, drawing it, Ryan was sure, all the way from her toes. The tears disappeared and her lips firmed. "If the U.S. won't help me destroy Ivanov, and find my grandmother," —her gaze shifted from Ryan to Truman— "then I'll find another country that will."

Wait. What? Ryan jerked the phone back and pressed the speaker against his chest, doing a little mental cursing, and then something clicked in his brain.

He looked at Anya again, gripping the phone hard and using every ounce of control he had to keep from launching it at the far wall.

Conrad had recruited a Russian princess who'd been hiding in America. Russian spy or American asset, it didn't matter. What he'd gotten was a bombshell of an international incident.

4

EVEN THOUGH RYAN'S face was unreadable, his eyes were hard as steel. A chill ran over Anya's skin that had nothing to do with the cold room.

Tough. She straightened her already straight back and returned his glare.

Still holding the phone, he walked to the door and reached for the knob, every muscle taught with anger. Truman moved out of his way and Anya jumped from the bed, yanking the blanket with her. "Ryan, wait."

She expected him to slam the door behind him. Instead he closed it with a soft, deliberate click.

Hope drained out of her. She was trying to do the right thing, and yet it seemed the harder she tried, the worse she screwed up. How was she going to get Grams away from Ivanov, *the bastard*, now?

A prickly awareness made goose flesh rise on her skin. Across the room, Truman watched her, examining and appraising her blanket-wrapped body from head to foot. Not ogling, just interested, as if he were examining a new sports car.

On the other side of the door, Ryan raised his voice to

Solomon. He was still on the phone, and even though she couldn't make out everything he was saying, it was obvious he was upset.

Damn it. She didn't want to care that he was angry. Didn't want to care about him, period. But he'd stitched up her wound, saved her from the police. *Don't trust until verified* rang in her brain, but it was hard not to trust such a decent guy. "What did I do to make him so angry?"

Truman leaned a shoulder against the wall. "Let's see. Might have been talking when he told you not to, or—over a phone line—threatening to destroy the Russian president. Or maybe it was when you threatened to give Queen and country your top secret information instead of him."

"It wasn't an idle threat. If the CIA won't make good on their promises to my grandmother, then I'll give the information to someone who will."

Truman stuck one hand in his pocket, ever so casual. "What's up with your nan?"

Anya plopped down, ignoring the pain in her side and mentally searching for some way to still save the day. She'd gotten his attention with the key, but she couldn't tell him everything. Not yet, though the secret about her true identity and her past was already out.

The only card she had left to play was the truth about Grams. "Ivanov kidnapped her from a hotel in Geneva two days ago. She was visiting a friend there. I came home from work to a cryptic message on my voice mail instructing to me to come to Moscow if I ever wanted to see her again. This all has to do, I think, with Ivanov's obsession with royalty. If I refuse to attend the summit meeting by his side, or refuse to go along with whatever charade he's playing, he'll kill her."

"I'm sorry." Truman grew appropriately solemn. "I'm sure there's a lot more to this story, but how exactly did you expect the CIA to help?"

In the beginning, Anya had been looking through a microscope, examining her grandmother's kidnapping from every angle and trying to figure out a way to get her safely back to America. After the initial meeting at the Kremlin with President Ivanov her perspective had changed. He'd paraded Anya around like a trophy, showed her the new lab he'd built for genetics, and made it clear he had some kind of plan for her. A plan for the next generation of Russians. Her microscope had morphed into a telescope.

While Ivanov had avoided answering her endless questions, she'd kept her eyes and ears open. She'd overheard him talking with his prime minister behind closed doors. Heard him acknowledge his plans for the future of Russia. That's when her focus had broadened. The rescue Anya had been planning could no longer be only about saving her grandmother. Now the safety and well-being of millions of people depended on her. Ivanov not only planned to build an arsenal of superior weapons to use against the world, but a race of superior Russians as well.

Still, it was the thought of her grandmother dying that made Anya sick to her stomach. Her grandmother was all she had left. The two of them had been on their own for so long...

Blinking back tears, she picked at a lint ball on the blanket. "She knows Solomon. Told me I could trust him if I ever had problems with the Russian government. As soon as she was kidnapped, I contacted him, and he told me to follow Ivanov's orders, and get in touch with him when I figured out where Ivanov had stashed Grams. But I can't find her. I'd hoped I could handle this on my own, but unfortunately, I have no idea how to take on a Russian president and get Grams back in one piece."

Without warning, Ryan burst through the door. All business as usual but with a slight strain in his voice. "Cops."

Truman straightened, his earlier casualness gone. "Ah, yes.

We expected them to return." He motioned at Anya in the blanket. "Where do you want her?"

"Bunker." In one swift movement, Ryan shucked his sweater and tossed it to Anya. "Put this on. Follow Truman. Stay quiet."

Ryan's upper body was a beautiful sculpture...muscles moving with fluid grace as he shoved the chair into the corner. Anya hugged the sweater, breathing in the scent of warm male mixed with sweat and deodorant. She should have been scared and yet Ryan's simple presence calmed her. Even under these circumstances, he appeared calm, cool, and in control. He'd helped her before. He was about to do it again.

Maybe she owed him a little more trust. Maybe he could handle one or two of her secrets.

Unless the cops arrested her before she could share them.

He sent a glance her way before giving more instructions to Truman. "Blindfold her once she's down there. Tell the others, including Del, to stay quiet and be ready to move on my signal."

With that, he was gone.

Truman turned his back while Anya dropped the blanket and slid the sweater over her head. The soft cotton fisherman's weave engulfed her, as did Ryan's scent. She smoothed her hands down the front, enjoying the feel and texture. The bottom edge of the sweater hung down over her butt and for that she was grateful.

While the red dress had been couture, it had come from Ivanov with the demand to wear it. He insisted that no matter where she went or what she was doing, she was dressed appropriately for a princess. In his warped mind, red silk was as suitable for the spa as for a formal dinner in Kremlin Palace. This new addition to her wardrobe of Ryan's sweater, even if only temporary, beat that one all to hell.

Truman tossed the blanket on the bed, snatched up Anya's passport and motioned for her to follow. They moved quickly through a living room outfitted with worn upholstered chairs, an old TV with rabbit ears, and a wood burning stove that looked like it had been around since the last World War. The other man she'd seen when she arrived stood with his side pressed against the wall, a large, black handgun pointed up as he drew back the curtains a fraction. He gave her one slight tip of his chin in acknowledgement.

A left turn took them into the kitchen. Outside the windows, the bleak Russian night was dark and foreboding. A weak fluorescent light over the sink threw shadows on dirty dishes, scarred cabinets, and a table with a card game in progress. Another man, also armed, stood at the back door watching the outside.

Ryan had put on a T-shirt and was leaning down by a trap door, talking to someone below. "How soon, Del?"

A sharp rap on the front door made Ryan's head snap up.

"Um, like, now?" a voice, sounding young and scared, whom Anya presumed to be Del, answered.

Ryan rose, his gaze giving her a critical once over as he handed a bandanna to Truman.

"Why do I need to be blind..."

One hand went over her mouth, the other behind her head. "One more word," he whispered, his eyes pools of determination. "And I will throw you to the wolves at the door. Understand?"

Trapped in the vice of his hands, nose to nose and anger radiating off him, Anya's heart thudded hard against her ribcage. Deep down, she wasn't frightened. Okay, maybe a little. More than that, she was hypnotized by his commanding force.

She nodded her head—not easy to do, his grip on her so strong.

Ryan released her head, spun her around and pushed her toward the opening, not intentionally rough, just hurried. A ladder extended into the bunker and four pairs of male eyes looked up at her. Four pairs of very curious eyes.

Bad enough Ryan had seen her naked. She was about to provide a peep show for the four men in the bunker. This day was just too much.

She turned to say so to Ryan, only to have him snap his fingers at the men below. The men's gazes cut to him, all of them looking like they'd been caught with their hand in the cookie jar. He made a whirling motion with his finger and all four turned their backs on the ladder.

Anya started to say thank you, but the second she opened her mouth, he placed a hand over her mouth. Ignoring the way her heart thumped again at his touch, she sighed, gave him a nod of understanding, and started down the ladder.

Truman followed. At the bottom, Anya barely had a chance to make out the collection of screens, keyboards, and what were probably hard drives, before Truman blindfolded her with the bandanna. One hand on her upper arm guided her to a chair and pushed her into it.

With her sight gone, her other senses went into overdrive. Above her, the trapdoor closed with a suffocating thump. Footsteps, keeping time with her heartbeat, hurried overhead. The scrape of table legs against the linoleum floor made her grit her teeth.

Her nose picked up the smells of the dank basement, nervous men, and old plastic. Bone-chilling cold seeped into her bare feet and up her legs. She shivered.

Thank God for Ryan's warm sweater.

She'd been right. He was a good man. Even though he didn't know or trust her, he'd given her protection and the sweater off his back. While her CIA contact, Solomon, had promised help, Ryan had actually provided it.

An image of him going to the front door to confront the

cops flashed on the backs of her eyelids. Her heart squeezed. He was right; she was putting them all in danger.

Especially him.

Around her, the other men moved like ghosts, packing up equipment, she supposed. Equipment Ryan didn't want her to see. Or the police to find.

She had to go back. Soon. She was supposed to be at a spa, having a full body treatment to make up for Ivanov's rough treatment before tomorrow's big shindig at the Kremlin began in earnest. Ivanov had given her the afternoon and evening off from his constant presence to allow her to shop and have a massage. Two goons had followed her around, but she'd been able to give them the slip once inside the spa. She'd climbed out a window, hotwired a car, and found the cabin. She'd reopened the wound while squeezing through the window, but she'd been so focused on escaping, she'd barely noticed the blood. If she wasn't back in her room before Ivanov came for his nightly visit, she—and Grams—would be doomed.

Footsteps sounded again above them, different this time. Heavier. Shuffling.

Clipped, razor-sharp voices echoed off the floorboards. Around her in the bunker, all motion, even breathing, stopped.

Anya stopped breathing too. Seconds ticked by as Ryan answered questions. Was he speaking Russian? There were crashing noises and more discussions, Ryan's voice remaining unflustered and cool as the officers combed the house searching for her

A flashback of the previous night's terrifying incident played like a movie in her brain. She tried to shut out the memory of Ivanov's hands on her arms, her waist. Tried to shut out the memory of his voice in her ear. The memory of what she'd seen in the second set of presidential quarters, hidden under the Kremlin in a bunker that was supposed to be abandoned but was adorned like Stalin was still in residence.

The cutting-edge lab that made GenLife look like a high-school chem lab. The high-tech command center filled with computers, satellite uplinks, and floor-to-ceiling flat screens. The military weapons room and full-scale army headquarters. Displays of launch keys, antique guns and other Soviet weapons everywhere she'd looked. All under Moscow, spread out like a post-apocalyptic sci-fi city.

Her mouth went dry, her teeth chattered. The memories consumed her, and she could no longer hear the sounds above, ears ringing as if she were inside a bell. Her lungs burned. She couldn't breathe.

Ripping the blindfold off, she bent forward, gasping as quietly as she could. Even with the blindfold gone, she couldn't see anything but darkness. Heavy as a wool blanket, it closed around her, pushing down, suffocating her. She was going to have a heart attack and die right there.

After all the trouble she'd caused, Ryan would probably go off and leave her body there to rot. Grams would die never knowing what happened. She'd die thinking Anya had abandoned her.

Vertigo hit and the chair seemed to roll sideways. Anya went down on hands and knees, the cement floor tearing her skin. Blood roared in her ears and she felt lightheaded, as if the room were now spinning.

On the brink of passing out, someone touched her back. Said her name.

They seemed too far away. Could they hear her reply? Her tongue was so thick in her mouth, she wasn't sure she could make one.

She slapped a hand across her lips. *No talking.*

If she talked, Ryan would hand her over to the cops. If Ivanov had figured out she'd stolen the key and taken it to the CIA, the cops would turn her over to the Federal Security

Agency, Ivanov's modern-day KGB. She would disappear, like so many before her, never to be seen again.

Strong hands gripped her shoulders and dragged Anya up off the floor. She heard her name being said over and over as the hands shook her ever so slightly.

She knew the feel of those hands.

Her eyes were closed and she forced them open. The room was lit once more. The men were packing up the equipment. Ryan held her and her knees buckled with relief.

His eyes searched hers for something she couldn't discern. She tried to open herself up and let him see how grateful she was.

"You're safe, princess," he said. His gaze dropped to her lips, down to his sweater, and back up to stare into her eyes. "At least from the Russians."

5

Anya banged her toe on a kitchen chair as Ryan led her around the table, his big, warm hand wrapped securely around hers.

Damn, that hurt. She sucked in a breath and kept going. No way would she act like a wimp even though her teeth chattered from fear, her feet were ice blocks, and her knees shook with pent-up adrenaline.

He hustled her through the living room and she nearly had to run to keep up. Her legs were long, but his were longer, and he covered the distance with quick, hard strides. Just adrenaline, she told herself, not anger, making him whisk her away from the hidden bunker. Away from his men.

Well, maybe a little anger. Fear too?

What a position she'd put him in, protecting her over the safety of the men. Even now, his group was removing equipment from below and scurrying out the back door with it. Loading up to leave.

Was he leaving as well?

Propelling her into the bedroom, Ryan closed the door behind them. He released her hand and cocked his chin at the bed. "The best I could do. They'll be big on you."

Clothes. Thermal underwear bottoms, a pair of gray sweat-pants. Socks.

Ryan's clothes.

Anya wasn't a hugger–who would she hug besides her Grandmother?–but her arms went around his neck of their own volition and she pressed herself against him. He was warm, and solid, and so handsome, she almost kissed him. Out of gratitude, she told herself. Not because she wanted to touch all that heat and strength and solidness. "Thank you," she murmured against his neck. "For everything."

He stiffened at first, then relaxed, one hand coming to rest on her back. "They're just clothes. Nothing fancy, but they're clean."

Just clothes. The irony struck her and she smiled into his shoulder. If only he knew what a few items of clothing had cost her in the past few days.

He gently pressed her away. "We need to talk."

Her turn to stiffen. Embarrassed at her display of emotion, she kept her eyes averted and faced the bed. The supply of clothing didn't include a shirt, so it looked like she got to keep the sweater.

Good. She hugged herself and rubbed the soft cotton. Her teeth chattered and she clamped her jaw to stop them. Grabbing the long underwear, she tugged them on, then the sweats. Flopping down on the bed, she raised her knees to her chest and rubbed her red toe, resigning herself to telling Ryan at least some of the truth. "What do you want to know?"

Seemingly without thought, he bent down and took over the rubbing, and massaging, of her injured toe.

Her breath caught at the shock of his warm hands against her cold skin. *Oh, God.* She'd never had a man touch her feet before.

So good.

Too good. Her brain went fuzzy. On his knees in front of

her, the action appeared to help him concentrate, his forehead creasing as the wheels in his head turned.

He stroked the injured toe, base to end, over and over. The fuzziness left and her thoughts became clear once more... although they were anything but appropriate. Ryan and her in this bedroom – on the bed – doing more than talking...

He glanced up, met her eyes. She blushed but he didn't seem to notice her embarrassment. Mr. Business had other things on his mind. "Truman told me about your grandmother and Ivanov. Solomon believes you can be an asset for us, and retrieve certain sensitive information from the Kremlin. You help us, we'll help you. We need evidence Ivanov is a real threat."

Anya hugged her knees, tried to focus. "I brought you the key. How much more do you need?"

Ryan's face was impassive, though his fingers moved to massaging her whole foot. Warming it up. Warming *everything* up. "Launch keys for nuclear weapons are old school collectors' items. What we need is some kind of evidence Ivanov is actually violating the NPT."

Concentrate, Anya. "NPT?"

"Non-proliferation Treaty for nuclear weapons." He counted off the items on his fingers. "Non-proliferation, disarmament, and the right to peacefully use nuclear technology. We're concerned about the first two obviously."

"He's amassing everything. Weapons, royalty, genetic research."

He quirked a brow, stopped massaging. "Genetic research?"

Oh, god. Don't stop. "I think he wants me to do more than play the role of his princess at the summit. And I'm a two-for-one special."

"Meaning?"

She wiggled her toes and he started kneading her foot again. *Nice.* "I'm a geneticist. From what I saw in the underground lab he showed me yesterday, I think he wants me to help him create a super race."

Ryan's brow dipped in confusion.

"He believes royal blood is superior, and wants to bring royal genes back to Russia."

Ryan released a low whistle under his breath and absently began rubbing her other foot. "Based on your blood?"

"Possibly."

Hemophilia ran rampant in the royal genes, but Ivanov didn't know about her disorder. She'd been cursed with Von Willebrand's, a hereditary blood abnormality that was fairly common and rarely fatal. Only she had the more dangerous Type 3 variety. Less common, sometimes fatal. Definitely not super-race material.

Ryan's gaze dropped to her side where her wound lay hidden. "Did he do that to you? Cut you?"

Anya pinned her gaze to the floor. The memory of Ivanov's rage, his attack with the dirk, slamming her hard. "I refused to wear the clothing he picked out for me. Couture dresses and shoes he believes a princess should wear. They're all ridiculous. I look like a bridesmaid or a prostitute in them. When I said no to the red dress, he got mad, and cut off my shirt to teach me a lesson. In the process, he nicked me with the blade. Afterward, he claimed it was an accident. I'm not so sure."

Brief silence descended. A deep silence charged with anger. "He got that upset over clothes?"

And there it was. The difference between a man like Ivanov and a man like Ryan. "He's obsessed with me. With how I look, what I wear. I have to be a princess twenty-four-seven, no exceptions. Appearances are crucial."

Another silence. This one longer. Anya thought she heard Ryan's teeth grinding. He released her foot but stayed on his knees in front of her. He scanned her face searching for more answers. "How did you escape him to come here, Anya?"

She preferred Anya over princess, especially when Ryan said it. "After he cut me, Ivanov freaked out and apologized. He called in his personal doctor who bandaged the wound, but I refused to talk to Ivanov. I was..."

Should she admit she was terrified of him? That he was a madman? Oh, hell, she'd come this far. "I was scared. Terrified, actually. He thought I was playing hard to get. He thinks this is a dream come true for me, being a Russian princess." Hate charged her next words. "It isn't."

She rocked back and forth on the bed, caught herself and stopped. Straightening her back, she grabbed the socks and shoved them on her feet, then set her feet on the floor and wiggled her toes.

Wool socks.

Ryan's wool socks. Not as good as his hands, but still nice. "In the bastard's warped mind he decided a spa day would appease me. Every princess needs one of those, right?" Bitter laughter escaped her lips. "A massage, a mani-pedi, and all's forgiven. He lined up a complete package...hair, nails, sauna, makeup. Had to get me ready for the summit tomorrow. So he sent me to a private place that caters to his cabinet members and their wives. I used a pair of earrings he gave me – he claimed they were family heirlooms – to bribe the spa manager for a few hours alone. Then I climbed out a bathroom window while I was supposed to be in the steam bath and stole the car."

Ryan got to his feet and sat on the bed next to her. The bed sagged from his weight. "Industrious."

His approval filled her with pride. "Grams always said you have to work with what you've got." *And I don't have much at the moment.*

Except she did. She glanced at Ryan from the corner of her eye.

Sitting close enough their shoulders touched, he crossed

his arms over his chest and stared at the door. Even his thinking was charged with tension.

But, she had to admit, all that energy coiled in his body was fierce and...sexy. "We need to get you back before they notice you're missing."

I don't want to go back. Anya's knee bobbed. "Inga – my babysitter – told me lots of the wives sneak out of the spa and meet lovers on the side. That's how I got the idea to bribe the manager with the earrings. The manager will cover for me as long as possible, but not forever."

More thinking.

You help us, we'll help you.

Anya stayed quiet. The thought of returning to the Palace, to Ivanov, made her skin crawl, but Ryan needed her to find proof of Ivanov's plans. What was he going to ask her to do?

He shifted to look her in the face. So brown, his eyes. So serious. "Anya, you don't have to go back if you don't want to. I'll make some calls. Get you into some type of protective custody."

What? She met his stare. "No way. I have to go back to the Palace. Ivanov will kill Grams if I don't."

"You're sure he's got her? Have you seen her?"

A sick dread crept into her stomach. "No."

He uncrossed his arms, attention dropping to her lips as he leaned on the bed with one hand, his casualness belying the gears churning behind the calm, impassive face. "This type of undercover work is rough. Things could get...intense. More intense than an accidental slip of Ivanov's knife"

She raked her teeth over her bottom lip. Ryan's eyes flashed with a bit of heat at the gesture. She forced her knee to stop bobbing and put her hand over his. She could do this. *With his help.* "I can handle it."

They stayed that way for a long minute. Anya's face heated from the intensity of his stare. Her heart beat fast, echoing in her ears. Would he trust her? Would he stay in Russia and help her find Grams if she helped him nail Ivanov?

Suddenly, there was more to the heat in his eyes. More than the adrenaline from the close brush with the police and the anger over Ivanov's rough treatment lingering in his body. The tension changed, morphed into something else. Something that made her smile, unexpectedly feeling very female.

He blinked, and just like that, the heat was gone. He slid his hand out from under hers. Stood and moved toward the door. "Your assignment will be two-fold, then. Obtain proof of life regarding your grandmother and evidence against Ivanov regarding the nukes. I'll be attending the summit meeting, so I can help you. There's not much we can do at this point about his playing God with genes, but we sure as hell can stop him from adding to his nuclear arsenal." He turned back and looked at her. "I'll give you a quick rundown of evidence to look for before we drive you back to Moscow. Think you can handle it?"

Of course she could handle it. Didn't mean she wasn't freaking out inside. "I pocketed a launch key from Ivanov's collection, escaped his security goons at the spa, and made it all the way here in a stolen car and a red dress with a bleeding wound. What do you think?"

The side of his mouth quirked. "I think you're resourceful as well as industrious."

Anya couldn't stop the satisfaction that flooded her. "Exactly. I'm the one person who can get up close and personal with Ivanov. So tell me, Eddie..." She used the code name to make her point. "What do you need me to do?"

6

Moscow

    Twenty-four hours later

"I WANT YOUR ASSURANCE," AMBASSADOR LUTZ SAID FROM behind his massive cherry desk, "you're not going to screw up everything we've accomplished with Ivanov in the past seven months."

Ryan stared out the US Embassy window and absently watched snow fall thickly from the heavens, wishing he could see the Great Kremlin Palace.

The Palace was an enormous complex, and Anya was one person, all alone, inside. If she'd kept his sweater, he'd have no trouble finding her using the miniature tracking device he'd planted in the seam. The MTD—the size of a pin head—would only transmit when activated. Ryan just hoped he wouldn't have to turn it on.

The nuclear reduction summit was scheduled to start the next day, but his mission would begin tonight, within the hour, at the opening ceremonies.

If, that was, he could get the US Ambassador off his large backside and into the waiting limo outside. Ryan turned from the window and gave Aldridge Lutz his director of operations face. "Of course, sir. My only goal is to assist President Pennington."

The ambassador's heavy jowls worked up and down above the tight collar of his tux as if he were chewing over Ryan's words. "Ivanov is a friend to the United States. Hell, he's *my* friend. I want your assurances everything will go smoothly during the summit. If you, or the president's entourage, step on Ivanov's toes, you make my life a whole lot more difficult. Understood?"

Five thousand miles from D.C. and Ryan still couldn't get away from diplomatic ignorance, or the State Department's misguided ideas about the way the real world worked. Lutz's attitude was more dangerous to his mission than being inside the Kremlin surrounded by Ivanov's secret police. Lutz didn't know Ryan was the CIA's Director of Operations in Europe and Asia, and wouldn't benefit from knowing the truth about Ryan's covert mission any more than he'd benefit from Ryan showing him the sixty pages of transcripts, faxes, and eye-witness accounts, including Anya's, suggesting Ivanov was no friend to the United States. So Ryan lied. "I assure you, sir, I'm only acting on behalf of the President, and we have no intention of stepping on anyone's toes."

"And your two assistants?"

Lutz said the word *assistants* like he was talking about a couple of rats.

Come to think of it, Del and Josh were rat-like in their intelligence and sneakiness, but that's where the similarities ended. The computer geek and weapons expert were more like Ryan's left and right hands outside the Kremlin once he went in. They'd outfitted his tux with a button camera, a doped-up optical fiber communication system in his cummerbund, and a smart card reader in the heel of one of his Bruno Magli's. Since he couldn't openly carry a weapon, Josh had loaded Ryan up with a few everyday items that would double as such. From the keys on his keychain to the buckle on his belt, he was a walking WMD.

He hadn't planned on needing a weapon since recruiting an asset was tedious work but rarely dangerous. However, this was Russia, and the asset he was targeting was a deputy prime minister in Ivanov's cabinet. With any undercover op, things could get dicey, and in Ryan's world, 'Be Prepared' wasn't just the Boy Scout motto. Combined with the accusations Anya had made about Ivanov and his New World Order, Ryan wasn't taking chances.

The ambassador stood, signaling the discussion was over. He snagged his long wool coat from a hook and motioned for Ryan to follow him. "Just don't embarrass me."

The casual air of the opening ceremony would give Ryan the perfect chance to meet the deputy prime minister and strike up a conversation. It might take the entire week of summit meetings, dinners, and parties to gain the man's trust, but if he was as disgruntled as Ryan's sources claimed, the time would be a worthy investment. Keeping an eye on Anya, and figuring out if Ivanov truly held her grandmother captive, was his second mission. She hadn't told him everything, he was sure of that. Just enough to persuade him with that damned launch key into believing he was saving America, as well as her grandmother, if he helped her out.

Ryan shot his cuffs, and gave the ambassador a slight nod. Time to go to work. "After you, sir."

Half an hour later, Ryan was in Georgievsky Hall, otherwise known as the Hall of St. George, along with a mass of American and British diplomats. An appropriate place to host the trilateral summit welcome ceremony, its massive columns were crowned with statues exemplifying Russian weaponry. Marble plaques built into the walls showcased commanders who'd received their highest military decoration—the Order of St. George.

Russian architecture fascinated Ryan. Fresh out of the farm, he'd once navigated Moscow by the intricately designed buildings on a field test sans map. He'd learned Russian as a second language and fell in love with its art work. The Grand Kremlin Palace was his favorite site in Moscow, but he wasn't there for a sightseeing tour. As his gaze scanned the room, he counted fourteen of Ivanov's security guards stationed at the room's archways, and another dozen plainclothes police scattered amongst the U.S. president's secret service detail and the British prime minister's security unit. Ivanov had guaranteed the visiting dignitaries the highest level of security available and apparently he was true to his word, at least on this subject.

What Ryan didn't see was Anya.

He told himself not to worry about her. Whoever she was— double agent, innocent Russian princess, damsel in distress, or all of the above—she'd made it clear she was capable of handling herself in this place. His first order of business was his official Agency mission. Ignoring his lingering worries about her, Ryan scouted for surveillance equipment. Amidst the interior structural decor were hundreds of places perfect for cameras, and although he didn't see any obvious lenses, he knew they existed and were tracking his every movement.

Waiters with trays of champagne, vodka, and hors d'oeuvres circled small groups of socializing dignitaries at the east end of the ballroom. On the opposite side, long tables covered with damask tablecloths, fine china, sixteenth century candelabras, and shoulder-high floral centerpieces, were laid out in a U shape for dinner. A blend of modern Russian rock music and classical opera added background noise from hidden speakers above everyone's heads.

Ivanov was nowhere to be seen. Ryan's target, however, was

at three o'clock, talking to his boss, the Russian prime minister. The balding deputy minister, Yuri Barchai, was sweating heavily, his gaze darting around the room as if he, too, were keeping an eye on all the security details.

Ryan followed his gaze, scanning the different groups of dignitaries, security personnel, and even the waiters. All seemed exactly as it had been.

With one exception. Someone was watching him watch Barchai.

Across the vast expanse of the hall, Truman Gunn caught Ryan's eye. He was standing near the British prime minister and talking to Ambassador Lutz, a clear drink in his hand, and a camera hanging from a strap around his neck.

Ryan couldn't acknowledge him as a friend or acquaintance since they were both undercover. When their paths crossed, they would pretend they were meeting for the first time. One of the many reasons it was difficult for operatives to have long-lasting friendships. In public, they had to ignore each other.

Truman understood the game well, and with a subtle tip of the glass that no one but Ryan would've noticed, he shifted his focus back to Lutz.

Ryan followed suit and returned his attention to his target.

Along with the photographs of the Palace and grounds, Ryan had studied Barchai in detail. Bank accounts, extramarital affairs, bribes, even his elementary school records had been gone over with a fine-tooth comb. The smallest of details could give Ryan the upper hand when turning him, and if anything, Ryan was thorough with details.

Even if he hadn't known the man was unhappy in his current job, it was easy to deduce the conversation he was currently having with his boss made him agitated. When people felt upset, they were easier to turn into an asset because they gravitated to a sympathetic listener. Another of Ryan's skills.

But something about the man's expression made Ryan step back into the shadows behind a marble column to watch him more closely. Along with the agitation, he seemed to be arguing a point. The set of his jaw, the directness of his gaze when it went back to the prime minister's face, told him Yuri Barchai was on a mission.

And a man on a mission was no one to fool with.

When turning an asset, the first encounter was crucial. No sense rushing it and blowing the one chance he had of uncovering the truth about Ivanov. The nuclear summit would last a full week, and although it was a time crunch, Ryan would wait for the right opening.

Just like he would with Anya.

Recruiting assets in Russia had been a priority of Ryan's since he was promoted to top-dog over the European and Asian sectors. Getting CIA operatives into Russia, however, was still risky business. Twenty years after the end of the Cold War, animosity toward Americans ran like an electrical charge under the surface of Russian culture, waiting for a spark to ignite it. Something, no doubt, Ivanov was counting on down the road.

The new Russian president pretended to be a friend of the United States, but the CIA suspected Ivanov of covertly funneling money and weapons into Iran and Afghanistan. The only reason he would do such a thing would be to undermine America's ongoing war with terrorism.

While Ryan had a bevy of spies he could have used in Moscow to recruit assets, part of being director of operations was identifying the best man or woman for the job. In an extremely sensitive case like this, the man for the job was him.

For the next half hour, he pretended to be the Pennington aide his backstopped identity said he was, all the while searching for any sign of Anya. He mingled and shook hands, wishing he could ask about the princess, but knowing it wouldn't be a good idea. Instead, he had a brief conversation with Thad Pennington, President of the United States, who had no idea Ryan worked for the CIA even though Thad's brother-in-law, Michael Stone, was the clandestine group's deputy director. Pennington believed Ryan was one of his endless government worker bees, and that was exactly what Ryan wanted.

While Ryan worked the crowd, he spotted Truman snapping photographs. It was doubtful Truman would compromise him in such a way, but he made sure to stay out of the camera's eye at all times. Continuing to mingle, he kept Barchai in sight, waiting for the opportunity to introduce himself. He also steered clear of Lutz who kept shooting him nasty glances. When the moment came to approach his target, Ryan snagged a shot of vodka from a passing waiter's tray and walked toward the deputy prime minister who happened to be talking to Truman.

But just as he was about to join them, Barchai checked his watch, turned on his heel, and left the hall, eyes once again darting over the posted guards.

Too late to turn around or pretend that he hadn't been headed in Truman's direction, so Ryan stuck out his hand, plastered on a benign smile, and introduced himself. "Ryan Jones, advisor to President Pennington."

Truman shook his hand, sipped his drink, and affected his snootiest British accent. "Bond. James Bond."

Ryan glanced around and saw no one was close enough to overhear them. They were also underneath one of the ceiling speakers so if a listening device was in the vicinity, the music would drown them out. "You need a new pickup line."

"Don't kid yourself. Russian women love that line."

There were all of two women in the entire place, one a British diplomat with Truman's delegation, and the other a waitress who had a distinct mustache. Neither of which

Truman had paid any attention to. "You didn't mention you would be here. What's your cover?"

Truman scanned the room as if bored, slipped a business card from his inside breast pocket to give Ryan. "Tony Westport. Journalist for the *Guardian*."

"Covering the summit all week?"

A single head dip. "Have you seen the princess?"

"No. You?"

Truman shook his head and Ryan's gut gave a twinge. Had Ivanov found out about the key? Ryan'd given it back to Anya with instructions to return it to its case as soon as she could, but what if Ivanov had discovered it missing or worse, discovered Anya'd gone AWOL on him? When she'd returned to the Kremlin, he could have been waiting for her.

Ryan swallowed past the sudden tightness in his throat. *Where is she?*

He steeled his nerves, shook off the worry. Anya had already proven she could think on her feet. "You're the only media here. Seems like Ivanov would have his own press junket covering the summit."

"They're tucked inside his right pocket." Truman waived off a waiter with a tray of caviar on toast points before speaking again. "They'll only come out when he's in the spotlight shaking hands with Pennington or Morrow over the new treaty."

Ivanov, like many world leaders, was a known control freak. "So why'd he let the *Guardian* in?"

Truman cut his eyes to the female British diplomat. Shrugged. "Ivanov would love to win Britain's friendship away from America, I imagine."

Ryan was about to respond when a bell rang, silencing everyone. All heads turned toward the sound. The security guards at each of the archways stood even straighter and the hair on Ryan's neck tightened in response.

A door, invisible from inside the hall, opened at the far end behind the dining tables. Barchai appeared in the doorway, pausing for a moment to be sure he had everyone's attention. "Ladies and gentlemen, I present your host for the evening, and this week, the president of the Russian Federation, Maxim Ivanov."

The deputy prime minister moved out of the way. A round of applause broke out as the other dignitaries and guests stepped forward en masse to get a glance of Ivanov as he entered the grand hall.

A showman who enjoyed making an entrance, the fifty-three-year-old leader was dressed in his military attire rather than the designer dress suits worn by his British and American counterparts. His hair, barely graying at the sides, was military short as well.

He extended his hands in a gesture not unlike an actor receiving a standing ovation. "Fellow world leaders, friends, welcome to the nuclear summit meetings, and welcome to my home. It is my pleasure to host all of you here at the Great Kremlin Palace. Suites have been readied for each of you and my staff has been instructed to take care of your every need."

As more applause echoed in the hall, Ivanov made a little bow, and then raised a hand for silence.

Ryan and Truman stood at the back of the crowd. A flash of peacock blue behind Ivanov caught Ryan's attention and he strained his head to get a better glimpse.

"With me tonight," Ivanov continued, "and all of this week, is Grand Duchess Anya Maria Alesandrovna Romanov Radzoya. Her bloodline traces back to Paul I of Russia." He shifted to the right, turned and held out his hand.

Murmurs rippled through the crowd as Anya stepped to Ivanov's side. Ryan's breath stuck in his chest. Gone was the wind-blown hair and wild-eyed countenance. In its place, her white-blond hair fell elegantly around her face, and her eyes, which barely glanced at the crowd, showed tempered resistance. She was almost Ivanov's height in the heels that matched her blue dress. This dress, like the red silk one, stopped mid-thigh, accentuating her long, slim legs.

Black hole, here we come.

Ivanov took her hand as more clapping welcomed her to the event, and Ryan gritted his teeth at the intimate gesture. "Czarevna Anya and I welcome you to Russia!"

Czarevna. Interesting term. As if Russia was still lead by czars.

The attendees applauded and milled around to find their assigned places at various tables, many of them stealing glances at Anya as Ivanov escorted her to the head table. Waiters appeared with shoulder-lofted silver trays. The sound of conversations again filled the air.

Truman raised his camera and took a photograph of Ivanov and Anya. "There's your Russian princess." He lowered the camera and glanced at Ryan. "Before she showed up at the cabin, I didn't realize there were any Russian princesses left, at least none so young and pretty. Wonder where he dug her up?"

Ryan pressed a finger into a cufflink on his left sleeve, engaging the camera hidden in the button of his shirt. Thad Pennington approached Ivanov, greeting the leader and shaking his hand and Ivanov in turn introduced Anya. Her eyes brightened at meeting the President of the United States. She eagerly shook his hand and smiled openly as he chatted with her for a moment. She looked almost star struck.

Beautiful. Ryan angled his chest and pressed the cufflink to get a shot of her smiling.

When Pennington moved off to Ivanov's right, however, Anya's smile faded and she flinched at Ivanov's touch—a subtle movement Ryan would have missed if he hadn't been watching her closely. Ivanov guided her to a chair next to his.

"There are three living females descended from the original

Imperial Houses," Ryan murmured to Truman. "One is a widow in her forties who lives in the south of France and claims to be waiting for the Russian people to reinstate her as their ruler. The second woman of royal blood disappeared with her granddaughter—the third and youngest Russian Grand Duchess—back in 1995 after the girl's parents died in a tragic auto accident outside Moscow."

At the time, no one in- or outside of Russia had said a word about the disappearances, as if they feared questioning them might result in their own disappearance or untimely accident.

"And Ivanov found her," Truman said.

"That, or the Russian president knew her whereabouts all along."

At the head table, Anya ignored the commotion around her. Her head was tilted down, attention locked on the china. Tense lines framed the corners of her mouth. Through the throng of waiters and the rustle of people taking their seats, she seemed to feel Ryan's gaze. Slowly, she lifted her head and met his eyes.

For the second time that night, Ryan recognized the expression staring back at him. Like the deputy prime minister, Anya Radzoya was on a mission.

Only hers was a deadly game of treason.

And if he wasn't careful, she'd bring him down with her.

7

HE WAS HERE. Finally.

And damn, he cleaned up good. The soft light from the overhead chandeliers made his wheat colored hair—now trimmed and neat—glow. Cheeks smooth, stubble shaved off. The tux added bulk to his already broad shoulders and emphasized his natural air of complete invulnerability.

He was put together and in control of himself. Hell, in control of everything.

Which made her less freaked out about her situation, and more freaked out that she was so attracted to a spy.

Ryan's direct, unwavering gaze held hers across the room. His presence reassured her, although she wasn't sure why—he'd been less than encouraging about her plans to save her grandmother and stop Ivanov's treachery. Having him there took some of the weight off her shoulders though. If she got into hot water, he would be there. She could trust him, even though he still didn't quite trust her.

He continued to stare, his gaze traveling down her body, his eyes dark and unnerving. As if he suspected she was more than a kidnapped woman trying desperately to put her shattered world back together. As if he suspected she was screwing him over.

As if he didn't give a damn if she was.

Her cheeks heated. *You're paranoid, Anya. Stop it.*

She had a right to be paranoid considering what had happened in the past few days. Since arriving back at the Kremlin, Ivanov or his protection guards had watched her every move. Not just goons following discreetly behind her, but full-on security details shadowing her every step. He hadn't said anything to suggest he suspected she'd done something besides spend six hours at the spa, but she was now under 24/7 surveillance. When she'd asked, he'd said it was simply because of the all the foreign guests arriving for the summit. The mass of strangers presented more risk, and one couldn't be too safe. Fortunately or unfortunately, depending on how she looked at it, he'd been so busy preparing for this joke of a summit, he'd barely given her ten minutes of his time, and in those ten minutes, he'd refused to discuss her grandmother.

Grams. *God, I hope you're okay.*

While Natasha Romanov was healthy for her age, she'd had mild heart trouble. The one and only time she'd been in the hospital was for an angiogram, which had uncovered a blockage and resulted in the insertion of a stent, and daily heart medication. It hadn't slowed her down, as evidenced by her constant traveling to see friends, but how long could she go without her meds?

Have you seen her? Ryan's words echoed in Anya's brain. The thought Grams might be suffering, or even dead, fired up the constant dread sitting in Anya's chest. It also fired up her determination. She bobbed her knee under the table. From across the room, she met Ryan's stare, forgetting the heat in her face. No one—not Ivanov, or the CIA—was going to stop her from carrying out her plans.

Eyes locked with hers, Ryan suddenly smiled, full on

charm, and all traces of scrutinizing gone. Anya swallowed. For a second, she forgot she was sitting next to Ivanov in a room full of dignitaries. She forgot all her problems. That smile...*damn*.

He really should smile more often.

Her knee slowed. Ryan's body language combined with that smile made her believe for half a second that everything was going to be okay.

He'd instructed her to act like they were strangers at this dinner. Well, duh. She might not be a spy, but she knew better than to tip her hand to Ivanov, or endanger Ryan in any way by acting like they were friends. Ryan, Eddie, whatever the hell his real name was, they *weren't* friends. Anya didn't even know his last name. He probably had several of those too.

Like her.

Yes, their secrets were better left alone, but how was she supposed to ignore the warm, tingling in her lower stomach? The fact that she had to keep looking at him to calm her nerves?

Truman, the British spy, said something to Ryan, and he responded without breaking eye contact with Anya. Reassuring her that he was keeping an eye on her?

Another place, under different circumstances, she might have returned his smile with something more than reserved hope. She couldn't keep her heart from jumping around, though, and struggled to keep her face solemn. The only way to suffocate her very female reaction to him was to break their eye lock.

Drawing a determined breath, she forced her gaze to the sweeping arches and towering pillars of the room.

Georgievsky Hall was awe-inspiringly beautiful. From the grandiose arches to the highly polished floors, the hall's magnificent and elegant design reminded the men and women attending tonight's celebration that Imperial Russia lived on in the heart and soul of the capital, even if the country was now led by an elected president.

Everywhere Anya looked, light reflected off gold, crystal, marble. And everywhere she looked, ghosts rose in her mind.

The hall had hosted dozens of important foreign diplomats since the end of the Cold War. It had also been the site of official domestic ceremonies. When her father, a favorite member of then-President Yeltsin's cabinet, and her mother, a geneticist who'd worked for Yeltsin in a special government laboratory, had been killed in an auto accident, the president had arranged a formal wake in Georgievsky Hall for them.

Fifteen years had passed since Anya had been in Moscow, in this very hall, a dark abyss opening at her feet at the loss of her parents. Eleven years old and staring in shock at the ornate caskets, closed due to the damage done by the fire when the car went up in flames. Or so they told her. Anya knew the truth. Both her parents had been shot. Murdered. Before her eyes. The car had gone up in flames to hide the bullet holes and destroy the bodies beyond recognition. She'd been there, having run from the car and hidden in the woods at her mother's insistence. She'd seen the masked man dressed in black approach the car. Heard her trapped mother's screams before the car exploded.

If it hadn't been for her stoic and regal grandmother moving Anya through the formalities of shaking hands and accepting condolences from Yeltsin and her parents' peers, Anya would have been a basket case. Even now, a thousand tiny razor blades of memories assaulted her. Buried emotions threatened to flood her chest.

Never tell, Grams had said. *Or the man in black will find you too.*

Anya averted her gaze from the spots where the caskets had sat. Averted it from where she'd watched Grams, after everyone had gone, throw herself on top of her son's casket and weep.

Where Anya had cried silently, shaking so hard she could barely stand, as the bells of Dormition Cathedral rang a death toll in the distance.

Ivanov's booming voice jarred her from her depressing walk down memory lane. It rang with unchallenged authority. "A toast."

On her right, he stood and raised a crystal glass full of champagne. He continued to speak in English, his Russian accent thick as his words hushed the guests. "This week marks a historic event, as Russia, Britain, and all of our allies join together in the quest to reduce nuclear weapons. We achieve a safer place for all our peoples and create a world of peace."

He paused, briefly meeting the eyes of his counterparts in the room. Anya chanced a glance at Ryan. He now studied the Russian president with the same intense scrutiny he had given her. "Tonight we lift our glasses in solidarity."

Truman snapped a picture. Next to her, Ivanov's prime minister mimicked the president's raised glass. Like a ripple of water, the seated diplomats down both tables did the same, clinking glasses together to echos of "hear, hear."

Ivanov smiled down at Anya and her stomach dropped. Nothing at all like Ryan's smile, his was of the conqueror, the subjugator. *The cat who'd swallowed the canary,* Grams would have said. He was in his glory in the glow of the limelight, and his eyes told her what he expected her to do.

Her throat went dry.

Do it for Grams.

Biting the inside of her cheek, she raised her glass and let him clink his against it. Under his scrutiny, she put the glass to her lips and pretended to sip. The champagne fizzed on her lips, but she refused to swallow. Drinking a toast with her sworn enemy would betray every moral and ethical element of her being.

Ivanov returned to his seat wearing a satisfied smile. As the first course was served, he touched her hand under the table. Anya flinched, his cold skin so different from the warm, steadying hands of the spy across the room. "We will enjoy a traditional Russian feast tonight, Czarevna. I've instructed the chefs to represent each region of Russia during the various courses. You will enjoy it."

He was old enough to be her father, and although she loathed him, she had to admit he was a striking man. His salt and pepper beard, mixed with his graying hair and dark eyebrows reminded her of Sean Connery in *The Hunt for Red October*, only thirty pounds heavier. Grams loved those movies as much as the Clint Eastwood ones. By outward appearances, Ivanov was polite, attentive, and charming. Women must have swooned over him, but Grams would have said he was *velik telom, da mal delom*. Big of the body, but small by his deeds. Why he wanted her by his side was exceedingly clear.

Czarevna.

Princess.

The title he used so frequently burned her ears. His touch sent goose bumps racing over her skin.

He noticed her shaking. "You are cold?"

Even though the hall was drafty, and the dress Ivanov had insisted she wear wouldn't cover a twelve-year-old, the chill in her bones had little to do with either.

Five more days. She only had to endure the game until the end of the summit.

A waiter slid a bowl of steaming borscht in front of her. Grateful for the distraction, she drew her hand away from Ivanov's and picked up the spoon next to her plate, hoping it was the right one. "The soup will warm me."

Seeming content with her answer, he snapped his napkin open, and dug into his own bowl of beet soup. Anya stared at the liquid, the color of blood, and bile rose in her throat. She hadn't eaten since sometime Friday, and her stomach growled in anticipation of food. She raised a spoonful to her mouth, but her lips refused to open.

Appearance was important. Stirring the soup, she continued to bob her knee under the table, trying to release the pent up anxiety coursing through her body. Once or twice she glanced at Ryan to calm herself. He was there, his gaze steady and encouraging. Holding her breath, she lifted the spoon to her lips once more. No way could she pretend to eat the soup like she'd pretended to drink the champagne.

But the thought of swallowing borscht turned her stomach. *I can't do it.*

She returned the spoon to the bowl.

Ivanov spoke in her ear. "Is there something wrong with your soup?"

Startled from his sudden nearness, she jerked her head back. "Oh, uh, no." Peering down at the soup, she swallowed hard. "I just...um. I'm allergic to beets. Beetroot," she amended. Only in America did they refer to the vegetable as beets.

Allergic to beets? *Who in the world is allergic to beets?*

She could have slapped her forehead, but Ivanov only seemed embarrassed. He looked down at this own soup, coughed into his napkin. "I did not know."

A snap of his fingers at a nearby waiter and the borscht was replaced with a mushroom soup that smelled exactly like her grandmother's version. The earthy aroma filled Anya's nostrils, memories of eating Grams's soup pushing out her anxiety.

Beside her, Ivanov watched her closely. "This is more to your liking, *da*?"

There was true concern on his face like a child wanting to please a parent. Where was the madman lurking behind the clear blue of his eyes? Why did he care if she liked the soup when he was causing her such torment over her grandmother?

For a split second, Anya considered standing up and announcing to the entire group that the Russian president was holding her grandmother hostage. Would Thad Pennington demand Ivanov release her? Would Brad Morrow charge Ivanov with international crimes?

Grams' life wasn't worth the risk. Ivanov would deny Anya's claims, and since he was probably the only person who knew where Grams was, it was imperative Anya not force his hand until she discovered the location herself. Then, hopefully, Ryan and the CIA would come through. If they didn't, Anya had no qualms about rescuing Grams on her own. She had no idea how she'd liberate an ailing seventy-year-old woman from Ivanov's clutches and get her out of Russia safely, but she had five days to figure it out.

Five days to show the world that Maxim Ivanov was nothing less than a modern day Hitler.

Reaching deeper into her willpower, she took the clean spoon the waiter provided and tasted the soup. "This is delicious."

The statement wasn't untrue. The soup was good. Not as good as Grams', but good enough to eat.

Pleased by her response, Ivanov returned to his borscht and resumed a conversation with Pennington as if nothing had happened.

Which was fine with Anya. The hum of conversations rose and fell as people ate and drank freely. When Ivanov wasn't watching her every move, she could block out reality and pretend she was out to eat at a fancy restaurant by herself. With a handsome man in a tux making eyes at her across the room.

Until the foie gras arrived in a purple sauce that looked like grape juice. Tiny pine cones were strewn across the plate. She would never order that, fancy restaurant or not. She didn't even try to force down the pâté, only moving some around on the plate to look like she'd eaten it. Seeing others try the edible pine cones, she nibbled on one. While the pine cone itself was delicious, the texture in her dry mouth made her choke.

Thankfully, Ivanov didn't seem to notice.

Ryan did. Across the room, he glanced at Ivanov to make sure the man was distracted, looked down at his plate, and drew the edges of his mouth down in a comical frown of disgust. His focus came back to hers and he winked.

He winked. At me.

It was so unexpected, a soft bubble of laughter escaped her throat before she could stop it.

"You like the food? Next will be sturgeon. *Mnoga.*"

Her laughter had drawn Ivanov's attention. He followed the direction of her gaze, saw Ryan—who'd had the good sense to look away from Anya and return to his conversation—and narrowed his eyes at her.

Grams needs you. Play your part. Maybe if she pretended to have forgotten her native language, and seemed to be more American than Russian, it would turn him off. "*Mnoga* means 'a lot', right?"

One small act of defiance, but it worked to make Ivanov forget about Ryan, and warm to instructing her. He stretched his arms out to demonstrate. "*Da. Mnoga,* many. Big."

He lifted his vodka shot glass and tapped it against her champagne glass. "The longer you are here, Czarevna, the more you will remember your Russian ancestry and learn about your Russian future."

The longer you are here. His summons had only required her presence for the summit, but every minute with him confirmed the truth about his true intentions.

He downed the shot and slapped the upturned glass on the table. "You and I, together." He smiled, and in that smile she saw something that made her heart hammer and her knee bob like crazy. "*Mnoga.*"

For years after Grams had removed her from Russia, shadowy monsters followed Anya everywhere. In her imagination, in her dreams. The man in black was always there.

Sinister and threatening like the Grimm tales. The older she'd gotten, the less she'd noticed them. Now, staring at Ivanov, the Grimm tales had come to life. The monster of her youth had materialized in front of her.

Worse, she was at his mercy. Grams wasn't there to wake her up and tell her everything was all right.

Everything was *not* all right.

But Grams had trained her well during her years in America. Showing fear or uncertainty would send a fatal signal to the monster, giving him the upper hand. To win the game of survival, Anya had to pretend she wasn't shaking from head to toe. Pretend she knew what she was doing every second of every day.

The reality was, she was a nobody, and Ivanov was the president of the Russian Federation. She had something he wanted, though. Something no one else could give him.

Her imperial Russian genes. Defective though they were.

During her years in America, living under a false name and keeping a low profile, she'd had to pretend her royal blood didn't exist. But, here in the place of her birth, the blood of her ancestors swirled in her body, alive and vibrant, and fighting to resurface. The princesses who'd come before her whispered in her ear, bolstering her for the coming five days of torment.

For Grams, she would survive. For Grams, she would face the monster and win.

Fighting the urge to throw her champagne in Ivanov's face, Anya instead raised her chin and smiled back at him, Ryan's steady presence reassuring her.

8

He'd finally gotten a smile out of the princess. More, she'd laughed.

A small thing, but it made Ryan's chest warm with a sense of accomplishment.

Even though he couldn't hear the laugh, the effect had been mesmerizing, transforming her face like it had back at the cabin, and his imagination had happily filled in the sound. Before the night was over, he wanted to see if the real thing matched the soft, sexy resonance his brain had conjured.

The laugh made her body language do a complete one-eighty. From the curve of her lips, the change rose up her cheek bones to her eyes. The rigid determination he'd seen in them earlier disappeared, and in its place, a conspiratorial look of appreciation. The chain effect then slid down her body. Her tense shoulders relaxed and she took another deep breath.

While the entire metamorphosis took less than a heartbeat, Ryan registered every component.

But then Ivanov spoke to her and the satisfaction brewing in Ryan's chest had dissipated. Irritation took its place.

Luckily Truman had been sitting on his left, carrying on the conversation without him, and asking questions as if they were indeed new friends. Before Ivanov could follow Anya's gaze, Ryan had answered one of Truman's benign questions. When he dared look back, she was talking to Ivanov.

A dangerous emotion took root in Ryan's gut. Anger.

Anger was generally born out of fear, sometimes out of revenge. This anger, however, came from jealousy.

Emotions, good or bad, made an operative vulnerable, and a vulnerable operative was a dead operative.

Ryan shoved the jealousy behind a steel door in his mind and slammed it shut. Jealousy, mission or no mission, had no place in his life.

He couldn't, however, pull his focus away from Anya.

The change he'd affected was still present. The smile she gave Ivanov was reserved, almost demure, and yet there was an edge to it. A sharp edge. As if she'd realized something that renewed her self-confidence.

While the Russian president didn't seem to notice, Ryan saw it in every expression on her face, every move she made over the next few minutes.

Waiters served an apple tart along with coffee. Anya dug into her dessert with an odd gusto lacking during the previous courses, and once again, a sense of satisfaction took hold inside him.

Truman spoke around a mouthful of tart. "You really think Ivanov's new play thing is a credible asset for the U.S.?"

Ryan sipped his coffee, ignoring the way his gut rebelled at *play thing*. "If I say no, you going to proposition her?"

"I wish. Unfortunately, I'm stuck with an internal affair." Truman cut his eyes toward the female British diplomat at the nearby table. From the way he emphasized 'affair', Ryan figured the woman was probably selling or sharing national security secrets with a lover.

He made a mental note to put his own eyes and ears in

London on her in case she was jeopardizing U.S. security as well. "You staying in the Palace?"

"No. You?"

"That's the plan. Pennington wants me at his beck and call. Not sure why, other than he's completely out of his safe zone here."

"I assume Michael Stone planted a bug in his ear. Gave you a gold star and all that."

"The deputy director wouldn't tell the president that I'm a spy, even if he is his brother-in-law. Lutz has his suspicions, but he's been around a long time. Seen a lot of spies posing as various aides and advisors. I think I've convinced him I'm not, but if he tips my hand, he can kiss his ambassador title goodbye."

Polishing off the last of his tart, Truman followed Ryan's gaze to Anya. "Anything you want me to pass on to Langley about her?"

After seeing firsthand the extent of Ivanov's 'security' measures, Ryan was sure even with his high-tech communication gear, he couldn't get anything in or out of the Palace without Ivanov's people intercepting it. Truman could very well be his only safe link to the outside world.

Ryan didn't like being in another spook's debt, but this time, the risk might be worth it. "I've already asked Stone to confirm Anya's story about her grandmother's kidnapping. Conrad's still out of commission, so check with Del and see if he's heard anything. Tell him not to risk contacting me yet. He's only to send information in with you."

Truman gave a brusque nod.

"In return, what do you want from me?"

The British spy played with his fork, thinking it over. "I'll let you know."

After dinner, they were led to a salon off Georgievsky Hall which continued the gold, marble and crystal theme. A group of young children hovered around a grand piano at the far end, while a twenty-something man in a tux complete with tails sat at the piano, playing soft show tunes. A large arched window framed the group, and outside the window, snow continued to fall.

British and American security details fanned out around the perimeter. There were fewer Russian guards inside the salon, but the rest were outside the doors. As in any situation, worst-case scenarios ran through his head. Even with all the security keeping outside dangers from getting in, the people were sitting ducks if the danger came from within.

Ryan trusted Ivanov about as far as he could spit. Crazy Russian dictators were a cliché for a reason. As nonchalantly as possible, he watched Ivanov's every move. Anya's too.

The seating in the salon was less formal and Ryan snagged a spot next to Barchai. The deputy prime minister was still keyed up, fiddling with his cufflinks, straightening his tie over and over again. Ryan took the opportunity to introduce himself and made a few polite comments about the evening's meal, but Barchai's responses were short and pointed, as if he weren't really listening. Ryan let further socializing go.

An older woman, a grandmotherly type in a pale yellow dress, gathered the waiting children into a semi-circle and cued the accompanist to begin. The oldest of the children looked to be eight or nine, and yet the quality of their voices as they sang traditional Russian folk songs for the dignitaries was truly amazing.

As the children's voices echoed through the room, Ryan glanced at Anya, who was at the front beside Ivanov. From his vantage point behind her, Ryan couldn't see her face but her body language continued to demonstrate confidence. At the end of the concert, she clapped heartily.

Each of the children in the chorus held a white rose. After accepting the applause, the first young boy on the end stepped forward and presented his flower to Anya with a small bow. The other children lined up behind him to do the same.

Next in line was a short, thin girl. With her blue eyes and white blonde hair, she could have been Anya's sister and seemed to know it. Her eyes rounded with awe as she handed Anya the rose and curtsied. *"Dlya vas, Czarevna."*

For you, Princess.

Anya's surprise over the presentation was genuine, and even sitting three rows behind her, Ryan could feel it as well as see it as she wrapped the young girl in a hug and praised her singing.

Truman dutifully snapped pictures as the children filed by, Ivanov beaming at Anya with a strange kind of pride.

Once more something dark and dangerous flickered deep in Ryan's gut. A need to protect Anya, shield her from the Russian president, spread through his veins like a drug.

He checked himself. He was there to do a job. Get in, find out what he could about Ivanov, and get out. He would help Anya and her grandmother if he could, but ultimately, the soap opera antics of the Russian president took second place to his mission to gain a bonafide asset inside the Kremlin.

As the children continued to file by, each glowed under Anya's praises. Ryan concentrated on listening to her softly spoken words, automatically analyzing the cadence, vocabulary, and accent. She'd been well-schooled in American English. Her Russian accent so faint, only he would notice. Probably because he found it so damn sexy.

Pieces of the puzzle fell into place. The princess and her grandmother who'd disappeared from Russia in the 1990s had apparently made the United States their home. The CIA had no doubt orchestrated their relocation and assimilation into American culture.

He made a mental note to check into that as well, but his gut told him another element of Anya's story rang true.

After the last child handed Anya his rose and received a

hug, the woman in the yellow dress herded the children out the door. As they were leaving, the Russian prime minister, who had been absent during the concert, rushed in and approached Ivanov. He whispered something in Ivanov's ear and drew him aside. Ryan's instincts went on high alert.

Barchai jumped up, hurried to the front of the group and announced the evening's entertainment was concluded. The dignitaries would be shown to their apartment suites inside the main building as soon as President Ivanov said his parting words. Then he turned to the piano player and motioned for him to play. The young man seemed caught off guard, but soft music soon filled the salon.

Ivanov and his right hand man continued conversing in the corner. People stood and broke into smaller groups, both Pennington and Morrow gathering with the embassy dignitaries to discuss the next day's meetings.

The woman in the yellow dress returned and took the roses from Anya's arms, said a few words to her, and hustled out the door with the flowers. Anya, now alone, glanced around the room, obviously unsure of what to do or who to talk to. She met Ryan's gaze, gave him a small, sad smile, and walked to the arched window behind the piano to stare out into the snowy night.

Without taking his eyes off her, Ryan nodded to Truman. "See you tomorrow."

He started to walk away, only to be stopped by Truman's hand on his arm. "Surely you're not about to chat up Ivanov's new toy right in front of him."

Ryan slid his arm from Truman's grasp. "Surely not."

Adjusting his bow tie as if he couldn't wait to get it off, Truman smirked. "Right."

He abandoned Truman and skirted several of the talking groups, a plan already forming. Turning Barchai into an asset inside a week was a pipe dream. Anya, already close to Ivanov, and willing to spy on him, was at Ryan's disposal. If he agreed to help her with her grandmother, she'd do anything he wanted.

The window overlooked a courtyard filled with statues, trellises, and walkways, all carpeted in white. Anya's face reflected in the glass as she stared out into the night, not seeming to see it. She leaned a shoulder against one side of the arch as if needing the support. Ryan edged closer, mindful of Ivanov, who continued to be engrossed in his conversation with the Russian prime minister. He was also mindful of the guards stationed around the room who kept a steady eye on the princess at all times.

Up close, he could see how pale her skin was under the cover of makeup. How tired she looked. The curve of her bare shoulder was enticing, but the rapid beat of her pulse at the base of her neck kept Ryan from enjoying it. Her fingers, folded together in front of her, twisted as she worried a ring on her left hand.

For all her display of bravado at the cabin and during the evening's proceedings, bottom line, she was scared.

One last step and he faced the window, pretending not to stare at her reflection. "Beautiful night."

Her startled reaction confirmed she was indeed a million miles away in her thoughts. She turned from the window and gave him a weak smile before looking outside again. "Beautiful, if you like winter."

She was following his lead, making small talk. Good girl. "Hard to escape winter in Moscow this time of year."

"Mmm-hmm. Harder still to escape fois gras."

Score. The lady had a sense of humor. He faced her, drawing her attention to him. "Ryan Jones. Russian affairs advisor for President Pennington." He held up a hand, put it back down. "I'd offer to shake hands, but I'm not sure what the proper protocol is for introducing oneself to a modern Russian grand duchess..." He leaned in conspiratorially and shot his gaze around the room. "And I wouldn't want to be shot by Ivanov's police for violating it."

Her smile had more punch to it this time and her eyes held a definite spark. "A Russian affairs *expert* who doesn't know protocol when it comes to royalty? Seems like your schooling needs supplementation."

Another direct hit. He chuckled, and damn if it didn't feel good. "Having a direct royal source for guidance would certainly help."

She extended her hand, still pretending they'd never met before. "Well, I never saw the brochure on How to Be A Princess, so I'm afraid my own education falls short of Russian protocol." Now she leaned toward him and lowered her sexy voice another notch. "But don't tell, okay?"

Flirting with her was a terrible idea. A terrible, horrible idea. It could get them both in serious hot water.

But Ryan couldn't stop himself. Didn't *want* to stop himself.

Her fingers were slim, nails short and manicured. He took her hand in his and was surprised when she gave him one firm, all-business shake. Like at the cabin, there was nothing demure or hesitant about it.

"How does it feel to be back in Russia?" he ventured, opening the lines of conversation subterfuge. He needed to confirm she was all right.

She shot a glance in Ivanov's direction and tensed. Ryan jerked his gaze to the right and saw the man headed their way. His small, hard eyes narrowed into jealous slits.

Approaching enemy. The age old response of fight or flight kicked in and adrenaline rolled through his limbs. He'd had training to neutralize facial reactions the instinctual response generated, so he ignored the instinct, returning his focus to Anya. She, on the other hand, hadn't had the same training.

Her eyes darted from Ivanov to Ryan and then out the

window. Her breathing sped up and her body quivered. Flight was definitely on Anya's menu.

Then, just as quickly as she'd given thought to it, she took a deep breath, and brought her gaze back to his. In her eyes, Ryan saw the same resolve he'd seen earlier. She was staying because she had a job to do, and she would handle Ivanov, whatever that job entailed.

Too bad he hadn't time at the cabin to give her more training about how to act around the bastard.

The Russian president was two steps away. Anya smiled at Ryan, a detached smile, as if he were nothing more than another politician she had to make nice to. Her eyes were just as impartial. "Nice to meet you, Mr. Jones. I hope you enjoy your stay here at the Palace."

She may have lacked training, but she definitely could stand on her own two feet. She couldn't suppress the shudder that rolled through her, though, as Ivanov slipped his arm around her waist.

The emotion Ryan most feared ignited deep in his gut. He nodded in response and acknowledged Ivanov's presence. "Tonight's dinner was exceptional, as was the entertainment."

Ivanov didn't even pretend politeness. He gave Ryan another scathing once over. Translation: Ryan was nothing more than an ant under Ivanov's boot.

Ivanov swept Anya away, moving her to the center of the room before releasing his hold and calling for everyone's attention. He waited until the crowd quieted before thanking the leaders of Britain and the United States for attending the dinner. "The summit will begin tomorrow morning at eight o'clock sharp in Georgievsky Hall," he said.

As he spoke, Anya took several steps back and to the left, sneaking a look over her shoulder at Ryan. Her face was no longer impassive, a hint of real fear in her eyes over the fact, he presumed, that the evening was done. At least the public part of it.

The resolve she'd had up to now was fading fast. She gave Ryan a half-smile as if letting him know she was sorry for the chilly brush off. He winked at her in response.

Give em hell, sweetheart.

His silent message registered. She forced a little more courage into her smile before facing Ivanov, as if assuring Ryan, or possibly herself, she was okay.

Ryan didn't believe her.

Whatever lay ahead for the night scared the crap out of her, and it wasn't hard to guess exactly what she feared.

The anger in Ryan's gut burst into flame.

9

ONCE SHE CROSSED THE THRESHOLD, there was no turning back.

"Make yourself at home, Grand Duchess." Ivanov opened the double doors of the presidential suite and made a sweeping gesture with his arm.

Every fiber in Anya's body rebelled as the previous two nights' memories assaulted her. Every warning bell in her head clanged. The muscles in her neck tensed and her feet tried to move backwards. The wound on her side itched. Maybe it was finally healing thanks to Ryan's expert care.

Would the security guards on each side of the doors grab her if she tried to run? Would Ivanov force her inside? Yank out that stupid vintage Russian dirk he carried like a security blanket and cut her again?

Stupid man. The wrong cut at the wrong time and she could potentially bleed to death. *Wait 'til I tell him that.*

Gritting her teeth, she lifted her foot and stepped into the spider's web.

Like all the various halls and rooms in the Palace, the Throne Chamber, or Czar's Study, was a stunning example of architectural splendor. Domed ceilings painted a brilliant white and trimmed in gold made her think of a painting she'd seen in the Smithsonian depicting gold-edged clouds with cherubs resting on them. The deep blue walls, curtains, and upholstery of the chamber mimicked a late-afternoon summer sky. The dark wooden floor shone with multiple layers of heavy polish.

The effect would have been mesmerizing if not for the dread beating in her chest.

Antique guns and dirks were on display in glass cabinets everywhere she looked. Ivanov led her past his desk, a smaller version of the massive one made from Ural malachite in his official office, to a 19th century Italian sofa in front of the white marble fireplace. Above the fireplace, a wooden clock told her it was after midnight. Orange flames simmered behind the iron grate giving off little heat but adding charm to the overall effect.

Reluctantly, she sat on the sofa while Ivanov poked at the fire and added a log. The flames twitched and shuddered, climbing up the logs to reach for air. Satisfied that the fire was once more active, he headed to a sidebar filled with liquor bottles, decanters, and crystal classes. Removing a bottle of chilled vodka from a hidden cabinet refrigerator, he poured two glasses and brought one back to her.

She took the offered glass, even though she had no intention of drinking the vodka. By her estimation, Ivanov had downed half a bottle already, plus the champagne he'd used to toast over dinner. He was an inch or so over six foot tall, and probably weighed two-twenty or more, but the alcohol so far didn't seem to be affecting him.

He sat on the edge of the sofa, entirely too close for comfort, unbuttoning his military coat with one hand, and swigging the vodka with the other. He smelled like alcohol and a thick, musky aftershave.

Anya shifted backwards. The dress inched up her thighs, revealing more of her pale skin. She slipped her left hand down to the side and tugged at the hem as casually as she could, trying not to call attention to the fact her legs were so bare. Her knee bobbed ever so slightly.

"What did you think of the dinner tonight?" Ivanov scanned her face, looking for approval. His accent was heavier, thicker. The alcohol was affecting him after all. "Did you enjoy the children?"

She didn't want to discuss the dinner or the children's chorus, but as Grams had taught her, the best defense was a good offense. He wanted her approval, so that's what she gave him. "The evening was a success, and I'm glad we finally have a chance to talk. About my grandmother..."

"President Pennington and Prime Minister Morrow were impressed, *da*?"

"Everyone was impressed."

Ivanov smiled his Cheshire cat smile and lifted his glass to her. His eyes reflected the flames of the fire as he gulped the vodka. "I have special events planned all week. For you."

His meaning was clear, his intent as well. The heat from the fire might as well have been the north wind blowing outside. Anya's blood ran cold. "I need to know my grandmother is okay."

Ivanov heaved up from the sofa, empty glass in hand. "There is something I want to show you."

Her heart leapt. Was he going to take her to Grams? As he grabbed the bottle of chilled vodka from the refrigerator, she rose from the sofa to follow him.

The trip was disappointingly short, ending at the bookcases near his desk. He refilled his glass and offered to top off hers as well. Since she hadn't even sipped her vodka, she shook her head, and set her still half-full tumbler on the malachite desk.

Ivanov threw another shot down his throat. Then he faced the books on the nearby shelves and skimmed his fingers over the spines. The titles were in Russian and Anya strug-gled for a second to shift to her native language and the

Cyrillic alphabet. She was fluent in Russian, but after Grams insisted she purge the first eleven years from her memory, she was rusty.

He removed a twelve-by-twelve, leather bound book and set it on the desk. The book's Russian title was imprinted in gold lettering on the front—*Romanov Family Tree*—and Ivanov ran his fingers across it as if it were sacred. Opening the cover, he flipped through several pages, all of them encased behind page protectors. Anya tried to see what was on the pages, but she couldn't without moving closer to him.

Finding the page he was looking for, he ran a finger down the plastic protector. "Here." He tapped the page and glanced up. "Natasha Maria Romanov."

Curiosity got the better of her and Anya inched closer. Like the title, the words were in Russian, but she recognized the name she had printed out hundreds of times during her school years before moving to America. *Romanov.*

The page held a diagram, labeled with various names. A horizontal line ran from Gram's name to Anya's grandfather's name, Anton Radzoya. Below their union, a vertical line connected them to another name she recognized. Peter Romanov Radzoya. Anya's father. His name connected to her mother's, Ekateirna, and below them a new tier of the family tree held Anya's full name.

"The great imperial dynasty," Ivanov said, his eyes glowing with pride. With his empty hand, he motioned at a collection of books behind them. "I have researched and documented the complete ancestral history of each royal family dating back to the founding of our Russian monarchy."

Our Russian monarchy. The way he emphasized *our* made it sound like he and Anya shared dominion over it. And while she knew Russian history had been researched and documented by hundreds of scholars all around the world, she once again understood Ivanov wanted to impress her. He wanted her approval. He was bragging, as if he had done all the work himself.

She couldn't bring herself to flatter him, so she went with a generic response. "That's an impressive amount of work." *Probably all done by someone else.*

Her feedback egged him on. He reached for another leather-bound book and took it from the shelf, opening it on top of her family's history. Just like with the first book, he flipped through dozens of pages to find the one he wanted. He turned the book so it was easier for her to see, and pointed at the name he wanted her to read.

Maxim Yakovlev Ivanov.

Apprehension shivered down Anya's spine. He was a descendent of one of the imperial houses as well.

Or was he? This was his book, his supposed research. He could insert any name he wanted in it, and no one inside Russia would argue with him...if they valued their life.

Surely it wasn't a secret. If he was one of the last remaining Grand Dukes, the public, especially the one beyond the borders of Russia, knew it. Wouldn't the press have made a big deal about it when he was elected president? As prideful as he was, wouldn't he?

Maybe the press had. She didn't follow politics. Specifically, she didn't follow Russian politics. And while she'd spent the first eleven years of her life in Moscow, her parents had stressed math and science, not history, and pushed her to prepare for the future rather than fixate on the past.

Ryan. He was a Russian affairs expert. Would he know?

Possibly, but what good would that do her right now?

Up to that moment, she'd understood Ivanov was obsessed with her lineage. Now he'd confirmed what she'd feared since she'd seen the below-ground lab, and heard him say he had a plan for the future Russian generations. He didn't want her just for show.

Regardless of how American she appeared, he wanted her because he believed she was the only Russian worthy enough to produce his offspring. To start a new line of superior Russians.

The truth rang with gong-like intensity inside her head. He obviously wanted to sleep with her, and start his own family. But would he harvest her eggs to supplement the line? Stockpile her DNA? While she'd suspected his scheme, she knew it now with certainty. He didn't intend to let her leave when the summit was over.

And now that she was here, what reason did he have for keeping her grandmother alive?

The implication of his duplicity sunk in. Her head swam. She glanced up from the book and saw he was waiting for her to say something. His eyes shone with anticipation as if he thought she'd be ecstatic to learn he was a royal too.

She wasn't sure if she was going to throw up or take a swing at him. She opened her mouth to say something, but words eluded her. All she managed was, "I ...ah..."

Ivanov, however, took her stunned reaction as delight. He gripped her hands with his and drew her close. His breath reeked of alcohol and onions, and his eyes searched hers with a wild glee. "You and I are the last true heirs to the Russian monarchy. We can create a whole new empire of quality citizens. A whole new house of royals with superior blood, superior genes." He gave her hands a squeeze. "Together we will rule Russia and lead the world."

Anya choked back her response, letting the words dissolve on her tongue. *Not if you were the last man on earth.*

His grip was strong, so it took a bit of twisting to free her hands. She stepped back. "Russia doesn't need a new house of royals, and our ancestry does not make our blood, or our genes, superior to our countrymen. In fact, my blood..."

A flush rose up his neck and stained his cheeks. He grabbed

the vodka bottle and sloshed more in his glass. "We are descended from the Imperials. We *are* superior."

Without warning, he grabbed one of her wrists and dragged her toward the sofa. One of her ankles twisted, and she lost her balance, but he kept moving, and she struggled to keep from falling. He shoved her down onto the sofa and stood over her, glaring, as he downed the vodka. "You do not question me."

Her first instinct was to kick him in the knee, drop him to the ground. A sizable opponent, he was nevertheless threatening her with bodily harm, and she knew how to take down a man twice her size.

Fighting back at this point, however, would certainly doom her and Grams. She knew his threats were real. The wound on her side was proof. But it was better to use her brains to balance the playing field instead of taekwondo to make him back off. His obsession with the royals was the best place to start. "I've never seen my family tree. Will you show it to me again?"

The change in his demeanor was Jekyll and Hyde. Elation replaced the glare and his grip on the glass loosened. He retrieved the book from his desk, returning to sit next to her and flipping to the beginning where he had detailed accounts of her earliest ancestors.

"All the Imperial Houses began with a Norseman back in 862 A.D."

As Ivanov walked her through the various histories of each person descended from the Norse ruler Rurik, he translated the factual information as well as folk lore about them. A walking version of Ancestery.com, he was totally enthralled with the information as if it were the first time he'd ever read it.

After a few minutes, Anya found herself enthralled as well. Like the fairy tales of the princesses who'd come before her, these stories were part of her. She was learning as much about her past as she was about the future Ivanov intended her to have. While she couldn't forget his closeness, or completely ignore the fear still making her pulse race, she couldn't pretend she wasn't interested in her family's history.

And putting Ivanov in a better mood improved her chances of finding out about Grams.

An hour later, the leader of Russia, who believed himself a czar, passed out on the sofa next to her, his family history open in his lap and one hand resting on her leg. His head was back, mouth open, bad breath filling the air as snores rumbled from his chest. Anya wanted nothing more than to shove his hand off her leg and flee the room, but she'd come this far, in spite of everything. Now was the time to play cowboy if ever there was one.

The fire in the fireplace had returned to a soft glow. Biding her time and listening to Ivanov's breathing grow deeper and slower, she let her mind wander. The image of Ryan smiling at her surfaced, and the dark cloud in her mind lifted.

With slow, careful movements, she straightened her leg and brought her upper body forward. Ivanov's breathing maintained its rhythm and she gave herself a mental high five. She hated the idea of touching him, and wondered if she could simply slide her leg out from under his hand, but the odds were slim to none he'd sleep through that. Gritting her teeth, she stuck out her hand over his, letting it hover in midair. Her heart beat as fast as a hummingbird's wings. She took a silent deep breath to try and slow it. Ever so lightly, she touched the top of his hand, cutting her gaze to his face to see if he reacted.

He didn't.

The hardest part was still to come. Not only did it make her sick to touch him, she had to do a lot more than just touch him in order to remove his hand. If she squeezed his hand too hard or moved too fast, he'd wake up. If she didn't squeeze hard enough, she'd drop it.

With gentle pressure, she held his hand in place and shifted her thigh out from under it.

His hand was sweaty. While every instinct in her body screamed at her to drop it, she instead lowered his hand to the sofa with care.

Ivanov's chest hitched and he let out a grunt. The book on his lap slipped an inch, ready to tumble to the floor. Anya froze, her hand still holding his. A glance at his face showed his eyes were shut, but his mouth kept opening and closing. He swallowed, his lips parted, and a soft snore escaped.

The hummingbird turned into a jackhammer inside her chest. She counted ten snores, and then another ten, before releasing his hand.

Free at last, she debated taking the book off his lap. The slightest movement would cause it to fall. Should she risk waking him in order to buy herself time?

Deciding to chance it, she left the book where it was, removed her heels, and tiptoed to the desk.

A spark of hope ignited inside her. There were navy blue files, red folders marked with the Russian Federation emblem, and dozens of loose papers covering the desktop. As she poked around and tried to read what she could, the spark dimmed. There was so much information, it would take her hours to read it all.

Uncovering a map of Russia, her hope rose again. Black dots marked locations along the border and around major metropolitan areas, Russian names next to them. There was a set of blue dots around Moscow. A set of red ones around St. Petersburg. Could one of the dots represent her grandmother?

She tackled reading the map with gusto, but none of the words matched Natasha's Russian name.

Anya tossed the map aside and started on the blue files.

Frustration built as the words blurred and became meaningless. These appeared to be medical files of a dozen different people. What was Ivanov doing with those? This was taking too long and proving futile. She had discovered nothing about her grandmother and no proof for Ryan.

She moved on to the red folders. Ivanov continued to snore on the sofa and Anya eyed the book sitting precariously in his lap.

A few more minutes, she begged the book.

A few more minutes and the Russian words once more blurred in front of her eyes. She rubbed them, blinked, and ignored the sinking feeling in her stomach. Where would he keep information about her grandmother?

Giving up on the desktop's mess, she carefully tried one of the desk doors. Expecting them to be locked, she was surprised when the file door popped open with a soft *schick*.

Five minutes later, she still hadn't found Grams' name in any of the files. She had, however, found two other names she recognized, printed on documents buried in a red folder at the back of the drawer. Not just any documents – they were KGB execution warrants.

Peter Radzoya - Executed.

Ekateirna Radzoya - Executed.

Anya's hands trembled. At the bottom of each document, the initials of the assassin were listed. MYI.

Maxim Yakovlev Ivanov

Crash!

The book on Ivanov's lap fell to the floor.

10

ANYA JUMPED, heart solidifying in her chest. Ivanov sputtered and choked, sitting forward, elbows on knees. Pure instinct made her want to drop to the floor and hide behind the desk, but what good would that do? She couldn't hide from him.

The fire in the fireplace was gone and the room was cold. Even so, Anya clearly saw the sweat on Ivanov's face as he coughed. Without taking her gaze off him, she slid the execution warrants into her lap and closed the red folder. If she was going to get caught, she damn well was going to confront the bastard about the truth.

Ivanov gave one more cough, wheezed a heavy sigh and tipped to the left, disappearing behind the sofa's high arm. When he didn't reappear after a few seconds, Anya sat up straighter, peering over the edge. The most she could see was Ivanov's body from the waist down. Too long for the sofa, his feet hung off the side at the far end.

Anya's heart started beating again. She counted the seconds as she waited to see if he would wake fully and get up. If he would find her snooping in his desk.

An eternity passed before she heard the loud, congested

breathing that told her he was dead to the world. She drew a thankful breath and swallowed the dryness in her throat. As quietly as she could, she returned the red folder to the desk. The click of the drawer closing made her flinch. Still Ivanov did not move.

Anya folded the warrants in half, then in half again, continuing until they'd formed a small square. *Executed.* She shuddered. MYI – those initials could belong to any number of former KGB agents, but she knew in her heart they belonged to one man.

The monster in the room.

She needed time to think. Needed to get away from Ivanov. Now.

Rising from the chair, a new thought struck her. The posted guards outside the suite's door might stop her. Might wake the monster.

How would she get back to her suite without passing the guards?

The connecting door. The czarina's suite was next to Ivanov's personal quarters. She'd noticed a hidden door in her bed chambers the day she'd arrived. The door itself was part of the wall, a pocket door, which slid back and forth on a rail. There was no lock on her side, but she hadn't been able to open it, which meant it was locked from the other side.

Kings and queens, czars and czarinas, had kept separate quarters throughout history, and yet they could come and go from each other's rooms without being seen by the rest of the Palace. If Anya's bedchamber had a secret pocket door, odds were it led to the presidential bedchambers.

Tiptoeing to the sofa, Anya scooped up her shoes and made sure Ivanov continued to sleep. She crept past him and the fireplace, remembering the layout of her suite and where it had to be connected to his.

A few steps later, she stood inside his bedchamber. Soft

light emanated from half a dozen wall sconces, spotlighting a massive bed, draped on all sides by heavy blue curtains. Anya ignored the dark premonition that rolled through her at the thought of Ivanov's plans.

While the connecting door on his side was also a pocket door, it was much easier to find amidst the furniture, oil paintings. and elaborate wallpaper, because his door had an obvious lock. An ornate gold one that stood out like a neon sign.

Holding her shoes by the straps in one hand, Anya slowly turned the lock. She was pleased to hear the click of the bolt sliding free.

Almost home.

Funny how even the smallest amount of freedom felt good. She slid the door back with a small smile. The smile fell off her face when the door made a high-pitched squeak.

She froze in place, listening for the sound of Ivanov's snores. The edges of the stolen documents scratched the skin under her breast as her chest heaved.

Her body demanded she fling herself across the connecting hallway to the door of her own suite, but she held still. She'd come this far, avoiding Ivanov's advances, snooping through his official papers, and stealing secret documents. She would not blow her chance of making an escape to her own room by panicking.

No shouts erupted from behind her. No sounds of marching feet coming for her. With trembling limbs, she stepped out of Ivanov's bedchamber, and with slow, protracted movements, slid the door closed. This time the squeak was minimal.

There was no way to relock the door from the other side, so she left it.

Sconces dotted the hallway, casting dim light and eerie shadows. Anya reached out and found the small lever she needed. As suspected, there was a lock on this side, but a twist of her hand released it. Czars could apparently visit czarinas at will; wives, however, could only visit their husbands if invited.

Anya slipped inside her dark bedchamber, closed the door, and leaned against it, pulse racing. As her eyes adjusted to the shadows, she dropped the shoes and collapsed onto the four-poster bed.

Two seconds later, she got off the bed and pushed a short, fat dresser in front of the secret door. The dresser—a 17th century Italian mahogany—outweighed her and she grunted with the effort. Once it was in place, however, a sense of calm pervaded her mind and body. She may not have been able to lock Ivanov out, but by God, she wouldn't be a sitting duck in case he decided to sneak into her room. He hadn't tried it yet, but that didn't mean he wouldn't.

She grabbed the bedside table lamp and several ornate silver candlestick holders, stacking them on top of the dresser for good measure.

Her muscles trembled from utter exhaustion. She had no intention of sleeping in the blue satin dress, but the bed called to her and she once more sank into the soft silk bedspread, drawing the white gauze curtains around the sides. While they were no real protection from prying eyes, they gave her comfort.

I'll just rest for a few minutes. Then I'll wash my face, take my pill, and put on my pajamas.

She tugged the documents from her bra. It was too dark in the room to read, but she didn't need to see the Russian words. She knew what they said and more importantly she knew what they meant.

In her tired mind, Ivanov and the man in black morphed into one.

Closing her eyes and swallowing her tears, she held the names of her parents close to her chest, missing them, and her grandmother, even more than her freedom.

11

Anya woke with a start to a hand gripping her shoulder and shaking her hard.

A woman's voice, strangely familiar, and thickly accented, spoke over her. "Czarevna Anya. Wake up, *puzhalsta.*"

Blinking her eyes open, Anya looked up to see Inga wringing her hands and frowning at her.

Inga had been assigned to her as an assistant by Ivanov. Bodyguard in sheep's clothing was more like it. Today the older woman was dressed in a dull brown suit, but her favorite color, yellow, was represented by a scarf. She'd helped Anya unpack when she'd arrived, kept her apprised of Ivanov's schedule, and been in charge of last night's entertainment. In some ways, Inga reminded her of Grams. Only Inga didn't have the same grace or regality.

Inga appeared to be the helpful personal assistant, but like it or not, Inga was trouble.

Two feet behind the woman stood Ivanov's Prime Minister, Fyodor Andreev. Short and boxy, he reminded Anya of a bulldog. He was also frowning.

Beda ne prikhodit odna. Trouble never comes alone, Grams would have said.

"What's going on?" Anya struggled to sit up. Her head hurt, her eyelids were rough as sandpaper, and she was lightheaded. She'd just fallen asleep. How could it be time to wake up already?

"Breakfast is being served." Inga's dark eyes cut to the side, over her shoulder, as if fearing Andreev would yell at them both. "You must get ready, and hurry."

She was still wearing the blue dress and it was off-center, revealing a great deal of her right breast. Reaching up to adjust it, she realized she still had the papers she'd stolen from Ivanov's desk in her hand. Projecting modesty that wasn't all faked, she turned her back to Andreev and made a production of correcting the dress's top. As she did so, she once again slipped the folded documents into her bra. Standing up, she shooed Inga away. "Give me fifteen minutes." She sent an unwavering look to Andreev. "Alone, please."

Inga glanced between Anya and Andreev. The Prime Minister narrowed his eyes a fraction before nodding once and heading for the outer door. His gaze raked over the dresser before he marched out of the bedchamber.

"Please," Inga whispered. "Hurry." She followed on his heels.

Anya waited until she heard the outer doors close, then she, too, followed and locked them. While it obviously did no good in keeping anyone out if they really wanted in, pretending it did helped her sanity.

She didn't have to wonder what to wear to breakfast. Inga had laid out a conservative suit with a white blouse. Anya brought the suit and blouse into the bathroom and went to work on waking up in the shower.

Her wound was seeping. She cleaned it carefully, wishing again she hadn't forgotten her kit. Being a walking defect didn't mean she was helpless when it came to taking care of herself. After cleaning and rebandaging the wound, she took her birth control pill—at least she hadn't forgotten those. All she needed was to get her period and not have her pills.

The irony of the situation hit her all over again. She'd been taking birth control pills for over twelve years—not to prevent pregnancy, but to control the heavy periods her blood disorder produced—and the only man to have ever see her naked was Ryan. A man she didn't know, and who didn't know her.

She just wished she had her kit. The antibiotic cream Ryan had used on the wound had cleared up the infection, but without an infusion of clotting agent, the wound refused to heal completely.

Make do for now. And stay the hell away from Ivanov's dirk.

As promised, she was ready for breakfast in fifteen minutes. The Palace of Facets was the largest banquet room Anya had ever seen. Italian frescoes decorated the walls, mammoth columns and domed ceilings in a beautiful balance of blues and golds. Tiered candelabras hung from the high ceilings, each tier holding white electric candles.

There was no time, however, to take in all of the beautiful surroundings. As Anya entered the banquet hall, Inga on her left and Andreev on her right, she was at once under Ivanov's scrutiny.

He didn't look like a man who'd spent the night passed out on the couch. He didn't look like an assassin. Showered and shaved, he was dressed in a black designer suit, white shirt and red tie. The moment his gaze landed on her, he smiled broadly and opened his arms as if to hug her.

The sight of him made her queasy and angry all at the same time. Was he really the monster who had killed her parents? Under the still-curious eyes of the guests, she had to play along. She gritted her teeth and stepped into his embrace.

Always appearing the gentleman, he did nothing more than

lay his hands on her upper arms, and air kiss each of her cheeks in greeting. *"Dobroye utro."*

Lacking a better hiding place, and knowing her room might be searched while she was absent, she'd tucked the warrants once again inside her bra. They seemed to press into her skin like a brand as she forced a smile. She returned his greeting deliberately in English. "Good morning."

His eyes twinkled. "You look beautiful."

She very much doubted that, since her hair was still damp and the only makeup she'd had time for was one sweep of mascara and a coating of cherry Chapstick. But she couldn't have cared less whether he approved of the way she looked. The scent of buckwheat pancakes, sausage, and eggs filled the air. "What's for breakfast? I'm starving."

Immediately, he ushered her to his table where her order was taken by one of the waiters from the previous night. Inga and Andreev moved off. While Anya waited for her breakfast, she scanned the various tables of people and saw the person she was looking for. Ryan stood near one of the columns, sipping coffee, and speaking to the ambassador from the U.S. Embassy. He was dressed in a dark gray suit with a clean-cut, tailored edge to it, white button down shirt and pale blue tie. When he caught her staring, he gave her a slight nod.

"You slipped out last night," Ivanov said. "I am afraid I was a poor host."

Dropping her gaze from Ryan, Anya opened her cloth napkin, and placed it in her lap. Then she glanced at Ivanov. The guilt on his face surprised her. "It was a long day. We were both tired."

He seemed relieved. "Today the summit begins and I will be tied up with meetings. Tonight there will be another dinner, and afterwards, I promise to spend time with you and not fall asleep."

The chagrin in his voice was genuine. The desire in his eyes, seeking her forgiveness, was as well.

Maybe he's not the man in black. Maybe he didn't kill my parents. Maybe he can be reasonable.

In the bright light of day, the idea he'd once been an assassin seemed preposterous. The MYI had to belong to another man.

But as she picked up her coffee cup, the warrants bit into her skin. He *was* the man in black, she was sure of it. And his charm was nothing more than a façade.

The Belgian waffle she'd ordered arrived, covered in strawberries and whipped cream. It smelled delicious, but Anya no longer felt like eating. After her parents' murders, she'd told Grams what she'd witnessed, and Grams had panicked, making Anya swear never to tell another human being what she'd seen. She'd packed up her and Anya's belongings two days after burying her son and daughter-in-law, saying nothing more about it.

Anya had plagued her grandmother with questions about the man in black and why he had shot her parents, but Grams had refused to answer. She also refused to answer Anya's questions about why they had to move to America, claiming they simply needed a fresh start.

The impression that something was amiss diminished rapidly in the face of a new place with new people and experiences. Over time, Anya shut out the memories, did what Grams wanted, and threw herself into becoming an American. But the dread never left her, always lying under the surface of her new life, always reflected in Grams' face. She never stopped looking over her shoulder, even as she immersed herself in growing up.

Executed. The word ping-ponged inside Anya's brain. Her parents had been killed, murdered. The move to America, the change of their last name, the dread Anya always felt...the fear and remorse rushed back like a tidal wave.

The whipped cream on her waffle was melting. Anya picked up a fork and stuck it in a fat strawberry, imagining it was Ivanov's eyeball. While the documents weren't one-hundred-percent proof he'd killed them, Anya couldn't shake her suspicions. Was there a way she could find out if he'd been in the KGB?

Andreev returned with an official red folder and sat down next to Ivanov. The two men spoke in low voices in Russian, and the Prime Minister handed Ivanov a stack of papers and a pen. Ivanov signed the papers with bold, flowing strokes.

Anya forced herself to eat the strawberry she'd speared. As she chewed, she looked for Ryan. One of President Pennington's aides, Truman, and one of Ivanov's cabinet members were all standing around him talking. He was smiling and joking, and at one point, the whole group laughed in response to something he said. Even though she had no idea what the punch line was, she smiled along.

Absently she ate another strawberry, and then another, as she continued watching Ryan entertain his group. She wished she was part of them, listening to his strong, deep voice, and laughing at his jokes.

President Pennington wanted to be part of the group too. He rose from his chair and meandered over with several people in his party. He shook Ryan's hand and patted him on the back, and Anya saw a faint blush on Ryan's cheeks as he accepted some compliment from the president. A strange sensation of pride rose in her chest.

Fascinated, she ate a corner of her waffle.

A large, cold hand covered hers, interrupting the moment. Ivanov. He glanced once in Ryan's direction, studying the way Pennington joked with him, before his focus returned to her. "How is your breakfast?"

The flat tone of his voice told her he was upset. The tight hold he had on her hand told her he wanted her full attention.

He didn't like her staring at Ryan. Didn't like the fact Ryan was more entertaining than he was.

Andreev shuffled the papers into the folder, stood, and made haste to leave. The folded papers inside Anya's bra pressed into her skin as if in warning. She knew Ivanov's currency, what he traded in. If he was a former KGB agent, he was ruthless. What had she been thinking? Showing even an ounce of interest in Ryan could get him killed.

Throat tight, she forced down the waffle and gave Ivanov a pleasant smile. From this point on, no matter what, she had to ignore Ryan. "It's just the way I like it. Better than any I ever ate in America."

Once again, Hyde morphed into Jekyll. Ivanov's face went from controlled anger to childlike joy. The squeeze he gave her hand this time signaled his pleasure at doing something better than the Americans.

He rose from his chair, leaned down, and planted a kiss on the top of her head. "I will see you tonight."

Outwardly she simply nodded. Inwardly she recoiled as if he'd set a tarantula on her head.

———

Ryan couldn't get Anya to look at him.

Like a shepherd driving his flock, Ivanov ushered his guests ahead of him out of the Palace of Facets. The summit would take place back in Georgievsky Hall, where diplomatic meetings had occurred for centuries. Ryan had never attended a weapons summit and had been looking forward to this one. Now, as Anya wasn't following Ivanov but looking down forlornly at her waffle, Ryan had no desire to sit through hours of political posturing.

As Pennington and Morrow rounded up their respective groups and moved out, Truman sidled up next to Ryan and handed him a platinum pen. "Thanks for letting me borrow this last night."

The pen was one of Del's favorite toys. He'd probably loaded the hidden memory chip inside the cap with information about Anya. Without missing a beat, Ryan stuck it in the breast pocket of his suit coat. No one was within earshot or paying attention to them, but he played along. "Anytime."

"Interesting information about our princess and her grandmother your man dug up."

Ryan paused. Now she was 'our' princess instead of Ivanov's play thing. He tapped his pocket. "You read the contents of a CIA file?"

Truman grinned. "The price you pay for using me as your courier."

Truman knew more about Anya at the moment than he did. Fabulous. Still trying to catch her eye before he left, Ryan ambled back to the table where he'd left his briefcase.

Truman followed. "Piece of advice, mate. There are a thousand pretty women in this city who would shag you, and all a lot less dangerous that that one." He jerked his chin in Anya's direction.

Anya, dangerous? What was in the file Del had sent him?

Most of the room had cleared out. Twenty feet away, Anya sat motionless, face pale, bluish shadows under her eyes. Ivanov had stepped up his public display of affection toward her that morning, insinuating their relationship had grown over night. Ryan's gut churned at the thought.

He picked up his briefcase and gave Truman a pat on his shoulder. "Dangerous women don't scare me."

Truman laughed and hiked his thumb toward the open doors. "You coming?"

"In a minute."

Ryan left him standing there and walked toward Anya. The few people still in the room consisted of maids cleaning up dishes and a couple of Ivanov's security detail keeping an eye on Anya.

She glanced up at his approach. A smile broke over her face, but in the next instance, she slammed the door on her emotions, resetting her face to stone.

There was no time to figure out why, so Ryan simply placed his card on the table and slid it in her direction. "If you need anything, cell number's on the back." He lowered his voice to a whisper, using the card exchange as a simple way to give her a message. "Be in your room at midnight."

He didn't wait for her to answer. Turning on his heel, he spotted the reason for her sudden change of heart. Prime Minister Andreev had emerged from behind one of the massive columns and was watching. As Ryan passed by, Andreev fell into step behind him.

If Andreev wanted to intimidate him, he'd have to work harder than that. Ryan smiled to himself. As he passed through the doorway, he chanced a glance back at Anya.

The exquisite Russian architecture of the great hall paled in comparison to her beauty.

Now all he had to do was figure out just how dangerous she was.

"Good morning, Director. I trust your doctor officially released you from the hospital?"

Conrad Flynn waved a hand at his assistant, Katie, as he walked past her to his office. Good was relative, and who cared what the doctor thought. His stomach still hurt like a son of a bitch, and Julia was pissed he was returning to work so soon. To top it off, the power was out at their apartment, thanks to the fluky storms the area had experienced since Friday, and he was going to have to borrow the shower in Michael Stone's office to wash off the smell of the hospital clinging to his skin. "Morning."

As usual, Katie followed on his heels, giving him his messages and running through the day's agenda. "I called in John Quick, sir, to help with the Radzoya situation, since you promised Agent Morgan you wouldn't send Lt. Commander Vaughn overseas again until after the baby comes."

"I did?"

"While you were in the hospital. Don't you remember?"

How could a bout of food poisoning screw up his head so much? Katie looked inordinately happy about it. "Of course I remember."

"John will be here in fifteen minutes."

Conrad tossed his briefcase on the desk and shrugged off his winter coat. Johnny Quick was part of Pegasus, officially a search and rescue team, but more of a special ops team of former military guys used by the CIA, FBI, and NSA. "The Rad-*what* situation?"

Katie placed a cup of freshly brewed coffee on his blotter and retrieved a file from a stack of paperwork on the far corner of the desk while Conrad hung up the coat. She opened the file and laid it in front of him. "Radzoya, sir. Natasha Radzoya disappeared sometime Wednesday while visiting a friend in Geneva, Switzerland? Her granddaughter, Anya, flew out of Dulles and landed in Moscow on Friday. Director Smith asked us to follow up on allegations Natasha was kidnapped?"

Katie ended sentences as if they were questions. Whether she was questioning his memory or his competence, Conrad wasn't sure. Neither was working at full capacity, so he didn't blame her.

Anya Radzoya, Smitty's call. Snatches of their conversation came flooding back, but he was still blotto about the past week's events. One minute, he was enjoying a steak at his favorite steakhouse in D.C., the next he was puking his guts up with his ass hanging out of a hospital gown.

He glanced at the 8x10 photo clipped to the inside of the file's cover and scanned the information sheet opposite it. Natasha Radzoya had been a double agent, working for the U.S. government during the Cold War. After the war ended, she and her granddaughter had sought refuge in America. All of it taking place before his time as Director of Operations. Even before his time in the field "And why do I care about this?"

"I received word this morning from our source at GenLife Laboratories. Anya didn't show up for work and rumor has it she's taking time off for a *family emergency*." Katie made air quotes around the words. "The source reported she didn't know when she'd be back. Our source believes it has to do with her grandmother and President Ivanov."

Conrad prided himself on knowing everything about everyone directly or indirectly connected to his employer, but for some reason he'd entered a parallel world this morning with this latest intel. Hell of it was, he didn't think he could blame it on the aftereffects of the food poisoning. "Why do we have a source at GenLife Laboratories?"

A glint of mischief lit Katie's eyes. He knew she loved knowing something her boss didn't. "GenLife is the premier DNA lab on the East Coast, sir, handling the analysis for a large clientele of politicians, bureaucrats, and the rich and famous. Also has a specialized group of geneticists contributing to the Human Genome Project. Keeping an eye on Anya Radzoya is only a small part of our source's job description."

Conrad sipped his coffee and read more of Natasha's file. His predecessor, who had handled the Radzoyas' defection to America, had highlighted one particular section. As Conrad read the brief paragraph, the coffee in his stomach turn to acid. He glanced up at Katie, who was standing in the doorway, the phone call from Anya Radzoya suddenly coming back to him. "How soon will Quick be here?"

Seemingly pleased he'd finally caught on to the importance of the situation, the glint in Katie's eyes sharpened. "I believe he just arrived. Shall I show him in?"

"Yes." Conrad motioned toward the door. "And get Del Hoffman on the phone for me. ASAP."

12

The Great Kremlin Palace
Moscow

Anya's bra was getting entirely too full. She really had to find a better hiding place for all the surreptitious contraband she was carrying.

The warrants she'd stolen from Ivanov's file were hidden under her right breast. Ryan's business card, with his personal contact information, hidden under her left. Why he hadn't given it to her at the cabin was a mystery, but instinct told her he was starting to trust her.

Be in your room at midnight. What was he planning? Her body tingled in anticipation.

While uncomfortable, she had to admit the feel of Ryan's card against her skin was also reassuring. The heavy card stock, the raised lettering in bold print, the simplicity of his name, and the forwardness of his gesture all combined in an impressive cocktail. Believing he was her friend on the basis of what had passed between them was juvenile, and yet she couldn't help herself. She wasn't alone in the Great Kremlin Palace complex.

Of course, Ivanov's guards were always close by, as was Inga, so technically she wasn't alone. Even Andreev monitored her every move, and the way he'd purposely followed Ryan from the banquet room made her uneasy. He would report back to Ivanov about her and Ryan's exchange. Ivanov was a suspicious and distrustful person who obviously considered her his property. If Ryan continued to talk to her or show any kind of interest, his life would be in danger.

Alone inside her suite, she carefully drew the card out of her bra Flipping the card over, she admired the straight block letters and numbers carefully printed on the back. Her instincts continued to reinforce that he was a good man, a good person, and she'd be damned if she'd stick him in the crosshairs of Ivanov's Mr. Hyde personality.

Midnight was a long time away. Slipping the card back inside her bra, she considered her options. She could sit in her room all day and wait for the inevitable evening confrontation with Ivanov, or she could test the boundaries of her freedom.

While she had a lot to sort through in her mind, she wasn't one to sit and twiddle her thumbs. Opening the large mahogany wardrobe in the dressing room, she took out her coat, scarf and purse, and then she exchanged the heels she'd worn to breakfast for a pair of low-heeled boots.

By the door she paused in front of the mirror to adjust the scarf around her neck.

Even though she was under constant guard, it was time to see just how far being a princess would get her.

It didn't get her far. The minute she walked out the suite's French doors, the security guards stationed there stopped her.

"Where are you going?" one of them asked her in Russian.

Pretending she didn't understand, she gave him a little wave and walked down the hall. She had no idea exactly where she was headed, but it was away from Georgievsky Hall. At some point, she'd find a door leading out of the building.

"Czarevna Anya!"

The two guards hustled past her, cutting her off, one on each side. Taking another step would result in running into them.

Heart racing, Anya swallowed her alarm and called up as much royal indignation as she could muster. "What is the meaning of this?"

Out of nowhere, trouble known as Inga emerged. "Princess Anya, where are you going?"

Anya narrowed her eyes at the guards and lifted her chin. "The president will be in summit meetings all day. I'm going out sightseeing and I might do some shopping as well." She turned her gaze to Inga. "Is there a car ready for me?"

The old woman seemed more flustered than normal. In her arms was a stack of folders like the ones on Ivanov's desk. "I'm afraid that is not possible."

Wondering what the czarinas and czarevnas before her would have done, she flipped a mental coin and went with righteous anger. "And why not?"

Inga's gaze dropped to the files in her arms. "President Ivanov wishes you to stay inside the Palace. He would like you to look over these health reports and write a summary of each one."

Just as she'd feared. She wasn't going anywhere and Ivanov was making busy work for her. Once again, the blood of her ancestors churned in her veins. "I am Grand Duchess Anya Maria Romanov Radzoya. If I want to leave the Palace, I will."

She stepped forward as if to break through the guards' blockade, but all she managed to do was get both of her arms securely restrained.

"Abject apologies." Inga's gaze locked on the floor at Anya's feet. "I cannot allow you to leave."

With that, Anya was escorted back inside her suite by the guards and dumped across the threshold in a very un-princess like manner.

Inga followed, setting the stack of files on the czarina's desk. "If you would like, I could bring you tea while you work on these for President Ivanov. He's very interested in your findings."

Anya dropped her coat on the back of an elegant Queen Anne chair. "Just leave, please."

The woman bowed her head and disappeared, closing the doors behind her.

Huffing, Anya returned to the bedchambers and kicked off the boots. It was then she noticed the Italian dresser had been returned to its original spot along the wall. A new idea took root in her head.

Ivanov was more than a eugenics nutcase. He was a power-hungry manipulator, a control freak. If he would kidnap Grams in order to blackmail Anya, what other injustices and corruption would he wield to get his way? There had been more than her parents' execution warrants in that file. How many other secrets was he hiding in his office?

Removing her suit jacket, Anya eyed the door, a new seed of rebellion sprouting. Since she couldn't escape from the dreaded foxhole, she might as well dig herself in deeper.

She rolled up the sleeves of her shirt.

HE WAS DEFINITELY BEING WATCHED.

Ryan found his name card and gave an internal sigh. He sat down next to Lutz and pretended he didn't see Andreev talking to one of the security goons about him. Now that he'd called attention to himself, he'd have to be on his best behavior. The last thing he wanted to do was get Anya in trouble.

Georgievsky Hall had been transformed into an official lecture hall. At one end, a podium had been set up, Russian, American and British flags providing a backdrop. Off to one side, in ornate high-backed chairs, sat the three world leaders. On this first day of the summit, each of them would address the audience in the hall with opening speeches centered on the topic of nuclear arms reduction and the current and perceived future threats of world-wide terrorism.

Audience seating was divided into two sections: one for the attending diplomats and one for the media. Reporters from thirteen countries had been allowed access to these proceedings. Three major news organizations, hand-picked by Ivanov, had also been granted video privileges for the speeches.

Lutz glared at Ryan. "I thought you were staying at the Savoy during the summit."

Less than a kilometer from the Kremlin, Hotel Savoy was a common place for Americans to stay while in Moscow. Ryan clipped the provided nametag on his lapel and shrugged. "There was an empty suite available here. President Pennington insisted I take it. My language skills and history doctorate have already proven helpful to him."

The mention of Pennington stopped further needling. Lutz huffed and made a big deal out of gathering papers from his briefcase. Ryan withdrew a touch screen tablet from his that looked exactly like the latest one hitting the consumer market and turned it on. Right down to the famous logo, it mimicked the popular all-in-one flat pad. His, however, was CIA-pimped and field-operative approved. Amongst the apps for locating the best coffee house in Moscow and reading the Washington Post, were apps for translating the Cyrillic alphabet, instructions for creating a smoke bomb with sugar, potassium nitrate, and aluminum foil, and a facial recognition program, with the faces of six thousand known, wanted, or suspected international criminals. Another of Del's genius inventions.

Ryan intended to take notes using the keyboard, but he pulled out the titanium pen and fingered it. He'd give anything to have five minutes alone with the pen and his tablet. Whatever was encoded on its memory chip about Anya, though, would have to wait. He still had a job to do at the summit, and not just for appearance's sake.

Barchai was still an option for an asset, and Lutz needed reassuring Ryan wasn't spying on Ivanov. He'd have to play his part today full-throttle to get Lutz, as well as Andreev, off his back. The time would be well-spent. He had research to do on royal blood, DNA, and gene sequencing. Notes to take on people. Especially Ivanov.

Every gesture, every facial reaction, every tic. Ryan wanted to know it all, right down to how many times the man took a piss.

Because somewhere down the road, Ryan had no doubt he and Ivanov were going to tangle.

13

THE SECRET DOOR between the royal suites was locked. Of course.

Her plan to snoop through Ivanov's suite foiled, Anya slumped on the four-poster and considered her options. Option one: stay in her room like a good girl and analyze the medical records Inga had left behind. Analyze them for what, Anya wasn't sure, but there was no pretending she didn't recognize the gene maps contained in each one. What was Ivanov looking for? While everything from hair color to propensity for disease was contained in those records, royal blood could not be discerned from DNA.

Option two: she could morph into Nikita, overpower the guards and make a break for it.

Option three: channel Jason Bourne, disable the lock on Ivanov's door, find unquestionable evidence he was a sociopath, and *then* make a break for it.

Unfortunately, she wasn't Nikita or Bourne. Her options for the day's entertainment thus boiled down to analyzing those files or watching another day of Russian soap operas with Inga until Ivanov returned from the summit meetings.

Either way, she was getting out of the damn power suit and putting on her jeans.

In the dressing room, she ignored the clothes hanging in the walk-in closet with their designer labels and went straight to her suitcase. She didn't want to wear anything Ivanov had bought her, no matter how beautiful or expensive. She wanted to be Anya Radcliff again, if only for a few hours.

Changing into a pair of worn jeans and her favorite cotton sweater, she buried her nose in the sweater. The familiar smell of her laundry detergent. The smell of home. Even if she managed to get Grams released from Ivanov's grip, they would never again share a lighthearted conversation over laundry. They'd never eat at their favorite Italian restaurant down the block, or order in pizza and watch a French film, complete with subtitles.

Anya removed the warrants from her bra. Her fingers shook as she unfolded them.

Executed. The word jumped out at her every time, a cobra striking without warning. It made no sense. Why would Ivanov and the KGB have wanted her parents dead?

Losing her mother and father in such an abrupt way was like losing two of her limbs. In the hours and days after the accident, her world canted sharply to the left, body and mind limping along. Lowering herself into a plush chair, Anya drew up her legs and hugged her knees.

Enemies. They'd obviously been enemies of Ivanov's. People he saw as a threat to his master plan. But what was it about a member of Yeltsin's cabinet and a geneticist that threatened Ivanov's plans?

A knock came from the door and Anya jumped. Before she could hide the papers, the double doors swung open, and Inga appeared, tray in hand. "I've brought you tea, Czarevna Anya. Where would you like to take it?"

Inga entered without waiting for Anya's reply. Behind her, Andreev stepped into the room.

Trouble One and Trouble Two. Anya's stomach dropped, her first instinct was to hide the papers but any rash movement to do so would call attention to them. Instead, she sat up, put her feet on the floor, and simultaneously folded the warrants in half, slipping them under her thigh. "Thank you, Inga. Please set it here."

Inga obeyed, bringing the tray to the coffee table in front of Anya and pouring her a cup of tea.

As Andreev circled the room, eyeing everything, Anya raised up to her full seated height. Andreev's gaze cataloged every vase, piece of furniture and portrait hanging on the wall. What was he looking for? "Did you come to take tea with me, Prime Minister?"

He stopped at the bedchamber's French doors, glancing inside no doubt to make sure she hadn't moved the furniture again. Satisfied everything was in its rightful place, he snapped his fingers at Inga and shooed her to the door.

Andreev wanted her alone. Anya's stomach dropped another notch.

As the double doors closed behind Inga, Andreev faced her. His skinny mustache twitched above his narrow lips. "The card the American gave you this morning."

Should she play dumb? Act like she didn't know what he was talking about? He'd clearly seen Ryan slip her his business card and pretending otherwise would be foolish. "What about it?"

"Give it to me."

Anya leaned forward, picked up the cup of tea she didn't want, and blew on the hot liquid to buy time. No way she was pulling that card out of her bra and handing it over to Andreev or anyone else.

She gave a dismissive shrug. "I left it in the dining room. I have no interest in the upcoming American art exhibit in St. Petersburg."

Andreev's course brows drew together. "Why would he invite you to the exhibit?"

"Not just me. President Ivanov as well. First Lady Ruth Pennington will be there, and the president asked his aide to extend a personal invitation to us to come and show our support of the expanding American presence in Russia."

Andreev clasped his hands behind his back and paced the room. When he disappeared behind the tall back of the wing chair, Anya slipped the paper into the crack between the chair arm and cushion.

Andreev rounded the far edge of the room and returned to where she was sitting. Sipping her tea, she stared at the portrait of Catherine the Great hanging over the marble fireplace, and pretended she cared little about Ryan, Americans in general, or Andreev's concerns.

"The card was not on the table after you left." Andreev stopped in front of her, blocking her view of the fireplace. "What did you do with it?"

Even if she hadn't been a Grand Duchess of Russia, his tone was rude. Between the guards manhandling her, and Inga ignoring her refusal of tea, Anya was becoming truly annoyed. She may have been a prisoner, but she was not weak, stupid, or a pushover. "As I recall, you left the banquet hall this morning before I did." She rose with a grace instilled by her grandmother, placing herself in a face-to-face standoff with Andreev over the coffee table. "I left the card on the table, and I don't appreciate you insinuating I'm a liar."

"I came back and checked the table, Princess." He sneered the title as if it were a disease. "You took the American's card, and now I must insist you hand it over to me."

"It's a damn business card. I'm sure he has hundreds of them. Why don't you just ask him for one?"

Andreev held out his hand. "Give me the card."

"Even if I had it," Anya said, not bothering to keep the defiance out of her tone. "I wouldn't give it to you, Prime Minister Andreev. And if you don't leave this minute, I'll be sure to tell President Ivanov about your inappropriate behavior."

Her threat gave him pause, but he was undaunted. "Give me the card."

With Catherine looking down on her, Anya tipped her cup and poured hot tea over Andreev's outstretched hand.

Moscow

GI 42 Prison

EVEN WITH A BLACK EYE AND A DIRT-SMUDGED FACE, THE ELDERLY Natasha Radzoya was as strikingly beautiful as her granddaughter. Age had not diminished her looks, only heightened it, pulling her skin tight over her high, sculpted cheekbones and deepening the set of her blue eyes. Eyes that shot bullets at Maxim as he paced around her in the cold, barren jail cell.

The summit was keeping him busy. He didn't have enough time with Anya and he lacked time to properly torture her grandmother. A shame.

Natasha was a very verbal woman, although she'd refused to tell him what he wanted to know about the missile launch code. He'd grown tired of her insulting tone and harsh criticisms, and had taped her mouth shut. Now he enjoyed how this simple technique stripped away the last of her power, and she knew it. She could not fight him physically or with words, and it was killing her as sure as lack of sleep, food and water.

Since she wouldn't tell him where she'd hidden the information he wanted, he'd decided to torture her in a different, more strategic way.

"Anya is beautiful," he said, stopping in front of her. "Beautiful, intelligent...innocent."

Natasha was tied to a chair, hands and feet bound. As she struggled against the restraints, he smiled. She was as determined as ever to break free and castrate him, even though her strength was nearly gone. He admired her intense desire to save her granddaughter, although he didn't understand it. She could have saved herself all this and died a quick, quiet death if she'd come forth in the beginning with the information.

But he was a royal, just like she was, and used to getting what he wanted. "Also, she is stubborn. She refused to trade in her Western garb for appropriate Russian attire." He fingered the ornate handle of the dirk secured by his wide leather belt. "So I sliced the clothes off of her."

Natasha surged against her restraints, mouth moving under the tape. The noise she made came out sounding like a growl.

"My dirk slipped and *accidently* cut her. I thought that would be enough warning for her not to challenge me again. I was wrong. She ran off for a few hours. Did not get far outside of Moscow before she stopped and came back. Her loyalty to you is strong, as I surmised it would be. All I need do is strip the Western ideas about independence you brainwashed her with, and I can mold her into the next czarina of Russia."

Maxim strolled around Natasha, noticing that her whole body heaved as she breathed. She bowed her head, the physical strain of her predicament taking a toll on her aging heart.

"My personal physician attended to her wound, gathering her DNA while he was at it. The geneticists in my lab are running a full battery of tests on it. Paternity, gene mapping, everything. When we announce our engagement, I will show the world the proof she is a true Russian princess and that her blood is perfect.

Natasha's head came up, her eyes scrutinizing and fierce. Since she wasn't yet ready to give him the information he wanted, he would push her mental and physical well-being to the limit. It was risky to strain her heart to the brink of collapse, but he hadn't achieved the ultimate power of Mother Russia by playing safe.

Leaning over her bowed head, he lowered his voice. "Anya belongs here with me. You and her parents, in essence, sold her soul to me through your actions. For betraying Russia, you owe your homeland much. Anya is payment for that debt." He smiled. "What a delicious payment she is. I will enjoy every moment with her."

Natasha surged against her restraints, desire to get her hands on him so evident, he chuckled.

"I watched her for years, you know, waiting for the chance to bring her back. Once you are out of the picture, she will forget her time in America. She will reject the propaganda you have fed her. She will be mine, and together, we will make history. A history where Russia becomes the leader of the free world."

Natasha stopped struggling. Her eyes narrowed. She hadn't fully understood what her traitorous ways would cost her in the end. Whether she gave him the launch code or not, she was a dead woman, and she knew it.

Maxim stepped forward and patted her face. Retribution was a sweet pill on his tongue. She jerked away, but couldn't move far. He stood over her, giving her the full impact of his size and power. "Traitors to Russia must die a tortuous, lingering death. It will give you time to wallow in your guilt, to suffer for your crimes, and to miss your granddaughter. But I promise, she will never feel your pain because she is a true royal. She is already embracing her destiny, relearning her place in the history books. She will be true to me, and true to Russia. You can be sure of it."

For once, Natasha sat immobile, face pale as the ghosts of her dead ancestors.

14

Geneva, Switzerland
Hotel Montague
Twelve hours later

JOHN QUICK WATCHED THE REVOLVING DOOR OF THE HOTEL FROM a corner of the lobby, pretending to be on his cell phone. The moment Josh Devons sauntered through, John put his phone in his pocket and flagged him down.

Devons was tall, and as broad as the front end of John's Ford F1-250 back home. His brown hair was buzzed like a Marine's, and he sported a scar on his left cheekbone. He walked with the tight air of a bouncer and his dark brown eyes missed nothing, including John, when he entered the lobby.

"Hey, man." Devons swung his arm in an arc before making contact with John's hand and shaking it with a crushing intensity. Yep, definitely a bouncer or a bodyguard or maybe even a defensive end before the spy gig. "Nice boots. You're from Texas, right? Love the ladies down there. You a one-man team this mission?"

A one-man team who'd just returned from a grueling rescue in South America and was *so* not up for partnering with a spy who couldn't shut his trap. Five hours of sleep in the past three days made John light on patience and heavy on irritation. "Flying solo for now. Boss man wanted it that way. We find your asset and need to recover her, Pegasus will assist if necessary."

Devons leaned one beefy shoulder against the nearest wall. "The hotel bagged up Natasha's belongings and turned them over to her friend Francine Harris, an ex-pat living here in Geneva. I interviewed Fran and went through Natasha's stuff with a fine-tooth comb. Found nothing of interest."

"Search the room?"

"My next step. Or I should say, *our* next step."

The two of them walked casually to the main desk, asked the middle-aged woman manning it if they could see the manager on duty. Her gaze lingered on Devons before she disappeared into the office. A moment later, a skinny man with greased back hair and a crooked nose appeared, looking them over with obvious apprehension.

John was tipping six-one and boasted a lean one-ninety on his frame. But with his winter coat on, he looked bigger. Add to that the fact he hadn't slept and was wearing his *don't fuck with me* face, he and Devons made an intimidating pair.

"May I help you?" The manager's name tag read Stephan. He stopped a foot away from the desk, avoiding getting too close.

Devons flashed a fake badge of some sort. "Detective Andresen, remember me? We spoke yesterday about the woman who disappeared from Room 18. This is my new part-ner, Detective..." He scanned John and made up a name. "Johan. We'd like to take a look at that room."

"The police already went through the room."

The woman had followed Stephan from the office and now stood behind his left shoulder, her attention firmly fixed on

Devons again. He shot her a grin and she smiled back, raising one hand to touch her hair. "Detective Johan here is new to the case and needs to see the room himself."

Stephan stuttered. "The authorities ruled out any crime and turned the room back over to us. There are new guests staying in it."

The woman—Alana, according to her matching nametag—jumped in. "The Austens are out of the room right now. The maid is cleaning it."

Devons tapped the top of the desk with his fake badge and spoke to Stephan. "Perhaps Alana, here, could take us to see it then?"

Alana was already reaching for a key card on the wall behind her. "I'd be happy to assist the police in their investigation."

They left Stephan sputtering behind them.

The maid was indeed cleaning the room. Devons kept Alana chatting in the hall while John did a sweep, working around the shy maid as he checked under the bed, examined every piece of furniture, and inspected behind the pictures hanging on the walls. The maid was changing the sheets on the queen size bed when John decided to run his hand along the seams of the mattresses. If he ever wanted to hide anything in a hotel room, he'd sew it into a mattress.

Bingo.

His fingers encountered hard plastic buried under the fabric at the headboard end. While the maid hefted the dirty sheets to her cart in the hall, John slit open the edge of the seam with his pocketknife. A small, black cell phone appeared.

Undoubtedly, it didn't belong to the couple currently renting the room, but if it turned out it did, he'd make sure they got it back. He slipped the phone into his pocket, caught up to Devons in the hall, and gave him the sign to wrap it up. Devons thanked Alana for her time, and the two made haste to leave.

They didn't talk until they'd both crawled into Devons' rental car. John retrieved the phone and handed it to the spy. "Battery's almost dead."

Devons found the call log and scanned its history. "Probably a dozen missed calls, several from Natasha's granddaughter, Anya. Flynn thinks Ivanov blackmailed the girl into traveling to Moscow, and Del confirmed she's living with him inside the Kremlin."

He scrolled more and stopped, holding the screen so John could see it. "Natasha took a call Wednesday, February thirteenth, just after eight in the morning. The number's private. She must have disappeared after that."

"Any messages waiting in a voice mail box?"

Devons punched a couple buttons and put the phone on speaker. "Only ten."

Voice mail demanded a password. The two men glanced at each other and Devons shrugged. "Anya." He typed the letters in.

The soft, computerized female voice told them *incorrect password*.

He tried 'Francine'. No luck. Natasha's birthday and then Anya's birthday, which he'd apparently memorized. The voice mail box remained locked.

Brainstorming a password was an art but sometimes luck played an important role. "Mother Russia?"

Devons typed in 'Russia', and next thing John knew, they heard a woman's voice. "That's Francine," Devons told him.

They listened to all the new messages, most of them from Natasha's friend, one from Natasha's dentist telling her it was time to schedule a teeth cleaning, and one from a charity in D.C. asking her if she'd volunteer for their next fundraiser. When the new messages were finished, the voice mail box began coughing up the previous messages.

The first one made the alarm bells in John's brain ring like

Sunday Mass. The voice was male, Russian. The message was short, less than ten seconds, and the Russian words faded out in places where a low background noise interrupted them, either because the battery on the phone was nearly dead or because the original connection had just been bad.

Devons frowned. "You get any of that?"

John was skilled in search and rescue, medical training and a host of other special ops skills. None included being a Russian linguist. "Not a word."

While hitting a button with one hand to make the message repeat, Devons motioned at the glove box. "Grab that extra battery in there, would ya?"

Sure enough, a brand new, still-in-the-package instant cell phone battery was inside. John unwrapped it, and Devons plugged it in. They listened to the message again. Still in Russian and still fading out in spots.

Devons banged his fist on the steering wheel. "I'll have to send it to Del and have him run an audio analysis. See if he can filter out the distortion and translate the message."

John, feeling like a walking zombie, groaned. "How long will that take?"

His new partner, the fake cop, shrugged. "Few hours."

A few hours and he'd be face down on whatever surface was handy. "Surely the Agency has a spook around here who speaks Russian."

"I might know someone."

Devons took out his own phone, sent a text. The two of them sat in silence, waiting for a response. John nearly fell asleep before the phone beeped, and Devons stuck the car in gear even as he was reading the screen. "Got it. Friend of mine not far from here can help us out."

His *friend* turned out to be a tall woman with black hair, guarded eyes, and a distinct Israeli accent. She ushered them into a loft apartment, stuck her head out the door, and looked both ways before closing the door and glaring at Devons. John noticed a discreet bulge on her hip under a thick sweater. "Let me hear it," she said.

Fine by him. John removed the cell phone from his jacket, called up the voice mail message, and punched the speaker button. "Can you translate this?"

She didn't take her gaze off Devons as the harsh sounding words spilled from the phone over the sounds of the background noise. When the message was done, she said, "Play it again."

John obliged, and they all listened once more to the clipped Russian voice. The corners of the woman's eyes narrowed in concentration. "It's an address. Something near the Russian Church on Rue Toepffer." She took the phone from John's hand and repeated the message a third time, pressing her ear to the speaker. "A law office?"

John sent Devons a look. "What do you think?"

The spy shrugged. "Looks like we better go find ourselves a lawyer."

"I will go, too," the woman said, reaching for her coat on a hook near the door. "In case you need more translating."

Devons' insouciant body language disappeared. His hands went to his hips. "Not a good idea, Naomi. We don't know what we're dealing with here. Could make trouble for you."

She made a dismissive noise in the back of her throat. "If I ran from trouble, I would never have met you."

Definitely history between these two.

Devons gave John a pleading look, but John didn't feel like arguing with her, or letting the spy off the hook so easily. "She might come in handy. Let's go."

Naomi smiled at Devons. "I'll get my phone and meet you downstairs."

The spy started to argue. John grabbed him by the coat and shoved him out the door.

"Bad idea, man," Devons murmured under his breath as they hit the stairs.

"Why? Because she gets under your skin?"

"She's former Mossad."

Some agents never really left Mossad. Like a Marine was always a Marine, Mossad wasn't just an intelligence service; it was a way of life.

They headed outside, making their way to the rental car. "We won't be spilling national secrets to her, just using her to help us speed up this process. Soon as I've got what we need, we'll thank her, and be on our way."

At the car, Devons stared back at the apartment building's front entrance. Naomi emerged, and he tensed at the sight of her. "Don't count on it."

John opened his door. "What? That she'll help us?"

Devons shook his head and sighed. "That we won't be spilling national secrets to her before this is over."

15

Kremlin Palace
Moscow

Ivanov came for her at six that evening.

Anya was dressed in another designer gown. This one—a ball gown made of midnight blue silk—molded to her breasts and dipped low in the back, but at least it covered her legs.

Ivanov was dressed in a suit, although he hadn't completely forgone his military uniform. He'd eliminated a traditional tie in favor of a red ascot, complete with the Russian Federation's coat of arms.

The minute he crossed the threshold, she expected a reprimand. He took one look at her in the gown, however, with her hair swept into a low bun at the back of her neck, and said nothing about the earlier incident with Andreev. "I have something for you."

He held out his hand, and Anya reluctantly placed hers in it. *Traitor*, her mind whispered. *He killed your parents.*

Revulsion rolled through her, and it took every ounce of her willpower not to jerk her hand back. Oblivious to her horror at his touch, he gave her hand a squeeze and propelled her toward the bedchamber.

Why was he leading her to the bedroom? Her feet stumbled.

Gritting her teeth, she righted herself and prayed the 'something' he had for her wasn't what she thought it was. The very idea made her gag.

Ivanov bypassed the bed and a modicum of relief rushed over her. But then he strode to the hidden pocket door and opened it.

A new wave of anxiety sent a cold chill over her skin. "Where are we going?"

It was a dumb question. Obviously, he was taking her to his bedchamber. Unable to stop herself, she drew back, resisting the step that would launch her across the threshold.

His only answer was a knowing smile as he opened the matching door on the other side and forced her through it.

She had no choice but to give in and enter. The night before, she hadn't had the presence of mind to pay attention to the king size bed. Tonight, it took center stage. With certainty, Anya knew she would be face to face with that bed, and soon. She just hoped it wasn't tonight.

Ivanov skirted the bed and led her through his chambers to his office. On the wall opposite the built-in book shelves, a portrait of Peter the Great hung on the wall. Ivanov stopped in front of it, gazing at the oil painting as if it were his own reflection, and a prickle of intuition ran down Anya's spine.

She'd picked out several Russian history books from the czarina's library and read them that afternoon. One of the books had devoted an entire section to the famous Russian leader, Peter I, of the late 17th and early 18th centuries. The painting on Ivanov's wall showed a middle aged man dressed in military attire, a sword in one hand. the other lying on a map.

She'd seen the painting in the book, his pose suggesting he ruled the world by force. The symbolism and the light in Ivanov's eyes as he studied the oil painting suggested he saw himself as the next Peter.

Peter I had renamed himself Peter the Great, and while he initiated massive economic and foreign policy reforms for the times, he'd also been cruel and ruthless. He'd interrogated his own son, whom he suspected was plotting against him, and threw him in prison.

After a moment's pause, Ivanov swung the picture away from the wall, revealing the front of a safe hidden behind it. He pressed a selection of numbered keys on the keypad and pushed down on the metal handle. The safe beeped, opened with a click, and a soft *swoosh* that sounded like a sigh to her.

The deep, cavernous opening was high enough up, Anya stood on her tiptoes to see over Ivanov's shoulder. Once the door was opened, a small, recessed light in the ceiling of the safe lit the contents, illuminating another safe, this one the size of a shoebox. Along with the smaller safe, dozens of files, USB drives, and assorted guns filled the inside. The odd mix also contained what looked like several velvet jewelry boxes.

It was one of these Ivanov removed. Facing Anya, he held it out and lifted the lid. "This belonged to the Romanovs. As the rightful heir to the throne, it is yours."

The necklace had a center sapphire bigger than a half-dollar coin and was crowned by three rows of diamonds. The diamonds continued around the entire necklace, all the stones set in gold.

So stunning, it took her breath away, Anya couldn't help but admire the beautiful jewels and exquisite details. She'd never seen anything so glamorous up close. The necklace was made for a red carpet affair or inaugural ball.

Or a Grand Duchess.

Without waiting for her consent, Ivanov removed the necklace from the black velvet box and wrapped it around her neck. The weight of the jewels pressed into Anya's skin, matching the heaviness in her chest. Accepting the jewels seemed every bit as treasonous as accepting food from her enemy. As accepting his hand.

She did it anyway.

And just like eating to keep up her strength, she acted like a princess in order to fool Ivanov into trusting her.

Running her fingers over the stones, she smiled. "It matches my dress perfectly. *Spasiba*."

Her thank you garnered Ivanov's approval. He nodded his head, closed the safe, and ushered her toward the main door of his suite. "Dinner awaits."

She took his proffered hand, steeling herself for the coming evening. Three things were crucial to tonight's performance.

Eat as much protein as she could stomach.

Ignore Ryan Jones.

Endure Ivanov's advances.

As she entered the lavish hall set up for dinner, the smell of fish hit her nose making her stomach dive. At the same time, Ryan locked eyes with her, and her heart skipped a beat.

It was going to be a long night.

THE DAY HAD BEEN A DAMN LONG ONE.

Ryan had called up his benign, friendly, aide personality and kept it in place throughout the boring opening day speeches of the summit. He'd laid low, kept his head down, and done his damnedest to fall off Andreev's radar.

Unfortunately, President Pennington had taken a liking to him, inviting him to eat lunch with his group, and placing Ryan in the spotlight several times during the lunchtime conversation.

When someone learned you were a spy, their body language, verbal language, and personality changed. Ryan had seen it dozens of times. Trust disappeared and they stole glances at you from the corner of their eye, or blatantly demanded you share top-secret information as proof. Pennington's sudden interest in Ryan suggested he'd learned the truth about who Ryan really worked for. The president's body language, however, suggested otherwise. His interest was genuine. He still believed Ryan was one of his worker bees, but one whom Pennington found refreshingly non-political.

Pennington and the British prime minister were not exactly BFFs. And Pennington, who was used to being the star of every summit, found himself dwarfed by Ivanov's ostentatious performances from sun up to sun down. Seeking to impress someone, and regain his ego's solid footing, he'd decided to take Ryan under his wing. Which certainly helped Ryan's standing with Ambassador Lutz, but kept him in the spotlight where he didn't want to be. Whenever Andreev was around, his laser beam attention followed Ryan everywhere.

Between Andreev and Pennington, Ryan hadn't had one minute to himself. The information on Anya still sat on the microchip inside the pen in his jacket. He was dying to know what it said, and more importantly, he was dying to see her again.

Midnight. A few hours from now. If he could get away, and his plan worked, he would see her.

Georgievsky Hall was once more laid out for an impressive dinner. Everyone was in their assigned seats, talking, drinking, and laughing, as they waited for their host and hostess to join them. Where were they? What was taking so long? Was this another of Ivanov's pretentious displays of ego?

Ryan was lifting a glass of vodka to his mouth when Ivanov and Anya appeared in the archway at the end of the hall. His hand froze in midair, immobilized at the sight of her.

What a difference twenty-four hours could make. Gone was the awkward and nervous young girl from the night before, and in her place, was a poised, dignified woman. While there was still a look of determination on her face, her eyes glittered brighter than the sapphire and diamond necklace circling her neck. But her newfound vivacity had nothing to do with her jewelry.

She was every inch the princess. It oozed from the tilt of her chin down to the swagger in her walk. Had Ivanov finally gotten to her? Had the idea of becoming the Russian president's wife and ruler of Russia turned her?

Sadness and a certain amount of betrayal nipped at the careful control Ryan had on his emotions. He tried to catch her eye to no avail. She and Ivanov took their seats and dinner was served. The whole time she avoided looking in Ryan's direction.

Tonight he was seated next to the British diplomat Truman was investigating. Her high-pitched voice and wheezing laugh barely penetrated his awareness. He should have been working any angle he could to befriend her and find a chink in her armor for Truman, if not for the CIA. Instead Ryan picked at the evening meal and tried to block out everything but Anya while appearing oblivious to her.

One didn't need spy training to figure out her clear signals. She wanted nothing to do with him.

The logical director of operations insisted that was okay. Whatever game she was playing, she didn't want him to be part of it. She no longer needed or wanted his help.

But the illogical male inside of him wanted to punch the table. He'd given her his number and made it obvious he was available if she needed anything. Had told her he'd be by tonight to see how she was. Unfortunately, there was nothing left to do but his job.

The only problem with that line of thinking was the fact he'd made *her* his job.

Along with his stellar logic was fact number two: his instincts were staging a full rebellion. She could ignore him until global warming turned Siberia into a rainforest but he was not giving up. At least not while she was in his sights. *Damsel in distress.* She might not be acting like it, but she was definitely the underdog in this scenario. While she might not become his top covert Russian asset, watching her appealing Russian assets were now his top priority.

Since he wasn't prone to making mistakes, Ryan kept his direct attention off those lovely assets and watched her only from the corner of his eye. Andreev hadn't given up watchdog mode, and Ryan knew better than to chuck the day's work into the garbage by slipping up with anything more than an indifferent glance here or there at Anya.

By the end of the dinner, though, Ryan's patience was wearing thin. Even a silly conversation with Truman as they made their way to the salon for the evening's entertainment couldn't bring him out of his funk.

Once inside the salon, he sank into a chair in the last row, avoiding Pennington, Lutz and Andreev. While Truman sat next to him, the spy seemed to understand Ryan was in no mood for conversation.

The entertainment consisted of a troupe of jugglers, acrobats, and a performance of the classic bear dance. The bears in the dance were only male members of the troupe in costume, but Ryan didn't miss the way Anya put a hand on her necklace when the bears' handlers tugged on their chain-linked leashes.

That necklace was a national treasure. One that hadn't been seen in years, just like the princess wearing it. He'd snapped a photo of it with his button camera to research later. If he was right, that necklace was one of the items presumably lost after the Soviet Union crumbled.

Many of Russia's legendary Diamond Fund pieces had been sold to private collectors and museums at the end of the Cold

War. Others were supposedly lost in the shuffle, the Romanov contributions suffering the most. Anya's appearance with one of the lost pieces made him wonder: Had it been in her possession all along? Or had it been in Ivanov's?

More importantly, was it a peace offering or a marriage proposal?

Ryan's gut again rebelled at the thought.

The entertainment wrapped up, and Ryan clapped along with everyone else, gritting his teeth even as he pasted on his friendly face. Ivanov stood, dragging Anya with him, to take his place center stage as the troupe filed off. "Tomorrow's agenda will be the same. The summit will resume in Georgievsky Hall." He beamed at Anya, his hand entangled with hers. "The Grand Duchess and I bid you good evening."

For half a second, the light in Anya's eyes died. A shadow passed over her face and her smile faltered. Ryan sheared enamel off his teeth.

As the group stood and stretched, commenting about the amazing show before parting ways again until morning, Truman poked an elbow at Ryan. "Your bluff is good, but if I was a betting man, I'd call you on it right now."

Ryan stared at the back of the chair in front of him, not seeing it. Everyone around them had filtered off. "What bluff?"

"The one you've been playing tonight in regard to the princess. Pretending you're not interested."

"You *are* a betting man, but you don't understand the art of the bluff." Ryan rose from his seat, sunk his hands in his pockets, and stared at the floor. "A royal flush is nothing without the queen. She's the one who isn't interested."

"Is that so?"

Ryan glanced up, and Truman gave him a smug wink, before tilting his head in Anya's direction. Sure enough, as he tracked Ivanov's movements, his eyes caught hers. Ivanov was shaking hands with Prime Minister Morrow, his back half-turned to Anya.

Her throat contracted, as if she were swallowing hard, before she gave Ryan a covert thumbs up.

A sudden rush of pleasure buzzed his nerve endings. Not forgetting where he was and who might be watching, he took a cautionary scan of the room.

Andreev, hidden in the shadows of one of the columns, was regarding him closely.

Ryan had survived the CIA's training camp, danced toe-to-toe with gun-happy terrorists, and once gone rogue in order to flush out a mole inside the Agency. Unwilling to damn Anya further, he gritted his teeth again and did the hardest thing he'd ever done.

He turned his back on her and walked away.

16

Rue Toepffer
Geneva

THE GENEVA LAW OFFICE OF MARCHÉ, YORDANOV, AND BAKER
was an international firm dealing in everything from offshore
business transactions to divorce. Housed in a large multiplex
that had once been the Honduras Embassy, the law firm was
one of many businesses in the U-shaped structure.

The street between the law office and the imposing church
across from it was a one-way with parallel parking. Night had
descended, but between the street lights and the spotlights on
the Russian Church, the entire block was easily visible. While
John, Devons and Naomi waited for Del to run background
checks on all of Marché, Yordanov, and Baker's employees, they
watched the side entrance marked Employees Only straight
across from the church. John snapped pictures with a digital
camera of anyone who came or went from that entrance.

Devons' phone rang. He pushed a button and Del's face
appeared on screen. "Yeah, Del, watcha got?"

Del was sweating slightly and his glasses were askew. "Before we get to the lawyer, I thought you should know, I've heard chatter from inside the Kremlin. The prime minister is suspicious of a certain American that fits Smitty's description."

"How are you picking up chatter from inside the Kremlin?" Devons looked amazed.

"You have your skills, Jar Head. I have mine. What do you want me to do if things go bad?"

Devons shook his head, and chuckled as he said, "Stay at your keyboard. As soon as we know what's going down with Natasha, John and I'll head to Moscow in case Smitty needs help."

Del made a face, switched gears. "Grigory Yordanov is probably your man. Except he's not. Yordanov is an alias. His real name is Sergei Kutzeg."

John and Devons exchanged a look. John pocketed his camera. "What do we know about him?"

"He was part of the KGB during the seventies and eighties. Disappeared right before Yeltsin took power in the nineties. Resurfaced in Geneva ten years ago as Grigory Yordanov and became a partner with Marché and Baker. His last living relative, a grandson, died two weeks ago."

Devons shrugged. "And?"

"Natasha Radzoya bought a plane ticket for Geneva six hours later."

Naomi, who'd been so quiet in the backseat John thought she'd fallen asleep, spoke up. "They were lovers."

John and Devons both turned to look at her. Del frowned and squinted at the monitor on his end. "Who is that?"

She leaned forward to put her face in his line of vision. "Naomi Singer. And you are?"

"Never mind," Devons said, eyeing Naomi with speculation, or perhaps interest. John wasn't sure. "Why do you think Yordanov and Radzoya were lovers?"

Naomi gave Devons a look that said he was six kinds of dense. "A Russian secret police officer and a spy, working together in Cold War Russia? What could be more romantic?"

It was a good call in John's book, but Devons grunted. "You, of all people, viewing the world through happily-ever-after lenses."

Naomi rolled her eyes and sat back.

All righty then. John agreed with Devons. He didn't view the world that way either in his line of work, and while understanding what role Yordanov played in Natasha Radzoya's abduction and disappearance was important, if it didn't help him locate her, it was pointless.

Devons stared out the windshield. "So the grandson dies and Natasha books a flight to visit her friend here in Geneva. She arrives, receives a call, most likely from Grigory-slash-Sergie, but never makes it to the law office. Why did she really come to Geneva, and why did Grigory want to see her?"

Naomi again attacked his IQ with a *why else* gesture. "Because her soul mate was grieving."

"Her soul mate?" Devons gave a derisive laugh. "There's more to it than that, but what?"

On the video screen, Del shrugged. Naomi, frowning at the back of Devon's head, remained quiet, her irritation speaking volumes. John's brain continued to connect dots. "Ivanov's the third player in this game. Must be something to do with him."

Devons considered it, nodded. "Something big."

A new face filled the video screen. "Here's a photo of Grigory taken at his grandson's funeral."

Grigory was older than John expected and the strain on his face was visible in the shot. Whether from losing his grandson, or from something more sinister, wasn't clear, but John was willing to find out. "Unless he took another exit from the building, he's still inside. I say we go in and have a chat with him."

"Del, see if you can find a link between Yordanov, Radzoya,

and Ivanov during the Cold War," Devons said. "Any link, no matter how thin, got it?"

Del agreed and signed off. Before John and Devons could devise a plan for entering the building and finding Grigory, Naomi jumped out of the car and took off for the employee entrance. "Coming?" she called back to Devons.

"Shit," John said. "She can't come with us."

Devons pocketed his phone. "You were the one who said we might need a Russian translator. I tried to warn you."

An international lawyer in Geneva would speak English. John shot a glance at Devons as the man hauled himself out of the compact car. Devons was devising a plan. A plan that involved Naomi.

KREMLIN PALACE
Moscow

THE FIRE IN THE FIREPLACE BURNED AND CRACKLED AS IVANOV droned on about his childhood. Anya listened with one ear and made appropriate noises here and there while she mentally tuned out.

They were in the Czarina's Golden chambers, in the private suite, the fire casting shadows on the expensive Persian rug and ornate coffee table. The tea from earlier had been cleaned up, and now a tray of fruit, crackers, and cheese sat waiting for consumption. Anya had no appetite and it wasn't because Ivanov was in her suite.

Ryan wasn't coming.

The image of his broad shoulders turning and walking away from her was burned into her brain. He hadn't even glanced back. There was no way he was coming at midnight.

A stark numbness filled Anya's chest. She was alone again. *Don't be ridiculous. Ryan was never your friend. You didn't even know him.*

Ryan had given her hope and renewed her self-confidence. He'd been so forthright in reaching out to her. Or so she'd thought. Maybe it was all in her imagination.

But maybe, too, it was for the best. Even though no one had been watching them but Truman, it was better he ignored her. After all, she'd ignored him to keep him off Ivanov's radar. Ryan may have just been playing along.

Either that, or he thought she didn't need him anymore.

Her gut cramped. She did need him. More every hour.

"Did you know my parents?" she asked, interrupting Ivanov in midsentence.

Sitting across from her in a matching winged-back chair, he stuttered. She could see him mentally shift gears from his first experience shooting an assault rifle in the army to whatever history he had had with her parents. His eyes transformed from animated to dead, like a shutter coming down on a door. "I met Peter once. At a state dinner with President Yeltsin."

"What was he like?"

A muscle twitched under Ivanov's eye. "We merely shook hands and exchanged pleasantries. I did not know him."

The past few days had proven to Anya that even a simple meeting, a simple exchange, could tell you a lot about another person. Although she didn't understand why Ryan had turned his back on her tonight, she knew he was one of the good guys. "Did my father seem like a good person to you?"

Ivanov's eyes narrowed as he tried to figure out why she was asking. "I understand your need to embellish the memories you have of your father, but I am unable to help you with that."

Before Anya could respond, there was a knock at the door. Relieved at the diversion, Ivanov called out, "Enter!"

Andreev came into the room, forehead wrinkled, and lips

set in a fine line. He was going to tell Ivanov about her earlier impertinence, she was sure of it. Even if she hadn't already known of his plans with Ivanov to resurrect several decommissioned nuclear missiles, their exchange earlier that morning would have shown her he was not in Ryan's league of good guys.

But what could Ivanov do to her that was worse than he'd already done? He'd had her parents executed, pulled the trigger himself. He'd kidnapped her grandmother. He'd blackmailed her into returning to Russia. And now he held her prisoner.

Andreev asked to speak to the president in private, sending her another of his scalding glares. Anya tipped her chin up and glared back.

Go ahead. Do your worst.

The prime minister guided Ivanov away from the sitting area and into Anya's bedchamber, putting as much distance as he could between them. The thought of Andreev near her bed made her shiver. Ivanov near it was no better. The two were a formidable pair, no matter where they went.

When they disappeared from sight, Anya strained her ears, hoping to catch something of their conversation. Andreev had left the French doors ajar an inch, but no matter how much she willed her ears to hear their conversation, she couldn't. Rising silently, she tiptoed, step by agonizingly slow step, until she was standing to the right of the arched doorway. Pressing her back against the wall, she edged closer to the opening and held her breath.

Andreev's voice, low and secretive, spoke fluent, clipped Russian. Nowhere in his diatribe did she hear her name mentioned. No Czarevna.

Odd. Perhaps the prime minister had decided against ratting her out. But why?

Anya's brain skittered across half a dozen reasons, none of

them very substantial. Maybe Ivanov wouldn't appreciate Andreev confronting her. Maybe Andreev was embarrassed that she'd refused and poured hot tea on him.

Ivanov was a jealous man. Maybe Andreev feared what Ivanov would do if he found out Andreev had approached her in her private quarters and spoke with her alone...

It seemed like the silliest reason for Andreev to keep his own counsel, but perhaps the wisest as well.

Lost in her thoughts, Anya missed part of the conversation, only hearing the end of a word that sounded vaguely like *American*. Her pulse leapt. Andreev had referred to Ryan as "the American" during their earlier confrontation. Was he informing Ivanov of their confrontation after all?

As Anya forced every cell in her body to concentrate on the Russian flowing between the men, she realized she'd misunderstood. They weren't talking about Ryan, or an American, they were talking about the president *of Iran*.

More meaningful words jumped out at her. They were making a deal from what she could decipher. A deal involving...weapons?

Either that, or they were selling the Iranians a thousand semiautomatic cows.

Anya frowned. She must have misunderstood. Even though she didn't follow politics, she knew Iran had rubbed most of the world the wrong way for its involvement in terrorism. The Iranian president's focus on building nuclear weapons had everyone nervous. Why would Ivanov sell weapons to them?

She slid an inch closer to the doorway. The French doors were mostly glass, and even though they sported expensive white silk drapes, the men inside the room would be able to see her shadow if she stepped up to the doors. But they were deep in conversation, and a passionate one at that. She leaned her head to catch more words and hoped her shadow went unnoticed.

Missiles? Had Andreev just said something about launching missiles? Either her Russian was rusty, or she was listening to the president of Russia and his prime minister discuss the reactivation of not just a few missiles along the Russian border, but somewhere closer to a thousand.

They needed a code. A code for initializing the launch of a select group of missiles protecting Moscow and St. Petersburg.

A code that apparently Natasha Radzoya had and refused to give up.

Cold seeped into Anya's bones. Her knees went weak. She pressed back against the wall with her full weight. Grams was still alive, but why would she have access to missile launch codes?

Anya had known Ivanov was pretending to support the summit's goals while secretly undermining it, but reactivating *a thousand* nuclear missiles?

My god. Why would he do that?

Stupid question. Why did Ivanov do anything? He was a power-hungry egomaniac who believed he was destined to be the greatest leader Russia had ever had. Weakening America and Britain would only add to his power. Reactivating nuclear missiles along the border, and around Moscow, would secure, at least in his mind, Russia's place as world leader.

Once again lost in her thoughts, she missed the conclusion of the discussion. Without warning, a fat hand slid through the crack in the door to land on the knob and pause there.

Andreev. "The summit is over in three days." He pushed open the door. "We need the code before then."

Anya straightened at the exact moment his gaze landed on her. His eyebrows shot up in momentary surprise before crashing down over his steely eyes. He knew she'd been eavesdropping and opened his mouth to accuse her.

"Excuse me. I was just on my way to the bathroom." She pushed past him into the bedchamber, gave an equally surprised Ivanov a weak smile, and hightailed it for the massive bathroom en suite. She'd only made it two steps when a hand caught her shoulder, stopping her.

The iron grip forced her to turn around. She faced Ivanov with her best innocent expression. "Yes?"

For a brief second, he scanned her face, suspicion clouding his own. "A matter of state has arisen, and I need to attend to it immediately."

She gave him a curt nod. "Of course. And now if you'll excuse my rudeness, I really must use the bathroom."

She laid a hand across her stomach for emphasis.

Ivanov made a dismissive motion, not at her, but at Andreev. The prime minister let out a rude sigh and disappeared through the French doors. A moment later, Anya heard the outside doors of her suite open and close.

She was alone with Ivanov in the bedchamber.

His eyelids lowered slightly, and his lips curved in a lazy smile. He leaned toward her, his gaze on her lips.

Worms of disgust slithered over each other in her stomach. Clapping a hand over her mouth, she shoved Ivanov out of the way with the other, and sprinted for the bathroom.

She barely reached the gold plated toilet before retching.

17

Ryan STARED at the words on the computer screen, reading certain facts for the fifth time.

Anya Maria Romanov Radzoya. Born: July 5th, 1985, Moscow, Russia.

Father: Peter Romanov Radzoya, deputy prime minister to President Boris Yeltsin, 1990 – 1995. Computer genius. Assigned oversight position during transition from key launch to computer launch of Russia's nuclear missile system.

Mother: Ekateirna Yuri Radzoya, geneticist and genome researcher at Russian Academy of Medical Sciences, 1988 – 1995. Worked on top secret cloning project, REPLICA.

The facts about Anya and her parents were scant, Anya's life summed up in Agency-speak. Between the cold, detached words, was another story. A story about party loyalists killed in an untimely and suspicious—at least to Ryan's conspiracy-loving brain—car accident. A story that went back dozens of generations and hundreds of years to one of the original Imperial houses and included traitors, coups, and double agents.

Anya was the last, and youngest, of three royal princesses, the one who'd been secreted out of Russia in the middle of a frigid winter night, and disappeared with her grandmother into the ether.

A graduate of the Farm with top honors in spy lingo, Ryan read between the lines of Del's brief, confirming his other suspicion. The CIA had indeed been involved in the relocation and new identities of Anya and her grandmother.

Of course, the U.S. government and its spy group had a longstanding and deep-seated interest in Russian nationals, especially those with political connections, so it was no surprise they'd lent a hand in the relocation. They'd provided Natasha, Anya's grandmother, with more than protection. Detailed information about her government, and about Peter's job, had been traded for a chunk of cash. What made Ryan drum his fingers on the tabletop was the fact Del had put two asterisks next to Natasha Radzoya's name. There was no corresponding explanation in a footnote at the bottom of the page, but Ryan didn't need it. Asterisks were another form of Agency-speak Ryan was well acquainted with.

One asterisk meant spy.

Two meant double agent.

Natasha Radzoya had been a double agent. The only question was, for whom? Russia or the United States?

Ryan's fingers continued to drum the table. Where was Natasha now? Anya claimed Ivanov had kidnapped her, but where would he stash her? There were dozens of prisons and other hiding places in Moscow alone. Most likely, she was dead or close to it.

He studied the photo Del had sent with the information. It was from Natasha's passport, and resembled a driver's license photo. Not the best picture, but even so, the woman's eyes and tilt of her chin displayed her beauty and regal air to the camera lens. Her white-gray hair was boldly swept up to the top of her head, the royal blue scarf wrapped around her neck emphasized her porcelain skin. Her snapping blue eyes denoted a proud, confident woman.

From her hair to her facial features, Ryan saw Anya reflected back at him. The ghost of Christmas Future.

Why would Ivanov go after Natasha? Was it because she had been a double agent during the Cold War? Why would he care? Was it because her son and daughter-in-law had worked for Yeltsin? Again, so what?

And why had Natasha slipped her granddaughter out of Russia after Peter and Ekateirna's deaths? Was she saving her own spy skin or Anya's?

None of it made sense. He needed Del to dig deeper. Find the transcripts of Natasha's interviews. No matter how many times he read the facts, without the missing pieces, they didn't add up.

Ryan's fingers drummed faster.

18

MIDNIGHT. The appointed hour.

Anya paced her suite. Outside the French doors, the guards had been talking and laughing since Ivanov's departure, but now they sounded tired, groggy. Long silences stretched between them as the night grew deeper.

Inside the room, she was wired like a caged animal. Would Ryan come? If he did, how would he get in? She'd chased Inga off but her door was under twenty-four-hour surveillance from the guards and cameras.

After she'd thrown up, Ivanov had left her alone. Like most men, he had no interest in playing nurse. Instead, Inga had stepped in to tend to Anya, and Anya had played the sick card well enough to convince everyone she had a mild stomach bug. After an hour of Inga's incessant care, Anya insisted she needed sleep, and told the woman to leave. Then she'd lain in bed, wondering what to do about the conversation she'd overheard between Ivanov and Andreev.

Out of all the ideas she'd had, the best was to attend breakfast in the morning and tell President Pennington what she'd overheard. The problem with that approach was Ivanov and

Andreev would be watching her and know immediately what she was up to. She had no doubt Pennington would want evidence, like Ryan, before accusing his host of such treachery. And if Ivanov suspected her of treason, she'd never see Grams again.

She was back where she started.

Ryan would know what to do. Sitting in front of Catherine's picture, she stared at the door, willing him to appear. *Please come.*

The only light in the room was from a desk lamp. A soft glow lit that area, the rest was drenched in shadows. Staring intently at the door, she thought she saw the ornate doorknob turn. Jumping up, she squinted. Were her eyes playing tricks on her?

No, because in the next second, there he was. Ryan, standing in the open doorway. He wore dark clothes, and his face was in shadows, but she'd know that hair and build anywhere. She'd know the tight coil of his body anywhere.

He moved into the light, smiled at her, and stole a glance back out the door. Satisfied, he closed it with a soft click and his gaze swept over her, top to bottom. "You all right?" he whispered.

Flummoxed, Anya pointed at the door and lowered her voice to match his. "How did you get past the guards?"

He held up a finger, went to the radio sitting on the desk, and tuned it to an all-night easy listening channel. Then he stepped right in front of her, drew her to him, and placed his lips next to her ear. "They're asleep."

His warm breath in her ear made her shiver. "Asleep?" she whispered back.

He leaned away and searched her face, a hint of humor in his eyes. Brushing stands of her hair back, he pressed his lips to her ear again. "A little sleeping powder in their evening meal. An American chef in Pennington's retinue is easily bribed –

something I'll have to look into tomorrow. He dusted their evening meal with it. The guards won't be out long, so I only have a minute."

Her body automatically pressed into him, arms rising on their own accord to hug him like she had at the cabin. The memory of his cold stare and the way he'd turned his back on her early in the evening stopped her. "Why would you take such a risk for me?"

The memory faded as fast as it had come when he lifted his hand to her face. "I had to make sure you were okay. Ivanov hasn't hurt you again, has he?"

His fingers brushed her cheek, his sincerity so over-whelming her knees weakened. "I'm okay."

"What happened last night?"

They were still whispering. The radio played on in the background. The clean male scent of him filled her nostrils. She wanted to bury her nose in his neck.

Focus, Anya. "Last night?"

"You were so different this morning. I was afraid he..."

A noise in the hallway interrupted whatever Ryan was about to say. They both froze, gazes jumping to the door. As they listened, Ryan's arms went around her, tight and comforting.

Long seconds passed. The sound of a snoring guard drifted in. He must have tipped over or kicked the door. Ryan laid a hand on the small of her back, drew her close, and put his lips against her ear once more. "I was afraid Ivanov had turned you."

Warm breath, smooth skin, spicy aftershave. *Heaven.*

Mimicking his stance, she positioned her face against the side of his head and breathed deep. Let the breath out ever so slowly. She needed to tell him about the papers tucked inside her bra. About Ivanov and the Iranians. The thousand missiles... "Turned me into what?"

His soft chuckle sent goose bumps down her neck. "I was afraid he'd convinced you to embrace your royal genes and his plans for them."

"Oh." She tried not to giggle. The conversation wasn't humorous, but being this close to Ryan under the circumstances made her giddy. She pinched her silly internal schoolgirl and sobered. "I was trying to protect you. He's a killer."

Ryan's hand rubbed her back. An absent-minded gesture or a provocative one? Either way, she didn't mind. "My offer still stands. I can make some calls and get you out of here."

"Not going."

He hugged her then, their heads still close together, and his strong, warm body supporting hers. His lips touched her earlobe. On purpose? "Knew you'd say that. Any news on Grams?"

Running her hands up his arms, she wrapped them around his neck, giving into the temptation. She just needed a minute to feel safe. "No, but I think I found out something important about my family..."

In the hallway, the snoring stopped. A shuffling noise filtered through the door.

Ryan sighed soundlessly and broke her hold. "I'm sorry, but I have to go."

Already? "When will I see you again?" Panicked, her voice rose, and he touched a finger to her lips to shush her.

She got a grip, whispered, "I mean, alone, like this?"

One hand smoothed her hair. His mouth rested comfortably against her ear. "Soon, I promise. I'll figure something out. The sleeping powder's not enough for the time we need, but I couldn't risk knocking them out all night. Someone would notice, and they'd be checked for drugs. Once confirmed, Ivanov might move you or kick us–the visitors–out. A tiny thing like that could cause an international incident, and he's been itching to start one of those."

"What about the cameras in the hallway?"

"I arranged a temporary malfunction."

She grinned. "Now who's being industrious?"

He returned her grin. As he pulled away, she gripped his shirt and jerked him back to her. Rising on tiptoes, she planted a kiss smack on those delicious lips that had just been taunting her earlobe.

She meant it as a thank you. As a *be safe* message. To be honest, she wasn't sure what she meant it as, but it didn't matter. Ryan enfolded her in his arms, molding her body to his, and kissed her back.

The kiss was soft but demanding. Succumbing, she followed his lead, letting him take charge.

My first real kiss.

And boy, oh boy, it was one for the books.

The world spun for a minute, so she hung on. To him, to the feelings boiling underneath her skin. She wanted to forget the nightmare her life had become. Forget who she was and the choices lying in front of her. For that moment, the only decision she wanted to make was whether to trust Ryan's intentions.

I trust him.

His tongue teased hers and she melted a little more. If he hadn't been holding her up, she would have sunk to the floor, dragging him with her.

Another noise interrupted their embrace, and Ryan broke the kiss, glancing at the door. When no warnings sounded, he raised her hand and kissed her fingers, gave her a meaningful look, and headed for the door.

Once there, he listened for a long moment, body tense. Then he cracked opened one side of the French doors and checked the guard situation. Must have been clear, because he gave her a final glance and disappeared into the night.

19

MARCHÉ, Yordanov and Baker International Law Office
Geneva

"TRY TO BE CHARMING," NAOMI SAID TO DEVONS AS THEY entered the glass door of the law office.

I'm always charming," Devons countered smoothly.

Naomi snorted. John reserved comment.

The reception area was sleek and contemporary with black couches, metal chairs and black-framed modern art on the walls. Bushy green plants lent the only color in the otherwise monotone room. Large metal letters on the wall behind the crescent shaped reception desk spelled out the name of the firm. The receptionist was absent from the front desk, but it was late, so maybe she'd already gone home.

Light instrumental music came from speakers in the ceiling. Somewhere in the back, a copy machine hummed and spit out paper. Devons motioned at John to keep watch while he went behind the desk and scanned the papers lying on it. When nothing seemed worth his attention, he pulled out a keyboard drawer and woke up the computer. What he was searching for, John had no idea. All he wanted was to get the hell out of there.

John's ears picked up a sound before his eyes caught movement, and he snapped his fingers to get Devons' attention. Just as a man came down the hallway, Devons hopped the desk, and rang the bell on the counter, as if the three of them had just walked in the door.

The man was short and middle-aged, balding on top and spreading through the center. His gaze darted between John and Devons. "Mr. Imman?"

John grabbed Naomi by the hand and turned on his own charm. "No, Mr. and Mrs. Johan. We have appointment with Mr. Yordanov to set up an offshore account with our friend here..." He searched his brain for Devons' cop persona. "Andresen."

Devons' gaze dropped to John and Naomi's clasped hands, and he scowled. Naomi beamed at the squat lawyer and leaned into John's arm as if they were newlyweds who couldn't wait to get back to the marriage bed.

Devons' scowl deepened.

The man looked momentarily confused, but recovered quickly at the sight of Naomi smiling at him. "Sorry. Thought you were my evening appointment." He glanced down hall. "I didn't know Yordanov had a client scheduled for tonight. Let me check and see if he's here."

He disappeared, and Devons shot John a tight smile. "You're good on your feet, man. Nice cover."

Good didn't have much to do with it. Impatience did. He wanted to get in, find out why Grigory had left a message for Natasha, and get the hell out.

On the receptionist's desk, the phone buzzed softly. A few seconds later, the short lawyer returned and motioned them down the hall. "Yordanov's office is the first door on your right."

So Grigory was there, but he had to know this appointment

was bogus. As the three of them filed past the lawyer, John wondered how long he should keep up his false identity.

He didn't need to worry. The moment they entered the large suite filled with overstuffed leather chairs and massive mahogany furniture, Devons shut the door behind them, and got right down to business. "You speak English?"

Grigory, who'd been staring out the window at the church, eased his office chair around to look at them. "Is she dead?"

The Russian accent matched the one on the phone. Like in the photo Del had sent, Grigory had heavy bags stacked under his eyes and hollow looking cheeks. His hair was completely gray. His eyes a light gray as well.

"Who?" Devons said.

"Natasha, of course." When none of the three of them answered his question, he returned his gaze to the window. "You are not FSB. So that leaves CIA, yes?"

Devons stepped up to the window, scanning the Russian Church and street from Yordanov's viewpoint. "You left Natasha a message Friday with this address. Why?"

Grigory shook his head and ran a hand over his face. "They got her, didn't they?"

"Who?" Devons asked again. He was starting to sound like an owl.

"Ivanov's secret police. Who else? She never made it here. I assume you're here looking for her."

Nice to know they were all on the same page. John asked the most important question on his list. "Where would they take her?"

Grigory turned his chair so he faced John. His accent grew a little stronger, even as his voice grew weaker. "Ivanov has a dozen different locations for interrogations and..."

When he didn't finish, Naomi stepped forward, frowning. "Please go on. And what?"

The man swallowed, his watery gray eyes not seeing her but

something else. Something distant and in the past. "Torture chambers. He was in the KGB, then a secret black ops group when the Cold War ended. They called him the Emperor. He conquered and destroyed many good people, either by torture or assassination."

Naomi glanced at Devons, brows dipping further. Her eyes filled with angst. For a former Mossad operative, she was awfully soft.

She put a hand on the old man's shoulder. "You loved Natasha, didn't you?"

His gaze dropped to the floor, his head moving in an affirmative nod. "She was everything to me all those years ago."

John took out his cell phone to take notes. "Where are the locations of the torture chambers?"

Grigory looked up at him, a new light in his eyes. "You can find her?"

"Maybe. But I need to know where those locations are."

Devons hawk-like gaze never left the window, but he was watching Naomi's reflection. "And I need to know why she was meeting you. She wasn't just an old flame, was she?"

When Grigory didn't answer, Naomi knelt beside him and took one of his hands in hers. "You can trust us. We only want to help Natasha. And you."

The lawyer patted her hand, rose from his chair, and removed a large framed original oil painting from the wall. Behind it was a safe. He entered the code on the keypad, opened it, and drew out a small brown envelope. He held it in his hand for a moment as if making a crucial decision. Then he held it out to Naomi.

Devons was faster, snatching the envelope and dumping out the contents. A silver key fell into his hand. "What does this go to?"

"A safe deposit box at the Odier Bank here in Geneva."

"What's in the box?"

For the first time since they'd entered, Grigory pulled himself together and met Devons stare eye for eye. "The poor lack much, but the greedy, more. If you want to know what's in the box, I suggest you go open it." Rubbing a hand over his face, he switched his focus to Naomi again. "I have nothing left. My grandson is dead. Natasha is gone. Everything we did to protect our families was for nothing. Ivanov is unstoppable."

Naomi squeezed his hand. "These men here will find Natasha. You haven't lost everything."

Hoping she was right, John tugged Grigory's coat off the nearby coat rack and held it out to him. "You can give me those locations on the way to the safe house."

Grigory frowned. "Safe house?"

"It wasn't that hard for us to connect you to Natasha." Devons started for the door, grabbing Naomi with one hand, and lifting the key to dangle it in front of the lawyer's face with the other. "If there's something in that bank box Ivanov wants, he'll come after you for this. Tonight you'll stay in the safe house. Tomorrow, after you help us at the bank, you'll take an extended vacation to Aruba until this all blows over. You feel me?"

Grigory didn't have a chance to think it over. Naomi took his coat from John and forced Grigory's arms into it. "We'll get Natasha back, and the two of you can start over."

Devon rolled his eyes, but John could see he secretly admired her fairy tale determination.

20

Kremlin Palace

Anya's lips tingled, Ryan's kiss in last night's shadows lingering on her skin even in the light of day.

Touching them gently with her fingers, she sighed. What was she supposed to think of that kiss? There was something developing between them. Something more than their agreement to help each other. What exactly, she wasn't sure.

No time to worry about that now. Her time during the summit was running out. She needed to stay focused and get on with her job.

When Grams and Anya had moved to America, one of Grams' favorite pastimes had been picking up slang, new curse words, and various American sayings to add to her repertoire of Russian proverbs. Her favorite idiom was, *you have to eat an elephant one bite at a time.*

For the first several years in America, there were a lot of elephants to eat. After hearing her grandmother repeat the saying so many times, Anya had tuned it out. Now as she shoved back the covers and sat up in bed, body trembling from lack of sleep and tense nerves, she once again heard Grams' voice offering the sage Americanism in her head.

She walked to the massive walk-in closet, as big as her entire apartment back home, and went through the motions of getting dressed for breakfast. A black pencil skirt. White blouse. Black pumps.

Her grandmother had taught her to be independent above all else, not so much through verbal encouragement but by her example. Anya had never relied on anyone else for help, and it galled her to do so now, but attacking this elephant alone was sheer stupidity. A crazy Russian leader, missiles, and the Iranians. She was in over her head and had no idea what she should do.

Talk to Ryan.

But how? When?

In front of the mirror in the bathroom, she ran a brush through her hair and dabbed concealer on the bruise-like shadows under her eyes. The white shirt did nothing to counterbalance her paleness, so she added a touch of blush and some of her cherry Chapstick for color. Funny her lips felt so different after Ryan's kiss. They looked the same as ever.

She popped a pill, changed the bandage on her wound, and then went to the sitting room to wait for Inga, the memory of Ryan and his lips giving her strength. He wasn't the only one who could set up a secret meeting.

The older woman was surprised to see Anya up and dressed. "You feel better, *da*? Did you look at those files?"

"Not yet." Anya didn't feel like conversation, and the thought of food turned her stomach, but she needed to get out of the room. She had a plan. "Let's go."

When they reached the Palace of Facets, Anya zeroed in on Ivanov and asked Inga to bring her a cup of coffee. Inga tsked at her. "Tea would be easier on your stomach."

"I don't want tea, Inga. Coffee. Cream and three sugars." She was rarely so brusque, but she couldn't find the energy to be nice. Ignoring the stares of a nearby group, she walked past them, and goose bumps rose on her skin when she caught sight of Ryan from the corner of her eye.

Don't even look at him.

Andreev was nowhere to be seen. Ivanov sat with President Pennington, and both men rose as she approached, concern obvious on Ivanov's face. For her health or his, she wasn't sure.

"Twenty-four hour bug," she reassured him. It was important to keep the monster happy. "But just like you, I'm made from hardy stock. Nothing keeps us royals down for long, right?"

The change she'd seen when she'd played along with his fixation on their gene pool happened again. He returned to his seat and glanced around the room to see who was watching them, pleased that she was at his side. "Very good. Would you like to eat?"

She was already chewing the first bite of the elephant. "Inga is bringing me coffee. That's enough for now."

Inga appeared at that moment, carrying a demure china cup and saucer to the table. Anya sighed. She'd need three times that amount of caffeine to get through this morning.

Seeing the tight expression on Inga's face, Anya felt a prick of guilt at her earlier gruffness. The poor woman had a hard enough life as it was. "Thank you, Inga." She pointed at the buffet steaming with food. "Please have some breakfast while I talk to President Ivanov."

Inga glanced at Ivanov as if to get his permission. He gave her one downward nod, and Inga bowed slightly, and said a soft 'thank you' before heading toward the food.

Ivanov started to return to his conversation with Pennington. Anya laid a hand on his forearm. His attention swung back to her.

Sell it, Anya. "It's meant so much to me to be back here in

Moscow, here in the Palace, I'd like to create a scrapbook of this week. Perhaps I could speak to the journalist over there—" she pointed to Truman across the room "—and ask him to share some of his photos with me."

A flicker of distrust showed in Ivanov's eyes and Anya immediately went to work to squash it. "With your permission, of course. I especially want a copy of the photo he took of us at the opening ceremony. That will be the first item in my scrapbook."

Ivanov's ego trumped the worries forming in his mind. "I will enjoy seeing this scrapbook when it's done."

One bite down. Another hundred to go. "Thank you."

Anya drank half of the coffee cup's contents, letting Ivanov immerse himself in his conversation with Pennington while she carefully planned out what she'd say to Truman. All the while, she steeled herself from looking at Ryan.

Easier said than done.

They hadn't had a chance to talk last night. Really talk, anyway. And that kiss... it seemed so out of character for him, and yet, she once again reminded herself, she didn't really know what his character was like. The kiss probably meant way more to her than it did him.

Hot and cold, this spy game. If they couldn't meet to talk about her discoveries and his intentions, there was no way for her to explain her actions or figure out his. Clandestine meetings like last night's were great for her short-term mental health, giving her a break from thinking too much, but they were hell on her heart and her timeline. They needed a better strategy...and fast.

The crushing weight of his rejection the previous day hovered at the back of her mind. Would he go along with today's bold idea? If he refused, she was back to square one. She was probably screwed anyway...might as well take a chance and see what it got her.

Downing the rest of her coffee, she gathered her courage and left the table.

As she crossed the room, she felt Ivanov's gaze crawl over her back. Ryan's scanned her front. Ryan's attention was far more discreet, but it was as if he were more aware of her. As if just from the briefest of glances he saw her—who she really was, not some idealistic version. And where Ivanov watched her with a possessive eye, Ryan watched her with an inquisitive one. Guarded, but curious all the same.

Truman was shoving eggs into his mouth when she sat down across from him. He glanced up, did a double take, and nearly jumped out of his chair. "Princess Anya." He wiped his mouth with a cloth napkin, held out his hand. His British accent was heavy. "An honor to meet you."

She played along and shook his hand, motioning for him to return to his seat. His name badge read Tony Westport, and his camera sat to one side. "Mr. Westport, I'd like you to show me all the pictures on your camera."

He did nonplussed well, setting the napkin down, and looking her straight in the eye. "Pictures?"

"I'm starting a scrapbook of the week's events, and since I don't have a camera of my own, I wondered if you would share your photos with me. Please." She stressed the last word, and gave him her most charming smile.

"Yes, of course. Well, bugger." He frowned slightly and lowered his voice. "Technically, the pictures are the property of *The Guardian*. I'll have to get permission to give you copies, but I'm sure I can arrange something."

She didn't really need the pictures, but she did need a minute or two more of his time. "Could you at least show me what you have so far?"

Behind the neutrality of his face, she saw a growing curiousness. And behind that, a probing gaze with a healthy dose of skepticism. So much like Ryan's. Still, he shoved his plate out of the way, picked up his camera, and turned it on.

For the next couple of minutes, Anya browsed the collection of photos on the camera. After the first dozen, she realized none of them included Ryan. Hurriedly, she flipped through the next dozen. No Ryan.

Now *she* was curious.

"Is there something specific you're looking for?" Truman asked.

"Um, no. I wonder if you could do me a huge favor?"

"Besides sharing photos with you?"

She put every ounce of charm she could drag up into her face, and patted his hand like they were old friends. "I'm a demanding woman, aren't I? Must be my much publicized royal blood."

Truman seemed a bit dazzled by the pensive look and friendly touch, but he recovered quickly and chuckled along with her. "I'm at your service."

Anya flashed him a brilliant smile and took the next bite of the elephant. "Can you give your friend, Mr. Jones, a message for me?"

ODIER BANK
Geneva

TWO MINUTES AFTER EIGHT O'CLOCK THE NEXT MORNING, JOHN, Naomi, and Grigory Yordanov walked into the bank. John peeled off to the right, a newspaper in hand and a two-way radio device in his ear, and took a seat in the plush waiting area near the bank's floor to ceiling windows. Naomi and Grigory located the desk of the woman in charge of the lock boxes.

Devons sat outside watching the entrance and scanning customers for any signs of Ivanov's secret police detail, or Russian undercover operatives who might also be surveilling the bank. It was one thing to steal the contents of Natasha's safe deposit box. Another to walk out of the bank with it and not end up dead.

Which was why John was stroking out behind his copy of the *Geneva Times*. Naomi was impersonating Anya Radcliff, the only other person on the bank's files allowed access to the box, according to Del. During the night, Josh Devons, CIA spook, weapons expert, and fake Geneva cop, had suddenly become a paper pusher. With Del's instructions and supplies from a local forger, Devons had made Naomi a fake passport with Anya's information on it. Naomi had bought a wig and tinted contacts to change her appearance. Both women looked nearly identical on paper, and when Devons had offered the idea up, Naomi had jumped at the chance to play spy again.

John had adamantly argued against the pair to no avail. And he couldn't exactly call up Conrad Flynn and tattle, "Devon's former girlfriend" – or whatever she was – "is a Mossad agent playing *007* for us."

Personal feelings aside, the plan was solid. Even he could hardly tell the difference between Naomi in costume and the picture of Anya Radcliff. Naomi had obviously done under-cover work before. Sending her in place of Anya would get the job done, and John knew for a fact, Flynn would have probably recruited Naomi as well.

John wasn't happy about it, though. Naomi pretending to be Anya Radcliff *or* Anya Radzoya was asking for trouble. Shit would hit the fan at some point and his ass would be on the line. That was why he'd insisted on entering the bank with her and keeping as close to her and Grigory as possible. Nothing was happening to any of them on his watch. *Nothing.*

Grigory had morphed overnight into a smooth operator. He

chatted up the desk gal, barely giving her a chance to eyeball Naomi's passport and confirm she was on Natasha's list of approved key holders. Grigory also provided his own I.D., impressing the woman with more than his charm. While Naomi headed to the elevator that led to the underground vault, Grigory offered the woman his business card and his services. She wrote down his personal cell number and gave him hers.

Voices and the click of women's heels echoed off the marble floors and high ceilings of the bank. John hustled to follow Naomi into the elevator without looking like he was following her. Like a good operative, she ignored him behind her giant sunglasses, which boasted the Dior name on the sides, until the doors shut. Once they were alone, she snagged the glasses off her nose and glared at him. "Stop acting as if you are stroking out."

He didn't know why, but the American sounding expression mixed with her Israeli accent made him laugh. It didn't, however, stop him from wanting to grab her hand and haul ass out of the bank.

He adjusted his earpiece and spoke to Devons. "We're going down into the vault where the boxes are kept. Communication may cease for a few minutes. Whatever you do, cover us."

Devons' voice, cocky as ever, floated into his ear. "Got your back, man. Relax."

Ding. The elevator stopped as they reached the bottom floor. They stepped into a foyer with a table along one wall sporting a vase of flowers. Artwork lined the other wall, and a pair of chairs sat under it.

John took Naomi's arm and helped her across the threshold. "You remember the plan?"

She patted the large bag hanging from her shoulder. "I know what I'm doing."

With that, she hustled by the chairs to scan the directory at the end of the short hall. Finding the Swiss version of Safe Deposit Box Vault, or whatever the hell it said, she turned left and disappeared.

Setting his newspaper on the table, John noted a surveillance camera in the corner. He turned his back to it while speaking softly to Devons. "D, you there? Can you hear me? Come in."

All he got back was static.

A clock above his head ticked off the seconds as John leaned against the elevator wall, staying out of sight of the camera while he ran possible alternative routes out of the bank using the mental map in his mind.

After three minutes had passed, he wanted to pace, but held himself still. Patience was one of the requirements for the type of work he did and he knew the value of it in every situation.

Four minutes passed.

Five.

At nine minutes and seventeen seconds, voices echoed down the hall on the left. Naomi's and a man's. Naomi was speaking rapid-fire French, sounding like a native Swiss instead of an Israeli, but agitated. All of John's nerves went into overdrive.

The man grunted. A warning? A comment? The sound of Naomi's heels on the marble floor sounded wrong—*click, thud, click, thud*—but John could tell the two of them were coming fast, and he didn't have time to think. He punched the button for the elevator and reached around to the spot at the back of his waist for his gun.

Naomi came around the corner, a burly, dark-haired guy dressed in a guard uniform with a beard and an attitude in tow. His hand was wrapped around her arm.

John stepped forward, gun already clearing his waistband, when Naomi smiled at him and held up one of the heels from her shoe. "Broke my favorite Louboutins. Can you believe it, honey?" All traces of the Israeli accent were gone. She sounded European, hinting at French. "Monsieur Blanc, here, insisted on helping me to the elevator."

Monsieur Blanc looked less than excited about his escort services, but John eased the gun back into his waistband. The elevator's soft ding sounded behind him. He pasted on a fake smile, and hustled Naomi away from the man and into the elevator. "Thanks," he said to the guard and punched the button for the first floor of the bank.

Once the doors closed, Naomi leaned against the back panel, smiling and lopsided in her shoes. She pulled out an old floppy disc and handed it to John. "I miss field work."

John checked the disc over, his gut sinking. "This is it? This is all there was?"

Naomi's delight faded. "And these." She drew out a stack of old comic books. Seeing his frown deepen, she crossed her arms. "What's wrong?"

In his ear, Devons' voice crackled, stopping John's reply. He handed the disc back to Naomi. "Say again, D. I didn't catch that."

This time, Devons' voice came through loud and clear. "We got trouble."

"Inside or out?"

"Both."

Ding. Securing Naomi behind him in one fluid motion as the elevator opened, John reached for his gun.

21

Moscow
GI 42 Prison

IDIOTS. IRANIANS WERE FAR INFERIOR TO RUSSIANS. ALWAYS HAD been. He'd offered to sell them guns, and now they wanted missiles. As if he would actually sell them advanced nuclear weapons, plans, or warheads.

Natasha Radzoya, however, was as clever as he was, and as loyal. Not loyal to her country, but loyal to her granddaughter.

No longer gagged, she nevertheless remained silent. He'd switched tactics, allowing Andreev to give her water and bread. The cold, dank prison cell had been turned into a sauna. Instead of silence, screeching techno music filled the air. Natasha was ailing, but not close to dead. Not yet.

Her stubbornness was commendable. In the end, if he had to, he'd resort to physical torture. First, he'd play with the mouse a little more.

"Look. " He held up a Russian newspaper. A picture of Anya in the dark blue dress and Romanov necklace was front page news. He tossed an assortment of pop culture magazines on Natasha's lap. "Our princess is assimilating into her true culture. People want to know about her. All over the world, they speak of her. She has become a media sensation, stealing the spotlight from the tight-ass British royalty."

As expected, Natasha flinched at the idea. Drawn to the pictures of Anya, her eyes scanned the various photographs with a certain longing.

But she stayed quiet.

Fine. Patience was easy. He wanted the code, though, and soon. His plan, along with securing Anya, depended on it.

"Do you know why I killed Peter?"

Natasha didn't answer, only continued to stare at her granddaughter's picture.

"He knew all our secrets. The codes. The locations. Every detail about the missiles and warheads. Yeltsin thought the risk was too high. The CIA was too close. You were unstable. If the United States or Britain or those dirty, disgusting Arabs grabbed Peter, they would get all those details. So..."

He put a finger gun to his head and pulled the pretend trigger.

Natasha raised her gaze to his. Electronic bass thumped in the air between them. "That was your first mistake."

The music was loud enough and her voice strained enough, he almost didn't make out her words. He chuckled at her statement. "Mistakes? I do not make mistakes."

The old woman's eyes were hard chunks of ice. "You touch my granddaughter and that will be your last mistake."

Her threat was meaningless, but her attitude irritated him. Raising a hand, he slapped her face. "Know your place, traitor."

She rocked back from the blow but showed no remorse. Her chest heaved twice before she spoke. "The code you want died with Peter. You screwed yourself."

"Yeltsin claims otherwise. That you have the code."

"Yeltsin was a weak, power hungry man. Much like the man I see in front of me. He lied...as do you."

"Yeltsin treated you with more respect and dignity than you or your family ever deserved."

At that, she laughed. "We can talk Russian politics all day. Won't change the fact that no matter what you do to me, I cannot give you the code. Neither will Anya ever be your czarina."

Anya was already his. And there were plenty of ways to break the immovable object in front of him.

"Enjoy the music," he said, smiling as he left.

ODIER BANK
Geneva

WHEN THE DOOR OPENED, DEVONS WAS BLOCKING THEIR departure. He raised his hands, a typical response to a drawn gun, and smiled at John. "Easy, partner. The Russians aren't the problem."

John released the breath he was holding, and seeing Devons' causal air of competence, returned the Glock to its hiding place. "Then what the hell is?"

Devons shifted so John and Naomi could see the massive hall behind him, including the desk where Grigory had been chatting up the manager.

A dozen or more people crowded around a body on the floor. A guard waved them away while another tried to revive the man with a mixture of shaking, slapping, and CPR. The recipient's shoes came into view. Brown loafers that looked familiar.

Naomi recognized them too. "*Adoni shelei*, Grigory. What happened?"

Devons eyed Grigory and shrugged. "My guess is a heart attack. Ambulance is on the way, and the guard reviving him says he has medical training."

Naomi started forward. Devons grabbed her, guiding her out of the elevator and over to a nearby palm tree. "You can't help him right now. Let the guards do their job." He glanced at Naomi's bag, then at John. "Did you get it?"

Whatever *it* was. "Yeah, we got it."

"Secret codes? Diamonds? What?"

"A floppy disc."

"Huh?"

"Computer disc from the eighties."

"And comic books," Naomi added.

Devons' eyes lit up with a weird kind of admiration. Maybe he'd been a geek as a kid, spending his lonely days in front of a computer, a stack of Superman comics next to his desk. "No kidding."

Naomi continued to watch the show around Grigory. "This isn't the way the story is supposed to go. We're supposed to find Natasha and reunite them." She looked at Devons. "Do you think he'll die?"

"He's receiving medical care. He'll be fine. While he's in the hospital recouping, John and I will find Natasha, and we'll reunite them just like you want."

Naomi's tension eased as Devons seemed to finally be on board with her fairy tale.

John stood by, quietly amused at the spy's change of heart. "We need to get that disc to Del but we shouldn't leave Grigory alone. Ivanov's goons could still come after him, and lying unconscious in the hospital makes him a sitting duck."

"I'll stay with him," Naomi volunteered.

"No," he and Devons said at the same time.

Devons got her walking, leading her away from the scene and toward the front entrance. "You're not a bodyguard, Naomi."

John agreed. "Flynn can send someone to guard Grigory. For now, we all need to get the hell out of here and get that disc to a safe place."

"But he came in with me." Naomi planted her feet, one heeled and one not. "People will wonder why I'm leaving without him. And I don't want him to be alone at the hospital."

An ambulance siren screamed in the distance. Cops would arrive with it. People would ask questions. Naomi's passport and story wouldn't hold up to that kind of scrutiny.

Devons gave Naomi a hard look. "Game's over, babe. We can't take any more chances. We have to go. Now."

She caved, pissed, but understanding their dilemma, and the three of them started walking again.

John walked at Devons' side. "I'll contact Flynn and take care of the disc. You take Naomi back to her place."

"Ask Flynn to put eyes on Naomi for the next forty-eight hours as well, will you?"

John saw the quiet fear in Devons' eyes. Mossad or no, he was worried about the woman. John had the same feelings about a certain someone back home. "Sure, man."

Passing the commotion at the manager's desk, John peeked at Grigory, lying on the floor. The man's eyelids fluttered open, his gray eyes scanning the crowd...

And landing on John.

The old spy sat up like someone had pushed his start button, knocking the guard out of the way and coughing loudly. Everyone gasped and took a step back.

"Oh, dear," he said, looking around at the surprised crowd. "I'm afraid I've caused you all a fright. But it's all right. I'm all right."

The guard administering CPR looked as shocked as the rest

of the group, and didn't even offer to help Grigory to his feet. Outside, the ambulance and a police car swung into the parking lot. As the guard tried to get Grigory to sit again, the old man brushed him aside and waved at everyone. "I'm fine, I'm fine. Just low blood sugar. Happens all the time."

He made a shooing motion at Naomi, John, and Devons, staying on their heels as they exited the building. "Make haste," he murmured. "We need to get out of here."

"No kidding," Devons said with a hint of impatience.

The four of them jumped in their car, and Devons gunned the motor, waving at the police officer who was directing traffic in and out of the parking lot. "Mind telling us what the hell that was all about?"

Grigory chuckled, sounding quite pleased with himself. "Just a little fun, like back in the day when I, too, could deceive the enemy." He turned to Naomi and John in the backseat. "You took so long, I thought you'd run into trouble. I created a diversion to help you out. Did you get it?"

Naomi smiled slyly, enjoying Grigory's subterfuge. She removed the disc from her purse and showed it to him. Grigory let out a whoop.

"Put it back in the bag," John said. We're not out of the woods yet."

Naomi followed orders. and met Devons eyes in the rearview. He winked, and she rolled her eyes.

John looked out the window. Comic books and an old floppy disc. Whatever the hell was on that disc better be worth the drama and danger they were in now.

22

THE GREAT KREMLIN Palace
Moscow

THE PRESIDENTIAL LIBRARY. THREE O'CLOCK. RYAN CHECKED HIS
watch again and fingered the book he'd located on the pretense
someone discovered him here.

Four minutes before three. Would she show?

The bigger question was why she'd asked him to meet her
here. Had she discovered the evidence they needed about
Ivanov's plans? Had she discovered where her grandmother
was being held hostage? She'd claimed last night in her room
that she'd uncovered something about her family, but how
would that help him?

It wouldn't. And she was taking too big of a chance with this
meeting.

But, damn, he was here anyway, ready to hear whatever she
had to say, and cover for her if they got caught.

His mind returned to their meeting in her room. The dim
light, the music in the background, her utter trust in him. The

way she never hesitated to throw her arms around him and say thank you.

His ego liked that. Liked her. His body had never had such a strong reaction to a woman before. Forget his misgivings about her loyalties and her family's history of treason, he wanted to kiss her, to hold her, to make her smile. He loved the determination in her eyes, the straight posture she erected when she felt challenged. He loved everything about her.

The thought made him cringe. Falling for an asset was the ultimate no-no. The rush of adrenaline and secrecy could trick even the most experienced, hardened spies into inappropriate feelings. Sometimes followed up by inappropriate actions.

Like a kiss that never should have happened.

Two minutes.

Ryan tapped his fingers on a bookshelf. Anya had given Truman some half-baked excuse for needing to speak to him in private about a surprise cultural event she wanted to plan for President Ivanov. The only part of her message Ryan believed was that she had no phone to call the number he'd given her. She'd gone through Truman instead of coming directly to Ryan to avoid Ivanov's suspicions.

Truman had warned him against the secret meeting. Warned him Ivanov's eyes were everywhere, and he couldn't take the chance. But Ryan had seen the change in Truman, the way Anya had affected him with her simple requests and obvious pretense. Either she was a very good actress playing on both their sympathies, or she was indeed a desperate young woman who truly needed help. He believed the latter, but hadn't totally ruled out the former.

The fact her grandmother had been a double agent hovered in the back of his mind. If Anya had followed in her grandmother's footsteps, he was about to step across a line. A line there was no stepping back from.

One minute to go. He paced the floor near the back wall,

not seeing the Persian carpets, tall windows, or three stories of Russian literary masterpieces. He wasn't sure what he was about to take part in, or find himself trapped in, but he was here. And while his logical brain was screaming warnings at him, his gut was happy to have a few minutes alone with her.

As far as private meeting places inside the Kremlin complex went, this was a good one. Maybe the best in the entire Palace, outside of Ivanov's private chambers. No cameras. No listening devices. No guards when the president wasn't inside. The library was a sanctuary, more for show than use, and therefore off the security grid unless someone important was using it.

That didn't mean the cameras in the hallway hadn't captured his entrance. He'd pretended to be on his cell phone and looking for better reception, and then he'd scanned the shelves for a book just in case. If Anya entered via the same door and someone was actually paying attention, it might raise suspicion. She'd warned him about the cameras outside her room last night, but Ryan made a mental note to warn her to be more careful next time.

Next time? His gut did another dance. He hadn't gotten through this meeting yet, and he was already looking forward to the next one.

As the enormous clock over the fireplace bonged the hour, one of the double doors at the opposite end creaked open and slim fingers slipped around the edge, Anya's face appearing before her body as if she were hesitant to enter. Her eyes were huge, jaw set, and her full pink lips pressed into a straight line. Even though his pulse raced at the sight of her, Ryan stepped back into the shadows...a habit born of caution.

She scanned the room, looking for him, he guessed, then slipped inside. She closed the door softly, leaned her back against it, and let out a long, deep breath. A sigh of relief or disappointment?

Since she appeared to be alone, Ryan stepped out from the

shadows, his pulse double-timing it. Whether because the meeting was furtive or because he was simply anxious to see her, he wasn't sure. To have her alone for a few minutes, all to himself, had been all he'd thought about since last night. Even so, he put a clamp on his emotions and drummed up complacency. As Truman had warned him, he was playing with fire.

The moment Anya saw him, her face broke into a smile. A relieved, happy-to-see you smile, as if he were her best friend. She was wearing the black pencil skirt from that morning, which covered half of her long, slender legs. The upside was, the skirt's narrow hem emphasized her hips and forced them to swing wider as she walked. Coupled with her smile, the effect was megawatt glam.

Ryan's brain stuttered.

Without even telling his feet to start walking, he found himself meeting her in the middle of the room.

"Mr. *Jones.*" She was breathless and still grinning, and for split second, he forgot Jones was his cover name. For a second, he even forgot his real name. So much for complacency.

Searching his face, she looked away, pressed her lips together, and then spoke in a rush. "I didn't get to tell you what I found last night."

She didn't give him a chance to respond, hurrying on to cover her awkwardness. "What I am about to tell you is going to sound crazy, but I swear I'm not making this up. I'm not crazy. I have my moments, but..."

She stopped herself, pressed a hand to her forehead, and closed her eyes. "Of course if I was crazy, I'd still tell you I wasn't, so that doesn't help does it?"

Just like his feet had moved on their own accord, his hand reached out and touched her arm. "Anya, it's okay. I know you're not crazy. I'm here, and I'm listening."

At his touch, she opened her eyes and looked straight at him, her high heels bringing her within an inch or two of his height. She dropped her hand and took a deep breath. "It's worse than I thought."

As she worried her bottom lip with her teeth, the black hole in his brain opened a little wider. "Worse how? Is your grandmother dead?"

Her eyes widened. "God, I hope not, but this isn't about her."

She rattled off the conversation she'd overheard the previous evening in her bed chambers between Ivanov and Andreev. His body tensed at the thought of either man being in her bedroom, and he found it hard to concentrate on what she was saying. Weapons, Iranians, a code.

"We have to talk to President Pennington." She grabbed Ryan's arm and gave it a small shake of urgency. "There probably isn't anything he can do to find my grandmother, but he has to stop Ivanov from getting his hands on that code and selling weapons to the Iranians. Millions of people could die..." Her voice trailed off and she bit her bottom lip again. "I can't figure how or why, but the code seems to involve Grams."

None of what she'd said surprised Ryan. Grandma Natasha having a code to ICBMs? Big surprise. As a double agent, she'd probably stolen it...and other top secret information as well.

Anya's story, however, opened the door on his anger. The door he had so meticulously locked. Ivanov's treachery truly knew no bounds, and although Ryan wanted to march into the summit meeting and punch Ivanov in the face, years of experience had taught him the only way to defeat a sociopath was to outsmart him at every turn.

Ryan hated to dash Anya's hopes of a simple fix, but he wouldn't lie. "President Pennington can't accuse Ivanov of anything unless he has proof in black-and-white. It's your word against the president of Russia. We discussed this at the cabin. Even under better circumstances, your word doesn't count as much as his."

Setting hands on hips, Anya looked down at the floor, tapping the toe of one shoe in frustration, and chewing so hard on her lip, Ryan thought it would bleed.

He reached for something—anything—he could say or do to help her out. She had the potential to be the key that ended Ivanov's reign, and this was the opportunity he'd been waiting for, and yet he couldn't bring himself to point her in the direction she needed to go.

He didn't have to.

"Wait." Her head snapped up. Determination lit her blue eyes as she met his gaze again. "Evidence in writing, that's what you said. Pictures or anything that shows he's breaking the treaty. I know where to find it. In his office. His personal office in his private chambers. There are maps and files all over his desk. I just have to get back in there. Which shouldn't be hard since he's determined to do more than show me his genealogy books."

The anger roared low and hot in Ryan's stomach. He didn't want her in Ivanov's private chambers, didn't want her anywhere near the man. The cards were dealt, however, and she was willing to use her access to get the evidence he needed.

His training demanded he give her the rope but his heart refused to let her hang herself. "Ivanov's security is one of the best in the world, and he didn't get where he is by leaving evidence of his crimes lying out in the open. Even our meeting right now could cause us both problems. I'll help you however I can, but we have to be careful and smart about what we're doing. We need a plan."

Anya's megawatt smile blindsided him once more. She reached for his hand and squeezed it firmly. "I have a plan."

The black hole at Ryan's feet swelled.

23

YES! Relief flooded Anya from head to toe. She was going to stop Ivanov and Ryan didn't think she was crazy. He wasn't even acting weird over their kiss.

Maybe good, maybe bad. Had it meant so little to him?

Get over yourself, Anya, and quit wasting time.

The thought of returning to Ivanov's private chambers and searching for evidence about reactivated missiles, and his deal with the Iranians, kick-started the dread in her chest. But Ryan's hand was so warm, so firm against hers, she didn't linger on the unpleasant thought. The future—even if it was only a few hours away—didn't matter as much as that moment. He believed her; that was the most important part of her plan. They were together, if only for a few stolen moments once again.

She didn't want to release his hand, but had been holding it and squeezing it several seconds longer than necessary. Pure and simple, she was acting like a dork. Like a lovesick teenager meeting her boy-band crush. "Sorry." She dropped his hand and gave a self-deprecating laugh. "I'm exhausted, and freaked out over my grandmother, and, uh, a little nervous."

His lips quirked to one side. "Tell me more about your grandmother. Was blackmailing you into returning to Moscow the only reason Ivanov kidnapped her? What about this code?"

Stumped, she frowned. "I don't have a clue. Why would my grandmother have a nuclear weapon code? The idea is ridiculous."

He studied her for a moment as if giving her time to think. Her brain honed in on that, and the thought she'd had several times surfaced. Was Grams a threat to Ivanov? Did she have proof he'd killed her parents? Did she indeed know a code that could launch missiles?

Before her brain could answer, Ryan dismissed his question with a shrug. "I don't recommend stealing anything from Ivanov's office. We'll figure out another way to get hard evidence."

A spurt of panic ran through her. "I can do it. I've already stolen something. Here." She unbuttoned the top two buttons of her blouse, fingers shaking so bad, she fumbled with the job before retrieving the folded up warrants from her bra.

As she unfolded them, Ryan's eyes—locked on her display of cleavage—widened and his brows disappeared under the hair on his forehead. She'd shocked him. Because she'd stolen something from Ivanov, or because she'd hidden it in her bra?

Using her free hand to draw the edges of her blouse together, she handed the paper to him. "KGB execution warrants. For my parents, and initialed by one MYI."

Ryan tore his gaze away from her cleavage and took the paper. He scanned the first paper, brows returning to their normal place on his face, then sinking into a frown.

Anya buttoned her blouse and moved beside him to read the second warrant. The scent of soap, and that clean, spicy aftershave, enveloped her. The smell was so completely opposite Ivanov, it was, in and of itself, reassuring. She inhaled.

He glanced at her from the corner of his eyes, her close

presence seeming to make him nervous. Ryan, nervous? She must be imagining it. Embarrassed, she pointed to the word next to each person's name and was proud to see her fingers were no longer shaking. "See? That word right there. That's Russian for 'executed'."

"Yes, I know," he murmured, dragging his gaze back to the paper.

"Of course." She gently slapped her forehead, signifying a *doh* moment, and her shoulder brushed against his. For some reason, she wanted to impress him. Wanted him to believe she was not only sane, but capable of what she was proposing. Wanted to leave her shoulder up against his. "I forgot. You're fluent in Russian, aren't you? I heard you speaking it at the cabin."

Again, he did the eye slide thing, as if he wanted to look directly at her but didn't want to move, even a little, away from her. That was good. She didn't want him to move. "Where exactly did you get these? *How* did you get these?"

She'd stolen a launch key, and he was surprised she'd stolen a couple pieces of paper?

The library's antique clock bonged the quarter hour and Anya jumped. She'd been here fifteen minutes already? How could that be? She double checked her watch. Three-fifteen. Damn.

"Look, I left my babysitter sleeping in front of the TV. The guards take a break when she's there in the afternoon with me, but they'll be back any minute, might even beat me there if I don't hurry." She took a couple steps toward the door. "Can we meet back here tomorrow, same time?"

In the silence that followed, he seemed to ascertain the fact that she'd slipped away from Inga to meet him and was planning to do it again. "Too dangerous. I'll figure something else out. In the meantime, you can continue to pass messages through Tru...Tony. That was a good idea, by the way."

His praise felt like warm maple syrup running down her spine. "If we can't meet here, and you can't drug my guards again, then where?"

He seemed unconcerned about the security. "Do you know anything about Kremlin Palace?"

"Every school child in Russia learns the history of the Palace."

"Not the history, the layout. Hidden doors? Secret passageways? They exist throughout the entire structure. I'll figure out a way for us to meet undetected and let you know."

Hidden doors. "My room is connected to Ivanov's by a secret door. There's a narrow hallway between them."

A nerve jumped in his jaw. "Can you lock it?"

"Not from my side. I shove a heavy dresser in front of it."

He unclenched his jaw and for the first time since they'd started talking, she saw a light in his eyes. Hope? Happiness? She wasn't sure.

He handed her the warrants. "Just promise me you won't try to steal anything else from Ivanov until we meet again."

Taking the papers and a step back, she began walking away. Time was up and she had to get back to her chambers. "I can't promise that," she said over her shoulder.

"Grand Duchess?"

She stopped and looked at him, confusion churning in her stomach. She wanted to stay there, talk to him more, find out what he knew about her and her family. Find out more about Ryan Jones and his spying. But a growing unease fired up the dread once more in her chest. "Yes?"

"Be careful. Whatever you do, please be careful."

That she could do. Would do. "You, too."

Just as she stepped off the giant Persian rug onto the hardwood floor, a muffled voice called her name from the hallway. Inga. Trouble One had woken up early. Had she brought the guards with her?

With one swift move, Ryan grabbed her arm and hustled her behind a freestanding bookcase. Anya clutched at the shelf in front of her while one of Ryan's arms went around her as they stared at the door together through a crack over the tops of the books. He was so close, she could feel his chest rising and falling against her back as he maintained his protective stance. She missed wearing his sweater. It was buried in her suitcase. Maybe she'd sleep in it tonight.

The doorknob turned, and Anya's heart slammed against her ribs from fear. She had no doubt Ryan could protect her from many things, but this was one thing he shouldn't protect her from. She had to face Inga on her own and return to her suite. "It's okay," she whispered, placing a hand on his chest. "I can handle this."

He glanced down at her hand, back up at her face. Then he let her slip out of his arms. As the door opened and Inga called Anya's name once more, he grabbed her hand, stopping her, and slid a slim book into it. Their gazes held and he nodded at her. She nodded back.

"Here I am," she said to Inga as she emerged from the book-case. "Did you have a good nap?"

Inga's hand went to her chest in relief. "Czarevna Anya. I've been looking all over for you." She gasped several times and Anya feared for a second the woman might be having a heart attack. After another heavy in and out breath, Inga pulled herself together, and shook a finger at Anya. "You know you are not to leave the Golden Chambers without me."

Anya waved her off. "You needed a rest after I kept you up half the night. I came in here for some new reading material."

Inga's relief deepened as she saw the book in Anya's hands. She scolded her anyway, guiding Anya to the door. "Next time, you must wake me, and I will bring you here, *da*?"

As Inga propelled her through the door, Anya glanced back over her shoulder, a bit of panic fluttering in her chest at leaving Ryan. Behind the bookcase, he waited in the shadows. She wouldn't have noticed him if she hadn't known where to look. "Yes. Next time."

The door shut behind them with an audible click. The fluttering in Anya's chest kicked up. When she looked down at the book in her hands, though, she felt Ryan's presence still with her.

A Thousand and One Nights, The Tales of Scheherazade. In English.

He knows everything, she thought. *Even my favorite book.*

As if in response, the bandage over her wound tugged at her skin.

Not everything, she reminded herself. She touched her side.

No matter how good a spy Ryan was, Anya still had many, many secrets.

24

HIS GAME WAS OFF TONIGHT. Ryan shuffled the cards in his hand, but there was no making anything of them.

Tonight's entertainment was Vegas style gambling. Poker, Blackjack, even slot machines were available to the guests. Showgirls circled the floor delivering drinks and flirting. In one corner of the hall, a circus act was performing, complete with jugglers, fire eaters, and a set of performing cats and dogs.

Anya sat watching with Ivanov, outside of Ryan's view.

His card game sucked, but his luck was holding in other areas. He had his asset. She was as close to Ivanov as any of the man's cabinet. And she was willing to risk everything to obtain the evidence Ryan desperately needed to end Ivanov's reign.

Across the green felt table, Truman wiggled a toothpick in the corner of his mouth. Ryan considered mentioning the traitorous tell to him. A good poker player never gave his opponents the upper hand though.

The other three players—a Pennington aide and a couple of Ivanov's cabinet members—had already folded.

Ryan folded, too, and Truman raised a questioning brow while happily claiming the pot. New players lined up around the table to watch, and Ryan would have enjoyed taking their cash any other time. Tonight, he had a job to do. While everyone was enjoying Las Vegas, he needed to get to Georgievsky Hall.

"I'm done," Truman said beside Ryan as Ryan scooped up his chips.

"Quitting while you're ahead for once?"

Together, they walked across the room toward the cashier to turn them in. Truman scanned the area. "Think I'll try my hand at slots."

Ryan looked over the row of machines and saw a lot of unhappy faces with their near empty cups of nickels. "Save your money. Ivanov's got them rigged."

"Should we watch the circus?"

"No thanks." Ryan gave his chips to the cashier. "I'm turning in early."

Truman remained silent until they'd both received their money. As they walked past the slots, he spoke under his breath. "Need help?"

Across the room, a roar of astonishment went up from the circus audience as a dog jumped through a ring of fire. "With what?"

"Whatever you're about to do."

Ryan smirked. "Bored already?"

"My mark is playing it cool here. I haven't found a scrap of evidence against her."

A slot machine behind them finally paid off, buzzers ringing with good fortune for the player. "Well, you can give a message to Anya for me."

"So now we're playing bloody Chinese whispers?"

"The politically correct name for the children's game is Telephone or Grapevine."

Truman shook his head. "You Yanks make a fucking deal out of everything, you know that?"

A fucking deal was right. "Tell her to leave the dresser in its normal spot tonight if she can. I'll knock twice after midnight."

"Midnight meetings, how cliché," he said, as he pieced together what was happening with lightning quick speed. "You won't make it to the door to knock. She's under twenty-four-hour surveillance."

"I'm not going through the guarded door."

"Ah." Again Truman worked the details out in the span of a second. "The hidden hallways, then? Sweet setup. Do you have a map? Kremlin Palace is a logistical nightmare. Never know what torture chamber you might end up in."

Ryan tapped his temple to signify his mental map. "Give a message to Del, would you? Tell him to contact Stone or Flynn and find out if they've uncovered anything more about Natasha Radzoya's disappearance from Switzerland last Friday."

Jugglers took the stage at the circus to a loud round of applause and whistles. Truman watched them while he spoke out the side of his mouth to Ryan. "This is batty, mate. Ivanov will kill you himself if he catches you messing with his property."

"I know," Ryan said, and on the heels of that came a singular, damning thought.

She's worth it.

25

TWO HOURS later

Anya's knee bobbed incessantly under Ivanov's desk as she shuffled the papers covering the top. Ivanov was in the bathroom. She had a minute, two tops, to find something for Ryan.

The map. Where was that damned map she'd seen the other night? The one with weird names. Had those names been some kind of code?

Ivanov had suggested they return to her chambers after the evening's entertainment, but Anya had persuaded him into his apartment suite, using the excuse that she wished to see the family histories again. She'd also agreed to go over a few of the medical files Inga had dumped on her. At the mention of that, Ivanov had practically skipped into his chambers. She was so nervous, the image nearly made her laugh.

Her plan was simple. Get in, steal the map, feign exhaustion from her twenty-four-hour bug, and escape to her room before midnight.

Simple plans were usually the easiest. She learned that long-ago from Grams. Tonight, however, her simple plan didn't seem easy at all.

Where is that map?

From the moment they'd entered the room, Ivanov had put his hands all over her. *The hands of a killer.* She'd dodged, parried, and skirted them as best as she could, restraining her natural reflexes, and defying her defensive training to keep from punching him. Like before, he'd drunk too much vodka, and what few inhibitions he had disappeared as quickly as the alcohol.

The only perk was the fact he had to empty his bladder, allowing her time to search his desk.

Invoices, half-written speeches, and dossiers of the visiting dignitaries claimed the top. Red folders, manila files, and spreadsheets were mixed in. Apparently the wheels that turned to make the Russian government work were made of paper.

From the distant shadows of Ivanov's bedchamber came the sound of a flushing toilet and running water. Time was up. She shuffled faster.

A doorknob rattled. Knowing she was out of time, Anya grabbed the leather bound family history she'd brought with her to the desk, slouched back in the chair, and opened it.

Ivanov shuffled into the room, and when Anya glanced up, she did a double take. He'd exchanged his expensive suit and tie for silk pajamas and a matching robe.

Lovely.

"Oh." Anya stood, closing the book and setting it down. "You're ready for bed. Forgive me for keeping you up."

"Nonsense." He eyed the book, patted his stomach. "I only wanted to be more comfortable. Which history are you reading?"

As Anya came around the side of the desk, a light blue paper caught her eye. The corner of the map she'd been looking for stuck out from a file at the far corner. It was ready to fall to the floor. She stepped in front of it, and leaned her butt back against the desktop. "Yours, of course."

Ivanov nodded, happy over her choice, and stopped at his built-in bar where he withdrew an icy bottle of Jewel of Russia from the fridge. He set up two shot glasses, unscrewed the lid, and poured, idly humming a song from the circus.

She couldn't take a chance he would head to the bathroom again before she had to make her way out from under his pawing advances. While Ivanov retrieved *zakusha*—bite sized snacks to go with their drinks—she used one hand to tug the map the rest of the way out from between the folders, folding it behind her back and sliding it into the waistband of her skirt.

Ivanov brought the *zakusha* and vodka to the coffee table in front of the fireplace and gestured for her to join him. Her stomach rebelled, both at the smoked fish on black bread, and the thought of getting within reach of his hands.

She grabbed the book from the desk. Approaching the fireplace, she opened it, and flipped through the pages as if looking for something. "Where are your parents, Maxim? They must be very proud of you."

"Like yours, they passed many years ago."

"I'm sorry to hear that. Any siblings?"

He eyed her from the sofa, his attention lingering on her breasts. He licked his lips. "One brother."

Flipping another page, she found his name. "Abram?"

His grin made the hair on Anya's neck rise. "I enjoy the way you are now embracing your homeland."

"Does Abram live here in Moscow?"

A heavy sigh escaped Ivanov's lips. "He is a businessman. He has no home, but travels all over the world."

Apparently a touchy subject. One, Anya was determined to pursue. "You must miss him like I miss my grandmother."

Ivanov's eyes narrowed before he busied himself with the vodka and food. No way would she go through with his plans to marry her, but she needed to drive home her point. "Family is important to me, and I hope important to you. It will make me very happy to have my grandmother here in the Palace with us when the time comes."

Ivanov raised a shot glass in acknowledgement, even though it was obvious his heart wasn't in it. "To family."

The clock on the mantle chimed eleven o'clock. One hour until Ryan would come. Smug that she had the map securely hidden, she took the second shot glass and clicked it against Ivanov's. "To family."

He sent his vodka down his throat and picked up one of the *zakusha*, patting the sofa next to him in invitation. His blood-shot eyes again zeroed in on her breasts and Anya checked her gag reflex.

"I'm sorry." She set down her untouched vodka and the family history. "But that twenty-four hour bug really zapped my energy. I think I'll retire early. We can go over those files you asked me to analyze tomorrow night."

Before he could swallow the food in his mouth, she was on her way to the door. She didn't get far, however, before he grabbed her upper arm and turned her around to face him. His grip was iron-hard and just as tight. "You are beautiful, Czarevna."

His lips came down on hers without warning, cold, wet, and soft. Revulsion filled her senses. She jerked backwards while at the same time pushing against his chest with her hands.

He released her and she stumbled, but caught herself before she fell, continuing to back toward the door as she put space between them. The look on her face had to be disgust. She didn't care.

He smiled sweetly, advancing on her until her back was against the door. He brushed his thumb across one of her nipples. "You are welcome to spend the night."

Her immediate fear was that he could feel the warrants through her shirt and bra, but the lecherous look on his face didn't change. That fear aside, sickening disgust rose from her stomach into her throat, and spread through her body. Everything about him, from his touch to his suggestion, horrified her. Loathing burned in her veins.

Reining in the urge to slap him, she felt around for the ornate door handle with the hand behind her back and gave it a twist. "Goodnight, President Ivanov."

She assumed he would stop her from going out the door, but he didn't. Inga was not waiting in the hall for her, confirming Anya's fears that Ivanov had indeed planned to seduce her, and keep her in his bedchambers until morning.

Another wave of disgust rolled through her. and she marched down the hallway toward her suite, oblivious to the guard who walked two paces behind her.

Once inside the Golden Chambers, she locked the French doors. and pushed the dresser in front of the hidden door in the bedroom. Ryan wasn't due for another twenty minutes, and she needed to clean up without worrying a drunk Ivanov would decide to spend the night by force. He would one of these nights, she had no doubt.

In the bathroom, she turned on the hot water in the gigantic, jetted spa tub, and while it filled, she poured mouthwash from a crystal decanter and rinsed her mouth over and over to get the taste of Ivanov off her lips.

Stripping off her clothes, she dropped them on a nearby chair, securing the map, warrants, and Ryan's business card in between a couple of folded plush towels on the rim of the tub. Then she sank into the water, easing down until it came up to her chin.

She removed the bandage from her side and the water soothed the skin of her wound. A light scab had formed over each end, but the middle still seeped blood now and then. "Heal, dammit," she whispered.

While she longed for her tiny, cramped bathroom at home, with its old-fashioned, claw foot tub, this one was still a welcoming place after fleeing her captor. A lot had happened, and yet, there was still so much of the elephant to eat.

With a sinking feeling in her stomach warring with the hope Ryan sparked in her chest, she tried to numb her overloaded brain. When Ryan got there, they'd figure out their next move. She'd show him the map, soak up some of his calm demeanor, and everything would be okay.

I might even kiss him again.

Avoiding her wound, Anya scrubbed the rest of her body hard and fast, wishing that was all it took to scrub Ivanov from her life forever.

26

HE WAS RUNNING LATE.

Georgievsky Hall was pitch black except for shafts of faint moonlight falling from the towering second floor windows. The giant columns towered over empty floors, throwing massive shadows. Vague sounds rose and fell from elsewhere in the Palace, but inside the hall, all was suffocating and silent.

From his left breast pocket, Ryan removed a pair of glasses and slipped them on his face. The special glasses looked like a normal pair of transition lenses, darkening in sunlight and returning to clear when not. This pair, however, had been engineered by Del Hoffman. Night vision, here we come.

To avoid the security cameras in the more public areas of the Palace, Ryan slunk into one of the many service corridors adjacent to the grand hall. Staff, guards, and waiters used the service corridors to get from one area of the Palace to another without disturbing or interrupting the president and his guests. None of these narrow passageways had cameras.

Several of the grand halls concealed kitchens and elevators behind their imposing structures in order to serve fresh, hot meals during events such as the summit. Georgievsky Hall was one of them.

Since it wasn't being used for entertainment tonight, the kitchen and staff areas were vacant. Leaving the kitchen behind, Ryan slipped into the hall, keeping his back against the ornate wall, and out of view of the six cameras he'd logged in his mental map of the place from the first night of the summit. That night, Ivanov and Anya had appeared as if out of nowhere on the east side of the hall, and Ryan was only a few feet away from that entrance. His challenge, besides staying out of the camera eyes, was to find the door release, which was no doubt concealed as expertly as the door itself.

While he was no stranger to covert ops, fieldwork had for the most part been left behind since he'd become Director. His pulse beat steady and strong, if a little faster than normal, as he searched with his hands for any telltale bump or ridge around the nonexistent doorframe. There had to be a release from this side as well as the hidden interior.

His nimble fingers found a super thin wire, as fine as one of his hairs. Probably invisible to the naked eye. Even with the night vision glasses, he couldn't see it, but he could feel it, and his fingers followed it to its source, a tiny, raised button on the right side of the door.

Bingo. He pushed the button and gave himself a mental high-five when the door slid open with a soft *whoosh*.

The secret hallway was barely a yard wide and lit by sconces every ten feet, before the passage turned at both ends. Definitely plain Jane compared to the grand hall he was leaving. The low lighting messed with his night vision, so removing his glasses, he took a cautious scan to the right and left and concentrated, using his eyes and ears to determine if anyone was nearby. All was quiet, but since he could only see to the end of the passage, and there were no hiding places, he had to take it slow, and keep all his senses engaged so as not to be caught unaware.

After waiting a full minute and hearing nothing, he stepped into the secret hall, shut the door behind him, and released a pent-up breath. He pressed the button on his watch to light up the face. Twelve-oh-six.

Better late than dead, he told himself, and followed the path to the Golden Chambers.

———

TWELVE MINUTES LATER, HE STOOD OUTSIDE THE DOOR HE thought was the right one. Across the hallway was a matching door, and on either side of that, larger, elaborate sconces that gave off more light and looked as old as the Palace itself. These, he guessed, were for the president.

The door in front of Ryan sported sconces that were more feminine and opulent, with jewels and crystals embedded in gold, suggesting he'd found his mark.

The deadbolt on the door was in place. To keep Anya locked inside.

Thunk, thunk, thunk. The heavy fall of footsteps echoed down an adjacent hallway. The hidden passageways were nothing more than tunnels that twisted and turned in many directions, making sounds travel in odd patterns. The footsteps could be literally around the corner or fifty yards away. There was no way to tell.

Because of that, Ryan couldn't risk knocking. Flipping the deadbolt back with one hand, he watched over his shoulder as he slid open the door with the other, and hoped against hope he'd picked the right bedroom.

He stepped into the room without looking and ran into something hard.

An antique dresser. Anya had moved the dresser in front of

the door. Apparently she hadn't gotten his message. At least he knew he had the right room.

The bedchamber was bathed in soft white light, barely visible from a nightstand on the far side of the four-poster bed. Sheer, white material hung from the posts to shield the bed, but he could just make out a form lying on it.

Thunk, thunk, thunk. The footstep echoes grew louder. A guard perhaps? Didn't matter. Whoever those footsteps belonged to was definitely coming this way.

Moving the dresser would be noisy and take too much time. Ryan hoisted himself onto the top, and slid the door closed as quickly as he could without making a sound.

He ran his hands and vision over the doorframe. There was no way to relock the deadbolt from the inside. Placing one ear against the door, he listened to the footsteps' approach. They paused right outside. Ryan held his breath while reaching into another pocket, concealed inside his jacket, for a knife he'd stolen from the kitchen. He didn't pull it out, but waited, every nerve screaming with tension. Sweat beaded on his forehead, and he strained to hear sounds from the other side.

Behind him came the rustle of bedclothes. "Ryan? Is that you?"

In a heartbeat, he slid off the dresser, and dove for the bed, where Anya was drawing herself up into a sitting position. Her eyes went wide, and she started to speak again, until he clamped a hand over her mouth and pulled her body to his. "Shhh."

27

Anya's heart thumped hard like it always did when she was close to Ryan. He was so big, so dangerous, so...in control. Face to face, his eyes bored into hers, willing her to trust him, to stay silent. Someone was listening.

On the other side of the door? Was it Ivanov? Her brain cried a warning, and she struggled for a second against Ryan's tight grip, but he wasn't hurting her, only holding her still. If he thought Ivanov was coming through the door, he'd most likely be looking for a hiding place, wouldn't he?

He was so close, he invaded all her senses, and yet the invasion was calming, reassuring. Like in the library, and at the cabin, he was protecting her.

Determined not to act like a wuss, she forced oxygen in through her nose and breathed deep to calm her nerves. No aftershave smell tonight. Instead, he smelled like soap that reminded her of a summer day. Green grass. Sunshine.

Warm male.

The female inside her kicked in. Summer was her favorite season, and she was suddenly sure she would spend the coming summer back home in America. With Grams.

Relaxing against his hand across her mouth, she smiled underneath it.

Ryan must have felt her lips move. She registered a small amount of surprise on his face. That made her smile broader. He took his hand away, placing a finger to her lips to signify she should stay quiet. She nodded her understanding, wishing he'd leave his finger there, and fighting her natural response to kiss it.

Sliding off the bed, he turned his ear toward the door and listened. After several heartbeats, he bent across the top of the antique dresser and listened for another long moment, body as motionless as the bust of Peter the Great in Ivanov's study. Anya listened too.

Another minute passed. Ryan relaxed. He met her gaze and did the finger to his lips move. Anya frowned, not understanding this time. If the threat outside the door was gone, why couldn't they talk? She almost opened her mouth to ask when Ryan started scanning the furniture, running his hands over and under the dresser, the nightstand, the lamp. He got down on the floor and looked under the bed, then climbed on the bed and began feeling his way over the back of her headboard. She scooted out of the way to allow him access, the female in her appreciating the way his shoulders and back muscles moved under his dark suit coat.

What was he looking for?

Spy. The word rang in her head. He was looking for bugs or cameras or both in her suite.

Why hadn't she thought to that? That's why he'd turned on the radio the previous night. Not because someone in the hall might hear them. Someone listening in on her room might have. She thunked the palm of her hand against her forehead. So much for watching all the Bourne movies. She would never get this spying thing down.

Watching Ryan in full spy mode sent a thrill of excitement

racing along her nerve endings. She ran to the letter desk in the main room, retrieving a compact flashlight and bringing it back to him. Comprehending her attempt at help, one corner of his lips lifted as he took the flashlight, and something passed between them. Anya felt it, and by the expression on his face, so did he. She swallowed hard and wondered if it was a spy thing, this easy silent communication between them.

Not a spy thing, her feminine instincts told her. A man and woman thing.

That kiss...now *that* had been a man and woman thing.

Ryan broke eye contact, turning back to his inspection, and leaving Anya a little lightheaded.

As he continued to comb the rest of the bedchamber looking for bugs, she did, too, not sure what one looked like, but ready to find out.

They moved from the bedchamber to the bathroom, gave it a once over. When Ryan came to the air vent, he removed a pair of glasses from his jacket, pressed his thumb against one tiny screw, and suddenly, the ear piece was a small screwdriver.

He removed the metal cover, inspected the vent, and then did the same thing to the bathroom fan before replacing the covers and progressing to the main living area.

The size of this room made their search more time-consuming. Anya didn't mind. Watching Ryan in action as he ran his hands and eyes over every single object, door frame, and fancy molding in the room was mesmerizing. She caught herself wishing he would do the same to her.

Before she knew it, her wish came true.

Sitting at the czarina's white and gold desk. checking under the drawers, she sensed him moving closer. She glanced up and there it was...that probing gaze. Just like at the cabin in the woods, his brown eyes deepened with a hundred questions. Was he sizing her up? Wondering what the hell he'd gotten himself into? Thinking about kissing her again?

If only she could reassure him like he had her.

Strolling toward her, he seemed satisfied there were no hidden bugs, but he flipped on the radio anyway. He kept his voice low and discreet since he knew guards hovered outside the French doors. "Find anything?"

Anya replaced the last drawer and lowered her voice to barely more than a whisper. "There was a false bottom in one of the drawers." She waved a hand over the recovered items...an antique revolver no bigger than her hand, a stash of cigarettes, and bejeweled lighter. Two envelopes, brown around the edges from age and sporting postmarks from the early 1900s. A child's drawing of four stick figures with the words *I love you, Mother* scribbled in Russian. "No bugs, though."

Ryan picked up the revolver, flipped open the chamber, and scrutinized it from one end to the other as if he were a connoisseur of antique guns. Someone who appreciated their intricacies, and not just for collecting in display cabinets. Maybe he was. "Any bullets?"

"Unfortunately, no. Otherwise, I'd tuck it under my pillow, fully loaded."

He smiled, closed the chamber, and returned it to the desktop, glancing over his shoulder at the French doors. Seeming to decide to move their conversation away from possible detection, he took her hand and led her into her bedchamber, guiding her to the bed and sitting next to her. The room was so quiet, she could hear herself breathing. Or not breathing, since he was suddenly next to her in such an intimate setting. Her heart beat loudly in her ears, and she wondered if he could hear it.

He didn't seem to notice. Didn't seem to be bothered at all. He leaned forward and continued to speak in low tones, which seemed appropriate for the midnight venue. "Sorry about the rude awakening earlier. Someone was in the passageway. The walls are fairly soundproof, but the door I'm not sure about. I didn't want them to question who you were talking to."

The memory of him so close and so intense on the bed at the cabin, combined with his current closeness, made her shiver under her pajamas. "I'm the one who's sorry. I didn't mean to fall asleep. Guess I was more tired than I thought."

Ryan smiled his crooked smile again, reaching out, and touching the collar of his sweater. "You sleep in my sweater?"

Heat flooded her cheeks. She'd gone for comfort over sexy, needing to feel Ryan's presence, and ignoring the provocative silk nightgown and robe hanging on the hook in the bathroom. After her soak in the tub, she'd felt relatively free of Ivanov's manhandling, but the silk boudoir set made her skin crawl. She'd opted for soft cotton and heavenly Ryan scent instead. "I meant to throw on jeans and a T-shirt before you arrived."

"Thought you were going to leave the dresser where it belonged instead of in front of the door. Or didn't Truman deliver my message?"

His leg was up against hers, warm and solid. What would it feel like to run her hand over his thigh? Press her body closer? She blinked the inappropriate thoughts away and cleared her throat. "Ivanov was aggressive tonight and drunk like usual. I didn't want to find him standing in my bedroom instead of you, so I pushed the dresser in front of the door while I bathed. Not that a dresser would stop him, but it would've given me a few seconds to get a running start in the opposite direction."

His smile faded. His eyes went hard. "Did he hurt you?"

"Grossed me out big time, but no, he didn't hurt me. I can't believe he can run this country when he's always drunk."

"Lots of leaders have been alcoholics. Boris Yeltsin was famous for his drunken antics."

"Yeltsin?" Her memory of the man had faded over time, but she didn't remember him ever appearing drunk. "Seriously?"

Ryan nodded. "Did you know him?"

"Not well. I was too young. But my parents worked for him, and my grandmother..." Anya's breath hitched in her chest. *Grams.*

"What about your grandmother?"

Anya swallowed the tightness in her throat. "I think she knew him well. She rarely mentioned anything about Russia, but a few times, I got her talking about her life here. She mentioned Yeltsin was a power-hungry mole. Rooting and destroying things under the surface while wearing a smiling face on the outside. She never mentioned he was an alcoholic."

The mantel clock's second hand ticked softly in the background. The radio played soft Russian love songs. Ryan reached out, this time touching her cheek. "We'll find her, Anya."

Saying it didn't make it so, and yet hearing the utter confidence in Ryan's words made it seem possible. Sometimes possible was all you got. A swell of emotions flooded her chest, swirling in a crazy tornado of desire from Ryan's touch, the surreal situation she was in with Ivanov, and the dread that Grams was in pain, or worse, dead at the maniac's hands. "Do you have any idea where Ivanov is holding her?"

He started to say something, then hesitated, as if it were less than happy news. The confidence in his voice this time was forced, and he dropped his fingers from her face. "I'm working on it. I'll figure it out."

Shifting back, she closed her eyes, and ran her hands over her face. "This is all my fault. Ivanov kidnapped her to get me here. He knew I'd never come on my own. If it weren't for my damn royal genes, he wouldn't even care about me."

"Don't forget, she supposedly has that code he needs, and you have no control over your genes or your heritage. Your grandmother wouldn't want you feeling guilty about this. In fact, she's probably feeling guilty herself for putting you in this predicament."

"Why would she feel guilty?"

He shrugged one shoulder. "For not protecting you better, hiding you better."

"I thought we changed our last name to fit in when we moved to America. Now I wonder if we didn't change it because she suspected this might happen down the road."

"Do you remember much about your childhood here in Moscow?"

"Some things. School, friends, music lessons. My dad loved comics, just like I did, and he would bring me a new one every Tuesday when he came home from work. My mom had this great voice, but she would only sing 'Love Me Tender' when she cooked dinner. Once Yeltsin promoted my dad to his cabinet, things got crazy. Dad came home late every night. My mother couldn't sleep, and she roamed our apartment, pacing and waiting for him. Grams took care of me a lot, even then."

"Do you remember Ivanov at all?"

She shook her head, seeing the masked killer in her mind.

Ryan looked like he wanted to see inside her head. "Never heard your father or grandmother talk about him?"

"Ivanov? No." Was she missing something? Did Ryan know something she didn't? Had he confirmed the man who'd assassinated her parents was now the president of Russia? "Why?"

He glanced at the floor, seemed to think something over, then changed the subject. "Did you get another look at that map you told me about?"

The map. Anya grinned. "Better than that." She stood, tugged on the drawstring of her pj bottoms to untie them, and removed the folded map from the waistband, where it had been poking her. "I stole it."

Ryan's eyes widened as he took the map from her hand, and a measure of satisfaction ran through Anya's blood. She might not be versed in covert operations, but she did okay in the kleptomaniac department.

"See?" She retied the pj bottoms and sunk back down on

the bed. "All those black dots? I think they represent the missiles he plans to activate when he gets that code. They all have names. I didn't get it at first, so I thought the names referenced people, but now I think he's named the missiles. Like they're pets or something. Too weird, huh? I didn't count how many there are, but there are hundreds."

She pointed to a group of dots surrounding Moscow. "These are different. No names, no codes, and they're in red. Another set of blue ones surrounding St. Petersburg. Maybe the code he needs activates these missiles?"

"Those are most likely defense missiles designed to protect Moscow and the Kremlin in the event of a nuclear war. But the government would have those codes. There must be something else to this." He stared at the map, lost in thought. "Wait. These must be the ones he claims to the world are decommissioned."

"Huh?"

"The decommissioned missiles. They're not active only because he doesn't have the code to activate them."

Ryan turned the map over, read the legend and the other wording in the upper right hand corner. "But we need more info, something concrete. There is nothing on this map that proves Ivanov is reactivating missiles or selling weapons to Iran. We couldn't even prove this is his map."

The satisfaction and hope building inside her popped like a balloon. "What do you mean? I took this from his desk, of course it's his map, and I overheard him and that weasel of a prime minister talking about reactivating all those missiles, and..."

Her voice had risen and Ryan put up a hand to remind her lower it. "I know. I know. It sucks, but this is circumstantial at best, and again, Ivanov's word against yours won't hold up anywhere."

Biting her lip, she tried to hide her utter disappointment. "I risked my neck to steal a map that means nothing."

"Pretty ballsy move if you ask me, and it doesn't mean *nothing*. It means we're on the right track. We just have to pile on some more concrete proof before I take it to Pennington and the CIA."

She kept the exasperated sigh in her throat from bursting out. No sense acting like a four-year-old. "What's it like being a spy?" The words were out before she could stop them.

He chuckled, but his face became shuttered. "Contrary to pop culture and the movies, it's not all women and futuristic gadgets."

"But I bet it is exciting and the women are pretty hot, right?"

He met her gaze. While the shuttered look was still in place, an amused light shown in his eyes. "Only the genetic research scientists who steal maps from a Russian president's personal chambers. Totally smokin' hot. That kind of risky move is usually only something spies do. You're not a Russian operative are you?"

Anya's pulse sped up. He thought she was sexy. *Smokin' hot.* The woman inside her did a whoop of joy.

There was real concern in his question about her being an operative, however. "I'm no operative, believe me. I'm conflict adverse, not risk adverse, and I'd do anything for my grand-mother. Besides, it was pure luck, not skill, helping me steal those documents."

"Either way, you need to hide them in a safer place."

He rose from the bed and went to the wall closest to the bathroom door. There he knelt on the floor and retrieved his glasses. Using the screwdriver, he pried the five-inch wide molding from the wall on a short section spanning the right side of the door.

Standing behind him, Anya saw where the plaster didn't go all the way to the floor and an old paint color peeked through. Ryan took the screwdriver and dug it into the plaster. Within a minute, a small pile of soft plaster rose on the floor, and a tiny opening now existed in the wall. A square just big enough to hold her contraband.

As Ryan folded the map into the same shape as the hole in the wall, Anya tugged the papers and business card from her bra. "Here." She handed him the items and noticed how he hesitated for a heartbeat when he saw his card. "Andreev tried to take it away from me," she told him. "I refused to give it up."

That crooked grin lifted the right side of Ryan's face, but he didn't say anything as he shoved the card and paper into the hole with the map. He replaced the molding, giving it a little tap to secure it.

He stood, stuck the glasses back in a pocket and retrieved a cell phone from another one. "This phone has a camera in it. If you get back into Ivanov's chambers, and you have a clear opportunity, take pictures of any documents you find. There may be tangible physical evidence in his office we can use if you get a picture of it, but don't take unnecessary risks, okay?"

Playing spy was growing more and more fun. Seeing Ryan make a safe for her in the wall reminded her of Ivanov's. "There's evidence all right. Do you know how to crack a safe, Mr. Spy Man?"

"Yes."

Another valuable skill. "Will you teach me?"

"No. No safe cracking. Just take some pictures if you get the chance."

He walked toward the dresser and the door to the passage-way, checking his watch and lowering his voice to a whisper. "Now, get some sleep. Tomorrow's another long day."

Anya followed, watching him hop on top of the dresser and press his ear to the door. She climbed on the bed, clutching the phone. "Ryan?" she whispered and he turned to look at her over his shoulder. "I won't let you down."

He nodded and mouthed the words "Be careful."

Something passed between them again, that silent communication that seemed to say more than any words could. Anya slid off the bed, running on full instinct, and grabbed his arm to tilt him down. She kissed him smack on the lips. Then she mouthed back, "You too."

He hesitated, seeming a bit stunned, yet recovered quickly, taking hold of the back of her neck, and leaning his lips fully into her mouth. Not too soft, not too hard, the kiss was still forceful and erotic. Heat shot to the spot between Anya's legs.

Spying on the Russian president or kissing a princess, Ryan was clearly in control.

They broke apart, staring at each other and breathing hard. A second later, Ryan was gone, the door sliding shut behind him.

Anya sunk into the soft mattress, happiness over their plan mixed with worry at the thought of him in the dangerous passageway alone.

He'll be fine.

The cell phone was warm in her hand. her lips buzzed from his kiss. After touching her lips with her finger, she turned on the phone and began searching through the functions. The address book was empty. The call log was empty. The picture files were empty.

Spies. Talk about secrets.

Anya touched her lips again and smiled.

28

U.S. Embassy
Moscow

When the call connected to Langley, Devons put Conrad Flynn on the speaker of the encrypted phone. "What'd'ya got, boys?"

Devons looked at the ancient computer monitor and made a face. John knew how he felt. The head of Operations wasn't going to like his answer. "Letters and numbers. That's all we got off the floppy. Took me hours to hunt down a computer to read it, and all we got was a string of letters that make no sense, and four columns of numbers that also make no sense."

Flynn's tone was brusque. "They mean something. Radzoya had that information for a reason. What's Quick think?"

John faced the phone, ignoring the look Naomi shot Devons from the corner of her eye . As per her MO, she'd refused to stay in Switzerland and was now in Moscow with them. Devons had told her not to say a word while he and John spoke to the director of operations or he would kill her. Seemed like the only way they'd get rid of her at this point.

Grigory was also there. The two of them were currently sitting with Del at the conference table, flipping through the comic books they'd retrieved from the safe. "There's only four letters used in that string, and like Devons said, they make no sense, no matter how you rearrange them. The numbers aren't longitude, latitude, or any kind of coordinates for air, sea or land."

"They're probably a code," Devons added. "But none I've ever seen."

There was a long, strained pause on the other end. Then Flynn's voice lowered a notch. "I didn't send my weapons expert and best tracker on a wild goose chase two thousand miles away for nothing. What's your gut say, Devons? Why would a former operative of the Soviet Union, who worked for our side, hide a bunch of numbers in a safe deposit box twenty years ago in Switzerland, that only she and her granddaughter could access?"

Devons shook his head, gaze scanning the ceiling as if the answer was written there. "The numbers are a code."

"No shit. A code you *have* seen before." Flynn drew an impatient sounding breath. "Look at 'em again, and tell me what they're for, weapons expert."

The term seemed to flip a switch in Devons' brain. His eyes lit up, and he stared at the screen. His focus intensified as his gaze flew back and forth across the columns. "Goddamn," he whispered under his breath. "There's at least a thousand of them."

John stepped toward him and looked over his shoulder at the numbers for the fiftieth time. "A thousand of what?"

"Missile launchers," Flynn said from the speaker at the same time Devons said it too.

"Like as in nuclear warhead missile launchers?" John asked.

Devons tapped the monitor with a finger. "These are missile launch codes for a thousand different sites."

Flynn sounded pleased at his pupil's assessment. "Missiles pointed at England and the United States. If Ivanov grabbed Anya Radzoya, he's trying to cut a deal to get those codes back."

John didn't get it. "Why doesn't he already have them? And what about the nuclear arms reduction summit? Those missiles from the 1980's were decommissioned, weren't they?"

A chuckle came from the speaker phone. "Decommissioned doesn't mean destroyed. The missiles are still there, just sleeping, and Ivanov wants to wake them up. Natasha Radzoya either stole those codes, or Yeltsin gave them to her for safe keeping. I assure you, that floppy disc is the only surviving copy, and if Ivanov gets his hands on it..."

Devon slapped the table next to his phone. "We're gonna be toasty critters before the year's out."

"Exactly." A squeak came from the speaker as Flynn shifted in his chair. His tone once again took a brusque manner. "Get those codes to Del, and destroy the disc, Devons."

"What about the funky letters?"

"Those too. Del will figure them out. Oh, and, Quick?"

"Yeah?"

"Find Natasha Radzoya. Now."

"Yes, sir."

"What about Anya?" Devons asked. "She knew about this. She brought us that launch key."

"Natasha is our priority right now. You got any leads, Quick?"

"Three, actually."

"Don't give me three," Flynn said, impatient again. "One. Where's Ivanov got her stashed?"

John planted his feet further apart, rubbed a hand over his face. Devons' intense focus was on him now. "The Kremlin. My best guess is she's under the Palace in GI 42."

One of Devons' brows lifted. The speaker was eerily quiet.

Another squeak from Flynn's chair broke the silence. "Better figure out a way to get into the Kremlin, boys. Smith's going to need all the help he can get."

The phone line went dead. Devons, Grigory, and Del stared at John, looking like they thought he was suddenly going to pull a fool-proof plan for crashing the summit meeting party out of his ass.

Naomi, still reading the comic book in front of her, flipped a page and frowned. "What is this?"

John and Devons gathered on either side to get a better look. A piece of paper with an unusual graph on it was folded into the comic book's pages.

The graph had headers and footnotes, some typed and others handwritten. All of it was in Russian.

"Beats the hell out of me," Devons said.

"I've seen one of these before." Naomi unfolded it, laying in on the table and pressing out the creases. Below the graph were a couple of spreadsheets.

"What is it?" John asked.

"My mother had one of these done when she was trying to prove my paternity."

O-*kay*. "It's a paternity test?"

"Mine looked different than this, but yes, there are three DNA profiles." She pointed to the first spreadsheet. "This column shows the mother's, this one, the child's, and this one, the father's."

She trailed a finger down the page to the second, and more extensive, spreadsheet, translating the Russian softly under her breath. "But this is something else. The child's genes appear to have been tested for various markers."

"Markers?" Devons asked.

Naomi nodded. "A marker is a gene or DNA sequence that can be used to identify individuals or species."

Grigory seemed to choke. "Is there a name on the paternity test?"

Naomi shook her head, pointed to a handwritten line at the bottom. "The child's marker letters are combined into one, here."

"Let me see that," John said. He took the paper over to the computer. Sure enough, the string of letters on the screen matched the genetic markers.

Devons saw it at the same time. He whistled under his breath. "The kid's DNA is some kind of code? Why would it be listed with ICBM codes?"

"Oh, dear." Grigory wiped his forehead with a handkerchief. "Peter, what did you do?"

"Peter?" Devons asked.

"Natasha's son was brilliant...and he designed the first computerized system to launch nuclear weapons."

Naomi closed the comic book. "The paternity test belongs to Anya Radzoya, doesn't it? Her gene sequence is somehow tied to the missiles."

Grigory nodded. "I believe you may be correct."

Anya. Natasha. They were both in big trouble. And if John didn't find them, he'd have more to worry about than Flynn riding his ass. "We need to get into the Kremlin. Better yet, the bunker underneath it. We need to come up with a solid plan, and fast."

Devons grinned. "I've got an idea."

"Playing a fake cop won't cut it this time. Breaching the bunker is impossible, and the Kremlin isn't much easier."

"Not a cop." The grin grew and he patted John on the back. "Terrorist, my friend. We're going in as terrorists."

THE NEXT MORNING AT BREAKFAST, IVANOV AND ANDREEV WERE MIA. Worse, Anya was also missing.

Ryan's gut churned. Had he compromised her last night? Had he been seen coming or going from her room? Or had it been their meeting in the library?

No one had spotted him last night, he was sure of that. But what if the library meeting had raised someone's suspicions? What if Anya was at that moment fighting for her life?

Not one to overdramatize, Ryan shook off that last assumption and bit into his toast. They were late. Big deal. Anya had arrived late for breakfast before, and he'd kept her up until nearly three a.m. last night. Ivanov and Andreev were probably dealing with normal, everyday government issues. Pennington and Morrow had been doing the same in between the endless summit meetings.

Truman pulled a chair out and sat beside him. "Good God, you look like my Aunt Edith showed you her knickers."

"Good morning to you too."

A waiter arrived, poured Truman coffee, and took his breakfast order. Once he left, Truman slipped Ryan an envelope and lowered his voice. "From Del. Your specialist believes the package is in one of these spots."

Ryan opened the envelope. A slip of paper was nestled inside. John Quick had narrowed the possible locations for Natasha to three. One made Ryan whistle under his breath.

"Where is it?" Truman asked.

The most obvious place for Ivanov to be holding Natasha Radzoya was also the most dangerous. At least in terms of rescuing her. "GI 42."

Truman set down his coffee cup without drinking. "Government Installation 42? But that's..."

"Here," Ryan finished for him. Government Installation 42 was a secret underground intelligence center built by Stalin during the Cold War. A presidential bunker. "Under the Kremlin."

At the height of Stalin's rule, it had housed fifteen hundred soldiers working round-the-clock shifts. The tunnels were steel plated to absorb electromagnetic fields and conceal radio waves. One tunnel connected to the Moscow train and subway station, allowing for evacuation of Stalin and his top officials if necessary. Outfitted as a command center, it was the ideal place for him and his group to survive a nuclear blast.

The Russians claimed it had been abandoned. At the cabin, Anya had insisted there was a new, improved model, complete with a lab. Ivanov had showed it to her. Had she been within spitting distance of her grandmother and not known it?

The silverware next to Ryan's plate of half-eaten breakfast suddenly rattled as if someone were shaking the table. Truman's cup trembled in its saucer. The movement and sounds were so minimal, the two might have missed them if they hadn't been silently contemplating how to pull off a rescue extraction from the world renowned bunker hidden deep underground.

Truman set his hands flat on the table. "Bloody hell, do you feel that?"

Ryan did. There was a vibration leaking up through the floor. Before he could answer, the tremor stopped. In the room around them, only a few other people seemed to have noticed and had the same perplexed look on their faces.

"Earthquake?" Truman wondered out loud.

Ryan had experienced small earthquakes in India and China. What he'd just felt was similar and yet not. It was a shockwave of some sort, but seemed too short lived for an earthquake.

Half a dozen cell phones began ringing. The people in the room grabbed for them, puzzlement spreading among the group. In the next few seconds, as Ryan studied the looks of shock on Pennington's and Morrow's faces and more ringing phones escalated the noise in the room, his blood ran cold. He knew the look on the President's face. It wasn't an earthquake.

"Bomb," he told Truman.

Which meant only one thing.

"Terrorists?" Truman's eyes widened a fraction as his own cell began ringing. He rose from the chair to snatch the phone off his belt. "God save the Queen," he whispered to no one in particular.

God save the princess, Ryan thought, and ran for the doors.

29

Bang. Bang. Bang.

Anya jumped at the sound of someone pounding on the bathroom door. She stepped out of the shower, grabbing the plush towel off the heated rack. She'd overslept again, and Inga was about to have a heart attack. "Give me a break, Inga. That wasn't even three minutes. I'm going as fast as I can."

"Grand Duchess," Ivanov's voice cut through the heavy door as if it were no more than cotton. "There has been a terrorist attack. I must insist you move immediately to my chambers for your own protection."

A terrorist attack? On the Grand Kremlin Palace?

Oh, no.

Ryan. Was he okay? Anya started drying as fast as her hands would move. They shook so badly, she dropped the towel. Twice. "Dammit," she muttered under her breath, and then to the door, she said, "I'm coming. Just give me a minute to get dressed."

The door knob rattled. Thank God she'd locked it. Ivanov swore in Russian. "There is no time, Anya. You must come with me. Now!"

"Two seconds," she yelled back, throwing on Ryan's sweater, and snatching up her dress pants. She didn't have time to bandage her wound.

He banged on the door again, frustration evident. "You may dress in my chambers."

Why was he so adamant about getting her to his chambers? Were the terrorists inside the Palace?

Still barefoot, but fully clothed, she yanked open the door and ran her fingers through her wet hair to comb it out of her face. "Where are they?"

Ivanov barely glanced at her, grabbing her arm, and hustling her through the dressing area and across the bedroom floor to the secret door connecting their rooms. Andreev stood guard, and when she came into view, his gaze swept her from head to toe. His attention seemed to linger on the too-big men's sweater.

"The terrorists bombed the train station," Ivanov said.

The train station. So they weren't in the Palace. A smidgen of relief washed over Anya. "How many were killed? Injured? Which group is behind it?"

Ivanov either didn't hear her question or chose to ignore it as he led her into his bedchambers. Guards with ugly black assault weapons hurried by in the connecting secret hallway. Behind them, Andreev followed, closing the door to Anya's room. He entered Ivanov's chambers and shut that door as well, snapping the lock into place.

A set of red suitcases and a briefcase sat on Ivanov's bed. Beside them, a collection of his dirks.

He hadn't answered her questions. "Were many people hurt?" she asked. "Is there anything I can do?"

Ivanov let go of her hand as he headed for the sitting area. "My guards will escort me to the presidential office to meet with my cabinet. You will stay here until I return. There is TV and food. Inga will be here shortly. If you have need of anything else, it will have to wait."

Andreev passed by her and began gathering papers on Ivanov's desk. Ivanov moved the picture of Peter the Great out of the way and punched buttons on the safe's keypad.

Ivanov was worried. More than worried, frightened. Under the tightly reined in emotions, he was freaking out. The suitcases and valued antique dirks told her he was ready to run. A natural reaction to a terrorist attack, but the thought unnerved her. He was president of Russia, after all. Shouldn't he be more composed? More in charge? More concerned about the people who'd been hurt?

More concerned about the world leaders inside the Palace under his protection?

A hundred and one questions ran through her brain. What kind of bomb had the terrorists used? Nuclear? Biological? She didn't know how far away the train station was, but if they were in danger, she at least wanted her shoes on to face it. "Why can't I stay in my room?"

Ivanov extracted a leather case and shut the safe door hard before turning to her. "The safest place for you is here."

Andreev piped up. "In case of evacuation, time is of the essence. You will stay in this room until further notice."

Evacuation. So maybe he was concerned about the safety of everyone in the Palace, not just his own. If they were considering evacuation, however, the situation must have been dire.

The dread in her chest had been sitting there, waiting. Now it exploded to life. Terrorists were trying to stop the summit, and they'd done enough damage to make Ivanov consider leaving the presidential Palace. No wonder he was freaking out.

But why would it be faster to evacuate if she were in Ivanov's chambers rather than across the hall?

Her first instinct was to run. But run where?

Her second instinct was to find Ryan. But, again, where was

he in all this mess? And how would she find him if she was trapped here?

Caught up in her thoughts, she watched mutely as Ivanov and Andreev raced out the door and past the ever-present guards, leaving her and her questions alone.

Fighting the urge to run back to the Golden Chambers, she slumped down on the sofa and stared at the charred logs and ash in the fireplace grate. What was she going to do now?

The bombing was certainly unexpected, and while part of her wanted to run far away, another part wanted to do something to help. She wasn't a doctor, but people needed all kinds of care when something like this happened. If only she knew more about what was going on.

The suite was too quiet, and for a minute, she considered turning on the TV in Ivanov's bedroom. But besides the fact that being in there for any reason appalled her, a new thought rose to the surface. She was alone in Ivanov's private quarters, and would be until Inga showed up to babysit her.

A sudden calm mixed with a weird excitement came over her. There was nothing she could do about the terrorists or the destruction from the bomb. What she could do, however, was help herself, and maybe a lot more people as well.

She pushed off of the sofa and eyed Ivanov's desk. A thorough inspection would surely give her all the evidence she needed against him.

If only I'd grabbed Ryan's cell phone...

Well, why couldn't she go back to her suite and grab it? Socks and shoes too? No one would know if she used the secret hallway between the rooms, and it sure beat doing nothing. *In for a penny, in for a pound.* Another of Grams favorite sayings, this one British.

The four steps between the doors was microscopic compared to the size of the entire Palace, but for some reason, they seemed like the great divide to Anya as she eased through

Ivanov's private door and scanned the hallway. Voices drifted to her, distant but getting closer. More armed guards? Afraid she'd lose her nerve, she slid the president's door closed, hopped across the divide, and opened hers.

Ivanov had given her a golden opportunity to case his personal quarters and get any kind of damning information she could scrounge up. She didn't want to waste too much time grabbing her shoes and the cell phone, so she hustled past the bed and over to the hiding place with focused determination. If she and the others inside the Palace were in any kind of danger from the terrorists, she'd at least have a way to communicate, and the small piece of proof that Ivanov had killed her parents.

Ryan's business card and the paper went back into her bra, but the phone was a problem. While it was slim and no longer than the palm of her hand, it nevertheless weighted down the light fabric of her linen and wool slacks when she slipped it into a pocket.

Anya jammed the elaborate trim back into place and entered the enormous walk-in closet. Combing through her belongings, she found her dress belt and wove it through the belt loops of her pants. She tightened it and slipped the phone into the waistband at the small of her back. Tight, but manageable. Ryan's sweater draped low and was bulky enough to hide any telltale bulge.

Next she grabbed dark wool socks. Ryan's socks. She'd put them and her boots on once she was back in Ivanov's quarters. Inga would arrive any minute, and Anya wanted as much time as possible alone.

Ivanov seemed to trust the old woman more than anyone else in the Palace, maybe even more than Andreev. Anya wondered why. Was Inga related to him? Didn't seem likely, but there was definite loyalty on both sides. She'd have to ask Inga a few questions and see if she could figure it out.

As she turned to find where she'd stowed her boots, a hand

came around her mouth, cutting off her startled gasp. An arm locked around her midsection, pressing her back against a hard stomach and chest.

Reflexes kicking in, she drove her elbow into her assailant's ribs. He grunted, but didn't let go. She raised a foot to slam her heel down on his just as he spoke in her ear. "Hey, it's me, Ryan."

At the last split second, she tried to rein in her heel, but it was too late. Adrenaline was shooting through her veins like a caffeine and sugar cocktail. She made contact with the top of his foot, although with slightly less force than intended. Which was good, since she wasn't wearing shoes and he was.

"Damn," he muttered, dropping his hand from her mouth. "Even barefoot, you're dangerous."

She sputtered a soft laugh and eyed him over her shoulder. His face was tense, tight lines pinching the corners of his eyes. He was worried.

Well, that made two of them. "That's what you get for sneaking up on me. I thought you were a terrorist."

His arm was still secured tight around her waist, his body heat soaking through the sweater. Now it was his turn to chuckle. "I've been a traitor but never a terrorist."

The moment the confession slipped out, his gaze dropped to the floor, and his jaw tightened. He hadn't meant to say that, so even though she was suddenly dying to find out what he meant, she saved her questions. There would be time one of these days to put him on the spot and make him reveal his deep, dark secrets. She hoped.

Relaxing into his body, she heaved a sigh and wondered why he hadn't turned loose of her yet. Although, she didn't want him to. Like everything else about him, his solid, sheltering body reassured her, gave her confidence.

He made her legs weak and her pulse erratic. That

wonderful man-woman thing they had going. The kisses they'd share didn't hurt either. "What are you doing here?"

As if he realized how intimately he was pressed against her backside, he dropped his arm and released her, taking his glorious warmth and shelter with him as he stepped back. "My plan was to protect you if necessary. Apparently you're capable of protecting yourself."

Instead of evacuating the Palace, he'd come back to make sure she was okay. To protect her. Anya's heart skipped. On impulse, she turned, threw her arms around his neck, and hugged him. For what he was. For *who* he was, even though she still wasn't quite sure of either. "From Ivanov or the terrorists?"

He covered his startled reaction well, only hesitating a split second before he gathered her inside the safety of his arms and hugged her back. "Either," he said softly against her hair. "Both."

Goose bumps trickled down the back of her neck and tightened her nipples. He was lean muscle and sinuous strength. Power and control, mixed with an underlying intensity that took her breath away.

After all she'd been through in the past few days, he was the one enigma that didn't scare her. The one mystery she wanted more of.

She shifted her head to look at him, not taking her arms away from around his neck, and gave him a grin. His handsome face was so close that even in the dim lighting she could see flecks of amber in the rich brown of his eyes. Slanting her head up for better access, she pressed a soft kiss to the side of his face, grazing the corner of his lips. "I'm glad you're okay."

For a second he didn't move, as if paralyzed. His already wide pupils widened a touch more. At the spot she kissed, his lips lifted. In surprise? In happiness?

Whichever, he stroked her back with one of his hands,

running his fingers up her spine, and giving the base of her neck a reassuring squeeze. "Ditto."

She kissed the other corner of his mouth. "I appreciate you wanting to protect me."

There was no hesitation this time. The hand at the base of her neck slid up under her hair and cradled the back of her head like he'd done in the early morning hours. His thumb massaged her scalp, making the warmth in her stomach rise up through her chest and into her face.

He lowered his head to kiss her. His lips, however, stopped a hair's width from hers. "Makes no sense, since I barely know you, but I'd risk my life to save yours."

It made no sense to her either, but it felt right, from the top of her head to the tips of her toes. She searched his face, saw the honesty there, and fixed her gaze on his mouth. "You may live to regret that."

His mouth closed the distance, lips coaxing hers to respond. She didn't need coaxing. She wanted Ryan with every cell in her body. Wanted his smile, his lips, and his strong arms to get her through the next few hours, the next few days.

Intoxicating need shook her. She opened her lips to taste more. His hands slid down her back and over her sides, pressing her firmly against him while his tongue slipped between her lips. She met it with her own, running a hand up the back of his neck and drawing his head closer.

There was so much she wanted to tell him. So much she wanted to ask him. It wasn't fair she didn't have time...

Anya jerked back, heart galloping. *Time.* Inga was on her way. If she didn't find Anya in Ivanov's chambers, she'd look in here. Here, where Anya was making out with a CIA spy posing as an aide to President Pennington.

Ryan looked dazed from the sudden shift, but immediately tensed and looked around. "What is it? Did you hear something?"

Only the blood rushing in my ears.

The creases in the corners of his eyes had almost disappeared. Anya wished she could take time to further erase the concern from his face, but she couldn't. This might be her only chance to search Ivanov's quarters. "I'm supposed to be next door. Ivanov demanded I hang out in his private chambers with Inga, in case of an evacuation. She's on her way to babysit me, so I have to get back. But, as for the terrorists, who are they? Do you know?"

Ryan's grip on her waist eased and he shook his head. "I have several theories, but nothing concrete."

"Do you know why Ivanov wants me in his chambers if we have to evacuate?"

"Highly unlikely he'd leave the Palace, but there's a secret passageway that runs from his bedchamber to Government Installation 42."

"Like the one I saw." Growing up, Anya had heard the stories about the hidden bunker Stalin had built in case America attacked with nuclear weapons. From what she'd seen firsthand, Ivanov had created an entirely new one, complete with all the modern conveniences any tyrant might need. The entire Russian cabinet and hundreds of soldiers could hide down there from an attack of any kind and survive for months, if not years. "When he showed me the modern bunker, we accessed it from The Cathedral of the Annunciation, not his room."

"There are at least four entrances, so he can escape to the bunker no matter where he is inside the Palace grounds."

Another thought came on the heels of that one. "Is it possible my grandmother is down there? In Stalin's old section?"

"We're talking about a crazy Russian president. Anything's possible."

They shared a grin before Anya turned to snatch up the

wool socks and shoes. "Sorry, but I have to go find that passageway."

Ryan grabbed her arm. "Not now. You could be in real danger, and not just from Ivanov's guards. Government Installation 42 is linked to the subway system where the bomb went off. Whoever the terrorists are, we can't underestimate them. Ivanov's security is airtight, but if any of the terrorists got into GI 42, they might kill on sight, or take hostages. You can't risk that."

For Grams, she'd risk anything. "She's my grandmother."

Determination and exasperation lit Ryan's eyes. "And she raised you to be logical, cautious, and sensible. What would she tell you to do in this situation?"

He had her there. Grams would never let Anya sacrifice herself. "Fine, but I have to get back to Ivanov's quarters before Inga finds me missing. I want to search his office and maybe even his bedchambers."

Ryan barely hid his eye roll from her. "This isn't a game. It's for real. If Ivanov or Andreev catches you—"

She shushed him with a finger to his lips, giving him a dose of his own silencing technique. His eyes darkened, heat and passion barely contained. "They won't. I promise."

With that, she took her boots, and ran for the secret door.

"Hey," he called softly after her.

She turned back. "What?"

Three strides and he was in front of her again. He ran a hand down her arm as if he couldn't stand not touching her. "If they don't evacuate everyone, I'll meet you back here tonight, after things calm down."

A bubble of excitement rose in her chest. She slung one arm around his neck and kissed him. "I was hoping you'd say that."

They shared a final grin before she went through the door.

30

THINGS DIDN'T CALM DOWN.

Another bomb went off near, but not in, a train packed with morning passengers. A third destroyed an entire substation that had been closed for maintenance. The death toll was at zero and the casualties were so minor, they barely needed a Band-Aid.

Didn't matter. Panic was rampant. Ivanov and his cabinet had been forced to shut down the entire Moscow train system. Not that anyone was using it after the bombs.

An attack on Moscow was an attack on Mother Russia, and the whole country seemed to be holding its breath.

Or instigating more trouble.

Using the political climate of the summit, Anya's reappearance, and the terrorist attacks as excuses, several nationalists groups took to protesting in Red Square. On the heels of that, the media reported threats had been made against Pennington and Morrow. The news showed limited coverage, which seemed to heighten citizen concerns and cause more unrest. By ten a.m., the Russian Interior Ministry had held a press conference and stated security measures were in place. From what

Ryan could see, the assurance was lost on those inside, as well as outside, Kremlin Palace.

Aside from Ivanov's initial insistence that everything was under control, the Russian president was AWOL. He was said to be behind closed doors with his advisors.

Whatever the case, everyone inside the Kremlin was effectively cut off from the outside world. Sitting ducks.

Ryan entered President Pennington's quarters shortly after the second bomber struck, adding his knowledge to the brain bank surrounding the flustered leader. It was the first time Pennington had been to Russia, and the first terrorist act in the world on his watch. Top priority was his safety. After that, the safety of his American counterparts with him, and those Americans in the city. At the same time, he had to lend public, if not private, support to Ivanov. Behind the scenes, he and his advisors had to extrapolate who the terrorists were, and if they were planning more acts, especially aimed at America or its citizens.

Pennington had to decide, would he stay or would he go? The threats to his and Morrow's lives could not be easily verified, but they were nevertheless taken seriously.

If the president chose to stay, the spin would be that Pennington was showing solidarity with the Russians. If he decided to go, the spin would be that his departure allowed all security looking after Ivanov to be dedicated to investigating the terrorist attacks.

Ryan's knowledge of Russia had him dead center in Pennington's circle, which was where he needed to be, even if he preferred to be with Anya. However, Ryan knew far more about the Chechen terrorists staking claim to the bombings, and their MOs, than a typical worker bee in the president's employ. He couldn't blow his cover to the men and women surrounding Pennington, but he needed to advise the president as a highly-trained counterterrorism expert, not as a Russian affairs authority.

Yet full disclosure wasn't an option. As an employee of the CIA, his job was classified, so the morning crawled by in a quagmire of politics as Ryan confirmed information from the State Department on the Chechens as well as hinting there was more going on behind the scenes. Ryan considered asking to speak to the president in private, but discarded the idea. He didn't trust the U.S. president, plain and simple.

As Pennington's other aides insisted the president should leave, Ryan pushed for him to stay, wanting Pennington to be there if Anya found proof about Ivanov violating the NPT. Soon, Ryan was hedging questions he could no longer answer.

And that pissed off the President of the United States.

Big time.

So be it. While Ryan was concerned about the state of emergency they were in, and he'd do all he could to help his Commander in Chief, he was also worried about Anya. Admitting who he was, and who he worked for, would only endanger her more. He had more critical things to worry about, and yet she dominated his every thought.

Which was ridiculous. He was a trained operative. She was an asset. A beautiful asset, but a dangerous one nonetheless. He tried to focus on details of the bombings, but instead of seeing the destruction flashing on the television, he saw Anya's face, glowing with excitement.

He wondered if she'd found anything in Ivanov's quarters they could use against him.

Remembered how incredibly good she'd felt in his arms.

How soft her lips had been against his.

Imagined how her long legs would feel wrapped around his waist...

What the hell was he doing, falling for her? The CIA files didn't tell him more than a few pertinent facts and a whole lot of useless ones—or what her real game plan was in all this? He couldn't shut down his cynical side. The grandmother was missing. The CIA had verified that. But had she been kidnapped in order to bring Anya to Russia, or was this whole mess over a code? Possibly both, if what Anya had overheard was accurate.

The TV running with the evening news popped up a photo of Anya in her peacock blue dress from the night of the opening ceremonies. Ryan's heart rate sped up. His pants grew tight.

Like the night at the cabin, he would meet the terrorists at the door, smooth talk Pennington in his fluent CIA language of denial, and take on Ivanov barehanded if necessary to save her.

His feelings for her were completely illogical. His imagination, running wild with ideas about the coming night, equally so. He wanted her on that damn four poster bed in all its Russian glory, with her legs spread wide, her full lips open, and her hands reaching for him.

Anya might have followed in her grandmother's footsteps to become a double agent, and was even at that very moment blackmailing him, but Ryan didn't care. He wanted her and he wanted her bad.

If she was using him, he didn't want to know. If she was a double agent, she'd end his career and put his life in danger, but he refused to go there.

Problem was, if Ivanov went to ground and tucked himself away in his bunker, he'd take Anya with him. Ryan might never see her again.

Under the guarded eyes of the president, Ryan left the suite and headed for the hidden door of a secret passageway.

31

"GET YOUR HANDS OFF ME." Anya stood rigid against Andreev's manhandling. "I'm not going anywhere."

Inga drew in a sharp breath. The woman stood off to the side, nearly hiding behind the blue draperies of Ivanov's suite. Once the president had left, taking his protection detail with him, Andreev had locked the door.

The prime minister's small, dark eyes bore into Anya, amused at the challenge rather than angry. His grip tightened on her upper arm, and he shook her. "You ungrateful bitch. My orders come from President Ivanov. He insists on placing your safety above his own."

Yeah, right. Psychopaths didn't put anyone's safety above their own. Anya pried Andreev's fingers off her bicep and shoved him away. "I should be doing something to help my fellow Russians, not hiding in that bunker."

"You are royalty! The Emergency Security Plan calls for..."

"I couldn't care less what your plan says. I'm staying here."

He charged her, grabbing her by the wrist this time, and backing her up against a wall. "This is not America." He turned his head and spit on the floor. "You will do as I say. Go into the bunker. Now."

She was going into the bunker, all right, but on her own terms, not to be locked away in Ivanov's private quarters down there where she couldn't search for her grandmother. "What do you think they're going to do? Overrun the Palace? Hang me from the rafters? This isn't the Middle Ages. Besides, if they're unhappy with anyone, it's you and the president."

Andreev jerked her toward him, prepared to yell another curse at her. With her free hand, she smacked him across his bulldog face. Then she raised her leg and kicked him in the shin.

He talked a good game, but he was weak. He barked a cry of pain and outrage, letting go of her for a second before raising the back of his hand to strike her.

So much for being royalty. She dodged the blow, kicked out, and swept his legs from under him. For half a second, his body seemed suspended in air before it dropped like a rock.

Inga sobbed at her to stop in both English and Russian.

Hell with that.

Anya had endured all she was going to take. From Andreev and from Ivanov. She was done cowering and playing stupid ass games. Where had the game-playing gotten her anyway? She didn't know any more now than she had three days ago, and in the meantime, her grandmother's heart could be giving out.

While Ivanov was tied up with the bombings and protesters, she was going to search the Palace from one end to the other for Grams. And then she was getting both of them the hell out of Dodge. Hopefully with Ryan's help.

Her first step would be Government Installation 42. But if she went with Andreev and Inga, she'd be locked up inside Ivanov's personal quarters. That wouldn't do her any good.

Andreev rolled to his side, cursing her in Russian, and

looking like a mad dog. The only way Anya was going to accomplish her search was to take Andreev out of the picture.

She hopped over his prone body, snatched a heavy malachite paperweight of the Russian Federation flag off Ivanov's messy desk, and brought it down on Andreev's head. The prime minister's body seized for a second and then went limp, blood trickling from the injury.

Inga sucked in another horrified breath and covered her mouth with one chubby hand, eyes wide. Anya expected her to call for the guards outside the suite's doors, but the woman seemed stunned into silence. Still, Anya raised the paperweight and started to tell her to be quiet, or she'd join Andreev in LaLa Land, when Inga's eyes rolled up inside her head and she fainted.

Takes care of that.

Anya was trying to decide if she should move the bodies, or simply stuff rags in their mouths and tie them up, when she felt more than saw a presence behind her. Whirling around, she threw the paperweight in defense. It was heavy, but her aim was true.

Thank God, Ryan's reflexes were outstanding. A few feet away, he caught the glass missile one-handed with the ease of a ballplayer. "Nice throw."

His gaze scanned Inga's limp body, and then Andreev's, in that typically unperturbed manner of his. Anya's pounding heart slowed a bit. "I came to save you," he said, casually tossing the paperweight up and catching it again. "But it looks like you're doing just fine as usual."

Anya laughed on a hard exhale, releasing the pent up stress building inside her chest. "Fine? Are you kidding? I just took out the prime minister. Pretty sure that's a no-no."

Ryan crossed the room, eyed the blood leaking from Andreev's head wound, and leaned down to check the man's neck for a pulse. Apparently finding one, he straightened. The paperweight went up in the air and came down again as Ryan seemed to turn the situation over in his mind. He was dressed in casual attire and wore a winter coat.

"Where did you come from?" Anya asked.

"You weren't in your room." The coat was unzipped and he rubbed the paperweight on his sweater, using the sweater to carry it back to the desk. Erasing both of their fingerprints.

Smart but probably pointless. He eyed the jumble of papers and files left on Ivanov's desk, rifled through a few of them. "Figured you were either here, or in the bunker already, so I slipped in the through the secret door."

Wearing a winter coat meant only one thing. "Looks like you're leaving."

"We're both leaving." Sticking a couple of the papers inside his coat, he grabbed her hand and led her toward Ivanov's bedchamber. "Go get your coat."

She didn't want to, but she tugged her hand out of his. "You know I can't go until I locate Grams. If she's in that bunker, I'm going to find her."

He reached out and took her hand again. He didn't propel her forward, only brought their entwined fingers to the center of his chest while he looked her in the eye. "Read my lips, Anya. I'm not stranding you or your grandmother here in Moscow. We'll find her together, and then we'll get the hell out of here. Until both of you are back on North American soil, I'll be by your side. Are we clear?"

Maybe it was the sincerity in his eyes. Maybe the complete control in the tone of his voice. Or the fact he was holding her hand so carefully, as if she would break if he squeezed too hard, or slip away if he held it too loose. "You're a good man, Ryan."

The subtle lift of his lips made her heart speed up again. "And, you're an amazing woman, Anya."

Amazing was stretching it, but she had her moments. "Inga

told me the presidential bunker has a direct rail line from the Palace to the airport."

"We can't take a plane out of here. Too conspicuous. And I don't know what condition Natasha may be in, so crossing land with so many checkpoints exposes us. We may have to float down the Moscow River. But whatever we do, we leave tonight."

He squeezed her hand and she squeezed back. A silent agreement.

Inga groaned from her spot on the marble floor. So much for grabbing her coat. It was time to move.

Ryan, hand still holding hers, swung them both toward the bedchambers. "Where's the secret entrance to the bunker?"

Anya half-ran behind him to keep up. She waited until they were out of the main room and the waking Inga. "In Ivanov's closet," she whispered, pointing toward two French doors that hid a walk-in the size of her entire apartment back home.

Overhead lights came on the second the doors opened, and Anya pointed to the back wall. She'd discovered the hidden door right before Inga had arrived that morning to babysit her. A large, gilded floor length mirror swung out to reveal the secret escape passage. Anya opened it, gesturing at him to follow.

For a second, Ryan hesitated, looking back at the closet rather than into the tunnel.

"What is it?" Anya asked. The dark, gaping tunnel yawned open in front of her. She ran a hand over the interior tunnel walls, searching for a light switch.

"Never in my wildest dreams did I think I'd see the inside of a Russian president's apartment, much less his private dressing room."

From the living area, Inga screamed. Trouble all right. High pierced, like an actress in a slasher flick, the sound made the hairs on the back of Anya's neck stand up.

Squeezing Ryan's hand, she jerked him toward the gaping

dark mouth of the tunnel. "When we get back to America, I'll show you a Russian princess's apartment, complete with a closet the size of a phone booth."

He touched her face in a gesture she couldn't quite read, but felt like a mixture of support and apology, sending a cascade of warmth over her. She caught his almost nonexistent grin as he closed the mirrored door and plunged them into darkness.

32

ANYA WAS WEARING HIS SWEATER. **Again.** That fact made Ryan inordinately happy. Logic had told him she'd be in Ivanov's suite, but he'd turned on the miniature tracking device in case she was still wearing his sweater. When the small red dot on his tablet computer had lit up and blinked her location, he'd had the same feeling. Inordinately happy.

And wasn't that the stupidest thing? He was standing in complete darkness in a tunnel that connected the private quarters of the Russian President to his presidential bunker system in the heart of Moscow, breaking at least a dozen Russian laws —as well as a few American ones— with not one, but two women's lives riding on his shoulders. His cover was all but blown, and the woman he was with had just assaulted the Russian prime minister and left him bleeding on the floor of the president's private apartment. Said woman was running away with him, and all he could do was grin into the heavy darkness because she was wearing his goddamn sweater.

The silence in the tunnel was as thick as the blackout. Soundproof walls, no doubt. Anya's breathing was light but there. He found her by touch, his fingers connecting with hers as if she were reaching for him at the same time he reached for her. There had to be a lighting system for the tunnel, but at that moment, he didn't much care that they hadn't found it. He could let his guard down, not worry about showing his emotions here in the dark.

He gripped her hand tight, drew her close, and whispered in her ear as he nudged her deeper into the tunnel. Soundproof or no, he wasn't taking chances. "Sorry I didn't get here sooner."

She kept her voice to a whisper as well. "I shouldn't have attacked Andreev, but I didn't know what to do. He tried to force me down here, and I knew if he succeeded, he'd lock me up somehow, someway. I'd never find Grams and..." She took one of those toe-deep breaths. "I'd never see you again."

Shit. Good thing he couldn't see her face, see the emotion on it. Her words alone were enough to swell his chest and shoot heat straight to his lower anatomy. He couldn't afford to think with his dick right now. The goatfuck of an international incident they were about to cause—had already caused—would get him fired from the Agency.

No point in worrying about that since he'd most likely be dead before he made it back to Langley anyway.

His vision fought to adjust to the darkness. It was so complete, all he could make out was a faint oval shape in front of him. Anya's face, hair. She was so pale, it was if she were an angel, her luminescent skin shining through the black gloom. Her hair nearly glowing.

Ryan slipped his night vision glasses from his coat pocket and put them on. Boom, there she was in front of him. Eyes wide, hair mussed, her skin, hair and clothing looking faintly green because of the lenses. The tunnel was cold, and he could see their breaths combining in the space between their faces. "Take my coat."

"I'm okay." Even as she said it, her body vibrated with a hard shiver.

He shrugged off the coat and helped her into it, ignoring her quiet protests. She couldn't see him or the coat, so he guided her arms into the sleeves, zipped it up to her chin. Immediately her shivering ceased. She sighed contentedly.

"You're wearing those glasses, aren't you?" Anya's fingers landed lightly on his face, touching the frames. The soft pads traced and explored like she was visually impaired, which she was, and *double shit*, his lower anatomy went sonic. "They help you see in the dark. Like night vision?"

Seeing was overrated when her fingers were so gently fondling his face. Two fingers landed on his lips, and he kissed them, once, twice.

Jesus God, he had to get his dick under control. "Anya, we have to get moving. Inga has probably already raised the alarm, and Ivanov's guards will be looking for you. For us."

Her fingers played over his cheekbones, drifted into the hair above his ears. Her face was turned up to his and even with sucky night vision, he saw her forehead crease in worry.

Damn.

"Why are you risking everything to help me?" Her voice, whisper and all, sounded so fragile, he couldn't stop himself from drawing her into his arms.

She came willingly, trusting him to protect her. But how could he answer that question when he didn't know why himself? Words never failed him, yet with her pressed close, and the worry on her face—not for her own predicament, but for him—shattered him to the bone. There were no words that could make her understand why he had just thrown his career, and possibly his life, under the bus.

So he lowered his lips to hers and answered her the only way he knew how.

She moaned under her breath, rising up on her toes and returning the kiss with her own soft lips. One hand slipped around the back of his neck, drawing his face down. The other curved around his waist and tugged him closer. Her lips played against his, pliant one second, aggressive the next. A give and take of tongues. All of it a loud and clear message that she understood what he couldn't say.

And he understood what she wanted. Him. As conspirator, as spy, as the man who gave her his coat. She didn't need to use sex to get him to help her save her grandmother. He was already here, already committed. He hadn't told her anything about himself, hadn't shared anything about who he was, or his past, and yet, that didn't matter. He wasn't Ryan Smith or Ryan Jones or Eddie or the other dozen alias and code names he'd developed over the years. He was just Ryan to her.

It was such a turn-on, he nearly backed her up against the cold tunnel wall, unzipped his coat—so totally bulky and too big for her frame—and went to work on making her the happiest woman in Moscow. What he did instead was intensify the kiss, going hard as a rock when she responded. Hot, wet, and deep, he probed her mouth and enjoyed her moan, even though it was loud enough to echo in the tunnel and give away their location.

The two functioning brain cells still active in his frontal lobe kicked in. She was alone and bravely standing up to an egomaniac who'd killed her parents and kidnapped her grandmother. Of course, she was crushing on him. He was the only friend she had in the world right now, and he'd be taking advantage of her if he let this go any further...

Crushing on me.

He broke the kiss. His heart rebelled at the thought, but his foggy brain cells didn't. Men and women in stressful situations often fell for each other, the adrenaline rush a natural aphrodisiac. Throw in some hero worship, the excitement of being on the run, and boom, the stress morphed into sexual desire. As soon as the danger passed, so did the emotional and physical high.

Was he freakin' stupid? Spies were trained to resist this. Taught never to allow a dangerous situation to cloud their thinking or cause them to let down their guard. Sex was the enemy's number one weapon. Plenty of agents, operatives, and assets had been done in by money and greed, but more had been done in by sex.

"Ryan?" Anya was breathing hard, her breath warm on his face. "What is it?"

No way should he be doing this. Taking her into the heart of GI 42, searching for a Cold War double agent, laughing in the face of his training and position in the CIA hierarchy. He should turn Anya around, march her back into Ivanov's quarters, and help her come up with a good story about how Andreev had attacked her. How she'd feared for her life. He should go to Pennington with the measly bunch of crap they had on Ivanov, and let the president handle the potential nuclear threat. He should call Conrad at Langley and tell him, and his army of super agents, to find Natasha Romanov.

Grasping Anya's hands, he removed them from his neck and waist, but held onto them. "We have to get moving."

The crease appeared in her forehead again. Without waiting for her consent, he dragged her deeper into the heart of the enemy's compound.

33

"How do you know which direction to go?" Anya asked, ignoring the stitch in her side.

They'd already hit several connecting tunnels, the one positive being that the intersections had lighting. Subdued, but there, allowing her to see Ryan and the path in front of them.

A weird vibe hung in the air, and it had nothing to do with the fact they were sprinting miles under the Earth in a catacomb of ostentatious steel tunnels that reflected the ugly side of the Soviet Union. Ryan had told her that a portion of Stalin's bunker had been opened to the public back in the early 1990's, but this section had been kept from the public since it connected directly to the president's apartments.

Regardless, it was hardly comparable to the beautiful subway system nearby. Where that system boasted opulence and pleasing architecture, this hidden bunker boasted sterile walls, terrible lighting, and cramped quarters.

In some ways, Anya felt a sense of pride in the Russian people, and those leaders who'd valued beauty and artistic expression in their transportation systems as well as their buildings. But just like in her life, outward appearances hid the unattractive truth. The hideous underbelly. These tunnels, still concealed from the public, attested to the horror of Stalin's reign.

Much of Russia's history was considered terrible by the free world, and Anya agreed there were many atrocities in its past, but life wasn't just about happy endings. There was beauty to be found even in the midst of strife and atrocities. Russians embraced that beauty and celebrated it. It gave them hope.

Right now, the shadowy tunnels gave her hope, even though they were far from beautiful. Or maybe it was Ryan's presence. Although the tightness of his face, and the fact he wouldn't look at her, made her stomach queasy. It was the kiss. Everything had changed since the kiss.

But why? They'd kissed previously, and he'd still been the imperturbable Ryan afterwards. Strong, sexy, unshakable. Why was he acting so weird now?

She stumbled, her legs heavy and weighted. Did she do something wrong? Well, duh. She'd done everything wrong since the moment she found Ivanov's note and the plane ticket ordering her to Mosco. Since the moment she'd confirmed Grams had disappeared. Tonight, she'd knocked out the prime minister, and from the amount of blood on the floor, he might be dead.

Her stomach went queasy again, and a ringing set up camp in her ears. Had she killed a man?

Now she was on the lam, taking Ryan with her. My God, how could she be so selfish as to incriminate him in this too?

How could she turn down his help though? She needed him.

Way to go, Anya. Ruin a man's life. A man who might have been the perfect prince to your princess if you weren't so damned screwed up.

He still hadn't answered her. Either he was ignoring her, or he was also lost in thought. She didn't blame him if he was ignoring her. "I'm sorry."

There she said it. No whispering it, either. She said it out loud, over the ringing in her ears. There was no one around, and they were miles under the Palace by now. Her feet burned inside her shoes from the furious pace Ryan had kept. Dots danced in front of her eyes.

He didn't stop, didn't even slow down. He did, however, respond. "For what?"

He was talking again. That was a good sign. She pressed a hand against the burning in her side and tried not to sound out of breath. "Getting you mixed up in this. I'm afraid something's going to happen—to you—and it will be my fault. I'm sorry for jeopardizing your men back at the cabin. I'm sorry for pushing your buttons and speaking when I should have kept my mouth shut. I'm sorry for all of it."

He stopped. Just like that. Anya, unprepared for the abrupt halt to their forward movement, ran into his back. Her heavy feet and weak legs caused her to lose her balance, but Ryan grabbed her upper arms and righted her with ease.

He rubbed his forehead and stared down the tunnel in front of them. He had to be cold, his breath fogging the air. "I have a map in my head of these tunnels."

Anya placed a hand on a column for support and took a few deep breaths, blinking away the dots. When had she gotten so out of shape? "Huh?"

"You asked me how I know where to go. A map. Up here." He pointed to his temple. "I memorized it a long time ago when I started with the CIA. Solomon, my friend, told me I was a dreamer to think I'd ever set foot in GI 42, but I memorized it anyway, just like I memorized Russian history and learned the language. I've spent my entire career wanting to be stationed in Russia, and ended up everywhere but, except for a brief stint right out of the Farm a dozen years ago. Now, here I am. Russia, the Cold War, Stalin...it fascinates me. All of it."

That explained so much. She hated to ask but she had to know. "Am I just another Russian fascination? Is that why you were so eager to help me get down here and look for my grandmother?"

He spun to face her, and seeing her seriousness, he laughed, grabbed her free hand and rubbed it between his. "You think I'm doing this so I can see GI 42?"

"Are you?"

He dropped her hand, and suddenly she was cold again. "What do I have to do, Anya, to prove to you I'm here because I want to help you and your grandmother? Write it in blood? Kill Ivanov? Go to prison for you?"

God, now she felt awful. She'd known since the moment she'd laid eyes on him that he was a good man, and here she was accusing him of using her to see a stupid Cold War bunker? It was the stress. She was losing her mind and her common sense.

She swallowed down the tears that clogged her throat. All she wanted to do was touch him again. Kiss him. Make him smile.

But none of that was going to work this time. "My whole life, I've spent looking over my shoulder. Running from things I couldn't stand up to, or fight head on. I can't trust anyone. That's what I've learned. So I don't. There's only been one person in my life I trusted and she's..."

Her voice wobbled. She cleared her throat. *I will not cry.* "Grams gave me a good life, but above everything, she taught me to be independent. Not to trust or rely on anyone else. Ever. I hope you'll forgive me for assuming the worst about you and your intentions. It's hard for me not to."

Ryan closed his eyes for a second as if he now felt awful.

Then he opened them and looked straight at her. "I don't trust anyone either. We'll learn to do that together."

He held out his hand, suspending it in the air between them.

Slowly, Anya raised her hand and slipped it into his. "That would be good."

He tugged her beside him, and they started walking.

"If my internal compass is right, we're heading northeast." He pointed. "There's an area ahead that was once used for interrogating Cold War spies. If Natasha is here, I'll bet money that's where Ivanov has her."

Interrogation? Anya gripped Ryan's hand tighter. Asked the question she had to ask. "Gram was more than just a Romanov, wasn't she? My father...I think Ivanov killed him because he thought my father might run for president after Yeltsin retired. I don't know why I think that, but it must be something he said when I was kid, and I buried it until now."

Ryan considered her theory. "Ivanov is obsessed with royalty so he probably saw your father as his one true competitor to the presidential throne."

"But why kill my mother too?"

"She must have known something that would hurt Ivanov's chances or maybe she was just in the wrong place at the wrong time."

Silence fell as Anya turned various ideas, including that one, over in her mind. Even walking, it was difficult to keep up with Ryan when she was so tired. Harder still to puzzle out her family's mysterious past. "When we find Grams, I'm getting answers."

"When. That's good."

"What?"

"You said 'when' not 'if'. That's good."

"Oh, we'll find her. Alive and spitting nails."

"She was a tough woman in her time."

"Still is."

He stopped and smiled. "I know where you get it from then."

Anya's ears rang, but she was grateful for the chance to catch her breath. "Oh, she's way tougher than me. She was heavily involved in politics, always in the middle of some debate, and advising Yeltsin behind closed doors. She and my dad talked politics a lot when I was young. I tuned it all out. When my parents died, she buried them, helped me with my grief, packed up everything, and moved us thousands of miles to get us safely to America. She answered hundreds of my questions and got me settled in a foreign country with unending patience and grace. It must have been terrifying for her. Sad, too. To lose her only son and his wife. To have to uproot herself and her granddaughter, leave everything familiar behind, and start over."

He'd seen the paper, seen "executed" beside her parents' names. But he didn't know everything.

"I was there that night." Anya let the memory come back to her, Ryan's hand warm on hers. She knew they needed to keep moving, so she started to walk. He fell into step with her. "We were driving, and I was in the backseat. The sniper bullet came out of nowhere. I didn't even know what it was. All I knew was, my father's side window exploded. His head fell forward. The car went spinning out of control."

A silent numbness set up in her chest. "The car went off the road and hit a tree. My mother was conscious, but her legs were crushed under the dashboard. She couldn't get out. She was crying and screaming for my father, but he was already dead. A man, wearing black from head to toe and a mask to cover his face, walked down the road. The rifle was slung over his back. My mother yelled at me to get out of the car and hide in the woods. I didn't want to leave her. Didn't want to leave either of them, but she insisted. So I climbed out and crept off before the man in black got to the car. I hid in the woods and saw him take a handgun from inside his coat." Her breath hitched. "He shot my mother in the head."

They'd come to a T-intersection. Ryan stopped, grabbed her in a fierce hug. "I'm so sorry."

They stayed that way for a minute, and then he released her, a deep frown creasing his forehead. "Did the man come after you?"

Anya sagged without his arms supporting her. She was so damned tired. She backed her butt against the wall, and set her hands on her knees. Leaning over helped get more oxygen into her lungs, and the burning in her side eased a bit. "I was in shock. The car exploded a minute later, so I ran. I had no idea where I was going. A part of me sensed the man was coming after me, although I never saw him. We were less than a kilometer outside a building my father had been working in. A compound of some sort. My mother had told me we all had to go to the compound to do something important for Russia, and afterwards, we'd go for pastries. It was one of the compound's guards who found me huddled on the ground the next morning."

She started to shiver hard under Ryan's coat. Even breathing deep, she couldn't make the dots disappear. "Can we sit down?"

She didn't wait for his okay, her butt hitting the hard floor as her legs went out from under her.

"Anya?"

His voice sounded far away. Like it was in a tunnel. *Duh, Anya. Of course he sounds like he's in a tunnel.* The thought made her laugh in jerky breaths, and she closed her eyes. Next thing she knew, she tipped over. Her head hit the floor.

"Anya!" Ryan's voice still sounded far away, but his hands were on her, shaking her, and she knew he was close.

Her eyes refused to open. "I just...need...a rest."

"Shit." One of his hands caressed her head, shifting it to the side. It pounded when he did that and she fought to move it back. "You smacked your head good. Why didn't you tell me you needed a break sooner?"

She loved the sound of his voice. She only wished he'd be quiet for a few minutes and let her sleep. Sleep would help...

"Anya, open your eyes."

Her head hurt, her side hurt. She swore under her breath in Russian. A little sleep, was that too much to ask for?

Suddenly, she was lifted into a sitting position, back against the wall. Ryan's voice was firm. "Don't you dare go to sleep on me."

So bossy. Forcing her eyes open, she found Ryan's face in front of hers, his dark eyes even darker in the shadows. Embarrassed at how weak she was, and that she was letting him down again, she fought through her body's lethargy. "I'm fine."

"You're not fine. You're weak as a kitten. When was the last time you ate?"

The fog in her brain wouldn't clear, and she shook her head. *Ouch.* "I don't know. Sometime yesterday?"

Ryan dug in the pocket of the coat she was wearing and accidently bumped her side. She flinched and sucked in her breath.

"What is it?" he asked, drawing out a granola bar from the pocket.

"Nothing. My side has a stitch from all the running."

He tore the wrapper off the end of the bar and handed it to her. "Eat this."

It was chewy and dry, but after nothing to eat in the past day, she wasn't complaining. While she snarfed it down, Ryan unzipped the coat and opened it. "Double shit."

He said it so softly, so subdued, Anya almost didn't catch the way his jaw jumped. She looked down and stopped eating.

Blood had soaked through Ryan's sweater.

He grabbed the hemmed edge and lifted it. "Your wound is

open and bleeding again. How is that possible? It should've healed by now."

Anya grabbed the sweater and tugged it back down. Like she wasn't embarrassed enough, how was she going to explain this? It wasn't something you laid on a guy you'd only just met and wanted as your lover.

"Anya." His voice was steady, comforting. Like he wasn't mad or frustrated or wigging out at all. "Did Ivanov cut you again?"

The granola bar turned to dirt inside her mouth. She forced it down, gave a small shake of her head. Hell, she was in this deep. Might as well tell Ryan all her secrets. "I have a blood disorder. Von Willebrand disease. It stops my blood from clotting correctly after an injury. Runs in my family. Usually the women are only carriers, but both my parents were carriers, so I have the full blown disorder. It's not a big deal."

Except that it could be. Especially when trying to escape a madman and his army of soldiers. Bleeding profusely left her lightheaded and wasn't exactly easy to take care of on the run. She opened her mouth to say, "I'm sorry," for the hundredth time when Ryan leaned forward and placed his forehead against hers. Such an intimate gesture, it totally caught her off guard.

"I'm sorry."

He was sorry? "For what?"

"For getting you into this goatfuck. I should have left you in the Palace. Taken you to Pennington and come looking for your grandmother on my own."

"No. I...Wait. You're not icked out about my blood disorder?"

"Of course not. I figured you were a carrier of hemophilia. Most of the royal women were. I just didn't realize you had a full-blown condition."

Relief flooded her. Blood icked out everybody. Even her and

she dealt with genes, mutations, platelets, and all that stuff, on a daily basis at GenLife. She'd never told anyone about the coagulation abnormality. Grams and her parents had been the only ones who knew.

Ryan's nose brushed Anya's. "You would've been warm in the Kremlin, had food. Bandages." He lifted his head and punched the wall behind her. "I should have thought this through. Should have made a fucking-ass plan. But no, I just grabbed you and ran. Very thoughtful. Very...stupid. God!"

He stood and paced, unbuttoning his shirt, and shrugging it off. Next, he whipped off his T-shirt, and stood there half-naked in front of her. She would have enjoyed it if he hadn't been castigating himself.

Imperturbable Ryan was gone. "I should have made sure you were safe. There's no excuse for this. You need a doctor, for fuck's sake. Not an incompetent operative who can't even make a viable escape plan."

He ripped a wide strip off the bottom edge of the T-shirt, folded it into a bandage, and dropped to his knees in front of her. "I've put you in incredible danger."

His fingers caressed her skin as he gently lifted the sweater and placed the bandage over her wound. So gentle. So opposite of his ranting and raving.

If this was incompetence, she'd take it over expert medical care any day.

Anya touched his face. "You think I would have stayed in the Palace and let you do this alone? Fat chance, buster. It was stupid of me to attack Andreev, but there was no way I was letting him imprison me. Ivanov either. If you hadn't shown up when you did, I'd be down here on my own, not knowing where to go, or how to find Grams, because I'm the one who can't come up with a plan. I'm safer here with you than anywhere else I could be."

He ripped a second strip off his shirt, the muscles in his

arms and shoulders bunching with the action. Winding the strip around her waist and tying it to hold the bandage in place, he avoided her eyes. "I did this all wrong."

Anya grabbed his hands to still them. His face was so close, she felt his warm breath on her cheek. She kissed the corner of his lips. "A horse has four legs, but still stumbles. Grams always says that. It means—"

"Even the most capable people make mistakes sometimes."

His expertise extended to old lady Russian proverbs. "Exactly. In my opinion, you did everything right, except for getting involved with me in the first place."

Some of the tension left his body. "Nah, pretty sure that's the part I did do right."

He kissed her then, another full out, make-her-want-to-moan-kiss. She slid into his arms, no longer feeling weak or embarrassed.

She wanted him. More than she'd ever wanted anyone. She'd lived behind a mask all these years. Hid behind it. Never able to let her guard down and love anyone. The few times she'd shown real interest in a boy growing up, her grandmother had firmly squashed her hopes of a relationship. Grams made her focus on her schooling, take piano, spend weekends on art exhibits and ballets, never letting Anya hang out with friends, and especially not boys.

Without coming right out and saying it, Grams had always had a way of making Anya feel like their family secrets were too dark, too dangerous to ever allow her the freedom her American peers had. Having a relationship meant sharing pasts, sharing personal information. Even casual dating was out because it might lead to something more intrusive. So Anya had made up fantasies from the time she was fourteen about the opposite sex. What it felt like to be kissed, to be held.

She crawled into his lap. Ryan's arms around her was nothing short of her wildest fantasy, and at twenty-six, she had some pretty righteous fantasies. He was hard and soft and warm, even with no shirt on, and he drew her closer, molding her body against his. One hand slipped up to cup her breast and she moaned into his mouth. The kiss was long and deep and so erotic, she curled her toes inside her shoes, wrapped her arms around his neck and ignored the voice inside her head, reciting Grams' rules.

To hell with rules. What had following them gotten her and her family anyway? Heartache, death.

She broke the kiss, looked Ryan in the eye. "I've been fantasizing about you since the cabin."

His eyes widened and he grinned. "I've been doing a bit of that about you."

Yes. She ran her hands over his shoulders, down his sculpted arms. He had to be a runner or a swimmer. Maybe both.

Muscles jumped under her fingers. "This—" she touched him on his chest just over his heart and then pointed at herself. "You and me, right here, right now, is better than any of my fantasies."

The grin on his face grew. "My top fantasy involves you with fewer clothes on."

She laughed, and he laughed with her. It was a warm, inviting sound in the otherwise cold, harsh tunnel. She traced a finger over his lips, and he kissed it. Between her legs, an explosion of sensations went off. There was still one last secret to share. "I feel a lot stronger now. Maybe we could act out a few of our fantasies."

He kissed her lips, three short, soft kisses in a row before he shook his head. "Not here in the open, under such dangerous circumstances. We need a place for you to rest up, and me to come up with a more solid escape plan."

Sliding her off his lap, he rezipped the coat. Then he helped her stand. Snatching up his button-down shirt, he threw it on, which was a shame, and stuck what was left of the T-shirt into her coat pocket. "How's your side? Do you think you can walk a little further? Stalin's suite should be just ahead."

The presidential suite. Anya shivered. Not Ivanov's, she reminded herself. His was a brand new, shiny version in another part of the bunker. She'd already seen that one first hand, along with the lab he'd built.

Ryan seemed to read her mind. "The suite hasn't been used in years. Not actively, anyway. But it may have what we need. Food, clothes, first aid supplies."

Knowing he was right didn't make her any happier that he was now his old self again. Calm, cool, unflappable Ryan.

But that was okay. She'd make him lose control again, and soon. "The new bunker is down here somewhere too. I've seen it. It definitely has supplies." Calling up polite, steadfast Anya, she pressed a hand against her side and gave him a nod. "Lead the way."

34

"I can't believe I let you talk me into this." John adjusted the face mask he wore to blend in with the other construction workers cleaning up debris left over from the latest bomb blast.

Devons chuckled, his own mask muffling the sound. "Becoming a terrorist or a disaster recovery specialist?"

John moved some rubble out of the way. "Since when are you friends with Chechen rebels?"

"I might have dated one of their sisters back in the day."

Why didn't that surprise him? Mossad agents, Chechen rebels. What next?

Devons held out a meter meant to read air quality. A low blipping noise sounded. "Guy owed me a favor and was more than happy to unload on the Ruskies. No one was killed. Injuries were light. Fast was what Flynn wanted, and fast is what we're giving him."

Stealth and efficiency were John's and Pegasus Team's motto. "Bombings? Protests? Total overkill for a search and rescue."

"Overkill? We're talking about a launch code for nuclear warheads aimed at Britain and America, and a total psycho with his finger on the button." Devons pocketed the meter. "And from the intel Del got from Truman Gunn, our operative is about to do something asinine that could put the Cold War and nuclear annihilation on today's menu. The MTD says he's down here, under the Kremlin."

John had never met Ryan Smith, only heard stories about him. He tended to stay behind the scenes, unlike Conrad Flynn, even though they had similar positions. Word was, Smith was every bit as cunning and devious as Flynn, only more likable since he befriended people rather than pissing them off. "Tracking device or no, my mission isn't about Smith. He's your job. My mission is to recover Natasha."

A heavy fog hung in the air, thus the need for air masks. Because the Russian government feared chemical or biological fallout from the bombs, the workers were dressed in full Nomex suits. Hot, sweaty suits.

Devons and John had sidled away from the main group, heading discreetly toward a maintenance door that ran behind the subway tunnels and connected to the hidden bunker. Or so Del had told them.

"This distraction gives us both the opportunity to complete our respective missions." Devons checked over his shoulder to see if they were being watched. Satisfied the rest of the cleanup crew was paying no attention to them, he motioned John toward the steel door. "You find Natasha, and I'll get Smitty and Anya out if necessary."

"Why would he blow his cover for this Russian gal?" John said before he thought it through. If it were Lucie – a woman he'd been crushing on for months - inside the Kremlin, he'd do the same thing. "Never mind. Let's just get that door open."

The steel door was locked, but when did that ever stop an

Agency operative? As John stood lookout, Devons used a hand-held lock pic to open it. The door was heavy and rusty from moisture, squeaking loudly as they shoved it open.

The squeak echoed in the crumbling tunnel. The heavy fog, full of debris still, helped hide them from any curious eyes. John heard a shout from behind them, so he pushed Devons through, jerked the door shut, and flipped the lock.

Next to the door sat a heavy cart filled with tools, a hard hat, and other paraphernalia the subway's maintenance workers used. Shedding his mask, John picked up a couple of hand tools. Devons, liking the idea, did the same.

John had been on plenty of dangerous missions, but entering the heart of a Russian Cold War bunker topped the list. As always, he had an entrance and exit strategy. It was what lay in between that made his palms sweat.

He drew out a map—courtesy of Del—from his coveralls, got his bearings, and motioned Devons to follow. "Half a kilometer west, we should find Stalin's official bunker. The torture chambers Grigory told us about are there."

"What if she's dead?"

Then the search and rescue mission became a search and recovery. "We bring her body back."

"And if she's not there?"

Ah, the fatal question that hung over every mission. The possibility of failure. "Then I'll keep looking until I find her."

They ran at a good clip, the slapping of their feet echoing in the tunnel as they covered the ground. Light from fixtures mounted on the walls gave the tunnel enough illumination for John to see Devons' face. The spy persona was gone. Not even the fake cop persona seemed alive.

At an intersection, Devons stopped, looked around. "You eat, breathe and sleep this special ops shit, don't you? I ever go missing? I want you heading up my rescue. Got that?"

Sincerity. That's what Devon's face revealed. John nodded. "And if I ever need a 'distraction' of this magnitude again, I'll call you."

Devons held out a hand. John shook it.

35

ANYA WAS asleep in Stalin's presidential bedchamber. There were no guards in this section, which worried Ryan more than he would admit. What he'd told Anya was true. GI 42 hadn't been actively used to the best of anyone's knowledge since Stalin. Didn't mean it wasn't kept functioning and ready for action in the event of war, even if Ivanov had created a new, improved version nearby. Made sense that there would be security there, but maybe not much at the moment. Ivanov needed all the security he could get above ground in the Kremlin and the connecting subways because of the terrorist bombings.

The shock-wave proof doors had been locked, of course, but they'd also been updated to a computerized system from the time Stalin had originally had them installed. Probably by one of his successors. Able to withstand a twenty-ton nuclear blast, the locks fell to an average computer geek who knew his way around a digital lock.

Inside the abandoned presidential bunker were three central rooms: the president's suite, a communications/weapons room, and a kitchen/utility area. Ryan had found a first-aid kit and doctored Anya's wound. When he'd asked her about her blood disorder, she'd clammed up on him and insisted it was nothing. Not wanting to upset her, he'd dropped the subject, even though it bothered him. She'd seemed embarrassed, as if she were ashamed. Of what, he couldn't imagine. He'd never heard of von Willebrand's, but intended to find out all he could about it if they ever got out of there.

Meanwhile, he'd found some MRE's stored in the kitchen. Ones created in the current decade, too, with fancy names. The fancy names did nothing to change the fact that the ready-to-eat meals were mostly canned beef. He also found tea and sugar. The beef tasted like hell, but Anya didn't complain. She ate what he fed her and drank the tea, which was a yellow color, but had no flavor outside of the sugar he'd added to the cup.

Anya was so damn tough. Hard to believe. She looked fragile on the outside, all pale skin, white hair, and lanky limbs, but she was tough underneath. A few vulnerable spots here and there, and yet, she didn't let those stop her from giving one hundred and ten percent. Strong-willed, that's what his mother had always called him. That's what he saw in Anya.

"Ryan?"

His body gave its normal happy response to the sound of her voice. Nerves tingled, his pulse sped up, and his crotch tightened.

Smiling, he paused typing on the keyboard in front of him, and turned from the control panel to face her. "You're supposed to be sleeping."

She'd wrapped a blanket around her body, hair sticking out on one side of her face. Free of makeup, her white-blonde eyelashes made her eyes look even more like blue crystals. He wished she'd leave off the mascara permanently. He liked her better this way.

Crossing the floor, she eyed the computer and the gun sitting next to his hand. Then she leaned forward and kissed him hello. Right smack on the lips. Possessive and sweet, and *ah, man*, his crotch wasn't just tight, it was painfully hard.

"That room, all that red." She drew the blanket tighter. "It gives me the creeps. Reminds me of all the Russian blood Stalin spilled."

For a geneticist, she sure had an aversion to blood. He motioned to a nearby chair even though he wanted to drag her down into his lap. "You look better."

"I feel better." She sat and harrumphed as she arranged the blanket to her liking. "I suck at this cloak and dagger stuff, in case you didn't notice. All this stress, no sleep, no food...again, I'm sorry for being more of a hindrance than a help with locating my grandmother."

Forcing himself not to stare at her incredible lips, Ryan cleared his throat, and clicked a few meaningless keys on the keyboard while it continued to boot up. He'd plugged a small, portable mobile access hub into the mainframe, hoping to find some kind of internet access. "Actually, you've been pretty impressive through all of this."

He stole a glance at her, and saw her eyes light up. "You're just saying that because you want to get my pants off."

The minute she said it, she blushed. Her flirting skills were so damn awkward, it turned him on. Hell, everything about her turned him on. "That is a strong possibility."

They both laughed. Anya nodded at the keyboard. "What are you doing?"

"Trying to make contact with the outside world. No one knows where we are and..." He fiddled with the keys.

"And if we die, no one will know what happened."

She caught on quick. "This bunker's communication system isn't as sophisticated as I had hoped." He pointed at the floppy disc drive, vintage 1990's. "But if I can figure out a few passwords, and this puppy has any kind of satellite—which it should since it was designed to send out messages to all the missile systems in case of an attack—I can get a message to Langley undetected."

"The CIA will rescue us?"

No. They wouldn't do an extraction from Russia for only Anya and Natasha. Conrad would, but Michael Stone, Deputy Director of the CIA, and maximum hardass supreme, would never okay it. Unless...

Unless his brother-in-law and commander-in-chief was in trouble.

Hmm. Ryan spun the idea around. What the hell. He'd already ruined his career. No point in doing it halfway. "If I send the right message, they'll come."

Anya scooted her chair across the floor, edging closer. "How can you figure out the password? It could be anything."

"Well, usually, I tell a supergeek at the Agency to hack it for me, but since that option is out, I have to be the supergeek, and do it myself. A password isn't that hard to crack, but it's time consuming since it can be any combination of numbers and letters. Personal passwords are easier because they mean something to the person who sets them up, so if you know a few details about the person, like their birthday and wedding anniversary, combined with their kid's name, bingo.

"In this case, we're dealing with a government organization —not a person. The passwords for this system were generated by a computer. The trick is, an administrator had to develop the system and tell the computer to generate passwords. With this old system, all I have to do is locate the administrator's password—which I can find with a simple DOS command—and..."

He typed in the last command, and *come to papa*, there it was. A fourteen digit combo of Russian numbers and letters in both upper and lower case used by the system administrator.

Which might have very well been Anya's father. Ryan had memorized the facts about Peter Radzoya from Del's file. He had a few theories on how deep the man had gotten himself, and his family, into a political scandal of massive consequences. "Now we use the admin's password and uncover the rest."

"Wow." Anya high-fived him. "Industrious and resourceful."

Not really, but he was glad she thought so. A more sophisticated system would have taken hours, maybe days or weeks to crack. "Back in the day, this computer system was high-tech, but the developers and administrator were only worried about an outside breach of security, not an internal one."

Logging into the center's infrastructure, he decided to see if he could breach another semi-secure, although human, site. "So tell me about your job."

Anya sat back in the chair, tucking her feet under her. "As you know, I'm a geneticist. I work at GenLife Laboratories in D.C. on special gene mapping for certain individuals. I do research on the Human Genome Project in my spare time."

"Gene mapping, huh?" He already knew all about her job—she'd followed in her mother's footsteps. But he wanted to keep her talking. "Heavy stuff."

Pride rang in her voice. "Some of it, yes. I help people, like a doctor, but in a different manner."

"Help them how?"

"I perform DNA analyses for a select clientele. For instance, my last case involved a high-profile female client whose sister was dying from a rapid onset of breast cancer. I did the workup and found my client's gene pool showed she had not inherited any mutation of the genes that suppress tumors in the breasts and ovaries. Her odds of contracting the breast cancer killing her sister were almost nonexistent. I gave her that news right before this whole thing with Grams went down. It was a good day."

Her last good day in a week. Ryan saw it in her expression. Somehow, he was going to make sure she had lots of good days in the future.

Words filtering across the screen in front of him showed the computer was still trying to connect with the satellite. At this rate, he could escape Russia and walk to Langley before his message got there. "That's cool. What about the client whose gene map shows they *did* inherit something ugly? How do you handle that?"

"Sharing that news is never easy, but what I'm doing gives them knowledge. Gives them the opportunity to be proactive and do something to offset whatever it is. I can give them hope along with the facts about their genetic makeup."

Ryan had met a few scientists over the years. He'd even smuggled one of out of North Korea in his younger days as a field operative. Granted, those scientists were of the nuclear weapons and biological warfare variety, but none of them had been a compassionate scientist like Anya. Where they'd viewed people as expendable, she viewed people as humans, and wanted to help them overcome their frailties and susceptibilities instead of capitalizing on them.

The computer beeped and hummed, another step closer to satellite hookup. Thinking about scientists and Cold War Russia triggered another thought in Ryan's already cluttered brain. "Did Ivanov mention anything directly about you resuming your work here?"

"It was more implied. Why?"

"We know he's obsessed with royal blood lines and racial ideology. Having you, a geneticist who can map people's genes and advise him on whose gene pool is clean..." He shrugged.

She straightened her long legs, practically coming out of the chair. Her socked feet brushed against his leg. "Oh, my God. That's it. I knew he wanted to cleanse the race, but I thought it was for future generations." The blanket fell from her shoulders and she nodded as if remembering something. "But it's more than that. Every time I was with him, he talked endlessly about restoring Russia to the way it used to be, bringing back pride in the country and respect for the leaders. But he only wants advisors and officials around him who are pure Russians, with nothing in their backgrounds that might mar his presidency. When he was talking about it, I thought he meant scandals and other political nightmares, but he was talking about their blood, wasn't he? That bastard! That's why he gave me those medical files. He wanted me to analyze their gene pools, make sure they didn't have any defects."

"A Hitler wannabe."

"Exactly."

Seeing her so animated was much better than seeing her faint. Better, even, than watching her sleep, which he'd done for the second time since the cabin, when he'd tucked her into Stalin's bed with its red sheets. He couldn't help it. He loved seeing her relaxed, the worry lines around her eyes erased.

Of course seeing her lying in bed, her white hair a tangled mess against the red silk had given him a hard-on for the record books. He'd had to leave her sleeping and take a trip through the weapons room to restore his logical thinking.

Now her cheeks were pink, hair mussed, and eyes bright with renewed determination to stop Ivanov's plans to use her. The blanket around her waist showed off the fact she was still wearing Ryan's sweater, the heavy cable knit cotton molding perfectly to her breasts.

God, he wanted her. Against all his logic and better judgment. Against the fact she'd been through hell in the past week. Against the fact they were sitting in a rundown operations room eighteen kilometers under Moscow without hope one of making it out alive.

Anya slid her chair closer, her feet intertwining with his. She touched his hand, then stroked the butt of the GSh 18 semiautomatic on the counter. Her slender, pale fingers contrasted against the hard, black handgun, and Ryan was suddenly jealous of an inanimate object. "Should I be armed, too?"

"Have you, uh..." She was looking at him so intently with those eyes that did him in, and now one of her feet was rubbing up and down on his leg. His brain was mush. "Have you had firearms training?"

She bit her bottom lip in a worried gesture as if he might be disappointed because she didn't know how to shoot a gun. "You can teach me?"

That imploring look combined with the lip biting and *shit*. Two seconds, tops, he was going to explode. "We could, um..." He knew what he should say, but for the life of him, he could not form words.

Gun, dipshit. She wants to learn how to shoot your gun.

And if that thought didn't send him into sexual tension orbit, what would?

"I can show you the, uh, basics, if you want. Firing, field stripping." Damn, when had talking guns become such a turn on? "But one thing you need to consider. Never point a gun at someone unless you're prepared to kill."

Her lips thinned.

Double shit. *Way to romance the woman you want to have sex with by talking about killing people.*

But it was true. He only used weapons as a last possible defense. Taking someone's life, even a psychotic maniac like Ivanov, wasn't child's play. It was something you lived with the rest of your life. Anya had enough scars. She didn't need to add another to her list.

She removed her hand from the gun, but her face was set with resolve. "I won't ask you to do anything I'm not willing to do myself."

Goddamn, she was a unique woman. "I'm trained in self-defense."

"So am I."

Surprise, surprise. "What type?"

"Taekwondo. Grams made me take lessons from the time I was fourteen."

"I like your Grams. She's one smart cookie."

Anya smiled and held out her hand. "You wield the gun, I'll wield hand attacks and kicks."

Ryan slid his hand into hers and they shook. "When we get you and your grandmother safely back to the States, I'd like to see you. You know, um...date you."

Her smile widened, and then she was pushing his chair backwards and climbing into his lap. The blanket fell to the ground, her legs sidled half on top of his as she kissed him. A sexier, wetter version of the hello kiss she'd dropped on him earlier.

That was Anya. Simple flirting seemed difficult for her, but she was full throttle when it came to kissing him.

A nice problem to have.

Her lips turned demanding, and Ryan forgot everything. The computer humming in the background. The stark communication center walls, low ceiling, and freezing air. He closed his eyes and kissed her back, letting his hands slide up her thighs, under his sweater.

And then that black hole opened up, not the one that had to do with her legs, but that black hole he hadn't seen since he and Conrad had gone AWOL from the CIA. The one where everything was spinning out of control and he was terrified.

"Wait," he breathed, drawing back. "This isn't the right time or place for this. You deserve better, Anya. You deserve..."

She pressed a finger to his lips to shush him. "I don't deserve any more than you or anyone else does. I'm not a princess who needs fancy things. This may not be the optimal time and place, but let's be honest. We may never have another chance. Do you really want to throw this away?"

Of course he didn't. He wasn't a fool. "You sure you don't want to use that princess angle? I've got this fantasy about being your eager and enthusiastic servant. Pleasing you and making you happy would be my number one job."

Anya laughed, full belly, head back. "Well, when you put it that way."

She kissed him again, and this time her hands got in on the action, unbuttoning his shirt and touching him everywhere. One hand slipped lower, and *hello*, she cupped him through his jeans, then stopped. Her head snapped back, and she looked him straight in the eye. "Now *that's* impressive."

There was a touch of awe in her voice, and Ryan felt heat creep up his neck. He opened his mouth to reply, but really, what could he say? Thank you? Glad you noticed? Even if he was able to string two words together, there was no right way to respond.

So he grabbed her ass and brought her closer, forcing her to straddle his hardness. She didn't seem to mind, pressing down on him and shucking off his sweater at the same time.

There they were. Breasts, glorious breasts. The bra she wore was utilitarian, but oh, so good at molding her porcelain skin into perfect mounds that just begged to be kissed, licked and sucked.

As she wiggled on top of him, her breasts jiggled. No way could he ignore all that beautiful skin. Ryan lowered his mouth and traced the line of cleavage between her breasts with his tongue. She urged his head down, eager for more.

He was happy to oblige. All the things he'd imagined doing to her, he did. He kissed the nipples inside the bra cups, drawing them one at a time into his mouth and sucking lightly. Anya moaned and ground her hips against his lap. She tossed her head back and ran a hand through his hair, egging him on. Releasing the clasp of the bra at the back, he was startled when several papers fell out into his lap, his business card among them.

Ah, yes. Her hiding place. Anya giggled as she shrugged off the bra, nipples hard and straining toward his mouth. "The contraband I stole from Ivanov's office. There's more in my pants and socks."

He tossed the papers next to the gun. "You'd definitely make a good spy."

A smile split her face, and she hugged him, pressing her breasts close to his face. He took advantage, lowering his lips.

He gave each breast his full attention before kissing his way up Anya's neck. He couldn't remember the last time he'd wanted a woman this much, and if she didn't stop grinding into his lap, she was going to push him over the edge.

He nipped her ear lobe with his teeth and whispered, "Are you sure?"

Her eyes were half lidded, lips parted when she looked at him. "I'm scared."

All the adrenaline pouring through his system came to a screeching halt. She was scared. Of him? Of having sex with him?

Jesus, God, what am I doing?

It took every ounce of willpower, but he called up his no-nonsense director of operations face, and said the words he needed to say, even though he wanted to shoot himself for even thinking them. "We can stop."

"No." She looked stricken for a second. Then laid her head on his shoulder. Her hair tickled his nose, but he didn't care. Anything to be near her was worth the price. "I don't want to stop. It's just...I..."

Wrapping his arms around her, he hugged her. "It's okay. We don't have to go any further. Like I said before, wrong time, wrong place. A military bunker is not exactly the most romantic place in the world."

She drew in one of those breaths that seemed to come from her toes, sat up, and met his gaze. "I don't want to stop."

There is a God, and somewhere along the line, Ryan had done something to earn the big guy's approval. "Tell me what you do want, Anya."

"Everything. All of it." She gave him that imploring look. "You. I want you. But there's something you need to know first."

His shit meter jumped into the red zone. Here it came. She had a boyfriend back in the States. She really was a Russian spy, double crossing him. There was more to her blood disorder than she'd admitted. "Anya, just so you know, I've never felt like this about a woman. Whatever it is, tell me, and I'll deal with it."

Silence hung between them for a few seconds. She swallowed visibly. "I'm a...virgin."

Whoa.

He managed to shut his gaping mouth. For a second anyway. "Excuse me?"

Brilliant, dipshit. The woman tells you she's a virgin and all you can say is excuse me?

She bit her bottom lip, hung her head, and started to slide off his lap.

He grabbed her by the hips and held her in place. "Where are you going?"

Avoiding his eyes, she shrugged. "I'm twenty-six years old and a virgin. It's understandable you think I'm a freak."

"A freak?" He tilted her chin up so she had to look at him. "I think you're amazing."

Her brows came together. "I've never had a relationship, never had a boyfriend. That's not normal."

"Screw normal."

Something flashed in her eyes. "I'd rather screw you."

Bright pink patches appeared on her cheeks. She laughed self-consciously. "I mean, I'd like—I want—to make love. With you. Right here. If you're not turned off by my..." She patted her bandaged side. "All my defects."

Defects. Freak. That's how she saw herself.

Time to change her self-image. Ryan had a good idea how to do that.

He traced his fingers up her spine, stopping at the back of her neck. Drawing her face close to his, he kissed her left eyelid, then her right. "You're the most beautiful woman I've ever seen."

He continued his assault, pushing hair behind her ears, and nuzzling her neck. "You're one of the smartest women I've ever met."

Down to her shoulders, sides, ribcage, and once again, those marvelous breasts. "I can't believe how lucky I am to be in the same room with you, much less touching you. Kissing you."

She might have been a virgin, but she wasn't shy when it came to using her hands and mouth. While he unzipped her pants, she did the same to his. He burst out of the opening and into her hand like a heat seeking missile. She stroked him with the finesse of a pro.

All the usual platitudes swam through his testosterone fueled brain. He should take it slow. Make it last. Her first time should be special. They needed a condom...

Birth control. Damn.

Her hand was warm and smooth, and stroking, stroking, stroking, and he was so gone, but he managed to step back from the edge. The only way to slow this down was to disconnect her hand, disconnect her body.

And why the hell would he do that?

"Anya." He lifted her off his lap and stood her up in front of him. Took a deep breath. "I don't have a condom."

Trying to shift gears, she gave him a perplexed look. "That's okay."

"No, it's not. While I'd love to throw caution to the wind one more time, I won't risk getting you pregnant on top of everything else."

She stepped toward him, but he held up a hand to stop her from climbing back in his lap. She laughed and grabbed his hand, moving it out of her way. "I'm on the pill. Have been for years."

Now it was his turn to look perplexed.

Realizing he needed an explanation, she looked slightly chagrined. "Because of my blood abnormality, I have really heavy periods. The hormones in the pills help control the bleeding."

After the longest, shittiest day of his life, his luck had turned around. Behind Anya's back, the antiquated computer beeped, signaling him it had finally located, and hooked up with, the satellite dish floating miles above the Earth.

Yes, sir, lady luck was his.

"As your humble servant, Grand Duchess Anya, let me send out an SOS to Langley, and then I'll strip those jeans off you, and we'll do anything your heart desires."

Already shimmying out of the jeans, she smiled big, and Ryan's heart thudded hard with happiness. "Make it quick." She kicked the legs of the jeans off her ankles and hopped up on the metal desktop. "A princess doesn't like to be kept waiting."

Taking his eyes off her long, glorious legs should have earned him a star on the wall at Langley because it nearly killed him. His message to Conrad was short and to the point:

Package and president are in trouble. Send help ASAP.

Before he was even done typing, Anya's hands were on him, pushing down his pants, removing his shirt. There was no way he could have written a longer message if his life depended on it. Which it sort of did. But he'd played his wildcard by including Pennington in the missive, and now all he could do was forget about it. If the Agency came to help, fine, but he wouldn't sit around waiting for them.

First, he had princess to please. Then he had to get her the hell out of Moscow.

36

RYAN WAS AMAZING.

Anya sat on the metal desk, her naked butt freezing on the cold, hard surface. She didn't care. Ryan stood before her, leaning over the keyboard, and concentrating on the computer screen next to her. She couldn't stop touching him. The muscles in his arms, the scant bit of blond chest hair that tickled her fingers, his flat stomach...she wanted it all.

And lower...

Heat rose in her cheeks from the sight of all that masculinity standing at full attention. She'd read romance books. She knew what was supposed to happen, but really? All of *that* was going inside her?

Reaching out, she skimmed his erection with her fingers, and Ryan sucked in a breath. He hit a final button, grabbed her wrist, and turned all that focused concentration on her. "Easy, princess."

Oops. Maybe she wasn't supposed to touch him like that. "Sorry."

"Don't be sorry. Your touch drives me a little crazy. I want to take this slow and easy and when you do that? Touch me like that? Well, that's going to get you fast and hard."

Fast and hard didn't sound so bad, especially when the spot between her legs ached for release. His gaze was so intense, she nearly exploded right there. "Please, Ryan," was all she could say.

Leaning over her, he placed his hands on the desktop on each side of her thighs, and caught her mouth with his. He kicked off his shoes, and the jeans around his ankles, while he kissed her, then broke the kiss for a second while he shoved several computer monitors out of the way, stretched the blanket out on the desktop, and kissed her down onto her back.

Their bodies connected in a long line of hot skin, her legs spreading instinctively to welcome him in. Shifting slightly to one hip, she felt him, hard and needy, land in just the right spot. Her body arched against his as a wild clash of emotions and craving crashed through her.

He felt it too. His hips jerked against hers, pinning all that hardness even closer against the sensitive area between her legs. Looking down at her, he drew a sharp breath. "Don't you want to take this slow?"

How could she know when she'd never done this before? She was only reacting to her body's need, its impulses. She wrapped her legs around his waist and his erection nudged past her slick folds, making her gasp at the sensation. Her hips moved on their own accord, rocking against him. "I don't think so."

He moaned low in his throat, vibrating his chest and hers. She rocked again, wanting him to lose control like she was. Willing him to stop thinking and let his body do what it wanted to her.

Running her hands down his back, she cupped his butt cheeks and pressed them down. At the same time, she arched her lower body once more into his.

"Anya—"

But it was too late. They were at the wall, his erection ready to breach. All she had to do was press a little harder and...

Pain, low and intense, hit her. She bit her lower lip. *Don't cry, don't cry, don't cry.*

Ryan kissed her, caressing her lips with a slow, sweet pressure. He didn't move except for the kiss, teasing her mouth with his tongue. As she focused on his warm lips and met his tongue with her own, the pain between her legs subsided.

Relax. He's in control.

Ryan stroked her hair with one hand, his other hand fondling one of her breasts, massaging it, and tweaking her nipple.

It was her turn to moan.

A new pressure filled her. Ryan, plus her desire, building again at his ministrations. He nuzzled her neck, stroked her thighs, and soon she was moving her hips again. Small rocking motions that began to build. She needed more of him, needed him moving with her.

He said nothing, just looked into her eyes as he drew himself partially out, and slowly pushed himself back inside. There was a burning sensation, but pleasure too.

Pleasure she'd never felt before. Meeting his strokes, she held his intense gaze. He filled her up. Not just her body, but her heart. Her mind. Her very soul. This was what it felt like to fall in love.

A new urgency registered down below and Anya met Ryan's strokes with determination. Something was building inside her. She needed him in a whole new way.

He shifted his hips, one hand moving into the space between their lower bodies.

"What are you..."

"Trust me." His thumb slid between her folds and hit an extremely sensitive spot.

Anya gasped. Once, twice, three times, his thumb built its own rhythm, working in time with his long strokes. But before it made a fourth caress, she exploded in a flood of sensation, digging her heels into his butt and her nails into his back. "Ryan!"

He continued to move, taking her to the brink, and over it. Continuing to move inside her until her nerve endings were raw. Whispering in her ear. "Are you all right?"

In the height of the orgasm, all she could do was whisper too. "I love you."

Ryan hardened even more inside her, his whole body tensing. She could feel his heart pounding against her chest, and his breathing was fast. "Anya, I..."

He detonated, his whole body freezing for a second. Eyes closed, his face a fierce mask of both concentration and sheer joy. Anya's heart swelled. Along with it, her body once again shattered apart from happiness under him.

For long seconds afterwards, they held each other. Seconds turned to minutes. Ryan's dead weight on top of her pressed her into the hard metal beneath the blanket, but when he tried to shift off of her, Anya held him still. "Don't leave me."

His breath was warm on her ear. "Never."

37

RYAN CAME AWAKE WITH A START, heart pounding, and a riotous blaring noise going off next to his head.

The computer.

Shit.

Anya was on top of him, so when he tried to bolt upright, he didn't go far. At some point after their lovemaking, he'd shifted them both around so he was lying under her. And then, like a true idiot, he'd fallen asleep.

But, damn, he'd felt so blissed out, and combined with the past week of little sleep, and an overload of stress, he hadn't been able to keep his eyes open. Holding Anya after sex had been the best sleep aid in the world.

A red light was flashing in the far corner of the room. The noise—still blaring like a fire alarm—echoed off the glass and stone walls. Anya's eyes flew open, confusion and fear on her face. Forget the warning blare of the alarm. The look on her face was all it took to get his brain cells firing. It wasn't a computer raising a fuss.

Every computer in the room was going off. Every alarm in the bunker.

Which only meant one thing.

Nuclear attack.

That's not possible.

But as Ryan and Anya untangled their limbs and went for their clothes, still scattered around the floor, Ryan's logic argued with him. *Possible, not probable.*

That particular argument didn't make him feel better.

"Have they found us?" Anya yelled over the alarm. Her fingers trembled as she tried to button her pants.

Ryan shook his head, shoving his legs into his jeans. "Something's set off an attack alert. As if an attack is in progress." He had a good idea what that something—or someones, *thank you Conrad and Del*—might have been. "My guess, it's a false alarm, a distraction we can use, so we need to get out of here. Now."

Anya pulled his sweater over her head. "What about my grandmother?"

Cad that he was, he'd been so caught up in making Anya's first sexual experience the best it could be under the circumstances, he'd forgotten all about the older woman. "Right. Okay."

Brilliant. Just brilliant. Tossing on his shirt, he slipped his feet into his shoes and scanned his memory for possible options. The gun went into the waistline at the small of his back. "Come with me." Grabbing Anya's hand, he tugged her after him.

Just off the communications room was a weapons room. Most of the inventory had been stripped, but there were still a few handguns, AK47s, and a ton of hand grenades. What the hell would you use a hand grenade for in an underground bunker?

He led Anya past the walls and crates, around a corner, and pointed to a room filled with rows of lockers. During the height of Stalin's paranoia, those lockers had held clothes for thousands of military personnel.

If he'd taken the time to scout deeper into the tunnels instead of having sex with Anya, Ryan might have found the actual barracks. As it was, he'd have to work with what he had. "Ivanov's probably stripped your grandmother of most of her clothes, so try to find a sweater, a coat, anything that'll cover her against the elements. There should be some items in those lockers. I'll be back in a minute."

"Where are you going?"

"We need supplies. Food, weapons, money."

"There's money down here?"

Not per se, but he was sure he could sell a gun or two topside and make enough to get them traveling funds. "Do you have your passport?"

Her face took on that *oh, shit* look. "I left it in my room."

He kissed her before she could bite her bottom lip, and added another weapon to sell to his mental checklist of supplies.

"All that stuff, and more, is in Ivanov's new bunker. Why can't we grab some from there?"

"I'm not sure how to get to that section, and it's probably guarded, especially now after the terrorist attack. Our best bet is to find what we can here."

She nodded, and he took off for the kitchen.

There, he found a military rucksack shoved behind the shelving unit stocked with more MREs. It was filthy, so he shook it out, dust and dirt filling the air. He swiftly cleared an entire shelf with his arm, guiding the canned meat and silver bags into the rucksack. There was no portable water, which sucked, but at least they'd have some food.

Gathering up a few guns and a couple of hand grenades was easy. Locating ammunition, more of a challenge. A few 9x19mm armor-piercing bullets lay scattered behind a garbage can. No doubt a guard had been reloading his gun clip and dropped them. Ryan pocketed the bullets, since they'd work in his GSh 18, but that was it. No clips, no other bullets, nothing.

He rubbed his forehead where a headache was setting up, thanks to the blaring alarms and the tension hardening every muscle in his body in a flight or fight instinct. The cold, hard fact of the matter was, guns were easy to come by anywhere in Europe. Ammunition was the real gold. Sure, he could still get a few rubles for the weapons, but not enough to buy fake IDs and new passports. Not good ones anyway.

Conrad, you better still have Josh and Del waiting for me on the other side of this godforsaken hole.

The trick was, while Del and Josh could both forge documents, it would take time and proper supplies. And did he really want to involve them in this going-down-in-flames project?

No. He wouldn't do that to either man. This was his mess. He would clean it up.

From the locker room, he heard banging and swearing over the alarm siren. Yanking a couple of mean-looking daggers from a display, he tossed them in his rucksack. Then he went to find Anya.

What a crappy interruption to his best laid plans to tell her the truth. About him, about his feelings for her. He didn't want to be in love with her—wasn't even sure this was love, but it sure felt better than anything he'd ever had with a woman— and maybe he wasn't. Maybe this was all a stress-fueled infatuation. Didn't matter. Whatever it was, he wanted more. He wanted it to last forever. If it didn't—and it probably wouldn't— he still wanted every second with her he could get.

Dozens of lockers stood open. Here and there, clothing and shoes dotted the benches and floor. "Anya?" he called over the noise.

"Here!"

In the back corner at the last row of lockers, he found her. Or what he thought was her.

She was wearing his coat, but had added an ushanka hat, the type with fur lining and earflaps that buttoned on top when the wearer wanted them out of the way. She tossed a woolen military jacket, complete with two rows of gold buttons down the front, at him, and then another ushanka. Soviet left overs, like the computers in the other room.

Grabbing a pile of clothes from the bench behind her, she showed him her bounty. "These should keep us all warm."

The hat was too big for her and canted to one side. She had the ear flaps down to try and drown out the alarm. Ryan put on the hat she'd given him, cinched up the rucksack, and hefted it over his shoulder. "Let's go find Grams."

According to his mental map, there were only the three main tunnels under Kremlin Palace. They mirrored the public subway tunnels on the northeastern side of Moscow.

But what they hadn't seen nagged at him. All the stuff Anya had told him about. The lab Ivanov had built, his personal quarters, a high-tech communication center filled with equipment. Where was all that?

Ryan heaved the massive door to Stalin's room open, peered inside. Once the place had been decadent. Now it was a sad relic, containing a bedroom, bathroom, and office, the once expensive furnishings covered in dirt and mold. The prison cells were reportedly somewhere nearby, and if Ryan was thinking straight, he figured Ivanov's presidential bunker was too.

He shifted the rucksack farther up on his shoulder. "Look for a secret panel," he told Anya, already feeling along the doorjamb. "Like in the Palace."

Without hesitation, she went to work, sliding her hands over every surface she could reach.

Come on, come on. Time was running out, and they still had to locate Natasha and break her out of whatever cell she was in. With all the alarms going off, it wouldn't be long before Ivanov's guards came to investigate, even if they had their hands full in the Palace.

Anya disappeared into the bathroom while Ryan went into the walk-in closet. He was shoving empty hangers and left-over clothes out of the way when he heard her call his name. Her voice held a definite strain, pinging his shit meter. Had she found something?

God, he hoped she hadn't stumbled onto her dead grandmother.

She called again. "Ryan! I need you."

And indeed, she did.

The moment he rounded the corner and ran into the bath-room, he knew something was wrong. She stood in front of a floor-to-ceiling armoire. One door was open, and Ryan could see it led to another room, Anya blocking the view. Her hat now sat perfectly centered on her head, but her eyes were wide as saucers, and her face was even paler than normal.

The underground alarm stopped without warning, and in the sudden silence, Ryan's ears rang with a blaring echo. "Anya? What is it?"

"Not what." She swallowed visibly. "Who."

Ryan reached for the gun in the hollow of his back, but a familiar, sadistic voice halted his movement.

"Mr. Jones." Ivanov pushed Anya forward. and she staggered before righting herself. Ivanov followed, stepping out of the fake armoire and pointing a fat, black gun at the base of her skull. "Did you think I would let a common American take my property and destroy my plans for the future?"

Ryan's shit meter blew.

38

ANYA DREW A SHAKY BREATH, locking her knees, and forcing her eyes to convey to Ryan that she was okay.

She was not okay. Not when Ivanov, *the bastard*, was jamming a gun into the back of her head. Not when they were so close to finally finding Grams and escaping.

And not when she felt a small trickle of warm blood under her shirt.

I'm fine, she conveyed to Ryan with her eyes, swallowing past the tightness in her throat. Whatever she did, she had to make him believe she was not freaking out like a girl.

Which was exactly what she was doing.

Ryan's gaze was as steady as always. A glint of anger, but no fear. No hesitation. Not even the slightest flicker of anxiety. Mr. Calm, Cool, and Drop Dead Dangerous was still in control.

He won't let Ivanov hurt me.

The last few days had been the worst of her life. Almost paralyzing fear, vexing guilt, harrowing revelations. Never had she imagined how bad things could get, and it was an experience she never wanted to repeat. For years, she'd wished she could erase the genes in her blood that made her an heir to

Russian royalty. The genes that made her blood not clot properly. All of it. The genes, the name, and all her imperfections. If she could just erase them all, life would never have taken this horrendous turn of events.

But she couldn't erase any of it. She was a Romanov. She was a Russian princess. She had imperfections—some visible, others not—and Ryan had looked past every one of them. He was her rock. She wouldn't let him down.

Show no weakness. No cowardice. This was her life, and she would meet it head on.

For Ryan. For Grams. For my parents.

Calling up her Grand Duchess façade, Anya whirled around and faced Ivanov, straightening her spine and arching a brow. "What the hell are you doing, Maxim?"

The barrel of the gun was now a breath away from her mouth. She heard Ryan's sharp intake of breath.

Ivanov reared back in surprise, but kept the gun trained on her face. His eyes narrowed. "How dare you lower yourself to run off with an American spy."

He knew who Ryan really was. Time for a big fat lie. "I wasn't running off with him, you idiot. I was playing him." She took a fortifying breath, and scrambled to come up with a convincing story. Which wasn't easy with a loaded gun pointed at her mouth, especially when she could smell liquor on Ivanov's breath, and see his hand tremble ever so slightly. "He's not just any spy. He's one who could cause a huge international incident. I brought him down here to keep him from leaving the Kremlin with all of our secrets. He knows everything. About you. About your cabinet. About the people you've had murdered in order to secure your place as president."

So lame, but it was the best she could do, and mentioning Ivanov's Achilles heel made him take a step back. All she needed was to throw his suspicion off her for a moment and make him think she was on his side. She'd done it before, she could do it again.

Even with an evil-looking gun aimed at her face.

"Do you really think I would give up becoming first lady of Russia for..." Anya glanced back at Ryan and gave a dismissive snort. "Him?"

A frown creased Ivanov's brow. "You're lying."

Bluffing wasn't her strongest suit. However, the gun lowered to her chin, and his voice held less certainty.

"What can I do to prove it to you?" She held her ground, this time trying to convey sincerity with her eyes. "I know what my grandmother did during the Cold War. Why you brought her here and won't let me see her. I know my parents were also traitors, and you had to take them out. I want to make amends for my family's deceptions and betrayals. Tell me what I can do to prove my loyalty to you and my country."

Ivanov's gaze cut to Ryan, back to her, seeming to ponder her offer.

She said the first thing that came to her. "Give me the gun, and I'll shoot him for you."

Ivanov smiled a slow, malicious smile, and pointed the gun at her forehead.

Okay, maybe she'd pushed her bluffing skills a bit far. "Fine." She threw her hands up in the air as if in surrender. "We could have it all, Maxim. We could rule Russia and bring it back to a state of purity. We could make our country the greatest nation in the world from the inside out. But if you want to kill me here and now and throw all of that away?" She glared at him. "You're the ultimate fool, and I'm ashamed I gave you so much credit."

The room swam, and Anya blinked hard to clear her vision. *I will not pass out.*

Ivanov didn't speak, only searched her face as if reading her mind. Then he lowered the gun and motioned for her to come toward him. He held out his empty hand to her.

He believes me! Anya flashed him her biggest smile yet and reached for his hand. She had to cross in front of him to grab it. *Now, Ryan.*

But as Ivanov tucked her into his side, and his alcohol and sweat scent filled her nostrils, she turned to find Ryan still standing nonchalantly in front of them, as if he didn't have a care in the world.

His gaze stayed on Ivanov, hard as stone now. He wouldn't look at her. Her heart slipped around inside her chest as if it had come unhinged. He didn't really believe her lies, did he?

She wanted desperately to go to him. To say his name. Anything to get him to look at her so she could wink at him. Let him know she was lying in order to buy both of them time and confuse Ivanov. He'd lowered the gun. If she could just get it away from him...

Ivanov's hand closed over her upper arm, tightening into a vise grip. He hugged her forcibly against his side. "You will prove your loyalty, Czarevna, by doing everything I say." He raised the gun once more. This time, the black barrel pointed at Ryan's chest. "But I will be the one to shoot this spy."

Her body moved before her brain registered Ivanov pressing the trigger. She grabbed his hand, but it was too late.

The gun fired. Ryan's body jerked and spun to the right.

As Anya screamed his name, he went down.

39

Son of a bitch, *that hurt.*

Ryan lay on his stomach on the floor of the ruined bathroom, blood running across the concrete in a steady flow underneath him. He ignored it, keeping his eyes closed and playing possum, in hopes Ivanov would think he was mortally wounded. That he was no longer in the game. No longer an issue.

The bullet had struck between his right shoulder and collar bone, and *damn it all to hell*, the pain was brutal. He'd spun to the right trying to avoid it, and as luck would have it, it missed his chest. Anya was partially to thank for that. She never stopped surprising him. One minute she was pretending she was double crossing him. The next, she was attacking Ivanov to save his ass.

Definitely keeping her away from Conrad. If I don't, he'll recruit her for his spy army.

The random, untimely thought almost made him laugh. He tamped down the temptation, refocusing on the pain to clear his head. Losing a little blood was no reason to get delirious.

His quick reflexes had landed him a prize. As he'd twisted away from Ivanov and Anya, he'd drawn the gun from his waistband with his right hand, and slid it around to his midsection before belly flopping to the floor. Now as he pretended to be dead, the gun dug uncomfortably into his stomach. He'd love to roll over, point the thing at Ivanov's head, and pull the trigger, but he only had two bullets. His right arm—his shooting arm—was out of commission, folded under him and useless from the wound. He was trained to shoot with either hand, but even after constant drills at the range, his left was less precise.

With Anya still in danger of getting between him and Ivanov, now was no time for imprecision.

Behind him, she was screaming at Ivanov in a mixture of English and Russian. She must have been giving him hell with her fists, and maybe feet, because Ryan heard the sound of punches and grunts from Ivanov. Finally, his deep voice boomed off the bathroom's tile walls as he told her shut up in Russian. The command was followed by the distinct sound of his hand hitting her flesh.

Ryan ground his teeth. Anger like he'd never experienced roared through him. Every atom in his body demanded he get up and beat the hell out of Russia's president, but logic laughed at the idea. No matter how much he wanted to kill Ivanov, the only thing he'd end up doing was killing himself. The way to save Anya was to play dead.

So he played dead.

Anya's screaming didn't subside after Ivanov's hit. If anything, she was more belligerent, and once again, Ryan found himself wanting to laugh. It was *so* not funny, but she was incredible, so alive and unafraid of anything. She seemed to be making up Russian curse words he'd never heard before. His heart swelled with pride. He'd never known a woman like her. Even other spies couldn't hold a candle to her fearlessness and grit.

He cracked one eye, stealing a glance at the mirror on the wall across from him. Ivanov had pushed Anya up against the wall, and all Ryan could see in the mirror was the back of the man's head and his bulky shoulders. Was he still holding the gun? Was Anya's distraction enough to warrant Ryan freeing his weapon and taking the best shot he could?

Where was Andreev? Ivanov's body guards? There had to be more people than just the president running around down here. They had to have heard the gun shot.

Patience. He needed more intel before he took a shot at Ivanov. There was still a chance he could rescue Anya and her grandmother, and get all of them out of Moscow without killing anyone. Sure the odds were equal to a snowball's chance in hell, but if there was any possible way to keep from bringing even more shit down on his and Anya's heads, he had to take it.

Slap! Ivanov struck Anya again and Ryan cringed. This time, she fell silent, and it took every bit of willpower he possessed not to come off the floor and tackle the son of a bitch. In the mirror, he saw Ivanov grab her and shove her through the fake armoire into the hidden door.

The room fell silent and Ryan drew in a steadying breath.

Ivanov would be back. Or he would send one of his minions to make sure Ryan was dead, and if he wasn't, put a second bullet in him, this one in his head.

Easing off the floor, he gritted his teeth against the pain radiating through his chest and grabbed the gun with his left hand. Blood ran down his right arm, down his chest. His shirt, already soaked, stuck to his skin.

The room swam before he locked his knees and blinked away the fuzziness. He stood immobile, opening up all his senses, and tuning out the pain. He should find a way to stop the bleeding, but there wasn't time to do any major first aid, and he didn't want to set down the gun in order to pull a shirt out of the rucksack.

He took two steps toward the door, realized he was leaving a bloody trail, and stopped short. Damn, that was a lot of blood, no matter how much he wanted to deny it. Definitely had to do something to stop it.

Since his right arm and hand were useless, he had no choice but to set down the gun and root through the sack with his left. There on his knees, he found a cotton shirt and a wool cap and jammed both under his shirt, one in front over his pectoral and one in back over the bullet's exit wound. Then he wrapped his belt around his upper chest to help secure the padding, struggling and swearing under his breath at his lack of dexterity with his left hand. Every few seconds, he stopped to listen and watch the armoire's doorway. No one came back for him.

Sweating and dizzy from the exertion, he managed to get on his feet a few minutes later, gun in hand. Leaving the rucksack, he double checked the gun's chambered bullets, and staggered through the armoire's passageway.

The change in décor was startling. A night and day difference. Ryan stepped from the cold, abandoned bathroom into a brightly-lit, modern facility that mimicked the beautiful Russian subway system. High archways, marble tiles, and rail tracks that ran west from the heart of Moscow, east to the airport.

This was what Anya had told him about. A completely new bunker upgraded and equipped like a miniature Kremlin. Ivanov's secret quarters. The lab. The computer launchers for the nuclear weapons.

Natasha Romanov Radzoya was here.

Ryan looked right, then left. No sign of Anya or Ivanov. No sign of any train either. He'd have to walk.

Would Ivanov take Anya back to the Kremlin or deeper into

the modern side of the bunker?

Before he could curse himself for leaving his tablet in the abandoned computer room behind them, a scream echoed down the corridor from the east.

Anya.

Forget walking. It was time to run.

40

Ryan's dead. Anya's mind reeled against the knowledge, but she'd seen the bullet strike him in the chest. Saw him fall. Saw the gushing blood and how still he'd lain on the bathroom floor. No one could live after losing that much blood, could they?

She'd always dealt with the semantics of blood. The science of it. DNA, genes, diseases. Not the actual details surrounding its life-giving force.

As she spit her own blood out of her mouth—the split lip Ivanov had given her was already swelling—she knew it didn't matter. She could have been an ER doctor, trained in saving gunshot victims, and she still couldn't have saved Ryan from bleeding out in an abandoned bunker under the Kremlin.

Ivanov shoved her into a chair. They'd entered his modern computer command center surrounded by glass, the sliding door behind them making a sucking sound as it sealed them in. The room looked similar to some of the university classrooms Anya had studied in. Tiered seats in a half-circular layout. Only these seats boasted individual high-tech computers, monitors, and printers, and the only person sitting at a computer was Andreev.

His head was bandaged. She should have felt relieved she hadn't killed him. Instead she felt the opposite. She wished she *had* killed him. An awful, but nevertheless truthful fact.

An assortment of flatscreens hung on the far wall, a Russian flag on either side. Andreev wore a headset and pecked at keys on the keyboard under his fingertips. Every few seconds, he glanced up at the flatscreens, went back to his pecking. He sneered at her once, and then ignored her.

A dozen different images played out before them on the screens. Live shots of Moscow, the subway station, and various buildings around the Kremlin. Images of other countries' capitols as well. Anya recognized London, Paris and Washington D.C.

The game was up. She should have been worried, but she couldn't dredge up the emotional energy. She was numb. She'd played her last card, trying to convince Ivanov she was on his side, and it had failed. She wanted to cry. For Ryan, for Grams. For all of them.

But she wasn't a crier.

Sitting up straight, she willed the numbness to fill her body like she'd done when her parents had been killed. It was time to end the game. "What are we doing here?"

Ivanov strutted over to the wall of flatscreens, put his hands on his waist and studied them. He was wearing his military uniform, looking every bit the part of the crazy leader surveying the war field. "America is responsible for the terrorist bombings in the subway. We must retaliate."

"America?" Anya couldn't help snorting. God, she was tired. "Americans didn't bomb anything. The Chechens did. Ryan told me."

Ivanov whipped his head around to stare at her for a moment, as if the idea she knew anything about politics and terrorists was shocking. Then he narrowed his eyes, letting her know he didn't appreciate her second-guessing him, throwing Ryan, and his opinion, in his face.

He went back to studying the board as Andreev continued manipulating images on the screens. "The Americans have backed the Chechens and other militia groups since the fall of the Soviet Union in an attempt to weaken Russia. My predecessors may have ignored such blatant terrorism but I will not. How dare Pennington and Morrow come here under the guise of being allies while they are helping my enemies destroy my homeland? Any country that backs terrorism on Russian soil will be dealt with and dealt with harshly."

Downtown Manhattan appeared on a screen next to the one showing the White House. On the other side, a U.S. naval base appeared. Anya surged out of the chair, no longer able to stay numb. "You're going to start a war with America over a subway bombing? Are you crazy?"

Stupid question. Of course he was crazy. "You can't do that. Innocent people will be killed, both here and in America. Don't you understand? You're starting a war you can't win."

He whirled on her, thumped a fist on a nearby desk. "I will win. All I need is the code to override your father's password. I won't kill a few innocent Americans – I will destroy every last one of them."

The monster of her dreams surfaced behind his eyes. "What are you talking about?" she whispered. "What does my father have to do with this?"

Something off to the left caught Ivanov's attention. "Ah, here we are."

In the hall, Inga appeared. With her was an older woman, bowed over at the waist and barely shuffling along. Inga seemed to be supporting her. The woman's gray hair stuck out in all directions, and she appeared dirty and unkempt. As the room's security door slid open with a soft *whoosh*, Anya's heart dropped to her knees.

Grams.

"Oh, my God." She ran and caught her grandmother's arm as Natasha and Inga cleared the threshold. "Grams!"

Natasha raised her head and looked Anya in the eye. Bruises covered her face and Anya couldn't stop the small whimper of distress that passed her lips as she hugged her grandmother to her, careful not to squeeze too hard.

With Inga's help, they guided Natasha to a chair. "Anya." Natasha patted her cheek and smiled at her, and Anya's heart warmed. Grams was in horrible shape, but she was alive. *I never should have given up on her.*

"I'm so sorry," Anya said, holding her grandmother's hand. "I'm going to get you out of here. I promise."

"You shouldn't make promises you can't keep." Ivanov stood behind her, the gun again in his hand.

Grabbing Anya, he spun her away from Natasha and Inga, and pressed the barrel of the gun to her temple. "Tell me the code, Natasha, or your precious granddaughter dies here and now."

Natasha's smile fell. Her eyes went cold, hard, but Anya sensed her hesitancy to tell Ivanov what he wanted to know. Grams would never put Anya's life in danger, so the code had to be something that carried enormous consequences. It had to be the one thing that would start the war with America. "Don't tell him, Grams. Whatever the code is, *don't tell him.*"

Natasha's gaze never left Ivanov's face. "My granddaughter is a braver soldier than you, Ivanov. Braver and smarter. As I told you already, killing her parents was your first mistake. Killing her will be your last."

Ivanov hesitated. Anya didn't understand her grandmother's statement any more than the president did, but it seemed like a good idea to keep him talking rather than shooting.

"Why is this code so important? And why did my father have it?"

"Do you want to tell her?" Natasha asked, seeming to settle into the chair. "Or should I?"

She crossed one leg over the other, looking for the world like the elegant woman Anya had known all her life, rather than the beat-up and tormented prisoner Ivanov had tried to turn her into.

Pride swelled inside Anya's chest. If Natasha could be so calm and regal in this situation, she could too.

Ignoring the gun pointed at her head, she shifted to face Ivanov. "Tell me, Maxim. I have the right to know the truth before I die."

The use of his first name, or perhaps the pleading look in her eye, made him lower the gun. He didn't release her, and she feared if she made one wrong move, he'd kill her on the spot. So she held still, held her ground. Willed him to start talking.

"Your father was in charge of *Prometheus*, a project to convert the launch systems from physical keys to computer codes back in the 1990s." Ivanov's gaze never left hers, but he wasn't seeing her any more. "The set of defense missiles protecting Moscow were some of the first to be converted. It all appeared to be spec. He set them up, converted their launch systems to an entirely encrypted and encoded system like the Americans had. They could only be launched by the president. Only, he inserted a backdoor code no one knew about at first. When I tried to upgrade his system, my engineers discovered that the defense missiles in Level A-155 will not launch unless that backdoor code is initialized."

Anya glanced at her grandmother. "Backdoor code?"

Natasha smiled. "A secret way of bypassing normal authentication. The code is like a password that opens up a program. A program that initializes the missiles."

She shifted on the chair, her face serious once more. "The

potential for nuclear war frightened your father, like it does all rational people. The Cold War was over, but the nuclear arms race was still going strong. He was torn about what he was doing, making it even easier for one man to start a nuclear war." She met Anya's gaze. "He had a daughter. A daughter he wanted to grow up and have her own kids without the threat of nuclear annihilation hanging over their heads."

Ivanov exploded in anger. "He had no right to tie the government's hands! To put us all in danger."

"He wasn't a power-hungry politician, Ivanov. He was a father, a son, a husband before he was a cabinet member. Things you'll never understand. He loved this country. *Truly* loved it."

"He was an abomination to Russia. A traitor, just like you. He died by my hand and you will too."

Natasha looked as tired as Anya felt. "Then you and Moscow will continue to be vulnerable, because I'm the only one who has the code now, and I will never, ever give it to you. 'Mankind must put an end to war, or war will put an end to mankind.'"

"How dare you quote that bastard Kennedy."

Ivanov moved, raising the gun as if to hit Natasha. Anya stepped between them, braced herself against the strike. "All these years, Moscow has been unprotected from a nuclear attack?"

He stayed the weapon. "Of course not. We have built other defensive missile shields."

"But those contain normal warheads, not nuclear ones," Natasha said. "They're designed for short-range interception. The last defense against nuclear annihilation. The ones your father worked on, Anya, are long-range ICBMs buried in silos surrounding Moscow and St. Petersburg. They're the forerunners of *Satan,* the one-hundred-ton warhead Ivanov has added to his arsenal this year. Those missiles are for attacking, not defending."

"My God." Anya took a step backwards, still shielding Natasha. Her grandmother's hand touched her back. Seeking reassurance or giving it? "You're making agreements with the United States and Britain to dismantle all these weapons, while behind their backs, you're building bigger ones?"

Natasha offered up more information. "Ivanov has listed the missiles as decommissioned since he realized they wouldn't work. If he can't obtain the code to initialize them, the missiles are worthless, but the rest of the world doesn't know that, do they Maxim?"

"Russia will be the leader of the world in this decade." Ivanov raised a fist and shook it at both of them. "And I will lead Russia."

Ivanov wasn't just the next Stalin or Hitler. He would take out anyone he perceived as a threat, regardless of the consequences. World domination was no joke to him.

Andreev's voice cut in. "Sir? We are ready."

Ivanov pointed his gun at Anya's forehead. "Tell me the code to Peter's backdoor, Natasha, or your granddaughter dies."

This was it. Anya reached back and grabbed Grams' hand.

"Forgive me, Anya," Natasha whispered. "I can't tell him."

"I'll tell you the code." The unexpected male voice made them jerk to look at the command center's door.

Ryan, bedraggled and bloody, wobbled precariously across the threshold. Inga gasped at the sight of him. Anya did the same. "Ryan?"

His calm, assessing gaze skimmed over her before it moved to the president. "Lower the gun, Ivanov, and I'll give you your precious code."

41

HE'S ALIVE.

He came for me.

Anya's knees buckled. Ryan was weaponless and appeared barely able to stand. And the blood...

His entire upper body was covered with it.

She swallowed hard and started to catapult herself across the room, wanting to throw her arms around him. As she stepped forward, her grandmother's hand tightened on hers, a death grip holding her back.

For a brief second, silence fell, Ryan's words registering with everyone. No one moved.

Ivanov hesitated, seeming to debate whether Ryan was telling the truth. Whether he should lower the gun.

He didn't.

"You need her," Ryan said, eyes steady on the Russian president. "For the code, and for the future of your homeland. Killing her would be a colossal mistake."

All eyes in the control room went to Ivanov. "What would you know about the code?"

"More than you. Let her come over here, to me, and I'll tell you."

The leader bristled, kept the gun trained on Anya's head. "Tell me, or I'll kill her."

Ryan drew a deep breath. Grams squeezed Anya's hand. In anticipation? Fear? Grams claimed she was the only who knew the code. Did Ryan actually know it or was he bluffing?

He was silent for so long, Anya bit her bottom lip. When Ivanov set the gun directly against her temple, Ryan raised a hand in a *wait* gesture.

"Her blood," he said, low and apologetic as he shot a glance at her. "The code is in her DNA."

As his words sunk in, Ivanov slowly lowered the gun. He either assumed Ryan was no threat in his current state, or the Russian president was as shocked as the rest of them at Ryan's announcement. Anya understood the words but not the meaning. How could her blood be the code Ivanov wanted to initialize the missiles?

Grams' voice, rigid and damning, came from behind Anya. "You're lying."

The acerbic tone of her voice got everyone's attention. Including Ryan's. He cut his gaze to Natasha, back to Ivanov, his steady demeanor leaving no doubt in Anya's mind he was indeed telling the truth. "You may be willing to risk Anya's life over this, Natasha, but I'm not."

Using Anya's hand as a crutch, Natasha leveraged her weight and stood. "I don't know who you are," she said to Ryan, "but you know nothing about my granddaughter."

Ryan's gaze flicked to Anya. "I know Peter Radzoya was a brilliant computer engineer with a penchant for writing unbreakable codes. His wife, Ekateirna was an accomplished geneticist. I got my hands on some information from the Agency about you and Peter, Natasha. I put that together with a few things Anya told me. The two of you came up with a plan to try and stop the use of nuclear weapons, didn't you? Peter and his wife hit on using a genetic fingerprint—a code as unique as the person—to guarantee it would take years, possibly decades, for anyone to figure out it was the key to Peter's backdoor setup. Then you went to work to manipulate Yeltsin into weapons reduction talks with America and Britain."

"The code has nothing to do with Anya," Natasha insisted.

"Yes, it does, and when you decided Anya's life was in danger if anyone found out about the source for the code, Peter and Ekateirna knew they had to come up with a different one. They were on their way to the lab to change it the night they were killed, weren't they?"

Snaking cold slithered up Anya's spine. Her grandmother didn't respond, didn't argue, and in that second, Anya knew it was true. All of it.

Her blood, with its defects, was a weapon of mass destruction.

Prometheus. The comic book antagonist her father loved. He'd given her all the issues the first Prometheus had appeared in, telling her the books held a secret. They'd been in Anya's school bag the night her parents were killed. When she'd slipped away from the car, her mother had insisted she take the bag with her. On their way to America, Grams and Anya had stopped in Switzerland, and Grams had taken the comics away, telling Anya she was too old for comic books now.

Was a copy of her gene map the secret hidden inside those books?

Her knees again threatened to go out. Her heart jumped around like a ferret caged inside her ribs. "How is that possible?"

Ryan's gaze stayed on Ivanov. "During the president's daily boring opening speeches at the summit, I did a little reading about genomes and DNA. Anya, your mother was a bright geneticist like you. Your father, a computer genius. Put the two of them together and..." His voice trailed off, letting her fill in the rest.

Ivanov chuckled, a low throated, humorless sound. "Even I would not have thought of such an ingenious code." He glanced at Anya with a new twisted glint in his eye. "Royal blood comes through once again."

Why was Ryan doing this? Telling such a secret to this madman? Giving Ivanov control over the missiles? Giving him control over her?

You may be willing to risk Anya's life over this, but I'm not.

Ryan knew Ivanov would put a bullet in her head if Grams didn't give him the code. Grams wouldn't do it, but Ryan would. Saving her...and damning them all in the long run if it were true.

Anya glared at Ryan. *How dare he—*

He winked.

At her.

So subtle, she almost missed it.

The wink was a message, but what? *Was* he bluffing? Buying time until the CIA arrived?

Andreev cleared his throat. "We have the tools we need here, sir. Your hand and retinol scans will activate the system. Her DNA—" he gave Anya a look of distaste "—will then unlock the system and initialize the missiles."

"I'm not your damn key to initializing anything." Anya jerked her hand out of her grandmother's. Bluffing or not, she wasn't going along with this plan. "And I'll never give you my blood."

Ivanov secured his gun in the waistband of his uniform. "I don't need blood, Czarina. I already have your genetic analysis."

"What?" Ryan said.

Anya echoed his shock. "How did you get that?"

"His doctor lifted your DNA," Natasha said, "when he treated your wound."

Ivanov snapped his fingers at Andreev. "Give me her medical file."

Andreev produced a black briefcase and withdrew a file from it, setting it on the desk.

Ivanov pointed at Ryan. "Remove him."

The prime minister took out a small black gun and aimed it at Ryan. "Move!"

Anya jumped forward to intercept Andreev, but Natasha once again grabbed hold of her, locking her arms around Anya in a bear hug. How could she be so strong after what she'd been through?

Ryan's eyes swung to Anya's and a flicker of doubt—the first she'd ever seen in them—appeared.

Ivanov opened the file and pointed his gun at her again. "Read the DNA sequence to me, Anya."

The smaller man gestured for Ryan to walk out of the center, and he took half a step backward. "Do as he says. Stay alive."

"Yes, Anya." Ivanov chuckled with a manic edge. "If you want to save your grandmother, read me the code."

"So you can kill millions of innocent people? *Poshol ti nahoo.*"

His laughter died at her derogatory use of Russian.

"President Ivanov," Inga stepped forward. "Surely, you're not going to set off nuclear weapons..."

The gun boomed and a round, red spot appeared on Inga's forehead. She froze, eyes wide for half a second before she toppled to the floor.

At the same moment, Ryan rushed Andreev. Whatever his plan, Anya had to help. She jerked forward, but Natasha hugged her tighter, refusing to let her go. Anya could have broken through her arm restraints, but didn't want to hurt her grandmother. "Let go, Grams."

"I won't," Natasha said.

The two men scuffled, Andreev throwing himself at Ryan and sending both of them out the door, and onto to the floor outside the center. Andreev's gun went off, echoing inside the room, and Anya flinched, screaming Ryan's name as the door whooshed shut, cutting them off.

Ivanov ran for the door, punching the computerized keypad on the wall to lock it. Just as he did, Ryan appeared on the other side of the glass, beating it with his left fist. His mouth moved, and Anya made out that he was saying her name.

Obviously, this was not part of his plan. She reached out a hand toward him, and squirmed in her grandmother's arms. He stepped back, raised a gun, and fired at the glass. Anya and Natasha ducked, but the glass didn't give.

Ivanov faced them, a smile lighting up his face. He tapped the glass with a fingernail. "Bulletproof. Fifty caliber armor piercing rounds cannot break it."

Ryan unloaded another bullet at Ivanov's head. A thin spider-web crack appeared but that was it.

Ivanov laughed. "Looks like it is just the three of us." He pointed his gun at Natasha. "Or maybe two."

Anya shoved Grams to the side as the gun discharged. Natasha hit the chair, knocking it over as she tumbled to the ground. The bullet missed her...

And nailed Anya squarely in her left hand, still in the air from pushing Natasha aside. The tiny missile ripped through flesh and bone, slamming Anya's hand back as it passed through and ricocheted off a nearby computer.

Out of the two of them, Grams had gotten the worst deal. Still, the burning in Anya's hand was intense. Using it to fuel her anger, she rushed Ivanov. If she was going to die, she was going down swinging.

Ivanov outweighed her by at least fifty pounds. She didn't

care. Even as his eyes widened and he raised the gun at her, she knocked it aside and jumped him. He stumbled backwards from the force of her entire weight slamming into him.

Together they hit the wall, the back of Ivanov's head smacking against the glass where Ryan had created the spider web. Anya caught a brief glimpse of Andreev lying on the ground, his head twisted at an odd angle. Ryan was nowhere in sight.

Had he left her?

Really, what could he do? The door was locked, the glass impenetrable.

Still, the realization stung as bad as the bullet wound in her hand. How could he leave her?

Anya shoved all thoughts of Ryan out of her head and aimed her thumbs at Ivanov's eye sockets. Her injured left hand didn't want to obey her commands, and Ivanov twisted his head to avoid her right, but she managed to smear blood across his face. Small victory.

He tried to hit her and the gun went off. Anya heard a startled intake of breath.

Grams.

Dropping off Ivanov, Anya hit the ground and whirled around to look for her grandmother. Natasha slid down the front of a desk, legs sprawled in front of her as blood leeched from between her fingers where they lay over her heart. "Anya?"

Anya scrambled to her grandmother's side. "Grams. Oh God." She pressed both hands over Natasha's chest. Blood gushed over their entwined fingers.

She eased her grandmother down to the floor, tears pooling in her eyes. "You're going to be okay. Everything's going to be okay."

Stupid words. Nothing was going to be okay. So much blood. Her grandmother was dying right in front of her eyes.

Natasha patted Anya's hand. Her eyes fluttered closed. "I'm...so...proud of you."

"Don't leave me, Grams. Open your eyes. You've got to stay with me."

"Your parents...would have been...so proud..."

"Grams, I need you. Please. Please don't leave me."

"Don't give him anything." Natasha gave her hand a solid squeeze. "I love you, Anya." Then she whispered, *"Vnooch-ka."* Granddaughter.

Anya squeezed back, tears pouring down her cheeks. "I love you, too, Grams."

Natasha's eyes fluttered closed one last time.

No, Grams.

Natasha drew one last shuddering breath.

Heavy footsteps sounded behind Anya. As grief overwhelmed her, another emotion rose with it. Cold rage.

There was nothing left. No one left. Just her and Ivanov.

Time to finish the game.

Anya raised her eyes to look Ivanov in the face. "Here." She held up her bleeding hand. "Give me the file."

42

GET TO ANYA.

That mantra looped over and over in Ryan's head, blocking out the pain and dizzyness. Logic, the one thing he'd always relied on, kept tacking on *before the bastard kills her.*

He had to ignore the logic voice because if he didn't...

Well, if he didn't, he'd fall to his knees and give up right there.

Logic had not been his friend inside the control room. Seeing Ivanov pointing his gun at Anya's head had screwed it up. Ryan's plan had been to distract Ivanov, get him to lower his weapon, and then take him out before he had the chance to hurt Anya or her grandmother.

Best laid plans...

He should have made something up about the code, instead of telling Ivanov the truth about Anya's blood. But he hadn't known Ivanov had a gene map of her blood. Ryan had figured he'd have to obtain one, and that would buy Anya— and Ryan — more time.

The only thing Ryan could hope for was that the president wasn't stupid. His fixation with genes and royalty made the truth the most effective weapon against him. Nuclear war or not, if Ivanov believed Anya was still worth something to him and the future royal dynasty of Russia, he'd think twice about killing her.

At least that's what Ryan had told himself. The reality was, in his light-headed state, he couldn't come up with a more believable story.

The lock on the command center door was computerized. Frustration had made him do stupid things, like shoot at the bullet-proof glass, but logic had finally come through and stopped him from sending a bullet into the keypad on the wall. Breaking the lock meant using his brain, not his brawn.

Sweat ran into his face as he stumbled into the old command center. The bulky monitors and antiquated keyboards called to him.

The spot where he'd made love to Anya mocked him.

Unhooking the nearest keyboard from its hard drive, he snugged it under his useless arm and turned to run back to the new GI 42. The sudden movement made the room swim and he lost his balance, knocking his bad shoulder into the wall. Good thing his arm was numb.

Get to Anya.

Before the bastard kills her.

Ryan pushed through the doorway and ran as fast as he could through the old presidential quarters, bathroom, and into the subway. His legs wobbled under him, and at times, darkness crowded his vision. He blinked away his fatigue, pushed through the pain, forced his legs to keep moving.

Get to Anya.

His shoe slipped in something slick and wet on the tiled floor of the subway, and he skated off balance for several seconds before falling on his ass. The keyboard shot out from under his arm and skittered across the floor. For a second, he just sat there, black spots dancing in front of his eyes, body racked with pain where it wasn't numb. He was so tired. If he could sit there for a minute—just one fucking minute—maybe he could recoup enough strength to get up again.

Anya doesn't have a minute. The world *doesn't have a minute.*

If Ivanov started a nuclear war, they were all going to die.

On a basic human level, he cared about that. But if he was being honest with himself, the only person he cared about in that moment was the princess.

His eyes closed for a second. Then he forced them open. Slapped his face with his good hand. Rolled onto his side and started crawling toward the dropped keyboard.

"Looking for this?"

Certain he was delusional from loss of blood, Ryan blinked twice at the sight of Josh Devons and another man in front of him. They were dressed in dark blue coveralls with Russian name badges sewn on them.

Devons held up the keyboard. He passed it to the other man and helped Ryan up. "Dude. You look like shit to the tenth."

He felt like shit to the nine hundredth. "What are you two doing here?"

"Saving your ass from the looks of things."

The man next to Devons nodded. "John Quick, Team Pegasus."

Get to Anya. Get to Anya. "I have to get back. Anya...is..."

He almost fainted. Devons caught him.

Quick grabbed his other arm. "Where's Natasha Radzoya?"

"East." He moved his head in the direction of the Ivanov's presidential bunker. He didn't have the energy to explain, nor did he have time. He shrugged off the men's steadying hands and grabbed the keyboard. "Follow me."

The keyboard safely under his arm once more, he pushed his legs into a run. Well, running was out of the question. It was more like a fast shuffle, but the rhythm worked with his mantra. Devons and Quick followed at his sides, ready to catch him if he fell.

"We brought you this." Devons held out a paper. "This ties into the Radzoya women and the ICBMs. Sounds crazy, but we think it's Anya's DNA code. And her gene sequence is also a launch code."

Ryan waved him off. "Already figured it out. It's a backdoor code—a password—that initializes the nukes."

Halfway there, an alarm went off, much like the one he and Anya had heard earlier in the old bunker. Lights in the tunnels flashed red, skittering and bouncing over the marble, stone, and metal. Ryan's pulse stopped for a moment.

This alarm, blaring like the Second Coming, meant only one thing.

He was too late.

Ivanov had declared war.

"I don't like the sound of that," Devons called over the blaring.

Ryan didn't bother to answer, a new rush of adrenaline fueling his legs. When they arrived at the glassed-walled command center and looked inside, Anya sat in a chair staring into space. She was covered with blood. Natasha was on the floor, dead by the looks of things. Quick swore under his breath.

Through the bullet-proof walls, Ryan heard a faint, computerized female voice counting down in Russian from thirty.

All the screens on the far walls showed nuclear silos around the outskirts of Moscow. Their steel doors were opening, launchers rising.

"Holy fucking cow," Devons said as he realized what was happening.

With his left hand, Ryan tore off the outer covering of the door's keypad. Breaking the code would take too long. He had to override it.

He jammed the end of the keyboard's cord into the USB outlet. Hit several keys and watched words file across the digital display. A warning.

Inside the room, Ivanov's head jerked up. Ryan met his gaze through the glass. The security system must have announced an intruder trying to override the lock.

Dropping the keyboard to the floor, Ryan wiped blood off his hands and fell to his knees in front of it. "Come on, come on," he pleaded with the keypad.

A moment later, he felt a heavy gaze boring into him. The Russian president ignored Devons and Quick and stared down at Ryan with a smile, egging him on. Ivanov's face was smeared with blood but Ryan couldn't see any visible facial wound. Was it Anya's blood?

Logic told him yes. She'd fought the bastard. Where was that hellcat now when he needed her?

Andreev's gun—the one he'd relieved the dead man of— was in the small of Ryan's back and fully loaded, but the minute he pressed the key to override the locking system and open the door, Ivanov would shoot him before he could pull the trigger.

"You two armed?" he asked Devons and Quick.

"We couldn't get weapons into the subway, but we have these." Devons drew a hammer from his coveralls. Quick drew a large, commercial-grade wrench.

Better than nothing.

Something happened inside the room. Ivanov looked over his shoulder at the screens on the wall. Ryan hit the last keystroke, and then paused a finger over the Russian word for Enter.

This was it.

Still distracted, Ivanov continued to look behind him, so Ryan drew the gun from his waistband and tapped the key with the end of the barrel.

Whoosh.

As the sliding door opened, Ryan raised the gun to fire at Ivanov, but the man was lying on the floor. Anya stood over him, chest heaving, and a fierce light in her eyes. The Russian flag, from pole to weighted bottom, was in her hand.

She'd belted the president with his own flag.

Tossing it on top of the unconscious man, she removed the gun from Ivanov's hand and palmed it like a pro. Her left hand was dripping blood all over the floor. "We have to stop the launch. I rearranged the code when I read it to him, but he figured out what I was doing and entered it himself."

As if to punctuate her words, the computerized female voice came from the speakers overhead, still counting down in Russian, "*Twenty.*"

Ryan staggered to his feet, stepped over the unconscious president, and hugged Anya to him. He buried his nose in her hair, but she pulled back, grabbing his arm to steady him as she led him to the main computer. "Can you stop it?"

"*Nineteen.*"

"Of course," Ryan lied. They only had a few seconds before the whole world changed. He wanted to spend those last few seconds holding her. Telling her that he loved her.

"*Eighteen.*"

Instead, he had to save the world.

And he had no flippin' idea how to override an ICBM launch program. Where was Del when you needed a super geek?

"*Seventeen.*"

His left hand flew across the keys even before he fully sat down, looking for any way to get inside the program. Surprise, surprise, like most of the modern world, it ran on a Windows based system. An extremely high-tech, highly-encrypted system, running on layers of Russian passwords that consisted of codenames and biometric scans.

"*Sixteen.*"

For the next few seconds, he worked at getting behind the program, finding some kind of administration log-in, password or other config system he could override. The alarm continued to wail, lights continued to flash. The system continued to count down.

"*Twelve.*"

He started to admit he couldn't do it, but when he looked up into Anya's eyes—as well as Devon's and Quick's—and saw confidence shining in them, he swallowed the truth. They all believed in him. Believed he could pull off a miracle.

"*Eleven.*"

"Get away from that computer!"

Anya whirled around, and Ryan saw Ivanov was on his feet, staggering toward them.

"*Ten.*"

What did Conrad always say? *When the shit gets too deep, pull the plug.*

Unfortunately, pulling the computer's plug wasn't that simple. And now Ivanov was once again getting in the way.

"*Nine.*"

Devons raised his hammer, but Anya stayed his arm, looked at Ryan. "You stop the launch. I'll take care of Ivanov."

The hellcat was back. She raised the gun and pointed Ivanov's own weapon at his head. "You killed my parents. You killed my grandmother."

"*Eight.*"

Windows was the easiest software in the world to hack for passwords. Ryan found the start menu, clicked shutdown. Miracle of miracles a window popped up and asked him what he wanted to do. Shut down or restart.

"*Seven.*"

Ivanov stopped in his tracks. Egomaniac that he was, he was smart enough to save his own skin. "I did what I had to for Russia."

"*Six.*"

Ryan hit restart. The system balked. He hit the F8 key. Windows took him to a safe mode startup screen.

Anya fingered the trigger on the gun. "Russia, my ass. You did this for yourself."

"*Five.*"

Control panel. User accounts.

Come on, come on.

Ryan searched the passwords.

"*Four.*"

There was no termination password, and he didn't have time to type in all the different passwords to find one that would override the system.

"*Three.*"

Pull the plug. But how? Blow up the computer? Remove the mother board? He grabbed the CPU. Screws held the protective plates in place.

"*Two.*"

"How do we stop the launch?" Anya demanded from Ivanov. A lump had appeared on the side of his head above his ear. "Tell us!"

"You can't stop it."

A dozen nuclear missiles sat locked and loaded for launch. Anya huffed out a heavy sigh, face scrunched in frustration.

"*One.*"

The screen in front of Ryan went to black. A DOS screen appeared. A screen with one directive. One beautiful Russian directive.

Prervat?

Abort?

Someone—probably the original programmer, Peter Radzoya—had had the good sense to give the president an out in case he changed his mind.

Ryan typed *DA. YES.* Windows took over again. A new screen appeared.

Stunned, he could only stare at the words as he mentally translated them.

Bioscanner confirmation needed. Twenty seconds to launch.

The counter flipped to twenty. The disembodied female voice started a new countdown.

Damn it. Ryan slapped the desktop.

Anya's gaze darted between him, Ivanov, and the screens on the far wall. "What happened? Did you stop it?"

The computer clock continued counting down. "Not yet. The bioscanner wants confirmation to abort."

"What kind of confirmation?"

"Fingerprints? Retina? I don't know."

Anya kept the gun trained on Ivanov as she scooted backwards toward the bioscanner. An outline of a hand was lit on the glass. She wiped her injured hand on her pants, laid in the scanner, and used the gun to depress a button. The scanner made noises and began working.

It only took a few seconds for it to process, but nothing changed on the screen in front of him. There was only six seconds until launch. "It didn't work."

"Damn it." She looked at her hand. "Does it need my genetic code, rather than my fingerprints?"

Ivanov chuckled in that condescending manner he had. "I'm the only one who can stop the launch." He waggled his fingers at them. "And I will never stop it."

Ivanov's fingerprints? Ryan doubted it would be that easy, but he was the president.

Anya laughed, a hysterical laugh full of frustration. "Of course. It's your fingerprints that it needs." Her hand firmed on the gun. "Put your hand on that scanner."

The Russian president flipped her the bird.

Anya stilled. Narrowed her eyes.

"Aim for his stomach," Ryan advised. "Bigger target. Plus the bioscanner reads for a pulse along with the fingerprint. Kill him and it won't work."

Without so much as blinking, she did as he instructed. She pulled the trigger.

The president's body jerked, and he stumbled backwards several feet before toppling to the floor. Blood oozed from his stomach and he cried out, clutching at the wound and rolling over. He came up on hands and knees, but went down again when Devons kicked him. Anya grabbed one arm and Devons grabbed the other. Together, they pulled Ivanov across the floor to the scanner.

Muscling him around wasn't easy. He fought them until Ryan knocked him in the head with the butt of his gun. Anya raised his arm, and Ryan and Devons shoved on his body until they managed to get his hand on the scanner to read his fingerprints.

The scanner hummed to life, read what it needed. Asked for a retinal scan.

They all exchanged a frustrated glance. Quick grabbed Ivanov by his short hair, Devons helped Ryan haul the man's face up to the scanner. A red line moved from top to bottom.

"Did it work?" Quick yelled over the alarms.

Ryan let Ivanov's body slump to the ground, the last of his own strength giving out. He stumbled to the chair, missed grabbing the back of it, and went down.

But not before he saw the screen.

Launch aborted.

The female voice stopped in mid-count. The alarm died away.

"Ryan!" Anya was by his side in an instant, her cool hands on his face. He smiled up at her as black shadows encroached on the edges of his vision.

She returned his smile, even though her brows scrunched

together in concern. "Did you learn that at the CIA? How to stop a nuclear missile launch?"

"YouTube."

Her brows smoothed out and she laughed.

The shadows grew bigger. The numbness in his chest began to spread. "Don't talk about what happened here to anyone but Conrad Flynn, okay? Nobody but him."

She brushed some hair from his forehead. "Conrad Flynn?"

"Solomon. Don't talk to anyone else, but tell him everything."

"Okay. Don't worry. I'll get you to a doctor. I'll fix this..." She glanced around at Devons and Quick, and did one of those deep intakes of breath. "I'll fix everything."

Before he could tell her he loved her, she kissed his lips.

Soft, warm, and the sweetest lips he'd ever kissed, he closed his eyes.

Anya was okay.

43

Don't die. Don't die. Don't die.

Anya watched Ryan's chest rise and fall. He was breathing. Shallow, but steady.

Always steady. Even unconscious, he was a rock of steadfast reassurance.

"Okay, Ryan Jones, or whatever your real name is, I'll make you a deal. You keep breathing, and I'll get us out of here."

She nodded at him as if he'd answered her. He was breathing, but he looked like hell. He was too pale for her liking, and his skin was cold.

The men who'd come back with Ryan tried to move her out of the way. She refused to let go of him.

The one that looked like a football player patted her shoulder and winked. She remembered him from the cabin in the woods. "Nice job. You did good. Great, actually. No wonder Smitty went off the reservation for you."

Smitty? Another name to add to her list. "Can you help him?"

"I can." The other man detached her hand from Ryan's with a gentle touch. "My name's John Quick. I've had extensive emergency medical training. We need to stop his bleeding and find something to cover him with to conserve his body heat. Think you can find a blanket?"

Anya stood and looked around. Her hand was bleeding profusely, and she needed to wrap it. She walked over and snatched up the Russian flag lying on the ground, ripped it from the pole. It was too silky and satiny to absorb blood, but it would work as a blanket. She pushed Quick out of the way so she could drape it over Ryan.

He and the football player exchanged a glance that said she was losing it, but she didn't care. She bent down and tucked the flag around Ryan's lifeless body. "Now what?"

Mr. Football drew her aside. "You're going into shock. We need to wrap your hand and warm you up too."

Shock. She'd been in shock mentally since this all began. Grabbing the other flag, she jerked it off the pole, and wrapped it around her shoulders. "Just worry about Ryan, okay?"

Quick used a chair to elevate Ryan's feet. "Find something to bandage your hand and stop the bleeding."

Anya's hat lay on the floor where it had fallen earlier. She took Ivanov's dirk from his belt, cut off the earflaps and chin straps. Then she went to work fashioning a padded tourniquet around her hand. A low buzzing set up shop in her ears, either a phantom echo from the alarm or she was going to faint.

I will not pass out.

One wooly earflap went on her palm, the other on top of her hand. She snapped the ends of the chin straps together, wrapped them around the whole concoction, and tied the ends using her teeth and right hand.

Natasha lay nearby. Anya scooted to her side, kissed her cheek, and smoothed back her hair. Took the flag and draped it over her body as she silently said a prayer for her grandmother's soul.

A set of phones hung on the back wall. Anya had no idea

who to call or even how to dial out. Ivanov lay on the floor unmoving. He was breathing, but losing a lot of blood from his stomach wound. He could bleed out for all she cared, but the fastest way to get Ryan to a hospital was to use Ivanov. Fighting a wave of dizziness, she made it to the bank of phones, picked up the first receiver and considered the keypad.

A male voice started speaking in her ear before she could figure what to dial. Fast, clipped Russian. Obviously, the man on the other end was topside in the Kremlin and could get her what she needed. "President Ivanov has been shot. He needs immediate emergency care. You'll find him in the new presidential bunker command center under the Palace."

There a slight pause on the other end, then she heard the man speaking to someone else before he came back on the phone with her. He continued to speak in rapid Russian sentences, so she spoke over him with a simple command. "Just hurry or he'll be dead before you get here."

As she hung up the phone, her body shook with exhaustion. Her eyelids drooped, too heavy to hold up. Her feet felt like hundred pound weights as she dragged herself back over to Ryan. She sat on the floor next to him and watched his chest rise and fall as Quick and the football player added another bandage over his chest wound. The steady rhythm of Ryan's breathing comforted her, and her eyelids threatened to close.

Still shaking, she lay as close to Ryan as she could get. It wasn't close enough, but she could reach out and touch his hair. The thought of sleep was tempting, but she forced herself to stay awake. If she fell asleep, he might die on her.

"Even after all of this, we don't know each other very well," she told him, ignoring the looks the other two men gave her. "So how about I tell you a few facts you might want to know? Like, I never had a dog growing up, and I really wanted one. You know, nothing fancy, no pure breed. Just a mutt from the shelter. A good dog with a scruffy face and silly ears. Did you ever have a dog growing up?"

Of course, he didn't reply, but Anya kept talking anyway. "So somehow you figured out that *One Thousand and One Nights* is my favorite book, but do you know why? It was my mother's favorite. I stole her copy when I was ten and read it straight through. Some of it, I didn't understand, but there were many great stories I did understand. Tragedies, comedies, romances."

Anya slid around so her head was next to Ryan's. "Help's on the way, but while we wait, how about I tell you one of those stories? Aladdin? Ali Baba? I bet you're a Sinbad fan."

She hadn't gotten far in the story before a group of men and women flooded the command center. Soldiers.security guards, Ivanov's personal emergency response team, and a handful of cabinet members. As they rushed in, saw the president and other bodies scattered over the floor, they yelled questions at her, and shoved Ryan's friends to the ground.

The guards immediately began to place them under arrest. A man who'd introduced himself as Deputy Prime Minister Yuri Barchai during the ceremonies stopped the guards and started talking. In Russian, he told the cabinet members he'd suspected Ivanov and Andreev had hatched a plan to start a nuclear war and blame it on the Americans. He said more stuff, too, but Anya found it hard to focus on anything until she heard him say she was innocent. That it was their job now to protect her.

The other cabinet members blustered and shouted, accusing Barchai of treason, and her of suspected treason as well. Barchai kept talking, continuing to smooth things over, and she ran interference as best she could. Each time someone asked her what had happened, she diverted their attention to Ryan. "Please, he needs to go to a hospital."

One of the medical team examined Anya's host of injuries while the others started IV's on Ryan and Ivanov, and put them on gurneys in order to transport them upstairs. Ivanov was wheeled out first, a host of guards surrounding him. Next to go was Ryan. Anya shoved a penlight out of her face, ignoring the EMT's sound of distress, and shrugged off the blanket the woman had thrown over her shoulders. "I have to go with him."

Several of the cabinet members exchanged glances. Barchai gave a nod, and said he would personally accompany her. The EMT protested, saying Anya was in shock and needed to have an IV and be gurnied upstairs like Ivanov and Ryan. Quick spoke up his agreement, and Anya glared at him.

"I'm going with Ryan."

Barchai took her elbow and helped her up. No further words were spoken, two soldiers falling into step behind them as they exited the command center. The Russian EMT grabbed her equipment and followed. So did both of Ryan's friends.

Barchai was a nervous man, but kind. He offered his sympathies for her grandmother. Asked if she would like him to accompany her to the hospital. Several times as they walked, Anya grew dizzy and had to stop. "I believe you do need medical attention," he said as he steadied her.

She wanted to trust him. Wanted to believe someone could be nice to her without wanting something in return.

But she didn't.

"I have to make sure Ryan gets to the hospital. That he's okay."

If Barchai was surprised that she didn't express concern for his president, he hid it well. "I give you my word as a Russian, I will make sure he receives the best care in Moscow."

The word of a Russian didn't mean much to her at the moment.

They were in the tunnel headed up. The ever-increasing slope pushed her already weak legs to the breaking point. "If anything happens to him..." Anya stopped and leaned against the tunnel's wall. Her heart pounded, and she felt lightheaded. "I will hold you personally responsible."

He gave Anya a troubled look. The EMT stepped forward, ignoring the drama. "You are in shock," she said in English. "If you do not allow me treat you, you will not be around to kick his ass if he fails."

John Quick nodded his head in agreement.

Anya couldn't fight it any longer. She sank down to the tunnel floor, damning her blood disorder, Ivanov, and anyone else she could think to damn. The EMT worked efficiently, though, and had an IV in her arm in under a minute. She gave her a shot of something and bandaged the wound in her hand. Since there was no gurney, Ryan's friends each took one of her arms, and along with Barchai, walked her through the last leg of the journey to the Kremlin.

Dozens of people waited for them top side, all of whom swarmed her with questions and demands. Thad Pennington was among the crowd, and by the look on his face, she guessed she looked quite frightening.

"What happened down there, Grand Duchess?" he said as she approached. Ryan's friends stayed at her sides like bodyguards.

Barchai spoke up, addressing everyone in the room. "The princess has been through a tragic ordeal. I'm sure she will be happy to answer your questions once she's received medical care and is feeling better."

Before Ryan's friends could drag her out of the throng, Anya grabbed Pennington by the arm. "Per Ryan's instructions, I'll only talk to Conrad Flynn. Can you get him for me?"

Pennington looked down at her bloody, bandaged hand on his sleeve, and then raised his gaze to her face.

Mr. Football leaned in and spoke in her ear. "He's already on his way. He'll be here before the night's over."

Anya released the president's arm. "He'll help Ryan, right?"

"And you," Quick said. "I'm sorry we failed to get your grandmother out alive."

"Not your fault." She patted his arm. "I couldn't save her either."

As she was strapped onto a gurney and secured in the ambulance, Anya closed her eyes. Solomon better damn well come through this time, or she was going to wipe the deck with his ass.

44

CONRAD JUMPED through all the bureaucratic bullshit necessary to get in to see Anya Romanov Radzoya. Smitty was out of surgery by the time he arrived in Moscow, but was heavily sedated. While the bullet had gone straight through, it had damaged tendons and muscles in Ryan's chest and back, nicking his collarbone before exiting. Conrad wasn't sure how his friend had gone from a simple asset recruitment to being underground in GI 42 and taking out the president of Russia, but he was sure it was one helluva good story.

And while he preferred to hear it from Smitty, he had no choice but to get Anya's side first.

She was a stubborn one. Sources reported she'd been interviewed, threatened, and put under arrest in the hospital, all in the past seven hours since she'd emerged from the bunker with Devons and Quick. Even with all that, she'd refused to say a word to anyone but him.

As Yuri Barchai, the asset Smitty was supposed to turn, escorted Conrad to the door of her hospital room, he stopped Conrad out of hearing range of the two guards posted outside her door and fiddled with his tie. "I believe Grand Duchess Anya was treated less than..."

He shook his head, stuck his hands in his pants pockets. "President Ivanov is still in surgery. We are not sure who shot him, but as you can imagine, the situation is a political nightmare. If it was the grand duchess, she will face serious consequences, as will your operatives. I suggest that no matter what she tells you, you consider all the possible complications her confession might cause and use wise judgment in making any accusations. I do not—I mean, *we*, the cabinet members—do not wish to cause the grand duchess further difficulties, but it may be inevitable."

Threat or warning? Conrad had already received a similar speech from Titus, Stone, and Thad Pennington. Interestingly, this man seemed to genuinely care about the Romanov woman. She and her grandmother had apparently made quite an impression on a lot of people.

Even Smitty, if his friend had drawn her into his mission as more than just an asset.

Now it was time for him to see what all the fuss was about. Giving Barchai a tight nod, he made his way past the guards, who Barchai commanded to let him in, and knocked on the closed wooden door of Anya's hospital room.

After a short pause, she called, "Come in."

He entered and found her not in bed, but sitting by the window fully dressed. Her bottom lip was swelled and he could see where it had been split. One eye was also swelled and sported a black bruise that looked particularly dark against her pale skin. Her hair was as white as the snow falling outside the window, and her arm was in a sling, the hand bandaged so thoroughly, he could barely see her fingers.

Light blue eyes met his, assessing him as much as he assessed her. "Anya Romanov Radzoya?"

She rose from the chair, wiped her good hand on the leg of her jeans, and held it out. "Solomon?"

He crossed the few feet to take her outstretched hand. "Any friend of Smitty's is welcome to call me Conrad."

Her handshake was brief but firm. Emotion flashed in her eyes. "He's a great man. He stopped a nuclear war last night."

Good story, hell. This was going to be a goddamn *great* story.

Conrad motioned for her to return to her chair. "I'd like to hear the details."

She stayed standing. "My grandmother always wanted to be buried here in Moscow, next to her son, Peter. I believe the U.S. government owes her that much, don't you? To take care of the paperwork and red tape necessary to make that happen?"

She wanted to bargain. Smart gal. And not for her own release, but for her grandmother's burial. "Consider it done."

"And you'll give me your word that Ryan will not be held responsible for anything that happened in that bunker, other than stopping dozens of ICBMs from launching."

Loyal to a fault. Another admirable trait. "Of course."

She drew a deep breath and bit her bottom lip, winced as she hit the cut. Moving to the bed, she continued to stare Conrad straight in the eyes as she sat down and cradled her injured hand. "Maxim Ivanov is a monster."

Tell me something I don't know. "What did he do to you and Ryan?"

"It's a long, complicated story. Most people will find it hard, if not impossible, to believe."

Conrad unbuttoned his suit coat, sat down in the chair she had vacated, and brought out a pocket voice recorder. He held it up and showed it to her. "For the record."

"No. What I tell you is between us. Once Ryan is awake, you can record his account if he agrees to it."

Tough negotiator. He slid the recorder back inside his coat, slouched in the chair, and crossed his legs at the ankles, trying to channel Ryan's friendly persona. "All right, but I want to hear everything, every detail. The only way I can help you out of this mess is if I have the full, unadulterated story. *Capice?*"

She didn't hesitate. "You can't get me out of this mess."

"Why not?"

"Because I shot the president of Russia, and if given the chance, I'd do it all over again."

45

THREE DAYS later
Novodevichy Cemetery

ANYA STARED AT HER GRANDMOTHER'S COFFIN, AND THE GRANITE mausoleum it was to be deposited in, a deep sadness permeating every inch of her mind, body and soul.

As promised, Grams was being buried in the Romanov tomb with Peter, Ekateirna, and some of the Romanov ancestors. Anya had passed the spot where Boris Yeltstin's body was interred, and his memorial raised, on her way to the Romanov mausoleum.

There had been no ceremony, no funeral, just the way Grams had wanted it. Anya wished her grandmother had wanted a lavish final send off because she deserved it, but in some ways, she was relieved that it was just her and Grams here in the quiet section of the cemetery for their final goodbye.

"You were right about Solomon, Grams. He and his associates have come through on all counts so far." Anya stubbed her toe on the snow-packed ground, wanting to draw out these last moments alone with her grandmother. "He tried to act like he wasn't shocked by my story—our story—but I could see it in the way his face tensed when I told him about Ivanov's plans to purify the Russian race and wipe America off the map. Guess even hardcore CIA agents can be surprised by the depths some men will go to.

"Ryan's doing okay from what they tell me. They won't let me see him. He's been on strong sedatives and pain killers, so until he's off those and can give his account of what went down with a clear head, they won't let me in his room. I miss him. And you."

Sunlight bounced off the snow and brightened the somber tombs nearby. Anya hugged herself. Even under layers of clothes and blankets, she couldn't get warm these days. "I'm no longer under arrest, but I am under surveillance. The Kremlin isn't even covert about it. Solomon put me up at a nice hotel near the U.S. Embassy, and there's this couple, Josh and Naomi, who are in the room next to mine. Josh helped rescue me. Him and John. Josh is a spy. I'm not sure what John is, but they both feel terribly guilty that they failed. They're all keeping an eye on me."

A crow cawed in the trees overhead. "Ivanov is still alive, unfortunately. While he was in surgery for the gunshot wound, he had a stroke. They're not sure how much damage it might have done to his brain, so they're keeping him in a coma until they think his body is ready to wake up."

She wished she'd aimed for his heart. "I don't know what will happen when he does."

If he was in his right mind, he would accuse her of attempted murder. He would also accuse Ryan of killing Andreev. The CIA might be able to keep Ryan out of prison, but it would be impossible to keep Anya from facing a death sentence.

As long as Ryan was okay, that was what mattered. She'd

take whatever punishment the Russian government handed her, and be grateful if Ryan walked away unscathed.

In her peripheral vision, she caught sight of an older man in a black trenchcoat making his way between the mausoleums. Another man, taller and skinnier, but no less aged, followed several yards behind. As the first man approached, his wrinkled face split into a smile. "Miss Radzoya?"

Anya looked around nervously. Who was this guy? A journalist? The media had been hounding her since she'd left the hospital. "Who's asking?"

He held out a hand. "Name's Titus Allen. Director of Central Intelligence. Solomon tells me you're as resourceful and astute as your grandmother was."

"You knew my grandmother?"

His gaze shifted to the coffin and rested there a moment. "She was an extraordinary woman." One hand went into his coat and produced a white business card with a single line of black type. "When you return to the States, I hope you'll visit me. I'd like to explore your career options."

She took the card and he started to walk away. "Tell me about my grandmother. About what she did for the CIA."

The director looked back at her, his gaze darting around the cemetery. The other man also glanced around as if Anya's words might produce unwanted company. Titus smiled, but it was a forced action, tightening the deep lines around his eyes. "I'm afraid much of that is classified."

Anya held out the card. "Then we have nothing to discuss."

His smile transformed into a real one. "Come see me. I'll tell you everything I know."

"I'm afraid I won't be able to leave Russia for quite some time, maybe never."

He didn't even pause. "Maxim Ivanov will be dead before the day's over, a second stroke that will prove fatal. Several cameras in the command center recorded what happened that day, so Ivanov's new prime minister will destroy that video, and the Russian people will be told nothing about what happened. You'll be free to leave Russia and resume your life."

He walked back the way he'd come, nodding as he passed the other man still waiting. That man, in an oversized winter coat, black fur hat, and wool scarf, raised a gloved hand to her.

When Anya didn't respond, he stepped toward the mausoleum, more tentative than the director had been, and shook his head as he stared at the casket. "Oh, Natasha. You always said you'd go out with a bang."

As he moved closer, Anya could only stare. The man was old, but reminded her of someone. He seemed to have her father's eyes, his bushy eyebrows. "Who are you?"

He stood proud. "These days, I go by Grigory Yordanov. Your grandmother knew me when I was Sergei Kutzeg."

She didn't recognize either name, but there was no mistaking the familiar eyes staring back at her. A new realization took root in her mind and bloomed with alarming speed. "You knew my grandmother...very well, I'm guessing."

A slight dip of his head told her he understood what she was insinuating, and her theory was accurate. "She swore me to secrecy. Refused to tell me where you were. All she would ever tell me was that you were safe."

A well of emotion grew in Anya's chest, pushing its way up her throat and behind her eyes. She blinked back tears she didn't understand. "She told me my grandfather was a man named Anton. That he died in the Soviet war with Afghanistan two months before my father was born."

He didn't say anything, just dropped his gaze to the snowy ground.

More secrets. There were always so damn many secrets. "Grams is dead. Nothing you divulge can hurt her anymore. I deserve to know the truth."

Grigory lifted his gaze to Natasha's casket. The sun's rays

spotlighted the smooth gunmetal gray of the interment vault. "Her husband did perish in that war, but he was not your grandfather."

"You are?"

He met her eyes and gave another of those barely-there nods.

Anya blew out her breath in a slow, steady stream, fogging the chilled air. She had a grandfather. A living, breathing relative who might be able to answer some of her endless questions now that Grams was gone. If there was anything she'd learned in the past week, it was not to take anything for granted. "Could we grab a coffee once I'm done here?"

"There's a coffee shop a few blocks east. I'll meet you there whenever you're ready."

They stared at each other a moment longer, and then Grigory touched his hand to his lips and laid it on Natasha's coffin. "She was the love of my life."

A tear escaped from her eye. Anya brushed it away, waiting patiently for Grigory to say his last goodbye. In the distance, she heard a car door slam. Grigory gave her one last nod and left her alone.

"Anya!" a female voice with a light Israeli accent rang out over the various mausoleums and tombstones. "Where are you?"

Anya smiled in spite of the sad moment. She waved to the woman who wore a bright red coat. "Over here, Naomi."

Naomi and Grigory met, said something to each other, and the woman gave him a pat on the arm. They parted ways, and Naomi tromped through the snow in a pair of ridiculously tall boots. "Come, come!" She waved a gloved hand at Anya. "Time to go."

"Give me one more minute, okay?"

She sighed with exasperation, and loitered at a large, marble tombstone with a giant angel on top.

"I did everything the way you wanted, Grams. No ceremony, no fanfare, not even a vase of flowers. But I'm getting you one of those angel monuments, whether you like it or not, for the top of the mausoleum. You were a silent hero for many people, including me, during your life. It's only fitting we recognize your angelic qualities."

This time, she didn't hold back on the tears. Grams would have hated her public display, yet the thought made Anya chuckle despite her grief. She bent over and kissed the casket. "Thank you for everything, Natasha Romanov Radzoya. I'm proud to be your granddaughter."

Backing away from the mausoleum, Anya used her gloves to wipe the wetness from her cheeks. She offered a silent prayer for her mother and father, then turned to Naomi. "What's up?"

The woman gave her a sly smile. "Come with me."

Naomi took Anya's hand and headed toward the cemetery's entrance, dragging Anya behind her. How could she walk in those boots?

A black, boxy SUV waited at the curb, engine idling. Josh was behind the wheel, and when he saw her and Naomi, he exited the vehicle and raised his hand in acknowledgement. Naomi opened the back passenger door. "Get in."

Anya slid inside.

And came face to face with Ryan.

46

Anya's black eye had morphed into purples and yellows but was no longer swollen. Her lip was nearly healed. She was devoid of makeup, just the way Ryan liked it, and although her eyes were bloodshot, she looked beautiful. A perfect ten.

"Ryan!"

She threw her arms around him, her voice echoing off the car's interior, and he grinned, hugging her back with his good arm, and ignoring the pain in his shoulder from her exuberant squeeze.

Her cheek was smooth as silk against his unshaven jaw. He breathed deep, drawing in her warm, fresh-air smell. Every nerve in his body rejoiced as he stroked her soft, fine hair with his hand. This was what he'd foregone the pain meds and ridiculous hospital rules for. "God, I missed you."

Leaning back, she scanned his face and the sling holding his arm. "What are doing here? You're supposed to be in the hospital."

He shrugged with his good shoulder. "A few stitches. No big deal."

"They wouldn't let me see you."

"I gave my statement an hour ago directly to Titus Allen and Thad Pennington. Devons and Quick backed up everything they witnessed. Although all of our stories match, Pennington isn't happy, and is calling for a quiet, but thorough, investigation. We'll both have to give our testimonies a few more times at Langley, and to a special congressional taskforce Pennington is setting up. I'm under orders not to see you, or complicate the situation even more, until we're both cleared. Titus arranged this meeting, but after this, we'll both be under constant surveillance until the investigation is over." He touched her cheek with a finger and swallowed the sudden lump in his throat. "Could be months."

She seemed to deflate, then resolve returned to her eyes. A wicked grin spread across her face. "We know how to get around constant surveillance."

He grinned back. He and Conrad already had plans set up to help Ryan see Anya as much as possible, regardless of who was keeping tabs on them. Her willingness to circumvent adversity to see him was the Jack in his poker spread. All he had to do now was play the rest of his cards right and reel in the winning hand. "I like the way you think."

"After I speak to President Pennington, you'll like the way I think even more."

"Why is that?"

"I have information he'll find very interesting about Russia's nuclear weapons program, remember? If he wants to harass us with a tax-payer funded investigation, he can kiss that info, and my willingness not to share a certain code with my homeland, goodbye. Not that I would, of course, but he doesn't know that. I'll also go to the press and spill everything I know, including his harassment."

Luck was with him and the winning hand was in sight. He

grabbed her chin and brought her face to his. "You would make one hell of a good spy."

"I like the way *you* think. In fact..." She kissed him, a quick but pleasant smack on his lips. "All of this has made me realize I'm more like my grandmother than I thought. Solomon and I have had several discussions. If I am cleared of all charges, like Titus claims I will be, I'm toying with the idea of joining the next class at the Farm. Solomon says I can keep my job with GenLife and also work for the CIA. He'll even tutor me to be in some special army of his."

Her excitement couldn't be denied. She wasn't just thinking about joining the next training class, she'd already made up her mind. He could tell. The Queen was now snug in his hand alongside the Jack and ten.

The King dangled in front of him. "I'm sorry I told Ivanov the truth in the command center. I didn't know he had an analysis of your blood. He was holding that gun to your head and your grandmother wasn't going to tell him, and..."

She shushed him with a finger to his lips, her eyes tearing at the mention of Grams. "I know, I know. She was strong, right up to the end. Refusing to tell him the truth. But I appreciate the fact you were trying to save me over the world."

He pinched his eyes closed, sighed. "But I couldn't save your grandmother. I've been over it a hundred times in my head, all the things I should've done differently. All the calls I made that were wrong."

"Ivanov is the bad guy here, not you. Or the others who saved us." She sighed and looked down at her bandaged hand. "But I've done the same thing. Gone over it a hundred times, thinking *if only I'd done this or hadn't done that, she'd still be alive.*" She raised her head. "Grams wouldn't want that. She'd want us to embrace life and focus on what we can do now to protect our countries from future tyrants like Ivanov."

"He'll be dead—"

"Before midnight, I know. Director Allen told me. I assume I don't want to know what the CIA is up to, but honestly, if they asked me to sneak into his room and do the job myself, I'd jump at the chance." Anya brushed hair from Ryan's forehead. "Grams would have liked you. Your quiet strength and willingness to do what needs to be done without calling attention to yourself."

The King was secured and Ryan did a mental fist pump.

But the Ace, that was the trickiest card to lay claim to. "As soon as the investigation is wrapped up—and from the sounds of it, it may be wrapped up very soon—I'll be heading back to my job at the Agency."

"Of course." A pause. Ryan held his breath. "What exactly *is* your job?"

"I'm Director of CIA Operations in Europe and Asia. I've been on temporary assignment in London, but Michael Stone – the deputy director – wants me back in the States. The CIA is recruiting, and he wants my input on new candidates for missions in Europe and Asia."

She whistled softly under her breath, sat back. "You're not just a spy, you're the *director* of spies in Europe and Asia?"

"There's a lot about my job I can't share with you. Even if you don't want to continue our relationship" —God he hoped she wanted to continue their relationship— "you won't be able to tell anyone the truth about who I work for or what I do. Are you okay with that?"

"I'm quite familiar with keeping secrets, even at my job. All of GenLife's cases are confidential. So I won't ask about your work, and you won't ask about mine. Deal?"

Time to lay everything on the table. "If you pass the Farm and become a spy, I may end up being your boss."

She was silent a long time, and Ryan's heart stuttered. It was one thing if she didn't want to be a spy but was still willing to see him. If she didn't want to be with him anymore, though, and he had to work with her...there was nothing he could do about that.

She glanced at him. "What's your real name?"

"Ryan Smith."

"Yeah, right." She chuckled as if that were a punch line. "Your real last name is Smith."

"Ask my mom."

She sat forward and leaned toward him, purpose hardening her voice. "I'm going to do that. And I'm going to talk to Solomon and Titus Allen and those two." She cocked a thumb at Josh and Naomi standing patiently outside the vehicle. "I'm going to talk to everyone under the sun, and find out all there is to know about you, Ryan Smith. I want to know your darkest secrets, your bad habits, and your favorite movies. I want to know everything."

Stunned, he couldn't decide if this was good or bad. "Or you could just ask me. On our honeymoon."

She sat back. "Are you asking me to marry you?"

"Sorry, I don't have a ring or anything. I've been a little tied up in the hospital after saving the world, and a damsel in distress, from a nuclear war."

Anya laughed, a soft, sweet sound that made Ryan smile. He knew before she opened her mouth that the Ace was his.

"Grams always said, 'life's not all beer and skittles' which is British, not Russian, but I think she may have been wrong. I beat the monster at his own game, I have a possible job offer from the CIA, and now marriage? You don't give a girl time to breathe. Sounds like beer and skittles to me."

"Is that a yes?"

She threw her arms around him, hugged him tight, and whispered in his ear. "Anya Romanov Radzoya Smith has a nice ring to it, don't you think? But we should run it by my grandfather first."

"Your grandfather?"

She beamed. "My *real* grandfather. He's waiting for me at a nearby café. I want you to meet him. He's going to tell me all about Grams and my family. I'm starting over with him." She delivered a quick kiss to Ryan's lips. "And you."

Ace. King. Queen. Jack. Ten. Same suit...hearts.

Ryan's luck had definitely turned around.

ENJOY THIS SNEAK PEAK AT
OPERATION: AMBUSH!

Chapter One

IN THE PAST TWO MONTHS, CIA operative John Quick had ridden a camel through the rough terrain of Afghanistan, set off a bomb under the Kremlin in Moscow, and spent time under-cover inside a Mexican prison. The bomb had been fun, right up his alley. The rest, not so much.

Still, it was what he did. He put his life on the line for his country every day. He lived and breathed this shit, and never doubted himself or his mission. Ever.

Standing in front of the Morgan family retreat in upstate New York, none of his recent special ops missions compared to the personal nightmare he was about to embark on. Doubts made him sweat, and he wiped some from his forehead. His feet involuntarily shifted and he leaned one hand on the door in front of him to steady himself for a moment.

What the ever-livin hell was *that* about?

Get it together, man. Don't lose your balls now.

His finger hovered over the doorbell. The Morgan vacation

home—one of six mansions owned by the billionaire financier, Charles Morgan—was more than your average cabin in the woods. From the intel John had gathered—and he never went into enemy territory without knowing the layout—the multi- story log and glass home situated on Otsego Lake boasted five bedrooms, an equal amount of bathrooms, a theater, a wine cellar, and a complete spa. The six acres surrounding it contained a boat dock, tennis courts, a pool, and a zip line in the woods behind the house.

Who the hell lived like this?

The cabin, like all the mansions, was the type of place Lucie Morgan—the woman of his dreams—belonged in. Not his simple, unadorned one-bedroom apartment in D.C.

She's so far out of my reach, I shouldn't even be standing here.

Conversation and laughter filtered through the window nearby. Soft music, the clink of glasses and silverware. The sounds of family and friends.

What was he doing here? This was no place for a man with no family, no home, no life outside his job.

You're on vacation.

Vacation. That's what Conrad Flynn, the spook in charge of Pegasus called it, but it was basically forced leave. Normal people liked time off. They looked forward to it. Sleeping in, hitting the beach, spending time away from their jobs.

Normal people went to fucking Disneyland. Or on a cruise to Alaska. The Bahamas.

While he wasn't actually a spook for the CIA, like the infamous Flynn, he wasn't exactly your average, "normal", Joe, either. While he'd never set foot inside Disneyland, he'd once done a search and rescue in the Bahamas and always thought he might go back someday. An ex–military operative with the highly trained and efficient Team Pegasus, he rescued lost spies, hunted down various folks trapped in foreign prisons, and acted as a bodyguard in third-world countries when certain covert deals were going down. Like all the men in Pegasus, he was on call 24/7.

Until now.

Vacation or not, he didn't belong here. He was adding fuel to the fire of his relationship with Lucie. His *non*-relationship with Lucie. Rehabbing an old house into a dance studio and spending a few nights together here and there was not a relationship, though Lucie wanted it to be. She'd made that clear. He'd tried squashing that crazy idea any time it came up, but here he was, because he just couldn't stay away from her.

She was his drug of choice. The way she smelled like lilacs. Her heavy and extremely sexy French accent. The way her big sky-blue eyes were always searching his, as if he held all the answers to life, or the Universe, or some such shit. The way her lips felt when she kissed him, the way they teased him when she laughed.

Everything about her sent him searching for those answers she wanted. Whatever her desire was, he wanted to give it to her.

Him. A guy with nothing to offer but himself. And that wasn't much, no matter how you looked at it.

He lowered his finger from the doorbell and cast a glance over his shoulder. On the sweeping driveway, his four-wheel-drive truck, rusty and ugly in the midst of BMWs and Mercedes, stood positioned for a quick getaway. It wasn't too late to turn around. Not too late to text Lucie and claim he'd been called away on a job—

His phone rang.

Maybe it won't be a lie.

Caller ID read "Boy Scout".

Lawson Vaughn, his boss. One of them, anyway.

Busted.

He debated hitting the button. What were the odds Lawson was actually calling about a mission? "Hey, man. I was just going to text you. Flynn's worried about one of his spies stuck in Syria. I'm heading to D.C. in case Pegasus needs to perform an extraction. The team and I—"

"Aren't going anywhere," the Pegasus leader said. "Get your ass in here with that six-pack, Johnnie boy, or I'm coming out to get you. That's an order."

John instinctively looked up. Lawson stood in front of a floor-to-ceiling window on the second floor. Inside enemy territory.

Lawson, Lucie's soon-to-be brother-in-law, waved. He was about to take the plunge and marry Lucie's sister. He was one brave—or maybe sick—man.

Setting down the beer, John waved back with a single finger. His favorite one, right in the middle. He moved away from the door a few steps and lowered his voice. "I can't do this."

"Bullshit. You can handle a simple party."

"A party with a bunch of strangers who mean nothing to me? Nothing I love better." He'd slapped a red bow on a six-pack of Bud as a gift to the expecting parents. They were going to need a whole case when the kid was born. "A party with Lucie's highfalutin' family? Send me back to Afghanistan, man. Shit, even another goddamn Mexican prison would be a fucking *picnic* compared to this."

"Suck it up."

How many times had they demanded that of each other in the past five years since John had taken over as Lawson's operations captain? "This isn't even a *party* party. It's a freakin' baby shower." He was so out of his element here, even his fingernails were sweating. "Family, babies...kill me now. Nothing I did with the Berets prepared me for this. I'm getting hives thinking about it."

"You want to see Lucie, don't you?"

Did soldiers love guns? He turned back and looked up again. "Awww, hell, Law." His Texas drawl, rising with his panic, turned one-syllable words into multi-syllables. "You know I do, but this is—"

"Normal. Family get-togethers and baby showers are *normal*. You should try it."

In Lawson's world, this *was* normal. In John's? "Sucks to be you."

A lie. John envied Lawson's upcoming nuptials and impending fatherhood, but no way could he see himself in Lawson's shoes. He'd seen other operatives lose their edge, worrying too much about those they'd left behind. He wasn't about to second-guess every decision in the field because he didn't want to leave a wife without a husband or kids without a dad.

So even though he'd wanted that elusive *something more* with Lucie since he'd rescued her from a terrorist the previous year—*what a way to meet*—it wasn't going to happen. She unraveled him...screwed with his brain, his emotions, his...everything.

He couldn't—no, he *wouldn't*—settle down. Not for her. Not for anyone. Whatever fantasy she was cooking up about them enjoying a future like Lawson and her sister, Zara, was just that —a fantasy.

No matter how much he wished it could be reality.

Then Lawson, the Yankee ballbuster who acted as honorable as a Boy Scout, said the one phrase John couldn't walk away from. "Do it for me."

Low blow. John turned his back on the door, on Lawson.

He scanned the frozen lake lined with snow-covered trees.

Picture postcard and all that shit. Stalling, he tried to think of something witty to say. "Who knew Flynn would allow one of his super agents like Zara to get pregnant?"

"Believe it or not, Director Flynn cannot control everything."

Dark gray clouds hung low in the distance. Another Canadian front swinging in. That could work to his advantage. A few minutes of face time at the party where he could drool over Lucie and log some mental pictures for future fantasizing, and then he could use the approaching storm as an excuse to cut and run. In and out in under an hour.

Disneyland was nice this time of year, right? Warm weather, Mickey Mouse, and not a Morgan family baby shower in sight.

Bailing on Lucie, after all she's been through, would be a shit-ass thing to do.

Not to mention disappointing Lawson, his best friend. Good thing John was an ace at disappointing people.

"Is that the best you could find to wear?" Lawson's voice held a slight air of exasperation.

Lowering his head, John looked down at the tips of his worn-out cowboy boots. Snow clung to the edges of his olive drab BDUs. Though he was no longer Army, he still wore the pants with T-shirts and flannels. They were as much a part of him as his social awkwardness around Lucie.

Maybe today she'd finally see him the way he really was. He didn't belong in her world, and he wasn't about to change in order to fit in with the Morgan family, no way in hell.

"I came straight from Dulles. No time to run home and put on my fancy clothes"—never mind that he only owned a total of one dress shirt and a single pair of black slacks—"but, hey, if I'm not dressed good enough for you and the future in-laws..."

Lawson issued a heavy sigh. "Speaking of in-laws, the sharks are circling in here. Lucie's sinking fast. She needs you, John."

The call to duty. *She needs you.*

Goddammit. Of all the people and relationships he'd walked away from in his life, he couldn't walk away from someone who needed him.

And Lawson—*damn him*—knew it.

Facing the door again, John glanced up at his boss. The

man he followed into the fire on a regular basis. The man who'd saved his ass more than once.

John owed him. He owed Lucie, too. "You better not be fucking with me, Boy Scout."

Three fingers rose in the air.

John shook his head, snorted. But something brewed deep in his gut. If the Morgans were giving Lucie a hard time, he'd clean the deck with them.

For kicks, he gave Lawson the Star Trek Vulcan salute. "*De Oppresso Liber*, man." *To Free the Oppressed*, the Beret motto. "I'm coming in."

Before he lost his nerve, he pocketed the phone and raised his mental shields—he had issues about his own dysfunctional family he needed to keep suppressed. Up went his impassive poker face, the one he preferred for awkward social events, as he snatched his gift from the spot on the deck.

He raised his finger to ring the doorbell.

Put it back down.

Fuck the doorbell. Guerrilla warfare worked best when you took the enemy by surprise.

READ NOW

ROMANTIC SUSPENSE & MYSTERIES BY MISTY EVANS

SEALS of Shadow Force Series: Spy Division

Man Hunt

Man Killer

Man Down

SEALs of Shadow Force Series

Fatal Truth

Fatal Honor

Fatal Courage

Fatal Love

Fatal Vision

Fatal Thrill

Risk

The SCVC Taskforce Series

Deadly Pursuit

Deadly Deception

Deadly Force

Deadly Intent

Deadly Affair, A SCVC Taskforce novella

Deadly Attraction

Deadly Secrets

Deadly Holiday, A SCVC Taskforce novella

Deadly Target

Deadly Rescue

Deadly Bounty

The Super Agent Series

Operation Sheba

Operation Paris

Operation Proof of Life

Operation Lost Princess

Operation Sleeping With the Enemy

The Justice Team Series (with Adrienne Giordano)

Stealing Justice

Cheating Justice

Holiday Justice

Exposing Justice

Undercover Justice

Protecting Justice

Missing Justice

Defending Justice

SCHOCK SISTERS MYSTERY SERIES w/Adrienne Giordano

1st Shock

2nd Strike

3rd Tango

The Secret Ingredient Culinary Mystery Series

The Secret Ingredient, A Culinary Romantic Mystery with Bonus Recipes

The Secret Life of Cranberry Sauce, A Secret Ingredient Holiday Novella

PNR & UF BY MISTY/NYX

Paranormal Romance

Witches Anonymous Step 1

Jingle Hells, Witches Anonymous Step 2

Wicked Souls, Witches Anonymous Step 3

Dark Moon Lilith, Witches Anonymous Step 4

Dancing With the Devil, Witches Anonymous Step 5

Devil's Due, Witches Anonymous Step 6

Dirty Deeds, Witches Anonymous Step 7

Wicked Wedding, Witches Anonymous Step 8

Urban Fantasy

Revenge Is Sweet, Kali Sweet Urban Fantasy Series, Book 1

Sweet Chaos, Kali Sweet Urban Fantasy Series, Book 2

Sweet Soldier, Kali Sweet Urban Fantasy Series, Book 3

Sweet Curse, Kali Sweet Urban Fantasy Series, Book 4

Paranormal Romantic Suspense

Soul Survivor, Moon Water Series, Book 1

Soul Protector, Moon Water Series, Book 2

Cozy Mysteries (writing as Nyx Halliwell)

Sister Witches Of Raven Falls Mystery Series

Of Potions and Portents

Of Curses and Charms

Of Stars and Spells

Of Spirits and Superstition

Confessions of a Closet Medium Cozy Mystery Series

(Coming 2020)

Pumpkins & Poltergeists

Once Upon a Witch Cozy Mystery Series

(Coming 2020)

Psychic Sisters Cozy Mystery Series

(Coming 2021)

ABOUT THE AUTHOR

USA TODAY Bestselling Author Misty Evans has published more than sixty novels and writes romantic suspense, urban fantasy, and paranormal romance. Under her pen name, Nyx Halliwell, she also writes cozy mysteries.

She got her start writing in 4th grade when she won second place in a school writing contest with an essay about her dad. Since then, she's written nonfiction magazine articles, started her own coaching business, become a yoga teacher, and raised twin boys on top of enjoying her fiction career.

When not reading or writing, she enjoys music, movies, and hanging out with her husband, twin sons, and three spoiled puppies. A registered yoga teacher and Master Reiki Practitioner, she shares her love of chakra yoga and energy healing, but still hasn't mastered levitating.

Get free reads, all the latest news, and alerts about sales when you sign up for her newsletter at www.readmistyevans.com. To find out more about her holistic healing practice, please visit www.crystalswithmisty.com.

LETTER FROM MISTY

Hello Beautiful Reader!

Thank you for reading this story! It is an honor and a privilege to write stories for you.

I hope you enjoyed this book, and I'd like to ask a favor – would you mind leaving a review at your favorite retailer? I'd really appreciate it, and reviews help other readers find books they will love too.

If you'd like to learn about my other books, sales, and special promotions, please sign up for my newsletter at www.readmistyevans.com.

Grab special edition box sets and get new releases before they come out at retailers by visiting my direct buy website www.mistyevansbooks.com.

I also have a holistic business, Crystals With Misty, and invite you to check out my website www.crystalswithmisty.com for information on my services.

Last but not least, if you enjoy clean, cozy mysteries, visit my pen name www.nyxhalliwell.com to see those books!

Thank you and happy reading!
Misty

CPSIA information can be obtained
at www.ICGtesting.com
Printed in the USA
BVHW031030280220
573637BV00001B/49